*Bill !
a little filler for*

MARTIN BOOTH

—

The Iron Tree

—

Iam shelves.

[signature]

Apr. 11. 94

POCKET
BOOKS

New York   London   Toronto   Sydney   Tokyo   Singapore

For
Terry and May

First published in Great Britain by
Simon & Schuster Ltd in 1993
First published in Great Britain by Pocket Books, 1994
A Paramount Communications Company

Copyright © Martin Booth, 1993
The moral rights of the author have been asserted

Simon & Schuster Ltd
West Garden Place
Kendal Street
London W2 2AQ

Simon & Schuster of Australia Pty Ltd
Sydney

A CIP catalogue record for this book is
available from the British Library
ISBN 0-671-71597-6

Typeset in Sabon 11/12 by
Hewer Text Composition Services, Edinburgh
Printed and bound in Great Britain by
HarperCollins Manufacturing, Glasgow

Not very far from here is a small temple.

It is not an elaborate place of worship, nothing like the gaudy, extravagant spots the tourists visit, disembarking from coaches with cameras slung around their necks, the women in floral print dresses and straw hats with the men in slacks and open-neck shirts, their hip pockets well buttoned. It has no message of welcome in English at the door, no sign prohibiting or encouraging photography, no request that the visitor respect it as a house of religion. There are no obtrusive alms boxes or grasping beggars, no hawkers selling Kodak film, boxes of out-of-date colour slides or dog-eared postcards. Indeed, if you did not know the temple was there, you might well pass it by in the street and, if you looked in its direction, you might assume the forecourt, in which there grows a low, wide banyan tree and a number of shrubs in dark-brown glazed pots surrounding a stone bench, was nothing more than a little garden set aside by the authorities to relieve the cramped panorama of tenements and shops, factories and street stalls.

The building is not in the least pretentious. It has a roof of green glazed pantiles with a frieze of dragons and mythical heroes along the ridge, all badly in need of repainting and hidden from the street by

1

the banyan. On either side of the door, the scarlet paint of the wooden plaques has dulled with time and traffic fumes to a deep red, like that of arterial blood. The gold characters have also tarnished to a dark brazen yellow.

Once inside, the atmosphere is thick with the smoke of joss sticks dropping, heavier than air, from the coils of sandalwood incense suspended from the rafters. The usual temple trappings stand dusty and mystical in the shadows of the side aisles: the scarlet and yellow drum with its taut hide skin, the bronze bell hanging in its squat frame like an inverted tulip head and, just inside the door, a huge model of a sailing junk in full sail protected behind a glass screen, the bottom right-hand corner of which is cracked.

It is always twilight in the temple. The sun may be beating down outside without a vestige of mercy but, in here, it is invariably semi-dark. The only illumination, apart from an early afternoon beam of sunlight cutting through the roof and the clouds of incense smoke, comes from a few guttering flames in lamps before the altars and a neon strip light tucked in behind the canopy hanging in front of the god to whom the temple is dedicated.

I frequently visit this place.

Sometimes, I light a few joss sticks and, placing them between my hands, make several noncommittal bows before sticking them in the urn of sand and ash which stands in the centre of the temple. On or just before festival days, I may light a red wax candle on a bamboo splint and, at Chinese New Year, I make sure to bring an offering of a miniature bottle of snake wine and four oranges which I place on the altar in the form of a little pyramid. There is an alms box hidden away beside the junk: I never fail to put a dollar in it, thrusting the note down through the slit in the top not because I feel anyone might come along and fish it out but just to make sure that it falls safely to the bottom and cannot be lost.

It is a peaceful place. Walking in from the day's heat, it is always cool, the thick walls killing the incessant sound of traffic. The incense also eradicates the dubious smells of the city.

If I have time, I sit in the temple. There is a folding stool to the right of the altar, just beside the statue of one of the guardians of heaven, a life-size warrior carved of wood. His eyes, the white made of bone and the iris of black soapstone, glare ferociously. His spear, tipped with a blade like a Victorian butter knife, is gilded. There is usually a spider's web connecting the tip of this weapon to the point in the centre of his elaborate helmet.

The old woman who is the temple caretaker knows me: she has seen me come here for years. As well as sweeping the stone flags and cleaning out the urn, tidying the offerings and getting rid of the ashes of burnt paper money offered to the god, she operates a tiny stall selling joss sticks, candles and small talismen shaped like fish or birds and carved out of plum stones. I am possibly her most regular customer and certainly her only regular European visitor. This fact, that I am a *gweilo*, no longer bothers her. The first time I visited the temple, she must have thought I was a tourist who had lost his camera and his way but now she knows I am a local resident and unquestioningly accepts me.

On occasion, she speaks to me. Her voice is weak

3

from age and possibly from spending much of her later life inhaling the pungent joss stick fumes. Our conversation is always the same. She asks if I am well, I reply affirmatively and ask after her health which she always reports to be fair, except for her rheumatism. Next she asks me where I live and I tell her: just a few streets away, near the rickshaw rank. To this information, she nods: yes, she confirms, she knows of it. It is not that she has forgotten where my home is, it is just good manners to enquire. This ritual over, she briefly comments upon a topic of the day. It might be the failure of her chosen horse to win at the races or the proximity of the next typhoon. It never concerns the temple, its fabric or its deity. They can look after themselves. More often than not she just nods to acknowledge my presence, sells me a bundle of joss sticks wrapped in red cellophane and leaves me to my own devices.

I think of nothing when I am sitting in the temple. I am certainly not a worshipper for I am done with gods. It is more that it is one of the few places left in the world where I can be alone with myself and forget my life. No one disturbs me. No one looks to wonder who or what I am. I am quite anonymous. Time ceases to pass and I can pretend, for a short while at any rate, that I am at peace.

In the winter, the Nine Dragon Hills of Kowloon catch fire.

By day, the only hint of this conflagration is a weak haze of grey smoke hanging above the skyline,

4

disseminating into the clear blue of the heavens. It has no more substance than a wash of water colour seeping into a heavy woven paper.

Sometimes, an eagle soars in the fire's thermals: more often the dots that endlessly wheel over the hillsides are shite hawks on the lookout for rodents flushed out of the ground, snakes making good their escape, the stones under which they nestle becoming hotter than the winter sun usually makes them. Below the shite hawks smaller birds dive and turn, picking off insects on the wing. They dart through the smoke, oblivious to the discomfort or proximity of danger. Some, the more agile or foolhardy, dip almost to ground level in their search to feed and their abiding desire to get the choicest morsels.

When night falls, the burning hills change. As the sun lowers, they shift from their daylight cloak of khaki into first a hint of purple then a blackness so deep that, unless it is a starry night or the moon is high and filling, their silhouette is lost. And it is when the darkness descends that the fires appear.

Each hill bears a ring of orange lights. From far away, a casual observer might assume them to be a newly opened road illuminated by sodium lamps. Yet watch them for a minute and they will be seen to part, disappear then suddenly rejoin themselves. And they flicker. This movement might be misconstrued as the last of the day's heat haze playing its shifty games but it is not. It is the greedy fire climbing inexorably up the slopes, consuming dried grass, scorching bushes and temporarily surrendering only when coming upon a bare gully or an outcrop of boulders.

Who is responsible for this orological arson is

unknown. The police never arrest anybody. The fire brigade invariably fails to apprehend a suspect. When the tenders arrive and the firemen reach the blaze, there is never anyone about. It is said that arsonists like to remain to watch the chaos and calamity their handiwork creates, but in the case of the burning mountains they do not.

It might be that the grass self-combusts. Perhaps a shard of broken glass amongst the rocks sets it off, or a thoughtlessly discarded cigarette end thrown away by a lorry driver crawling up the Tai Po Road: perhaps a charge of static electricity does it. No one can tell.

All that is a surety is that the hills of Hong Kong – and many others, throughout China, when the winter wind whips down from the Siberian north – catch fire once a year. For years I have pondered this puzzle. It is not the cause that is of curiosity to me: I am sure it is people who do it and that their actions are deliberate. It is their reason I want to discover.

I have asked others why the hills are torched and everyone has a different answer.

Mr Wu claims it is done by those whose ancestors are buried on the hills or whose bones are kept there in lines of urns. If, he deduces, they have relatives there, they would set the grass alight to clear the hillside so that, at the Festival of Ching Ming, when they went to tidy the graves, polish the bones and leave their annual offerings, they could more easily find their family plot.

On the other hand, Tsoi says it is the work of vandals. He laments the fact that Chinese teenagers listen to the music of Elvis Presley and that this is driving them away from their roots. They have to let off steam, he declares, because the music is made of destructive rhythms and contains no life force other than that of the primeval. The best way to release these emotions, he states, is to burn the hills. That the slopes have burned periodically for centuries seems not to dent his argument.

Other suggestions put forward are that the hills are set alight by the fire brigade to give their men practice, by the Urban Services Department to clear the brush, by charcoal makers or by the police in an attempt to smoke out opium factories. I have, however, discounted all these theories as either being too far-fetched or too simplistic. Besides the best explanation, in my opinion, is that suggested by Mrs van der Poehl.

She lives a floor down from me with a nondescript cat, a budgerigar and a pug dog she calls Pu Yi, so named because she once played tennis in Shanghai with the last emperor of China and declares he played the game like a lap-dog. He also, she recalls, swam like one with his arms paddling under him, but that is hearsay. I suspect much of what she says may be hearsay but that does not deter me.

'I will tell you why they set light to the hills,' she told me. 'It's to kill off the dragons.'

'Dragons?' I said.

I have for decades now had an abiding loathing of dragons.

'Kowloon hills!' she exclaimed. 'Stands to reason, man. *Kow loon*. Nine Dragons. They live up there. And they can do a lot of damage.'

'What about clearing the grass from graves?' I asked, playing devil's advocate to see if I could shift her attractively plausible line of reasoning.

7

'Graves? Up there? You've been on those hills?'
I nodded.
'You see graves there?'
I shook my head.
'Exactly! The *fung shui*'s lousy. No one wants to be buried on those hills. No necromancer would risk his reputation recommending it. No,' she lowered her voice conspiratorially, 'you mark my word, they're burning out dragons.'

And that is what I have chosen to believe.

Sometimes, on a winter's night, I sit quietly on the roof watching the necklace of destruction gradually rising to the peaks. I have never spied a dragon taking off, seen a shite hawk swoop on one in the dusk, watched one running with its back undulating like a carpet of scales being shaken, but that is by the way.

I choose to believe in her hypothesis, and that is enough.

Sometimes, to enter the tenement in which I have my dwelling, I must ring an electric buzzer to summon Chiu. He is the day- and night-watchman, always on duty and invariably to be found in a cubby-hole beneath the stairs, which space he has made his own by erecting a plasterboard wall and running into it an electric cable from which he operates a light, a small transistor radio and a single ring cooker. He has not installed a door for the simple fact that doors cost more than walls, requiring not just board and nails but also hinges, locks and handles. In lieu of such a convenience, he has hung a curtain of several layers of hessian sewn together with twine. His furniture is minimal: he has a narrow iron bed frame covered with a quilt, a folding stool, a wide shelf fixed to the wall with iron brackets which he uses as a table and several cardboard boxes which he keeps under the bed.

In this cubicle, he lives his life as happily as any man who might own a grandiose mansion. Unlike most of the residents, he pays no rent and his electricity is free for his cable is connected illegally to the street side of the junction box. No one begrudges him his luck. He has succeeded in part where we have failed and that's all there is to it.

Chiu is a quiet man, about forty years of age with thin, delicate hands. Plainly, he has never seen manual labour. When he looks at you, his eyes show a deep cavern within him where there might be a laugh echoing towards silence. His face is round and his eyes narrower than those of many Chinese, but he is not ugly in the fashion, say, of a Korean and his skin is pallid for he seldom ventures out of the building, even at night. He has made his little world under the stairs and is content with it.

He is always ready with a smile to unlock the street door after checking the bona fides of the would-be entrant by peering at him through the crack between the hinges. He has been given the keys not by the landlord but by Mr Pao, the middle-aged proprietor of the typewriter and cash register repairing workshop on the first floor. It is in his interest to see no thieves enter the building, break into his business and steal either the tools or the considerable stock of parts he maintains. It is also Mr Pao who pays the bulk of Chiu's salary.

Every Thursday evening, Chiu waits expectantly for the workshop to close. As Mr Pao leaves, he stops by the cubby-hole and a small ritual commences. Mr Pao reaches inside his jacket and removes a worn crocodile-skin wallet down the centre of which is a row of rounded scales. He opens the wallet, unzips a compartment and removes fifty dollars in ten dollar bills, held together by a paper clip. These he hands to Chiu who smiles broadly and makes a little bow. Mr Pao then utters a single phrase and Chiu bows again and says, 'Doh tse! Doh tse!' which is the required response when one is given a gift.

This done, Chiu holds open the street door for Mr Pao and, as he walks away towards the rickshaw rank, makes a show of locking up behind him, rattling the bolt and loudly snapping the locks.

If I am present, I wait until Mr Pao has gone and then I give Chiu twenty dollars. At some time during the evening, so do Mr Wu, Mrs van der Poehl, Tsoi and the woman called Pei whom I do not like who runs a secretarial agency in Flat 22 on the second floor. From time to time, we may also give Chiu food — some fruit or a bag of dried fish, some tea or a catty of rice — or some clothing we no longer require. The food he eats, the clothes he either stores in one of his cardboard boxes to be worn later or sells.

For everything, he is very grateful. Unlike many men, his gratitude is not expressed in the hope of receiving a greater benefaction. He smiles his thanks, bows to each of us and mutters his 'Doh tse!' in a quiet whisper. These are the only words I ever hear him say.

In my own way, I love this diffident, gentle man. He makes no demands of life, accepting whatever good fortune it might toss his way and being pleased his lot is better than it otherwise might have been. And I envy him. I would be as stoic if I could.

Like me, I am certain that Chiu has been through all the vicissitudes that human experience can provide. He arrived in our building in 1949, not long after the fall of China to the Communists, one of the tens of thousands who fled ahead of the Red Army, afraid of the doctrines, diatribes and cold revenges of Mao Tse-tung. Yet he seems unaffected by it all. He has taken the misery and loss in his stride, accepting his lot with as much resignation as a dog who, abandoned by one owner, takes up with the next. I cannot be like him, no matter how much I wish it. Where I am concerned, I have spent decades trying to reason, to seek to explain what I have seen, to set it in a context of history and belief. I have failed. He has not even embarked upon such a quest and is happier for his naiveté.

The street door of which Chiu is in charge is a sturdy affair made of steel sheets riveted onto a welded metal frame. It is held shut by two mortise locks and an industrial bolt with a hasp. It was painted silver some time ago but that has become chipped with age and the bottom is rusty. On the pavement beside the door is a tiny shrine like that to be found outside every building or shop in the street. It contains a small, brightly painted porcelain statue of Kwan Tai, a minuscule bowl of dusty rice wine and a tin can filled with dirty sand from which poke one or two glowing joss sticks. A shrivelled orange stands on the pavement in front of the wine bowl and

11

incense. Chiu is responsible for the shrine as well as the door: it is up to him to see the god is never without sustenance and the joss sticks never extinguished except at night, after everyone is asleep.

Whenever I stand by the door, press the button and wait for Chiu, the blue cords of smoke rise into my face until the draught from a passing pedestrian or taxi disperse them. The aroma mingling with the scents and smells of the street reminds me of wooded mountains and mysterious forests, of tiny villages and dark houses, of obscure gods squatting on their haunches with malevolent sneers and fat, jovial Buddhas in curio shop windows. It brings back the past, the first months I spent in China, a time of wonder and of happiness. And of sorrow. It also reminds me of death.

As happens these days with increasing frequency, I am startled by a voice on the stairs.

Sometimes the voice may be one I recognise but that still not reduce the level of surprise. I find I am becoming susceptible to sudden noises, that they increasingly catch me off my guard. There is no explanation: I have never suffered from shell shock or tinnitus and loud noises have never made me jump.

'*San foo*, my old friend. How you doing?'

I remove the key from my door and turn to find Mr Wu standing a few steps up from the landing. Quite often, the startling voice is his. I sometimes wonder if he does not lurk on the stairway waiting to pounce on me although I know this to be nonsense.

In the flat glow cast by the light over the lift door his face looks as if it is covered in parchment stretched across a frame of angled bones. Upon his nose is balanced a pair of circular spectacles with thin, black frames. They are not positioned squarely but askew, the right lens a good half an inch lower than the left.

'I'm doing okay,' I reply. I slip my key into my trouser pocket, placing my handkerchief over it as a defence against the light-fingered street operators one may encounter in the evenings. 'And you?'

Mr Wu has not been well for several months. He does not confide in me exactly what is wrong, but he drops occasional hints so I might be in a better position to sympathise. He thinks that as I am old like him I will offer him a greater sympathy than he might get from a younger man. He may be right and he may be wrong. I have never considered the matter.

'Better, better,' he responds.

When we meet, he likes to talk in English. This is not a pretension for his command of the language is good. He does it because he thinks it makes me feel at home. I have told him, over and over, it is not necessary. My home is here, I tell him, in Hong Kong. In China. He smiles benignly and nods his head but I can tell he only half believes me. Like many Chinese, he hopes to return to some distant nook or cranny in Kwangtung or Kwansi provinces to die with his ancestors and he mistakenly assumes Europeans will ultimately do likewise, going back to a leafy village churchyard in the shires of England to let their bodies rot in the mother soil whence they sprang.

13

'I been to see my doctor,' he continues. 'He has given me a prescription.'

He holds up a piece of flimsy paper on which I can make out printed red lines and a dense passage of characters in black ink. The paper has a similar texture to his skin.

'What is it?' I enquire, pressing the button for the lift.

'Herbs, spices. Deer's tail . . .' Mr Wu squints over his spectacles. 'You know, *san foo*, I can't see so well these days.'

I reach over and straighten the old man's glasses.

'That will not improve it. But thank you.'

'You need new glasses,' I say, not for the first time. 'You've had these for eight years at least.'

Mr Wu calculates time in his head.

'Now is 1961. I bought them in 1952. But they do me, my old friend. I need no more. New eyes, perhaps.' He holds the piece of paper out. 'See if you can read it.'

'Deer's tail is there,' I confirm, surveying the characters written with a calligraphic brush. 'And anis, ginseng, some other things I don't know the English for.'

'Do you think it will do me good?' Mr Wu enquires.

'I'm sure it will.'

'This is strange,' Mr Wu remarks, smiling at me. 'I am Chinese and you are a *gweilo* and I have to ask you to read my own language and then I ask you if you think the medicine will be good. You who do not believe . . .'

'I believe,' I interrupt him. 'I have seen Chinese

14

medicine working many times. Do not assume, because I am a *gweilo*, I take only aspirin.'

A tinny bell pings to announce the arrival of the lift and the doors rattle open. A metal grating sound can be heard: the lift is never serviced. I put my hand against the safety bar to prevent the door closing, signalling Mr Wu to go in first and we step into the lift.

'I should do that for you, my old friend. By your standards, I am a youngster. Why! When you first came to China, I could have been your pupil. Learned my English speaking from you.'

'You could not,' I answer, pressing the ground-floor button. 'You are the wrong sex. I taught only girls.'

I look up in silence at the numbers flicking slowly on and off. It is not my custom to discuss my affairs, even with those whom I know well, unless I choose to do so. There has to be a proper time and place for such intercourse and a lift is not one of them. A man must keep himself to himself unless he wishes his life to become public property. Not that I think Mr Wu would start blabbering about me. We have a certain secret in common which ensures we neither of us spill the other's beans. It is just that lift shafts carry sound, especially in an old tenement, with the efficacy of a tannoy.

'What were you doing on the roof?' I ask. 'In the daytime.'

'Nothing,' Mr Wu replies defensively. 'Nothing at all.'

He stares at the door as if willing it to open. I look at his profile and consider how much more quickly Chinese age than Europeans. Mr Wu is much my junior at seventy-three yet we look quite similar, racial physiognomy apart.

The old Chinese lives alone in Flat 36, third floor, one of the less salubrious quarters of the building for it looks out not on to the busy street crowded for eighteen hours a day with pedestrians and traffic but on to an alleyway at the rear in which dubious characters meet to carry on their suspect business and which, when there is no human presence, is the domain of some particularly large rats. Sometimes he curses these rodents and sometimes he feeds them. It all depends upon his mood or whether or not he wants to earn a credit in the account books of the gods. He has the idea that, if he shows compassion for his enemies, the gods might treat him kindly when he comes into their company. The rats being enemies, he sees feeding them as a good opportunity to be charitable.

The lift stops abruptly, my legs momentarily giving way then regaining their strength.

'Where are you going, *san foo*?' Mr Wu asks.

'You know,' I say, 'I am not a *san foo* any longer. That was a long time ago. I do wish you would call me something else.'

'What do I call you?' Mr Wu rejoins. 'There is nothing else. I am always a tailor, Tsoi will always be a cook, you will always be a *san foo*.'

Deciding not to follow this line of conversation, for it is one we have at least once a week without resolution, I say nothing. Mr Wu chuckles, a soft gurgling laugh I have grown to know well. At the street door, we part company. Mr Wu waves as we set off in different directions.

'I shall see you later?' he asks me.

'Later?' I consider his words. 'No, I think not.'

'You should come,' Mr Wu calls after me. 'Need to relax. You are too busy for an old man.'

Yet I have made up my mind, wave and walk away.

There are times when I do not want Mr Wu's company, and others when I need it. Tonight is one of the former. I seek only my own company in the presence of strangers, wish to be alone in the crowds, just another European wandering the streets.

Now it is evening, the tourists are out in force in Tsim Sha Tsui: their day excursions are over, they have had their hotel dinners and their guides have gone home. Left to their own devices, they have embarked upon a shopping spree in the brightly lit streets, pausing in front of camera and jewellery shops, being accosted by touts wanting to sell them silk ties and leather wallets. I mingle with them, watch and listen as they are persuaded, beguiled and cheated. One American, his tropical shirt decorated with palm trees and hula-hula girls hanging down over his belt, a Leica camera suspended around his neck, enquires into the price of a pair of binoculars.

'Six hund'ed eighty dollar,' the shopkeeper tells him. 'Good price. For you, first customer tonight, I say six hund'ed fifty. You wan' buy?'

'Six hundred,' the American bargains.

He has been told no one pays the asking price. It is the done thing, the guidebooks instruct him, to dicker with vendors, ignore the marked price on the label and go for the deal.

'Six forty,' the shopkeeper suggests. 'I make little p'ofit.'

'Six twenty,' the American demands.

'You hard man. Strike good bargain,' the shop-keeper congratulates him, smiling sheepishly. 'Okay! Six twenty.'

He grimaces, pretending to be a loser. The American grins and winks at his wife who is standing behind him clutching her handbag. He starts to remove traveller's cheques from his wallet, laying them out on the glass counter next to his purchase.

'Honey, give me a pen.'

'Okay. I got a pen,' says the shopkeeper and takes one out of his pocket.

The American's wife looks relieved. She does not want to open her handbag: she has read the Orient is awash with thieves.

'Say,' the American asks, 'is that US or Hong Kong dollars?'

'US dollar,' the shopkeeper says.

So the American signs six hundred and twenty US dollars' worth of cheques for an item he could have purchased for six hundred Hong Kong. I glance across the street at a money-changer's shop: the rate is four Hong Kong dollars and ten cents to the American buck. It occurs to me there should be another beatitude: blessed are the fleeced and suckered for they shall remain in blissful ignorance of their own stupidity.

In the side-streets, others are looking for a different deal. These would-be customers carry no cameras and are not accompanied by their wives. They walk in twos and threes, comrades-in-arms facing the thrill of the Oriental night. Some are visiting businessmen but most are sailors from the cruise ships, stewards from the airliners or soldiers posted to Whitfield Barracks in Nathan Road or Kowloon Tong.

Here, where the streets are narrower and the traffic slow moving, pimps are out in force. They are less strident than the silk tie hawkers but no less insistent.

'You want girl?' they enquire, walking beside a potential client for a few steps. 'Good girl. Young girl. Speak goo' English. Free beer for you.'

Some accept and are hustled down alleys: some refuse and are left alone for a few yards before another pimp confronts them. Only a few make it to the end of the street undecided or unmolested.

I am not accosted. I do not look right and am therefore left alone by both touts and pimps. There is something about me these canny operators can sense. Perhaps, in their eyes, I am too old. They think I am past it, have purchased all the silk ties a man can require in one lifetime and am too decrepit to lie with a woman young enough to be my great-granddaughter.

My perambulation is not to strike a hard bargain or to rent young flesh for an hour or two. I do not look upwards at the neon signs advertising the *Bayside Night-club* and *Eddie Shiu: Tailors*, *Rolex* and *Longines*, *Zeiss Ikon* and the *Opal Factory*. I am not here to swim vicariously in the wake of the more adventurous or foolhardy but simply to watch, to be with my fellow man as he makes an ass of himself, degrades himself, surrenders himself to base instincts. I do not criticise him nor try to prevent him going along the course he has set: I am not a judge or a jury, merely a lone spectator sharing in the quandaries of human existence, looking for truths which I know, deep within myself, I have never owned nor shall ever find.

Once, the tenement in which I live had been a chic apartment block in the modish style of its times: the corner of the building between Nanking Street and Woosung Street is rounded, this feature drawing much consternation from local residents. Sharp angles are bad luck and encourage evil spirits but a smooth curve makes life hard for them. Their talons cannot get a grip.

What seemed even more amazing to the local populace was the fact that the curved end of the building contained windows. It was a topic of considerable discussion in the local tea-houses and cooked food stalls as to how the building did not fold like a pile of rice wafers when the corner had no visible means of support.

It is five storeys high, six if you count them in the Chinese fashion where the ground is the first floor, with a communal flat roof. The whole structure was originally faced in cream-coloured concrete designed not to glare in the tropical sun like white-painted surfaces but to still keep the interior cool. The structural design allowed for no verandas but this did not deter residents: no one would want to sit out overlooking a street. Balconies were for those with gardens. Each apartment, in the old Colonial style, had a servants' quarters at the rear and spacious rooms. In the days before air conditioners, it was considered the bigger a room was, the cooler it would become in the hot months. The stairs were wide and there was no lift but the architect installed a winch system at the back to raise heavy loads into the apartments. It was by this route furniture arrived.

Each apartment had parquet floors, wide windows with typhoon-proof metal frames, solid mahogany doors and well-appointed kitchens. The bathrooms contained both a bath and a shower, and a western-style, sit-down water closet. The roof was paved with red quarry tiles and had an area set aside, with drain holes in the floor, where wash-amahs could hang the laundry and sit about to chatter.

The edifice was considered a marvel but I did not live here then. At the time, I rented two rooms in an wooden building in Western District, not far from the market and abattoir. Nanking Street, in those days, was above my station. By the time I moved into Flat 42 on the fourth floor, the building had come down in the world: it was no longer an apartment block but had become a tenement.

Today, the servants' quarters are self-contained flats occupied by families of up to six. The roomy apartments have been sub-divided into two, some-times three, and the stairwell has shrunk by the addition of the now decrepit lift which was installed up the centre, cutting out all light from the stairs and causing them to be rebuilt in a square spiral. Above each floor, a corrugated iron rooflet has been added over the windows: I suppose once the rooms were reduced in size, they became hot in the summer. The iron has rusted, staining the concrete facing which is no longer cream but blotchy grey and the window frames of every apartment, without exception, have also decayed, making their typhoon-proof abilities a matter for conjecture.

Mr Li, my neighbour in 43, realising the building's

deficiency in balconies, has knocked a window into a door and bolted onto the outside of the building a metal cage lined with steel mesh. It is three-feet deep, six wide and high, with a metal floor and a tin roof upon which the rain drums deafeningly and which, like the corrugated iron, has rusted. It can just accommodate him for, like his flat, it is chock-full with four kumquat and azalea bushes in pots, a green-and-white striped plastic chair, a folding table and a wooden crate in which there live two clucking hens and an indignant cockerel.

On the roof, the landlord has allowed an old woman to erect a shanty in the corner where the laundry area had been. It is a meagre, two-room shack of timber planks and packing cases nailed together under a sloping roof of plywood covered in flattened off-cuts filched from a metalworking business in Saigon Street. Once I saw her in the dead of night scurrying about the alley behind the workshop, tying aluminium sheets together with bamboo twine. In front of the shack is a small area of potted plants including a clump of bamboo which she claims is from the grove before her father's house near Swatow.

In the early hours of summer mornings, when the street is empty and the traffic temporarily stilled, the building hums with the spinning of old air-conditioner motors, the dripping of water sucked from the air, the buzz of neon lights with faulty connections and the belligerent, if muffled, crowing of the cockerel, which always begins its noise an hour before dawn. Not that it has much territory to protect nor any serious threat from an interloper. The nearest competition for his two scruffy hens is over two hundred yards away in Pak Hoi Street where there are a number of poultry sellers. Furthermore, the cockerels there are transients, en route for the cooked food stalls.

Yet I do not curse the bird. He has his life to live, just as we all do and, like us, is making the best of it.

My flat is not large but I am one of the lucky residents of the tenement for it incorporates one of the smooth corner windows. This has distinct benefits and equally manifest disadvantages. On one hand, it affords me a panoramic view of the junction between Nanking and Woosung Streets, brings morning sunlight into my abode and keeps the place cool in summer. On the other, the frames do not fit. Those sceptics who pondered on the wisdom of having an unsupported corner were right: the evil spirits cannot get a grip but neither can the concrete. The building has sagged under its own weight and buckled the window frames, some of which do not open, those which do opening too easily and letting in draughts when shut.

I live, by tenemental standards, in a plush residence of four rooms. What is more, I own it, having purchased the flat from Mr Poon on a fifty-year lease. He was a serious man with a limp who, like so many Chinese, was addicted not to opium or nicotine, alcohol or concubines but to gambling. He bet quite effectively on the horses and was a cool, quick-witted mah-jong player and these two sports, the one of kings and the other of coolies, brought him a steady if unspectacular profit. Yet, like any gambler, he was never satisfied: his life was empty without the big win and he could not understand, although I warned him, there was no such thing as the ultimate pot.

'I wan' one million dollars,' he confided one day as we met at a food stall in Temple Street.

'And then?' I asked.

'I stop, buy one more building, rent more flats. Maybe buy a Chrysler car. Big one. Sen' my son to school in America.'

He spooned his fish soup and noodles into his mouth as I watched him. There was a gambler's faraway stare in his eye.

'You cannot stop gambling,' I said. 'It is in your blood. It is a part of you, like doing business.'

'Sure, can do,' he answered, putting his bowl down on the wooden table. 'When I a rich man what I wan' to gamble for? I got my money.'

'No man gambles to win,' I replied. 'They gamble for excitement, for the thrill. Like drinking strong wine or having good sex.'

'How you know?' Mr Poon laughed. There was a hint of mockery in his words. 'You no gamble. You no drink too much. You no have woman.'

Yet I knew for I had seen the world and Mr Poon had not. His son never went to school abroad and he never bought another tenement. He gradually slid further into debt with the loan sharks and, one Sunday, after he had lost heavily at the Happy Valley races, he approached myself, Mr Wu and Mrs van der Poehl to offer us our flats. The asking price was below the going rate. He was desperate. We each spent the next day raising the money in our respective ways and, that evening, became the owners of our flats. We had attained the dream of everyone in the street — to own our own place, beyond the reach of rent rises and devious landlords. Mr Poon, however, did not pay off his creditors. He went immediately to Macau where we assumed he lost it all playing *fan tan* in the casino. He never returned. Rumour said he had made his fortune, cut and run, yet I know he did not. He loved his son too much if not his wife and daughter. He was probably killed by the loan sharks or at his own hand, going into the hills and swallowing caustic soda. One man's misfortune is another's good luck. That's the way it is.

The flat is not lavish. I have chosen not to live extravagantly. My needs are not excessive nor are my desires beyond more or less immediate satisfaction: at my age, the latter are reduced to the few plain luxuries which an old man might want to keep to ensure his life is made less difficult. A roof, sufficient food and adequate clothing are all I now demand of the world. And, of course, the security of mind to know these are mine without fear of imminent loss. I have a few friends whom I can trust or sit beside without endlessly talking cant and the good fortune to live where the sunlight is never chill and the world never boring. What is more, I have the inestimable luck of never being idle unless I so choose. An idle man dies quicker than a busy one.

However, I admit to having some weaknesses. I like beer in moderation and there is, of course, my occasional nocturnal indulgence with Mr Wu. These I consider my delicious little sins, weaknesses proving I am still alive. Should the time come when I no longer regard them in such a light, then that would be the hour to shuffle off this mortal coil and head for the next way point in eternity.

My home consists of a shower-cum-wc cubicle, an equally minute kitchen, a bedroom and a sitting room which is L-shaped. The latter is the only room with windows, the corner ones forming the heel of the L. I do not own a television although I have a third-hand air conditioner which keeps me awake just as the heat it is meant to combat does: it rattles incessantly and, after running for an hour or so, takes on the character of an old car, the motor stuttering as if changing gear. My furniture is simple – a bed and chest of drawers, a small round table to eat or read at with four chairs, some bookshelves, a cracked leather armchair I seldom sit in, a battered cane table with a glass sheet across the top and a matching chair which is my favourite, a scratched roll-top bureau and a large camphorwood chest. On the window sill is a kumquat plant in an ochre glazed pot whilst on the round table is a plastic cloth: on the cane table I keep a chipped Ming bowl and a pink-and-black soap-stone ashtray full of melon seeds.

I have allowed myself the luxury of a small refrigerator which does not come from the same stable as the air conditioner. The latter I bought from a stall in the market, the former from an electrical goods store in Sham Shui Po.

The floors are parquet making the place cool and I keep the wooden blocks polished therefore having no need of carpets. Having said that, I own a light blue Tientsin carpet in front of my arm chair. Just for decoration.

I am not a man for possessions. The older one

grows, the less one wants. The collecting phase of one's life ceases after fifty, objects replaced by memories. The mental trappings of the long voyage through the years are enough. Objects remind one of the past and in this they are beneficial for one can give them away and it is like shedding history. Memories are more cruel: they cannot be given away, only shared.

I have, however, retained three specific items from my past which sit on the bookcase. They are little mementos, totems of where I have been in my travels towards today. I do not need them as reminders. Why I keep them I do not really know for I am not sentimental. Sentimentality is a surrender to base emotions which I will not allow.

One of these *memento mori* is a trade dollar. On the face stands Britannia, her trident sharp and her Union Jack shield bold in her left hand. Her cloak billows in the wind. In the distance is a sailing ship, the might of commerce nestling under her protection. Beneath her feet is the date of issue – 1899. My *annus mirabilis*. The obverse is a geometrical design of curlicues and whirls set in a ring of Persian design with a central Chinese motif. The value is given in Arabic and Chinese and the coin is forged in silver, the figure of Britannia having lost its finer detail.

Next to the coin is a six-inch-high opium oil lamp with a thick glass bulb, brass fittings and a burnt wick protruding from the oil reservoir. From a distance, it looks like a small medicine bottle for the barrel of the straight sides is dark green: this is not glass but quality jade.

I rarely use the lamp and I cannot spend the coin. They are both, like myself, antiques. No one accepts trade dollars and few bother with the traditional rigmarole of opium smoking. Today's chasers of dragons make do with matches or a Zippo cigarette lighter.

And the third item: that is also jade, an exquisite carving no bigger than a thumb joint. The jade is off-white, the colour of clouds after they have shed their rain. It has a smooth, waxy touch: collectors refer to this as mutton-fat jade. Perfect in every detail, it is a tortoise's shell. The creature has left it: all that remains is the dome and flat base with a thin hole through the centre so one might pass a cord through and wear it.

This is not an ornament nor a piece of jewellery. It is grave jade. At some time in its past, it has adorned a corpse.

I do not wear such things. Not yet, anyway.

There are other possessions I own but, like unwanted relatives, I have farmed them out and they reside now in the vault of the Hongkong & Shanghai Bank. There they may remain. I am unable to bring myself to cast them off. Like unwelcome relatives, they are affiliated to me by blood. Not the blood that runs in my veins for this is but a convenient metaphor: their blood has already been spilled.

The bookcases are laden mostly with paperbacks. I mention this because the best judge of a man is to know what he reads: and what point is there in listing my few belongings if not to give an insight into my soul.

If a man reads nothing, he is a hollow creature: if he reads detective fiction, he has an errant mind and would prefer a puzzle to a truth: a reader of romances is a dolt unable to find love: an aficionado of adventure stories is a tired man who lacks the imagination to leave his room and run a risk: one who indulges in scientific works is a dullard. All may be acceptable fellows and staunch friends, their weaknesses indicated by their reading matter but not a cause for avoidance.

The only man to eschew is the one whose shelves bear books about religion, for he is a seeker after eternity, a pious fool, a self-righteous bombast and a moralistic toad. He may read this tripe, but be assured as readily as there are fish in the sea he has a mistress or a young boy in his past, has thieved or cheated, connived or killed. He cannot be trusted for he is lost and one lost man drags others after him into oblivion.

My shelves bear none of these although I admit that once they did: a Bible and the Apocrypha, religious treatises, *The Life of Christ* and *The Life and Works of St Paul* by Farrar, both volumes of Caird's *The Evolution of Religion*, Bartoli's *The Primitive Church and The Primacy of Rome*. No longer. I was lost but now am found.

At the end of the top shelf, on the right hand side, out of reach unless I climb onto a chair, a precarious action at my age, is a book bound in black leather. I have placed it second in from the end of the shelf so that I might never see the gold blocked numbers on the cover. There is no title visible on the spine, so one might assume it to be a prayer book.

I rarely take it down: in fact, I have not touched it for years, not even to dust it. I do not bother with the top shelf. No one sees the agglomeration of dead flies, desiccated mosquitoes and grey exuviae. And yet I know it is there, am unable to forget or ignore it. It squats above my room, above my life, like a small dark incubus which, every day, draws my eye to torment me.

I have not the courage to destroy it. I have thought to set it alight, watch as the brittle pages flare and char, or drop it over the side of the Star Ferry, not looking round as it floats away in the wake, but it holds too much I cannot refute, contains too many days I want to forget yet dare not. If I were to utterly destroy it, I would achieve nothing, for what it holds is in me, moving relentlessly about in me like cigarette smoke marbling in the still air of an empty room.

The gold numbers read 1900.

It is the diary of just one year of my life.

The hull of the steam pinnace *Lucky Moon* was black with a gold stripe and two golden entwining dragons painted on either side of the bow. They were not pretentious Chinese dragons with huge eyes, forked tongues and curving tails like scaly hawsers but small and discreet, somehow suggestive of considerable power. The black funnel was tall and thin with a brass collar which, being as highly polished as the deck fittings, looked golden: even the belching smoke was solidly black, not greyly ephemeral.

There was no cabin. Instead, aft of the boiler, there was a well deck stretching to the stern covered by an awning of blancoed canvas supported by a steel cross-frame which could be folded flat and transformed into a sort of shack by pulling a roof of wooden slats over the metal framework. The bench seats opened into beds, the lockers beneath them storing bedding and personal possessions.

She had a crew of two, a captain and a boy. The former was in his late middle-age and wore the threadbare remnants of a British naval officer's jacket with tattered epaulettes and a high collar he could not button up because of the prominence of his Adam's apple. Unlike most Chinese men, whose heads were shaven back to their long cues, he had a Western-style haircut with a few long wisps of bristle growing from a mole on his jaw. His responsibility was the sailing of the vessel, watching pressure gauges, taking the wheel, navigating and uttering guttural remarks to the boy between humming a tuneless music, his tongue making sonorous bell-like noises.

The boy was not more than thirteen, with his hair in a cue. His clothes were not as threadbare as his master's but just as incongruous, being a dark-blue Chinese jacket worn over a British soldier's pair of shorts which, being much too large, had been folded in a tuck in front and were held in place by a leather thong. What the captain did not do, the boy took on, swabbing decks, polishing pipes, stoking the boiler, coiling ropes and stowing painters.

The only other person aboard the craft, other than myself, was Ah Fong. It was he who had welcomed me aboard that morning. I had arrived by rickshaw at the dockside just before seven to be greeted by him bowing low at the foot of the gangplank.

'Goo' morning, master,' he had said, tilting his head back so he could see me. 'Me Ah Fong. Serwant, frien', compan-ee-on for you to go China side.'

His cue of hair slid to one side and he flicked

31

it deftly out of the way as he straightened his back.

'Good morning, Ah Fong,' I answered and held my hand out to him. He shook it firmly, just the once, the sleeve of his black cotton jacket swishing against his wrist.

'You come now, master,' he instructed, taking charge of my baggage and stowing it away in two lockers. 'Come on *Lucky Moon*. We go now.'

'How long is our journey?' I enquired as I stepped on to the gangplank.

'One two day, master. But goo' sea. Goo' wind. No rain, no womit.'

'Womit?' I replied.

'Womit, master. Womit.' He stretched his neck and gave a mime of retching. 'Womit. Chow come back topside. If sea too big. But now no big sea. No womit.'

I settled in the well deck as he indicated. The captain tinkered with some valves, the boy cast off, the steam whistle shrilled and the screw began to turn, threshing the water. We departed the dock, crossed through lines of sailing vessels riding at anchor then set off along a channel between rock-strewn, grassy hillsides falling steeply to the sea. Little beaches and headlands of boulders slid by until, after an hour or so, we passed a conical mountain to starboard and headed into the wide estuary of the Pearl River. Thus had begun the last stage of my journey from Dublin, upon which I had embarked three months previously.

For some time I stared pensively at the swirling wake but watching its convolutions made me feel slightly giddy. I turned my attention to the captain at the wheel, his jacket hazy through a jet of escaping steam: the boy knelt by the boiler operating a secondary firebox the door of which was open to display a trapped hell of glowing coals. Ah Fong stood over him.

We crossed the Pearl River estuary in three hours and, although the sea was not smooth, the swell was low and I was not discomforted. By one o'clock, the sun beating on the awning and striking off the sea, we entered channels of the river delta south west of Canton, passing a Chinese fort, the wide-mouthed cannons poking through battlements, bright red triangular pennants flying from bamboo poles which whipped in the breeze.

'For fighting,' Ah Fong had announced. 'Plenty bad men here in riffer. He name pywrat.'

'Shall we be troubled by them?' I asked apprehensively.

The pirates' reputation was bloody and extensive: given the opportunity, they would attack a sixty-gun man-o'-war. Only a few months before a band of brigands had stormed a Yokohama-bound clipper, murdering the crew, looting the vessel then setting her alight.

'No,' Ah Fong reassured me. 'We too small. No got much. He wan' catch big junk, big ship. Plenty people, plenty money.'

The delta lands were monotonous. Small fishing and cargo sampans drifted by, the banks lined by dense groves of bamboo with small matshed houses built by fishing nets suspended from poles. The further from the sea, the thicker the bamboo became and it was half an hour before we came upon a village. It was little more than a hamlet of

33

low, grey stone houses under roofs the eaves of which curled upwards at the corners. By a mud and shingle landing place grew a tree with branches hanging into the water reminding me of the scene depicted upon willow-pattern plates.

A mob of children, hearing the thump of the engine, ran down to the muddy shore to gaze at the vessel yet not one child waved and I felt sad. On the voyage out, wherever the ship had berthed, children had appeared to wave, beg, cat-call and laugh. They had gathered around me, their hands outstretched and their faces alight with smiles appealing for bak-sheesh, offering to be guides to mosques or iniquitous dens of pleasure. If the ship lay offshore they had swum out to dive for coins, their lithe nut-brown bodies disappearing under the sea like otters. Yet these children stood in a mute, solemn group, their eyes fixed on the *Lucky Moon*, following it intently as it passed. I waved to them yet drew not the least response.

Ah Fong stepped across the deck with a bowl of rice, an oval platter of fish and vegetables and a cup of tea. The eating utensils were a pair of bamboo chopsticks.

'I sowwy chow late come, master,' he apologised, placing the food beside me. 'No good cook before. Water too big.'

'That does not matter,' I said then, noticing his food was by the firebox, added, 'Get your food and sit with me. I want to talk to you.'

With Ah Fong squatting on the deck before me, I began to eat. The vegetables were a sort of pointed boiled mushroom the shape of an ink-cap, sliced crisp bamboo shoots and long strands of

34

green leaves which looked like spinach but tasted delicious. The fish contained an inordinate number of bones which I found difficult to separate from the flesh with chopsticks. I watched Ah Fong to see how he managed.

It was quite simple. He picked up a piece of the fish with his chopsticks, noisily sucked the flesh from the bones then spat the detritus over the side of the boat. I did likewise which produced a quick sideways glance from him which I construed as approval.

The fish and vegetables eaten, I was left with rice in my bowl, flavoured by a thin gravy. Ah Fong tackled this by placing his bowl to his lips, shovelling the rice into his mouth with a rowing motion of his chopsticks. I copied him.

'D'ink tea now,' Ah Fong suggested.

I picked up the cup which was like the rice bowl only smaller. It was hot and my fingers tingled as I sipped cautiously.

'Too hot for you, master? No matter. You d'ink, make noise. Make cold.'

Ah Fong took my cup, put it to his lips and slurped loudly.

'Now I get nuffer one.'

He went off and poured a second cup taken from a basin by the firebox. The tea was clear, weak and scented with jasmine flowers which hung above the tea leaves like tiny fish.

'Ah Fong,' I asked after imitating his slurp, 'why did those children not wave?'

'He no wafe. He af'aid.'

'Afraid?' I puzzled. 'Have they not seen a steam boat before?'

'Oh, he see. Plenty time see. *Lucky Moon* go up down Wuchow two time one mumph.'

'Do they think this a pirate boat?'

'No!' Ah Fong laughed. 'No pywrat boat! All pywrat Chinese man got junk. No engine.'

'So why are they afraid?'

'He af'aid you,' Ah Fong replied bluntly.

'Of me! They don't know me.'

'You fowener. Not Chinese man. You *gweilo*. Fowen devil. So he no wafe. If he wafe, you look him, can steal his soul.'

In mid-afternoon the hazy sky cleared to a hot blue and the delta countryside gave way to mountains. They were not a thousand feet high, as yet unweathered by time or sculptured by men. The steep slopes were wooded and the valleys cultivated with small paddy-fields. Villages appeared and the river, after going through a gorge a few miles long, widened to half a mile. The captain kept the *Lucky Moon* near the centre.

We made less headway, the engine straining against the current, the pistons vehemently hissing, the funnel gouting gobbets of smoke. About three o'clock, we passed a small town on the outskirts of which stood a seven-storey pagoda, its walls painted white with red piping, the roof crowned by a golden orb.

'What is that building for?' I asked Ah Fong, who was leaning over the side rinsing the food bowls by lowering them into the wake in a bucket pierced with holes.

'What for?' He was puzzled. 'Is pago-dah.'

'Yes, but why was it built?'

'To stop riffer d'agon,' he replied.

36

'River dragons?'

He pulled the bucket in, hanging it from a davit to drain in the scuppers.

'Water home for d'agon,' he explained. 'You see riffer bend come go? Because his tail bending.'

'How does the pagoda stop the dragon?' I enquired.

He pondered the question before answering, 'Pagodah tell d'agon no come here, we know you, you no make t'ouble for us or we kill you.'

Just as the sun was settling upon the mountains, the pinnace turned a bend to steam across a wide bay on which there was another town with a pagoda in its centre: on the opposite bank stood a second. The pinnace altered course to avoid a long, low barge-like vessel sailing up-river under a single brown square sail as ribbed as a bat's wing. When our bow swung round, the sun silhouetted the sail and hull, the river behind it a shifting cascade of gold light cast between the two pagodas.

I caught my breath and felt the strong desire to pray, to give thanks for such beauty at the end of a day that had seen me safely journeying into China. I knelt on the deck, placed my hands together and raised my face, the last rays of the sun warm on my skin. It was as if God were touching me.

'Thank you, Lord,' I said, 'for Your guidance and strength this day, for Your protection as I sail at Your command up the Si Kiang river to do Your bidding.' I paused for a moment before adding, 'And I offer my thanks also for this beautiful evening which is a manifestation of Your Holy Glory.'

Interrupting my devotions, Ah Fong called out,

'Master, here two pago-dah. Because too many d'agon in riffer.'

When Ah Fong served the evening meal, a thick broth in which floated pieces of anonymous gristly meat, I asked him when we would reach Wuchow.

'Long time, master,' was the reply. 'Next day we come Wuchow. Afternoon.'

As darkness fell, the river came alive with lights. At first, I thought these were houses on the shore but as we drew nearer they moved and soon we were in the thick of a fleet of small sampans hung with lanterns.

'He fishing,' Ah Fong explained. 'Make light. Fish come see light, like moff. When he come, fisherman catch him. Easy work.'

'Are we stopping tonight?' I enquired.

'We stop. But no here. Too many fisherman. Stop small time more, up near mountain.'

He pointed ahead: set darkly against the night was a range of hills. They could not have been more than a few miles away but it was an hour before we reached them, the captain throttling back the engine and turning the *Lucky Moon*, allowing her to drift with the strong current into a narrow creek grown over with tall bamboo and edged by reedbeds.

Once we were stationary in the creek, Ah Fong transformed the well deck into a cabin, covering the bench with a quilt.

'Sleep now,' Ah Fong said unnecessarily, as the boy attended to the boiler, raking out the hot ash to drop it hissing into the river. 'Tomorrow, we go before sun come.'

'I should like to stretch my legs,' I said. Ah Fong did not understand the colloquialism. 'I should like to walk. My legs,' I rubbed my thigh, 'are very sore.'

Ah Fong nodded and went into a huddle with the captain. They talked for several minutes before he said, 'Can do. But no go long way. No must meet people. If you see people, must hide. Capting say good you wear black cassock. No can see you easy. But if you see people hide come back quick quick. No talk him.'

The boy pushed the gangplank onto the bank, jamming it between some thick trunks of bamboo.

'Jus' here,' Ah Fong pointed through the bamboo, 'one parf. You walk parf, go only on parf. Go here.' He pointed up-river. 'No here.' He swung his arm down-river. 'How long you go?'

'Half an hour,' I suggested.

'Half hour can do. No more.'

I stepped along the gangplank but, as I reached the bamboo, Ah Fong advised, 'If you hide, look down you shoes. Put hand in pocket. White skin can see. People t'ink you ghost. No good be ghost.'

Struggling through the bamboo, I discovered the path and set off along it. I thought the need for caution to be overstated but appreciated from reports in Hong Kong that the hills harboured bandits. My baggage would constitute ripe pickings and, as a European, I could be held for a substantial ransom.

The moonless sky was clear, my eyes soon adjusting to the starlight. I could plainly see the path and was confident that if I were to meet someone I could easily step unseen into the bushes and bamboo thickets along the way.

I had walked for about ten minutes and was considering turning back when I smelt wood smoke. The path, which was narrow and not well-frequented near the *Lucky Moon*, was joined here by another

39

coming up from the river, the two forming a well-used thoroughfare. Past a clump of bamboo I found myself suddenly at a gate set in a fence of wooden planks.

Quickly, I stepped back and studied the gateway. The two pillars were made of stone across which was a wooden beam a foot square. Several vertical planks were set into a slot in the beam and a groove cut in the step which was carved of natural rock. In the centre of the beam was a circular mirror on either side of which was carved a Chinese character.

Through the gate, about thirty feet away, was a square, single-storey house before which was a hard, beaten-earth courtyard. To one side was a small shed of bamboo matting such as I had seen by the fishing nets on the river. Leaning against the building was a crude wooden plough next to which glowed several incense sticks poking out of a small glazed pot. The house was windowless but a faint light emanated from an open doorway.

I stood quite still and listened. Somewhere in a tree behind the house, a cicada was making its loud intermittent insect chirruping. From the shed came a restless shuffling which I assumed to be livestock of some sort. From the doorway came a low hum of voices punctuated by the sound of a liquid being poured. One voice was momentarily raised and someone laughed. They were male voices.

In the doorway appeared a woman. She materialised so quickly and so silently I had somehow not seen her. One moment the doorway was empty, the next she was standing there holding a lantern. I stepped into the shadow of the gate pillar. By the lamplight, I could make out her features. She was short and slim, wearing baggy trousers with a dark smock-like blouse. Her hair was raked back and shone across her scalp as if oiled. Her cheekbones were high but her eyes wide and not at all narrowed.

She moved to one side, set her lantern on the ground and, from the shadows, produced a small stool on which she sat. A child then came out of the house carrying a baby which it handed to her. Neither of them spoke and the child returned the way it had come.

The woman unbuttoned a flap at the shoulder of her blouse and, folding it back, lifted her breast out and gave it to the infant which began to suckle. I could see the soft white of the woman's skin and hear the contented suck of the baby. For several minutes, I watched this scene, captivated by its beauty, simplicity and wonder. Here was the work of God at its most basic: a mother feeding her child. All they needed, I considered, was to know the Word of the one God and have His Light shine upon them.

Another lantern appeared at the door held by an older woman. She rasped a curt command to the young mother who immediately put her breast away and, with a quiet word, handed the baby to the other who cuddled it. Then, by the old woman's side, appeared a dog. It sniffed the air, stepped onto the courtyard, sniffed again and growled in my direction.

Anxious not to alarm the animal, I stepped away. My sleeve snagged on a short sapling of bamboo but I was unaware of this: I continued to move until the thin stem broke free and snapped upright, rattling against the broader trunks of the parent plant like a pair of castanets. The dog began to bark furiously, raised voices accompanying it.

My cassock slapping against my legs, the sleeves flailing in the air, I ran. The heavy material snagged on thorns and snared on branches. I fled so quickly I missed the point where I had to turn down to the *Lucky Moon* and was obliged to retrace my steps for fifty yards, sweating with fear that I might meet a group out looking for me. When I reached the boat, I was breathless.

'You make dog bark,' Ah Fong whispered.

'Yes,' I stuttered, trying to find my breath. 'I don't think they followed me.'

'He no follow,' Ah Fong said matter-of-factly. 'Night time no follow. Too many ghost, too many d'agons.'

In the starlight, I could see Ah Fong and the captain grinning broadly.

'No more walk,' Ah Fong then stated quietly. 'Now sleep.'

I removed my outer garments and, in my underwear, wriggled under the quilt. I had the cabin space to myself, Ah Fong lying on the deck, the boy curled up and wheezing softly in his sleep by the engine: the captain sat on the gangplank listening to the night.

Just after dawn, I was disturbed from my slumbers by a gentle hissing of steam as the pinnace started to edge backwards. The roof and sides of the cabin were gone, the awning back in place. A faint wisp of smoke drifted out of the funnel to hang in the thick white mist settled upon the river.

'No noise,' Ah Fong cautioned me, pressing his finger horizontally along his lips rather than vertically across them. 'After you sleep, fisherman come look see for boat . . .'

As the *Lucky Moon* edged clear of the creek, the pull of her hull dragged a limp body out of the reeds. The figure lay face down, dressed in a blue jacket and trousers, a long cue of hair floating out from the head at right angles. Around the neck was a red weal where, I assumed, a garrotte had tightened. The body pirouetted about as it nudged a bed of weed. Twenty feet out from the bank a current took hold of the body, spun it ninety degrees and towed it quickly away.

'No good swim in riffer,' Ah Fong observed, as I watched the body vanish. 'D'agon take you downside. Eat you.'

A run of cold blood flowed down my spine: I could feel the hair rise on my nape. It was not the horror of death that filled me with such dread but the terrible matter-of-factness in Ah Fong's voice. Death was unequivocally accepted by him and the dragons were as real as the daylight.

'Did you have to kill him?' I asked.

'Must do. If no, people come, kill you, kill me.'

I looked at the river and thought of what I had witnessed the night before, the mother suckling her infant: if I had not gazed upon the sight, had not been so self-indulgent, the man would be alive and the infant would still have a father or an uncle.

'But will they not miss him?'

'He no know where he gone. They shout but no look. Too af'aid.'

'Will they not know it was us?'

'He no know!' Ah Fong said dismissively. 'He say d'agon eat him.'

43

Looking up at the funnel, I saw blacker smoke beginning to appear. The captain pressed a lever and the pistons began to hiss and spit, the propeller turning once more with its rhythmical thumping.

'They will hear the engine. They will smell the smoke,' I said.

'No, master. He say it d'agon. No can see boat, can smell fire, hear noise like snake. Like d'agon . . .'

I crossed myself and muttered a quick prayer for the poor heathen's soul but Ah Fong gave it no further thought and, as soon as we were under way, set about preparing a breakfast of thin gruel-like soup, little dumplings stuffed with fish and a cup of thick, dark tea.

'Man die ve'y quick, master,' he commented as he served the food. 'Captain ve'y good man. No noise, no pain.'

'He was not a dog,' I remonstrated, angry he could be so utterly ruthless and puzzled how a convert to Christianity could be so merciless.

Ah Fong, not understanding the analogy, said, 'No kill like dog. Hit dog with big stick on the head to kill him. Sometimes must hit five, six times before dog die. This one no hit. Just one touch and he finish.'

For the whole day, the *Lucky Moon* steamed up-river, the currents in places so strong the vessel barely made any headway against the flow, the captain standing in the prow to find a slower running channel. With him on lookout, the boy took the wheel, holding the vessel steady, a bright puerile grin of pleasure lighting up his face. Other vessels journeying upstream were overhauled very slowly whilst those going down-river sped by, their oarsmen struggling to keep the line of their course.

The sun beat down and, although there was a brisk easterly breeze, it was hot and carried no relief.

Throughout the day, I either sat and watched the mountain landscape move inexorably by or stood in the bow gazing ahead. I could not take from my mind the fact that a man had died so my own life might be spared.

It was true that I had not done the deed: indeed, I had been oblivious of it. Yet I could not escape the realisation that, even unwittingly, I had been the cause of the man's murder and that, if the divine plan to which I had submitted my life was that I come to China to bring the heathens to Christ then this was a very sorry start, and no mistake. It would have been better if I had been killed: as it was, an ignorant fisherman, trying to protect his family, had died without blessing, without salvation and, therefore, without hope.

The afternoon drew on to early evening. The sun set behind the hills, the sky turning the colour of ducks' eggs and, just as I was wondering if we were to spend another night moored secretly in a bywater, Ah Fong called out.

'Master! Wuchow come soon.'

I eased my back and, stretching my arms, massaged my fingers together. Every bone in my body seemed tuned to the throb of the pistons: my mouth tasted of soot and my skin felt grimy even though I had washed myself with a bucket of river water just after noon.

'Soon see Wuchow,' Ah Fong declared as I joined him in the bow. 'You see island?'

Straining my eyes against the dusk, I could just make out a small island about a mile and a half away. It was rocky by the shore but wooded higher up. From within the trees shone a surprisingly bright light.

'Yes, Ah Fong, I can see it.'

'He name D'agon Island.'

'Because a dragon lives there?' I asked with a hint of irony.

'D'agon live there sometime,' he confirmed.

'And the light is the dragon's eye, is it?'

'No, no d'agon eye.'

'His fiery mouth?' I suggested.

'No,' Ah Fong repeated pedantically, 'no mouth. D'agon mouth got flame. Got yellow light, not white light. Light come from Customs post.'

Remaining at the bow, I watched the island draw closer as the crew readied for arrival. The boy lowered painters over the gunwales, tidied the deck and re-coiled the ropes. The captain began to jostle the craft against the currents, spinning the wheel, speeding up or slowing down the engine. Ah Fong lit several lamps, stowed the eating utensils and removed my baggage from the lockers, lining it up on the deck.

The town was on the right bank, glimmering lights indicating its extent: on the opposite shore was a featureless darkness with only a few sparse, dim lights showing at the water's edge. Behind Dragon Island, their bows facing up-stream and their masts outlined against the sky, were three large sailing vessels, obviously trading up from Hong Kong or Macau, and a number of junks riding at anchor. All showed running lights whilst at the stern of one of the former was displayed a row of illuminated windows.

In less than half an hour, the captain spun the

wheel and the pinnace veered in to the right shore. Although it was now dark, I could see the bank was high and steep with a long flight of stone steps leading up to a sort of promenade which was lined for a hundred yards with a throng of chattering people, many of whom carried lanterns. At the foot of the steps was a wooden pontoon upon which were gathered five or six men.

As the *Lucky Moon* slid alongside, the boy jumped onto the planking, securing a line to a wooden bollard. Once the gangplank was out, I stepped onto the jetty and two figures detached themselves from the group to walk towards me, one behind the other: the second was a Chinese with a lantern hung from a pole which he tilted forward over the other's shoulder so that it swung, casting a mobile shadow across his face.

As he came nearer, I could see that the first man was short and ruddy-faced, wearing a black cassock. Around his waist hung a black silk girdle whilst about his neck was a silver cross suspended by a chain of the same metal. Despite the jetty being made of planking, he moved silently and, glancing down, I noticed he was not wearing the shoes of a European but the soft slippers as worn by Chinese men.

'Welcome to Wuchow, Father Stephen,' he said as he drew closer. 'It's good to see you delivered safely from your journey and the ravages of the river dragons. I doubt not that Ah Fong here's been regaling you with tales of submarine monsters breathing fire and stealing virgins from their beds.'

I could not help smiling.

'We have had mention of them,' I asserted, adding 'but we have been mercifully spared an encounter.'

Yet no sooner had I spoken than I saw again in my mind the heathen's body turning in the river and, with an awesome feeling of apprehension, considered that perhaps we had, after all, come close to one but had, this time, escaped its clutches.

The man offered me his hand and said with a slight Irish lilt which time and China had not quite eradicated, 'As you will have guessed, I'm Father Callaghan. To be sure but it's good to see you.'

☯

I halt by the flower stall at the entrance to the alleyway where I frequently stop, having done so for more years than I care to consider. It is on a short cut I occasionally take from the waterfront to Nanking Street and visiting it is almost a ritual, perhaps a part of growing old.

The stall consists of a trellis of makeshift wooden shelves arranged against the wall of a coffin-maker's shop, under an awning of moth-eaten tarpaulin stretched between the iron bracket of the shop sign, the framework of an asthmatic air conditioner and a lamp-post to which is attached a small galvanised cylindrical box for the collection of dead rats. The air conditioner is switched on, dripping morosely onto the tarpaulin, a steady trickle finding a hole and pock-marking the pavement.

Fumbling in my pocket for a fifty-cent coin, I smile benignly at the old crone who sells the flowers, squatting on a low three-legged stool out of range of the drips. She glances at me then, recognising me, stares wide-eyed as if surprised to see me. I raise my eyebrows in greeting but do not speak. This, too, is a part of our ceremony.

My hand shakes as I sort out coins in my pocket. They have begun to quake a little more recently and although this does not unduly worry me, for I accept it as a further sign that I am finally growing old, it annoys me. I tug my fingers free of the lining with an impatient jerk, grasping loose change.

'Good afternoon,' I greet the old woman, my voice calm now I have overcome my frustration.

My first words are always in English. There is no logic behind this for she speaks not a word of it.

Her response is to giggle: it is the giggle not of an old woman but of a young girl. I can see, in my mind's eye, how she must have looked as a domestic *saw hei* amah, vowed to celibacy and a life dedicated to the service of foreigners. Perhaps those words in English stir happy memories of polished floors and riding in varnished rickshaws, of missy in her cocktail dress, master in his white shorts and shirt, little missy with her hair in bunches and young master riding his tricycle. And of having a full rice bowl.

'*Nei ho ma?*' I enquire next, reverting to Cantonese.

She stops giggling and smiles, the lined skin about her eyes folding like those of an ancient reptile, two gold teeth glinting between her thin lips. Her arthritic hands lift from her lap. One half-waves to me, the other involuntarily stroking her tightly combed grey hair where it is severely dragged into a taut bun held by a jade and bone pin. The jade is weak green and semi-translucent: cheap jade, the sort coolie women wear.

'And what small, heavenly faces have you today?' I ask.

My Cantonese accent is so colloquial it might be a Chinese living within my body who speaks.

'Smiling faces, sad faces, sleeping faces,' the flower-seller responds. 'What do you want?'

She stops stroking her hair, her hand vaguely gesturing in mid-air in the direction of the shelves.

'What do you recommend?'

She ponders this problem, her eyes scanning her wares propped in tin cans, some carrying labels marked *Heinz, Cow and Gate* or *Crosse & Blackwell*. As always, I follow her gaze along the lines of multi-coloured petals, bunches of asparagus fern and twigs of peach blossom not yet open. Her gaze halts on some spikes of yellow and pink blooms.

'*Wong keung,*' she declares, seeing me looking at the same tin can.

I consider the ginger flowers. They are waxy, like the death lilies one sees on altars at Easter and I catch their heady, sinful scent even above the reeking perfume of Liuchow pine sap from the coffin-maker's shop and the faint, omniscient stench of drains which haunts the alley.

'*Kei toh?*'

There is no need for me to enquire for every bloom is always fifty cents. No matter if it is an Australian imported rose, a tiger lily from the market gardens near Yuen Long or a sprig of wild camellia picked on the hills behind Kowloon, it is invariably half a dollar, the sum the old woman assesses I am good for: it is not so much as to put me off buying but it is not so low as to dent her profit margins. I know she pays not more than fifteen cents for the blossom and that, had I been a Chinese, the cost would have been twenty-five cents.

'*Ng saap sin*,' she declares, confirming the price at fifty cents and looking me straight in the eye as if daring me to haggle.

Yet it does not matter. I do not begrudge her a living and I know any other European would be charged seventy-five cents and an American sailor a dollar or more.

'*Hai*,' I agree abruptly, shrugging to imply she has got the better of me. This is another part of the custom of our commerce.

The old woman turns on her stool and pretends to choose the best of her stock, rejecting several perfectly fine blossoms, clicking her tongue and muttering incoherently. Finally, she decides on the one I should purchase and wraps it in a funnel of Chinese newspaper, sealing the base of the stem with a rubber band. She does not need to ask how many flowers I want: I always purchase just one.

'*Ng saap sin*,' she demands again, holding the flower out with her left hand.

Opening my fingers, I display the coin and her right hand comes out, palm turned upward with her gnarled fingers bent not to grasp the money but from age, decades of laundering clothes and ironing uniforms, dusting ornaments and making beds, serving at table and minding a small, blonde-haired child she loved as if it had sprung from her own womb.

As her hand meets mine, I think how both of them have touched so much in their many years, blessed and cursed, struck and stroked, held other hands, chopsticks, rice bowls – all the impedimenta of three score years and ten, and a good few more beside.

She takes the money and passes over the flower. There is a sense of propriety in the exchange: we might have been making the trade-off at the end of a long kidnap or protracted marriage brokerage. Lifting the bottom hem of her white blouse, she inserts the coin in a canvas money belt. It chinks against other coins.

I nod and she smiles again. It is a golden smile not only because of her two eighteen-carat teeth but also because, in those lines of age, there still resides the tenacity to live, the soul of a young girl waiting to die: and I wonder if, in my own face, people can read my own past, assess my current state of mind.

The ginger flower in hand, I turn away from the bright array of flowers to face the dismal alleyway. It occurs to me that the flower stall is perhaps a little evil, a gaudy but deceitful display which camouflages the entrance to the dissolute world for which the alley stands with its garbage bins and detritus of human existence. If I gave credence to such thoughts, I might believe it had been placed there by Satan himself as an enticement into Hades, the old flower seller one of the fallen angels in disguise. For a moment, I pause and survey the way ahead.

It is not a long alleyway, perhaps twenty yards from the flower stall to the next street. On either side are tenements rising to four or five storeys. From some windows project bamboo poles resting on wrought-iron brackets and hung with drying laundry. As the alley is only ten feet wide, the poles reach almost to the opposite wall. It being early evening, the hanging flags of clothing are mostly dry: had I arrived earlier, I would have needed an umbrella to reach the far end without being soaked.

Doors lead into the tenements. Some are of metal construction and some wooden but all are substantial and carry hasps and padlocks or are fitted with double deadlocks; several have iron sliding lattice security gates across them. One, leading into the rear of a gold merchant's shop, is a grey-painted steel door like the door to a companionway on a warship. It might have been pilfered from such a vessel being broken up in the Lai Chi Kok scrap yards for it has lugs which could have taken watertight screw-clamps. The few windows at ground-floor level are grimy, glazed with frosted glass strengthened with wire or protected by iron grills. Wreathes of rusty barbed wire decorate the drainpipes.

Down the centre of the alley runs an open sluice leading to a grating. It never ceases to flow with a noxious, black liquid in which, over the years, I have seen floating, along with the usual effluent, drowned kittens with their fur spiked by the water, sleek grey rats with their spines snapped, khaki-coloured rubber prophylactics, two-inch long cockroaches trying to swim clear, dead geckoes and, once, an aborted human embryo not much bigger than a small doll and curiously misshapen.

I hate the alley for I can never enter it without recalling, even for the briefest moment, that half-made infant. I had cried at the time and, taking a length of plank from beside the coffin-maker's door, had stopped the stream in order to quickly bless the little corpse, making the sign of the cross over it and muttering what I could recollect of the Latin text of the Extreme Unction. I felt I had to do something to mark its passage from reality towards eternity.

That done, I had removed the plank and the build-up of filth washed the little body away, rolling it over and over towards the sluice opening and out of sight. There had been no grating then to halt its progress under the streets and into the harbour where the fishes would consume it.

It is a hot afternoon for so early in the year. I am slumped in the battered cane chair, my head tilted forward with my chin on my chest, my right arm folded limply in my lap, my left hanging out over the side. I am bare to my waist.

I am not asleep, nor yet am I fully awake. I am in that delicious limbo where the mind is alive but still divorced from the body. Transcendentalists spend hours trying to reach such a state. I can do it in minutes, on a hot afternoon, with the air conditioner off and the window ajar, the warm breeze wafting in the familiar reassuring sounds of Nanking Street.

As I have always been, I am a thinker. I was trained as such, taught to ponder the imponderable, my duty in life to grasp philosophical problems and seek to solve them. All the other responsibilities placed upon me I have long since shirked, cast off or ignored. Yet this, the act of thinking, is the one I have retained: it is the only one worth keeping.

When I indulge myself in these moments of quiet, one of the problems I pose myself is to consider the notion that a dying man sees, in his penultimate instant as a thinking being, his life flash before him. I do not subscribe to the theory.

Instead I believe that in the weeks leading to his final day he remembers his past: not all of it in some glorious fashion, like a cinema film being projected with interludes in which he may relieve or refresh himself. He merely sees incidents from it which recapitulate his personal history so he has an idea of what he has achieved, or failed to accomplish, found or lost along the way.

If my surmise is correct, then I have been dying for years.

My past does not flash before me but comes slowly by, dragging its heels, every action slowed so I might be aware of my every stupidity, every error, every fault laid bare, so I might look at it and know myself.

Perhaps this is a punishment, a chance at redemption in that, by seeing these scenes, I might renounce them or apologise for them. Yet it is too late for all that. I am an old man and those to whom I owe apologies have long since gone before me into oblivion.

My old leather-bound travelling clock rings. I come fully to myself, my mind joining my body again. I fumble for the switch, turning the clamour off and catching my finger in the clasp on the case. I am not yet in total command of my flesh. It will take a moment or two. I replace the clock a little too heavily on the table and a thin fluted vase with the now bedraggled ginger flower in it teeters dangerously. I make no effort to steady it. I would only knock it over.

The air in the room is sultry. I twist my head, casting an eye over the round, formica-topped table with its four chairs, the shelves of leaning books and the dark shadow of the passageway that leads to the door of my flat. Through the bedroom door I can see the upright wooden chair at the foot of my bed, my dark brown shoes resting one upon the other beneath it and my favourite cream jacket draped over the back.

Nothing has changed whilst I have been away.

I vigorously massage my neck: in dozing I have cricked a muscle below my left ear, tightening the flesh in a spasm which tics irritatingly. My skin is tanned but loose-fitting, as if I am shrinking within it. During my dozing, I have loosened my belt, undoing the top button of my trousers which have slid down to my groin, showing the elastic waistband of my underpants. My feet are unshod, my toes long and thin as if they have never been confined by shoes. As I breathe, I make a soft hushing sound, my chest barely moving. At my age, breathing takes little effort. I do not need the rush of oxygen demanded by the blood of young men.

I am not sure how long I have sat here. There have been occasions, occurring with increasing frequency of late, when the passage of minutes has gone by without recognition, without impinging itself upon me. Sometimes, I pause in the middle of an everyday action, like walking along the street, and realise I have not the slightest notion of what has occurred during the last few minutes. I look down the street at, say, a coolie in a conical rattan hat struggling under the swaying weight of his pole and baskets and find that I cannot remember having seen him pass me.

Tiny sections of my life are becoming blanks: it is like reading a book and discovering certain lines have been omitted, requiring the reader to make up what has occurred in the narrative in order to maintain the continuum of sense. These lapses do not worry me. They are a curious symptom of growing old, beyond my governance and therefore impassively accepted.

I glance at the clock. The numbers have lost their luminosity, the phosphorescent paint as pellucid as the eyes of a blind beggar. The enamel face is chipped beside the 4 and the hour hand has lost its point. The glass is beginning to oxidise, too, in the region of the 11 and 12.

'Half past four,' I remark. 'The boy'll be here soon.'

Quite often, I talk to myself. It is a trait I learned long ago and is not a sign of increasing senility or loneliness. It cannot be the former for I am fully aware of my action and do not seek to reply to myself. I make statements, not being so stupid as to pose questions. And it cannot be the latter for I am not lonely. Besides, self-conversation is not a wasted gift for it not only fills empty hours but often helps to reason out problems, assures and gives confidence. All it cannot do is quell fears.

I am hot, more so than I realised sitting still. Sweat runnels from my neck down the hollow of my sternum to my stomach. It tickles and I slap at it as if it is an annoying insect.

'Still firm!' I congratulate myself.

I smite my stomach again, the flat of my palm making a loud hollow report on the damp skin.

'Loose, maybe. Old. But not flabby. Not like one of those flaccid, languishing old pedants in the Kowloon Cricket Club. Bar-proppers. Mere *boulevardiers* . . .'

There is a knocking on my door.

'The boy,' I declare.

I tug up my trousers and, reaching under the table,

fumble for my shirt, pulling it on. The cotton sticks to my skin. Finally, buttoning it up, I walk down the short, narrow passage to the door. There is a repeat of the knocking.

'A moment, please,' I call out, a little exasperated.

Quickly, I check my flies are closed, discover my trousers are still open and hastily do them up.

'Never do to see the young gentleman whilst in semi-disarray,' I murmur as I slide the chain off the door.

Twice a week, I teach a private pupil. His name is Gerald Nelson and he comes to me for Cantonese lessons. He is English, a European, a *gweilo* like myself, about seventeen years old and a pupil at King George V School. It would be foolish to be discovered by him dishabille, as it were. That sort of thing can give one a reputation and Hong Kong is little more than a village where the earning of dubious celebrity is concerned.

I open the door.

'Good afternoon, sir,' the boy says.

He is fair-skinned with blond hair in a quiff hanging over his forehead with the rest combed back to what is called a duck's-arse at the rear. It is a fashion made popular by the film star Tony Curtis and adopted by many of the popular rock and roll singers. His eyes are intensely blue and, in spite of being fair, his skin is well tanned. Like my own.

'Good afternoon. Come in.'

I hold the door open and study him as he goes down the passageway. He is wearing his school winter uniform of a smart chocolate-brown blazer with a blue-and-gold badge of a rampant lion attached to the breast pocket, a white shirt and a blue-and-brown banded tie. Despite the heat, the boy seems not even to be warm: the crease in his trousers is still evident although he must have been wearing them all day. In his left hand is a small square wicker basket like a woven bamboo briefcase. He glances at his wrist-watch.

'I'm sorry I'm late, sir. The buses were held up in Waterloo Road. By an accident. A taxi had . . .'

'You could have got off there and walked,' I interrupt. 'It's not far.'

'Yes, sir. I'm sorry.'

The boy seems, to me, genuinely apologetic. I decide to let the matter rest. He is polite and appears considerate.

'Never mind,' I say curtly. 'Let's get on with your instruction. Enough time's been wasted.'

The boy looks quickly around the room then sits uninvited at the round table, putting his basket on the floor and, sliding aside the bent rattan clasps, opening the lid which creaks. From within he takes out a textbook and a black-and-red hardback notebook of the sort Chinese students use: from the breast pocket of his blazer he produces a Parker fountain pen.

'Page 15. Entering tones. Begin at the top.'

For a moment, the boy is silent as if gathering himself for some kind of performance. Then he commences.

'*Sìk. Sìk. Sík. Tsuk. Tsùk. Tsúk.*'

'Stop!' I order. 'Stop! Think, boy, think. Not *Sík.* Not *Tsúk.* What is it . . .'

The boy is silent. I watch his face. It is as impassive as that of a Chinese lad yet I can tell that, underneath, there is a struggle going on.

'Well? Do you not remember, boy? *Sík?*' I wait a

moment then, staring at the boy, say exasperatedly, '*Sîk*. And *Tsûk*.'

The boy avoids my stare.

I am impatient with him and cannot help it. I suppose I like the boy: at least, I do not dislike him. He means well, does his best but he sometimes lacks concentration, lacks the dedication such a study demands.

'Say them.'

'*Sîk*. *Tsûk*.'

'Again.'

'*Sîk*. *Tsûk*.'

'Good. Now note them down. Something written is never forgotten.'

Screwing the end off his pen, he opens his note-book. I sense he is glad to be given the opportunity to do something to show willing. He is not an unpleasant boy, unlike some pupils I have had: young bank or trading-house executives fresh out from public school in England with an imperious air about them; bored housewives who wanted to pass the time and communicate more accurately with their amahs and cook-boys; colonial civil servants struggling to master Cantonese before seeking promotion. Yet the boy is slow and forgets the basics too readily: in this failing he annoys me.

I cannot explain the reason for my vexation. Perhaps the boy's watch and fountain pen make me jealous, although I do not wish to own such prodigalities; perhaps it is his inability to remember his lessons, to apply himself and differentiate between a high-rising or low-rising tone, which anger me; perhaps it is an envy of his youth and future which I shall never see. There again, it might just be my character. Whatever the reason, I find the boy in turns infuriating and a frequent test for my patience.

The boy stops writing and lays his pen on the table, glancing briefly at me, avoiding my eye, seeking no contact.

'Done?'

'Yes, sir.'

'Very well. And remember – *sik* is the noun *colour* while *sîk* is the verb *to eat*. Tones in Cantonese – all Chinese dialects – are of vital importance. Don't forget this. Now continue, boy.'

'*Fat. Fàt. Fât. Kuk. Kùk. Kûk.*'

For an hour, I take the boy through tone exercises and simple sentences which use them. The sun leaves the room and the sky lightens as if making a final effort to cling on to the day before surrendering to evening. I do not switch on the light and the lesson ends just as it becomes too dim to see the text exercises.

'That will do,' I declare, turning my head pointedly in the direction of the travelling clock.

The boy, without speaking, pulls a leather wallet from his hip pocket and removes forty Hong Kong dollars in ten-dollar bills.

'Thank you, sir,' he says, giving me the money.

'Practise the tones before your next visit,' I reply, counting the bills with my fingers yet without looking at them.

'Yes, sir,' he replies.

From a single drawer in the table, I take out a pad of receipt forms and a plastic ballpoint which I bought in a stationery shop in Yunnan Lane. The pad is a cheap item made of flimsy paper with one

61

page printed and the next blank. Between the two is inserted a square of blue waxed carbon paper. I inscribe my name at the head of the page then, printing carefully, I write *Rec'd HK$40 (four-oh) in full pymnt for lesson*, followed by today's date. Over this I scribble what passes for my signature, fold the sheet and hand it to the boy. He says nothing but puts it in his wallet, gathers up his books and pen and places them in his basket.

As we part, he looks quite closely at me, as if studying my face for the story of my life. He does not stare rudely and the inspection lasts only a moment but it is positive and, as long as it exists, is deep and inquiring. There are times when I swear there may be more to him than meets the eye and I get the sense he wants more of me yet dares not ask.

As I close the door on the boy, I sigh. I am tired. My afternoon doze has not refreshed me and I feel an uncomfortable restlessness stirring in me, welling deep down inside like a hatred long felt and suppressed.

Or it might be a new kind of as yet nameless fear.

At the other end of the flat tenement roof from the old lady's lean-to stands the small concrete building housing a storeroom and the lift mechanism. The former is empty, a source of surprise to me that the landlord has neither let it nor has an enterprising person moved in to establish a small factory there. A similar construction three doors down Woosung Street contains a fluorescent plastic ribbon maker and the building beyond has a man who renders fat installed on the roof. I am thankful I do not live below his workshop: one can smell his operation in the street.

The roof space on the far side of the lift mechanism housing, away from the door, is ideal for Mr Wu and myself, being secluded and not overlooked. It faces north-west and there are no taller buildings between our tenement and the Yau Ma Tei typhoon shelter. The seclusion is aided by the fact that it is most awkward to reach: one has to squeeze between the housing and a large, rusting, galvanised tin ventilator hood, then edge along a parapet retained by a low wall.

I do not have a head for heights and whenever I make my way along this little rampart I feel the space over the wall calling silently to me. Its words are never distinct but I know their drift, heeding them if I do not accept their invitation.

Over several years, Mr Wu and I have equipped the space as our own little pleasure garden, installing two parallel benches three feet wide and made of planed deal planks: they resemble the ancient Chinese *k'ang*, with boxed in sides and a tiny lip around the edge, yet no source of heating beneath them. Around the area we have placed plant pots in which we grow chrysanthemums, marigolds, salvias and fuschias which Mr Wu tends: at his own admission he has a green thumb, an expression he has learnt from reading gardening books. By contrast, he states I have a brown thumb. What he touches grows whilst what I touch withers. Or so he claims.

We meet here at least once or twice a month but not by prior arrangement. We are both old men and that would be to tempt fate. We either knock on the other's door, suggesting we go up to the roof there and then or we meet during the day and agree we shall come together at a mutually acceptable time that evening. Also, we might go up alone: Mr Wu frequents the place more often than I do for his need is greater.

Today, we met in the market where he was purchasing some socks. He usually wears drab Chinese clothes — a jacket with a high collar buttoned by embroidered knots and loops, traditional trousers and a white vest with the label sticking out of the neck marked *Fruit of The Loom*. Mr Wu enjoys American underwear if he can afford it. His footwear, around his flat, is the traditional felt slipper: only when he is walking the streets does he wear leather shoes. Socks, however, are his indulgence.

'Well, *san foo*, what do you think?' he asked me as I came upon him at a stall selling socks, ladies' stockings and assorted hosiery.

He was holding a pair of knee-length woollen socks in brilliant yellow embroidered on the side with small red, white and blue sailing yachts.

'They are ostentatious,' I replied. 'Not befitting a man of your age.'

I took the socks from him and turned them over in my hand. The wool was of a good quality mixed with cotton. They would certainly keep his feet warm.

'Imperial yellow,' Mr Wu commented. 'If there were still an emperor of China, he would wear these socks.'

'With yachts?' I exclaimed.

Mr Wu studied them.

'Yes,' he admitted cautiously, 'the boats may put

him off. But,' he brightened, 'he could order a different decoration.'

'You, however,' I reminded him, 'are not the emperor of China. And you cannot buy these socks. How can a man of your age – of our age – command respect dressed in these? They are . . .'

I was, unusually, momentarily lost for words.

'. . . young!' Mr Wu snapped.

'Young,' I agreed.

'Well, there is a famous Chinese saying. An old peacock may draw the young hen if his feathers catch the sun.'

Mr Wu frequently does this. When he fears he is losing an argument he reverts to a maxim allegedly passed down through the ages from some wise old cove a thousand years before who had, by good chance, anticipated such a discursive problem.

'That is not an old Chinese saying,' I replied. 'That was invented by you this moment to support your argument. I know you too well, my friend. And you – a peacock! What hen do you hope to attract? There is another saying' – it was my turn to be inventive – 'which goes as follows: an old crow on a sturdy bough is better than a young crow on a twig. Which would you be at your age?'

He laughed then, taking the socks, rolled them up and placed them in their cellophane band. I believed I had won the argument but he took out his wallet and bought the loathsome things.

'What does it matter, *san foo*? I may have these bright feathers but I shall keep then hidden under my trousers.'

'I am not *san foo*,' I reminded him crossly.

I was annoyed he had got the better of me but he

ignored my reprimand. He cannot or will not alter his ways if he thinks he can use them to score a point over me. Whenever he is like this I am glad we are not bridge partners.

As we left the market, he suggested, 'Tonight, *san foo*?'

I looked at the clear blue sky, the sun shirking behind a cloud. The air was warm, a light breeze blowing through the stalls, ruffling the hanging clothing and agitating the tarpaulin covers and awnings.

'Very well,' I answered. 'Eleven o'clock?'

'Eleven o'clock,' Mr Wu concurred and studied his watch.

And so, now, we are in our little garden, safe from prying eyes and noses. A few minutes ago, a huge moon moth flitted past on pale, lazy wings, heading towards the lights of the street. It lingered for a moment over our plants, searching out any wayward blossoms but, disappointed, it vanished over the parapet. It is the first of its kind I have seen this year, a signal summer is coming.

'Will you go away tonight?' I ask, breaking a silence of some minutes.

'I think I shall,' Mr Wu answers falteringly then, as if gathering determination, says, 'Yes, *san foo*, I shall go away tonight.'

'Do you know where?'

'I do. Far away.'

'Tell me of your journey,' I ask.

'Well,' he begins, 'I shall fly. Not in the aeroplane. On the back ...' He pauses to consider his transport. '... of an owl. A white owl with black eyes. So black, they might be the onyx buttons on an old lady's coat. We shall not go high.'

'Where will you go?'

'To see my wife,' he says. 'To check she is well.'

'How was she the last time?' I enquire.

'Well. My offerings were welcome. The gods look kindly upon her. She has a new house. And a new servant. There are,' he adds as if to reassure me, 'no problems in heaven.'

'I am glad.' I say. 'And then?'

'My duty done for her, we shall visit the cloud country. You know the place?'

'I do not. Tell me.'

'There, everything is white. Not the same white, you understand. If that was the case, how could you see anything?'

He laughs very softly, like a young man in the first stages of seduction by someone he wants to love him.

'From there?'

'From there, I leave the owl and take a butterfly. The one we see in Hong Kong. Black with azure eyes upon its wings and emerald sparks set into its body. It will take me from the white place to the gardens. Here there is no white, just colours. Every colour. Colours with no earthly names. This, *san foo*,' he says quietly, 'is why I go to the cloud country first. To prepare for the colour.'

We fall silent. There is nothing we wish to convey to the other. We are lying side by side on our respective *k'angs*, which are close together so they are almost, but not quite, touching. Mr Wu is stretched out on his back staring at the sky whilst I am lying on my side looking at his profile. His face is outlined by

67

the glow of the street lights. He is breathing shallowly but I am not worried. This is a way of preparing himself for his journey. I, on the other hand, take deeper, more spaced breaths.

Both of us have a Chinese pillow under our heads, a block of lacquered papier maché with an indented centre. Mine is decorated with bamboo sprigs upon which perches a bird of indeterminate species: Mr Wu's has a white crane flying over an imagistic cloud.

'Are you ready now, *san foo*?' Mr Wu asks, sitting up and slowly swinging his legs over the far side of his bench.

'Yes. I am ready,' I say, propping myself up on my elbow. 'Let us go.'

Lifting a wooden case the size of a shoe box from the floor, Mr Wu puts it next to me, lying down on his bench. From the box, the wood of which is scratched and stained, he removes a small porcelain oil lamp which he lights with a match and places between us. The flame is at first smoky but quickly clears, its glow lighting up our faces. He then produces a pair of bamboo stems and two minute china pipe bowls which he fits to the stems, handing one to me.

Mr Wu keeps his opium in an ivory box with a sliding lid. It was not intended for such a use being in fact a chop box. Over a hundred years old, the ivory is yellowed with exposure to sunlight and carved with the relief of two copulating figures. I watch as he slides the lid and, by the lamplight, I can see the opium. It is a dark rich brown and looks like a mixture of bees'-wax and honey. I marvel something so innocuous-looking can produce such wonders.

With a little silver spoon, Mr Wu scours a scoop

of opium from the box, slides the ivory lid shut on his opium container and puts it to one side. Rolling the drug into a ball between his finger and thumb, he holds it in the spoon over the flame until it begins to melt: then he deftly divides it in two with his thumb nail, pressing half into my pipe and the remainder into his own. We both lie down on our sides, facing each other, taking turns to hold the bowl of our pipe inverted over the lamp flame.

The opium is of good quality, of Thai origin. Mr Wu is never foisted off with sub-standard dope. He does not purchase his supply from the heroin makers and the coolie suppliers but from a man of our acquaintance of whom we seldom speak.

The pipe lasts about twenty-five seconds: I suck in its promises with three long breaths. Mr Wu prepares another. As I suck again, a deep relaxing calm moves over me. My muscles do not so much slacken as grow light. If this is how the drug affects Mr Wu, I think, then the owl and the butterfly will carry no heavy burden this night. Staring at the plant pots, they are larger than before. If the moon moth was to appear now, I might hitch a lift on it. The downy hairs on its thorax would be a fine blanket in which to snuggle to keep warm as we gained altitude.

With the third pipe, the concerns of living and dying evaporate. I am a free man. All fear has suddenly abandoned me.

More relevant to the moment, I have no worries about being discovered smoking opium. A fleeting logical thought tells me we are safe, Mr Wu and I, for the perfume of the molten drug in my pipe is drifting away in the sky, lost amongst the myriad smells, scents and stinks of the city. It would be a different matter if we indulged our desires in our flats. The Pei woman with the secretarial agency would sniff us out and call the police: that is her way.

My pipe is empty and I put it down, the hot bowl hanging over the crack between our benches. Mr Wu has put his down too. His eyes are shut with his face devoid of expression. If he were not breathing I might think him dead.

I lie on my left side, my head on the hard pillow and tuck my right arm under my neck.

The crane on Mr Wu's pillow seems to be considering flight but, just as the thought occurs to me that it is about to follow the moon moth, it disappears and, in its place, I see an angel.

'These are some of the girls' quarters,' Father Callaghan explained.

We entered a spartan room with four bunks bearing only sleeping mats and quilts folded beside calico sheets. On each bunk was a square head-rest. I picked one up. It looked heavy but was as light as a loaf of bread. Painted on the end was an angel with a Chinese face and a faint white halo, not wearing the traditional smock of a heavenly being but the flowing robe of a wealthy Chinese woman.

'The girls decorate their own pillows,' Father Callaghan remarked. 'Just as they would if they were at home.'

Under one of the bunks was a wooden case which Father Callaghan pulled out. It was divided into four partitions each containing a few clothes. Beside the

70

box were four pairs of wooden sandals with leather straps. On the wall hung a small crucifix and, pasted to the door pillar, a red paper prayer-strip three feet long with gold characters written upon it.

'Is this not pagan?' I asked, pointing to the paper strip.

'It's a prayer flag,' he agreed, 'but it doesn't worship the God of War or the Goddess of Mercy.' He paused and smiled to himself. 'Well, in a way, I suppose it does. But not Kwan Yin.' He rang his finger down the characters, translating as he went. '*May the Blessed Virgin Mary, Mother of Jesus Christ, guard me safely as I sleep.*'

'Why not hang a sampler there?' I enquired. 'This is an heretical . . .'

'My friend,' Father Callaghan broke in, 'you will see and hear many . . . How shall I put it? . . . unorthodox things in China. In this mission. Not all might be approved by Rome. But I say this to you – is it not better to meet the people halfway than to be a dogmatist? Surely Our Lord doesn't mind how His message gets across. I see nothing wrong with using the ways of the heathen to preach the ways of God. Did not Our Saviour do just this?'

'Yes,' I began, 'but . . .'

'There's not a but about it. It's the way we must be. Did not the Jesuit Ricci, three centuries ago, permit his converts to worship their ancestors and images – and even Confucius – on the condition there was a holy cross upon the altar beside the idols?'

I made no response. His words were anathema and confusing to me yet I knew, in my heart of hearts, he must be right. Father Callaghan had lived in China for decades and I had to bow to his knowledge and experience.

We walked down a long corridor, descending a flight of stone steps at the end. As we went, there grew ahead of us the clamour of voices. They were young, lively and, it occurred to me as we approached, innocent and happy. Near the bottom of the steps, we stopped before a double set of doors closed against us.

'This is something which may shock you,' Father Callaghan warned as he turned the polished brass handle. 'Not at first but . . . Well, you shall see.'

I wondered what I was about to be shown: a roomful of lepers perhaps, or malformed cripples with misshapen limbs and the faces of mongoloid idiots.

As the door began to open, a silence fell. The merry chattering voices died away, the only sound remaining being a mechanical clacking noise. Father Callaghan entered and I stepped after him. The clacking sound slowed and ceased.

The room was large with open windows down one wall through which I could see the hills across the river. Seated at one end, on a dais, was an old woman wearing a Chinese jacket and trousers but with a starched, white wimple upon her head. The sight of her took me aback: I had not expected to see a nun in Wuchow.

'Sister Margaret,' explained Father Callaghan, 'speaks not a jot of English but has a command of Latin would shame many a monsignor. She was converted in Amoy in 1858. I guess her to be in her mid-sixties, but I can't be sure and neither can she. All she claims with conviction is she was born in the Year of the Horse. That comes round every twelve years in the Chinese calendar, and 1858 was a Horse Year, so I reckon my assumption is correct. She would have been converted about the age of twenty-four or five.' He paused, lowering his voice as if she could understand him. 'It's often hard to tell with them.'

Sensing she was aware we were speaking of her, I smiled at her and she gave me a gap-toothed smirk in return.

'Of course,' Father Callaghan went on, 'by saying she was born in a Horse Year she might be referring to her conversion. Born to Christ from her heathen past. In which case, she could be any age from about sixty to seventy-five. I try not to give such a quandary much consideration. There are sufficient conundrums in the Orient without adding another ephemeral one.'

Seated at rows of tables before the old nun was a large class of children ranging from the age of six up to about fourteen. They were dressed in a uniform of white Chinese blouses, black trousers and black slippers or wooden clogs with leather thongs. All had their hair tied back into a cue.

'*Cho san*!' Father Callaghan said in a loud voice.

'*Goo' more-ning, Farfer Ka Lai Hon,*' the children replied in a perfect chorus.

Father Callaghan laughed and replied in English, 'Excellent! Excellent! Carry on, my children, carry on.'

He waved his hand in the air with an almost grandiloquent gesture.

'*Yes, Farfer Ka Lai Hon,*' they responded as one and returned to their work, every one of them bowing their heads.

The clacking of the machine recommenced from

the rear of the room and I saw it emanated from a battered foot-treadle sewing machine operated by one of the elder pupils.

'What do you notice about them?' Father Callaghan asked me.

Not quite understanding the import of the question, I suggested, 'They are very obedient. And very diligent.'

'Nothing more?'

'Very neat, very polite, very . . .'

'Come, come! Look at them.'

I looked but all I saw were bent heads and busy hands.

'They're girls,' Father Callaghan pointed out. 'Every Jill and Jane of them. Not a boy in the lot.'

Casting my eye over them again, I realised they were indeed all girls. Although they wore their hair in cues, none had a partially shaved head as was customary amongst males and, here and there, I noticed one or two were developing breasts, their bosoms being pressed upwards as they leaned against their tables. In other respects, to my untrained eye, they could have been males. Their clothes seemed lacking in sexual variation.

'Do the poor Chinese not educate their sons?' I replied with some surprise: it was not what I had been led to believe in the seminary. There we had been instructed that Chinese boys were afforded the best education their parents could afford: indeed, they were given the best of everything possible.

'Sons they nurture and educate,' Father Callaghan confirmed, 'and molly-coddle and spoil and indulge and as near as worship. Girls,' he went on, 'they throw away if surplus to requirements.'

I stared at him. I was not sure if I had heard him correctly for the sewing machine, which had momentarily fallen still, had started up again and was joined by another.

'I beg your pardon. I don't . . .'

'It's simple,' Father Callaghan interjected. 'Boys carry on the family, the clan. They're the men of the future. Girls are good for nothing but household chores and the begetting of sons, to use a Biblical phrase. If you marry one off, you have to pay a match-maker's fee, a dowry and the Lord Himself knows what else. So daughters are unwanted.'

'And these?' I enquired.

'These are the lucky ones. They were all abandoned as babies . . .'

'Abandoned?'

'Dumped like rubbish,' Father Callaghan retorted curtly. 'In doorways, in the street, in the courtyards of temples. Wherever they see fit, I suppose.'

'And they are lucky!' I exclaimed.

Father Callaghan's voice dropped to a quieter, more sombre tone.

'Yes, Father Stephen, they're the lucky ones. Most, you see, are killed at birth. Infanticide is one of the biggest of Satan's arts rife in the Heavenly Kingdom.' He spoke with bitterness. 'And when I say killed, I don't mean quickly despatched as one might wring a chicken's neck or drown unwanted puppy-dogs. They're usually left out in the open, to die of exposure. Sometimes, their mothers love them and put them where they might be found and supported. For example, on doorstep.'

'And what happens to them then?'

'Sometimes they are taken in, raised then set to

work as domestic servants. A few – the comely ones – may become concubines. At other times, they're ignored and instead of dying in the fields, they die in the streets.'

He moved towards the door and I followed him. I thought we might be leaving, but he stopped beside it.

'When I first came to China, I saw a dead infant girl in the street. That was far away, in Kukong, but it matters not: it might just as well have been here. The poor little mite had been dead some time, I should guess. A part of it had been consumed. By dogs, I suppose. There are a lot of dogs in Chinese towns . . .'

I glanced at his face. There were tears lingering in his eyes, even after so many years. Then he rubbed his lower eyelid with his index finger, his mood brightening.

'Some, however, are saved by rich men. Of that I am certain. I know of at least two in this town. Living as servants but safe, well-fed and, in their own way, treasured by their masters.'

'Or saved by a mission,' I suggested.

'Yes, to be sure! I sometimes think Our Lord sent us here not to convert the heathen hordes but to save the little children and suffer them to come unto Him. And,' his voice was suddenly hard and cruel, 'may God rot the blasted population.'

He briefly looked upwards at the ceiling by way of apology.

'What are they doing?' I asked, looking at the rows of studious girls.

'They're learning to sew. Some of them to embroider,' Father Callaghan explained. 'Sister Margaret's teaching them. When they've become proficient and are about fifteen years old, we pack them off down the river to Canton, Hong Kong, Macau and our brethren there find them employment as sew-sew amahs. Some drift away, of course. They become whores or *mu tsai*. That's a sort of servant-cum-concubine. But the majority, I'm delighted to say, get gainful work and support themselves.'

Father Callaghan clapped his hands in a smart slap. Immediately, the work stopped, the girls sat upright in their seats and the sewing machines ground to a halt.

'There!' he said. 'Look at them, Father. Did you ever see such faces of innocence?'

I surveyed the room. Some of the girls were very pretty, some plain and a few ugly. As my gaze fell upon each of them, they smiled and shyly lowered their eyes. A few giggled. Father Callaghan then started to speak to them in Cantonese, his fluency such he sounded exactly like a Chinese with the words rising and falling, stretched out or clipped short in an exotic, linguistic music. As he spoke, the girls looked at him, occasionally glancing for the fleetest of moments in my direction, smiling and giggling again.

'What did you say to them?' I asked as Father Callaghan fell silent.

'I told them you were here to help us and I informed them of your name,' he said. 'At least, your Chinese name. Mine, you will have noticed, is *Ka Lai Hon*.'

'What is mine?' I enquired.

'Yours is *See Faat Han*. Stephen. It must be changed a little as there is no *st* phonetic in Cantonese.'

'*See Faat Han*,' I repeated, testing the name on my tongue.

No sooner had I spoken than a fit of giggles once more rippled round the room. A few of the girls nudged each other: others hid their faces behind their hands. As I looked at them, they turned away, giggling all the more.

'Why do they laugh?' I asked.

'They mean no harm,' Father Callaghan said. 'They are simple peasant girls, every one of them.'

'Are they laughing at me?' I enquired. I felt uneasy, embarrassed and sensed my cheeks beginning to warm and redden.

'Not at you, Father Stephen. Not at you.'

And he, too, chuckled, which set off another spasm of girlish titterings.

I thought for a moment then asked, 'What does *Ka Lai Hon* mean?'

'Nothing. It has no meaning. It is just a phonetic rendition.'

'And *See Faat Han*?'

There were more giggles verging upon being laughter.

'Itchy anus,' Father Callaghan replied, his face straight but his eyes laughing. 'It's a colloquial expression, not as unpleasant as it sounds. Quite often, it's a term of endearment of a mother for her child.'

He put his hand on my shoulder and guided me out of the doors which he closed behind us. The giggling subsided and the noise of sewing began again.

'You'll soon learn their language,' Father Callaghan said, adding reassuringly, 'then you'll discover other names have not so pleasant meanings.'

78

We went down the stairs, out of the building and across a smaller courtyard at the rear of the mission. The sun was warm but not oppressive. We approached another building, an ancient structure with no windows and a wooden door on either side of which were pasted more prayer flags, the sunlight glinting on the gold lettering.

'And these?' I asked, touching one.

'The same. Why not ask Christ to protect the place instead of Kwan Tai? What difference does it make in the long run?' He stopped with his hand on the wooden bar holding the door closed. 'I suggest to you, Father Stephen, we should ourselves have been better Christians, better men and done a better job had we heeded such concepts when we sought to convert the indigenous peoples of the South Americas.'

He raised the bar, leaned it against the wall and pushed upon the thick timbers of the door. As it swung back, I saw a short passage with a closed door to either side. The scent of burning pine and old stone hung in the air but there was no sound to be heard.

'Over a thousand years old,' Father Callaghan said in little more than a whisper. 'Once, it was a wealthy merchant's home. Our mission stands in what was the gardens. The man disgraced himself and his family, committing suicide and losing the family its position. The house is therefore considered unlucky, which is why we have been able to take it over. No one gives a farthing for what bad luck we foreign devils have dropped upon us.'

At the end of the passage we walked into a courtyard thirty feet square into which the sun was not shining, Father Callaghan pointing upwards. The yard was half-roofed with pantiles resting on bare, ancient trusses and spars. In the centre the sky could be seen but it was partially obscured by a drift of wood-smoke. As my eyes grew accustomed to the shade, I noticed many of the beams were intricately carved and blackened by decades of soot. A door opened and a young Chinese woman stepped into the yard, bowing to us.

'This is Ah Mee,' Father Callaghan said. 'She's one of our waifs but she came to us at about fifteen which makes her now twenty-six. She was not deserted but orphaned. Her parents – like so many others – were killed by brigands. She's our baby-amah. Follow me.'

I went after him as he stepped through the doorway, Ah Mee taking up the rear. Before us, against the wall, was a row of wooden cribs, in six or seven of which slept babies wrapped in swaddling sheets.

'Our nursery,' Father Callaghan explained quietly, a hint of pride in his voice, much the same as one might hear from a father pleased with his children's successes. When I looked at him, I could see his face softly smiling, reminding me of the half-smile upon the face of the Christ in a portrait by Alma Tadema, suffused with an inner joy he knew no one else could despoil or steal.

'Girls?' I asked.

'Girls,' he confirmed.

'How do you feed them?'

'You mean, how do *we* feed them?' Father Callaghan corrected me. 'They are your babies now, too.' He reached into one of the cots, gently stroking the sleeping infant's cheek. 'The Chinese don't drink milk. There are no cows in China. But they keep buffalo for ploughing and as beasts of burden. We buy their milk. Mostly though, we employ wet nurses, peasant women from outside the town who're glad to do it for a few grains of rice and a bit of dried fish. They feed our babies and we feed them. It's a fair business deal to me. And may God forgive me for saying this, but our girls are lucky there's still such infant mortality in China. Now,' he moved towards the door, pointing the way out, 'come and look at this.'

He led me into the courtyard and across to a high door barred with three thick beams. The timbers were studded with iron bolts and showed signs of charring.

'This leads to the *hutong* at the rear of the mission. By the way, that means alley. We never open it. The Tai Ping Rebellion,' he remarked, 'did the damage you see. The merchant's godown was set afire in the uprising and this was its main door. I had it placed here when we built the mission. You would not believe it but it weighs over a ton and took seventeen coolies with . . .' He abruptly stopped talking, putting his finger to his lips. 'Listen,' he whispered, 'to China's sorrow.'

I stood quite still. At first, no sound came to me except the trilling of a bird on the roof and the barking of a dog some way off. Then, gradually, I heard a soft sobbing coming from the other side of the door. Father Callaghan crossed himself and I did likewise, although I did not know why. For over a minute, we remained in silence while the sobbing continued.

'Should we not do something?' I urged finally in a whisper. 'There is someone in trouble . . .'

'There's nothing we can do, Father Stephen,' he replied quietly. 'The matter's in God's hands.'

81

At last, we heard footsteps in the *hutong* and the sobbing began to fade away.

'What was that?' I asked.

'A poor woman,' Father Callaghan responded, his voice filled with sadness. He pointed to a wooden box beside the door. 'What do you suppose this is for?'

I studied it. It was an oblong wooden box mounted into the wall, a simple handle on one end whilst the other was hidden in an opening in the stonework.

'You'll not guess,' Father Callaghan declared. 'Watch.'

He held a carved peg away from the side and pushed. The box slid through the wall on waxed wooden runners. Sunlight shone into it as it cleared the outside. After waiting a moment, he pulled it back in again, the peg falling in place to lock it shut and, at the same time, a length of string attached to it rang a small bell hanging on a coil spring. It was like the servant's bell one found in well-to-do houses in Europe.

'This contraption,' he said, 'was brought here by Sister Margaret from her convent in Amoy. They're common in nunneries in the north but I've seen few so far south.'

'What is it?' I asked.

'This,' said Father Callaghan, 'is a baby girl deposit box. It's here we collect our girls, posted to us like letters. And what we have just listened to was an incomplete delivery, one that will not come unto Christ.'

'What will happen to it?'

'That one, I fear,' Father Callaghan answered ruefully, 'will go the way of the puppy-dogs.'

I left my flat at ten and descended alone in the lift to the first floor where one of Mr Pao's minions entered it, carrying a cash register. He nodded to me and we continued down to the ground together where I held the lift door open for him and he thanked me politely. On the pavement, he loaded the register onto a hand cart, setting off down the street with it, the cart wheels squeaking, taxi drivers blaring their horns at him. Despite the modernity of Hong Kong, the streets still bustle with coolies carrying goods suspended from poles, rickshaws, hand carts, and even old-fashioned wheelbarrows with solid wooden wheels. The sight of a National Cash Register riding on a bamboo raft mounted on small iron wheels and being pulled along by a rope is but one of the paradoxes of the place.

After watching him disappear, I made my way to Pak Hoi Street, where there are half a dozen poultry stalls and shops, intending to buy a pullet and two eggs. One of the glories of Chinese shopping is one may buy just what one needs. There is no demand, as in European shops, for customers to purchase more than they require. Items are not sold in packs but singly. There is no waste and no shortage.

As I neared the street, I met increasing numbers of people carrying their purchases – clucking hens with their wings and feet trussed, complaining ducks and wicker baskets filled with a scrabbling clamour of feet and feathers. Fowls are sold live: an animal which still breathes, eats and defaecates is not going to deteriorate before it reaches the pot. For all their inventiveness, their discovery of comets, mathematics, gunpowder and magic, the Chinese never devised refrigeration.

I patronise one stall in particular. The man who runs it, whose name I do not know, has lost his left eye. He has not obtained a glass replacement nor does he wear a patch to cover the hollow orbit. Instead, he merely has a cavity in his face into which the eyelid has fallen and atrophied, giving him a grotesque appearance. He enhances this bizarre visage by occasionally fitting into this space a new fifty-cent coin. He then tilts his head to catch the bright light from the electric bulbs which illuminate his stall. Men laugh at this exhibition, women recoil from it, their children gawping in stunned amazement or hiding behind their mothers. Yet his customers return again and again. His showmanship is part and parcel of his trade, his inevitably Oriental way of turning a disability into an advantage. They may be revolted by his act but his clientele remembers him, which is the secret of successful business. If he had the money, no doubt he would install a flashing neon sign above his stall: but, being unable or unwilling to go to such extravagance, he has a flashing eye instead.

When I arrived at his stall, he was busy piling crates of hens on top of one another, catching them adroitly as they were tossed from a parked lorry at the kerb. A number of other would-be customers waited nearby for the delivery to be completed, and I joined them, surveying his stock.

One-eye does not sell only chickens. If it has feathers, a beak and a culinary use, then he sells it: which is to say he deals in every type of bird that does not have a fine song. Those are available from the song-bird sellers in Shek Lung Street. This morning, One-eye's cages and crates contained a wide assortment of fowl for the weekend is drawing near and he sells not only to housewives but also to restaurants.

By my shoulder were crates of common brown hens but next to these was a box of white silkies, chickens with long, hair-like feathers about their feet and delicate crests on their skulls lending them a supercilious expression: they reminded me of twenties flapper-girls bedecked in ostrich plumes. To the left of the silkies were two crates of ducks. These were not ordinary ducks but brilliantly plumaged teal shipped down from the far north of China. A common brown hen was priced at four dollars: one of these ducks would cost between thirty and fifty-five, according to the label hanging from the bars, depending on the sex and colour of the plumage. Another box contained several Lady Amherst's Pheasants.

This bird has my deepest admiration. Its plumage is brilliant with a red crown, silver and black cope on its neck, sea-green body, white breast, black wings and, at the base of the tail, a scarlet and yellow rainbow as if there was a fire encapsulated there from which the long white-and-black barred tail might be a petrified plume of smoke tugged out by a strong wind. Yet it is not the bird's appearance which captures my admiration but its courage. The other fowl cower, resigned to the chopper. This creature refuses to be cowed. It stands all the while, thrusting its head out of the bars, calling raucous defiance at One-eye.

At least, such is one interpretation of it – the

romantic in me speaking. The other might be that the bird is a fool and cannot guess from the blood and entrails in the gutter what its fate will be. Or perhaps it has entered into an unholy alliance with One-eye, taking a side part in his fifty-cent coin advertising gimmick.

The birds in the top cages are comparatively well off but, as one descends the pile, the worse the conditions get. Birdshit filters down through the barred floors, the cut-down tins serving as water containers grimed with dried guano and discarded belly feathers. Those at pavement level are a sorry lot and priced the cheapest.

I am inured to this state of affairs. Living in China for six decades has shown me far worse.

One-eye has to pay rent for his stall. It is erected on the public pavement and he has a hawker's licence but he also has to pay other dues, not a levy imposed by the government but by the 14K, the local triad gangsters who make their living operating cheap whores in Temple Street, selling drugs, conducting numbers games or mah-jong schools and running protection rackets. They own the streets around my tenement, no shop-keeper free of their graft. All profit margins take into account, hidden in the balance sheet, tea money, which is the colloquialism for pay-offs. This is the way of China, has been so and will remain so forever, regardless of who sits on the Heavenly Throne or which party flag flies over the police station.

It was obvious to me this morning One-eye has not kept up his tea money for, as I waited to purchase my pullet – in the third level down: not too expensive yet not too besmirched with shit as to be the cheapest – a *fei jai* approached him. Like spivs the world over, be they pimps or politicians, he walked with a swagger, his wristwatch the latest Rado on a steel bracelet, his shirt crisp and clean. He wore well-creased tailored trousers and his hair was trimmed, greased back then flipped up at the front.

There were only two customers left to be served at the stall, myself and a woman with a sleeping infant strapped to her back in a brightly coloured sling. She was half-way through her transaction and the spiv, waiting for this to end, began to study the cages in the polite, obliquely menacing way powerful men have of letting others know they are subordinate. He stroked a pheasant's head, felt the breast of a duck and, as One-eye watched him, purposefully knocked a water tin over, spilling the rank contents on a hen in the box underneath. The woman dealt with, One-eye glanced at me then turned to the rent collector.

'You've forgotten,' said the spiv, his voice quiet with menace: he spoke in Cantonese on the assumption I would not understand their intercourse.

'I have not forgotten, sir,' One-eye replied obsequiously. 'The money is coming. Business is not so good. Prices of chickens at Tuen Mun . . .'

'Four hundred dollars,' the spiv demanded. 'Pay me now.'

'I do not have four hundred.' One-eye fumbled in his jacket. 'I've got two hundred.'

'No good. Four hundred.'

The spiv was calm and I knew violence was imminent. I have seen this ploy so often.

'Tonight,' One-eye said. 'I borrow some.'

'Who you going to borrow from?' the spiv enquired.

87

'*Way Foong*,' came the prompt reply.

One-eye was quick with his answer. He named the bank because he knew, had he not, he would have been forced to borrow what he owed from the spiv: loan sharking is another of the triads' multifarious businesses.

'Okay,' the spiv said in English then, after considering his reply, continued in Cantonese, 'Six o'clock. Four fifty.'

One-eye nodded and the spiv turned to go. As he passed the end of the cages, he reached into one of them taking out a speckled Chinese partridge hardly bigger than a thrush. With a deft clenching of his fingers, he squeezed it to death. It chirped once then, despite the passing traffic, I heard its miniature bones shatter. Dropping the mangled carcass on the pavement and without looking back he departed. One-eye's face was blanched.

Human cruelty is far worse than that of the world of nature, which is to say the world of God if you believe in such a thing. It is gratuitous, premeditated and obscene. The cruelty which gods exact is more perfected, refined: that of man is crude, lacking the beauty of divine cunning.

For many years, I was taught man was fashioned in the image of God. Believe that and you will understand the situation as I see it.

The street in Kowloon Tong is a cul de sac ending in a low hill, the side perpendicular where rain and sun have in turn loosened and eroded it. On the top is a stand of pine trees behind which drift high clouds. All the houses are tucked behind concrete walls, the tops of which are lined with broken glass, rolls of barbed wire or spikes. They are low, two-storey buildings with deep verandas and broad-leafed sub-tropical trees shading the stonework. Every property has wrought iron gates, one bearing a steel shield painted gold and emblazoned with a rampant Chinese lion, its paw on a pearl. The tarmac is covered in fine gravel washed from the hill, which sparkles like semi-precious stones in the sunlight. From where I am standing under the shade of a bauhinia tree, I consider that if they were diamonds and not quartz, I would be a rich man with a huge responsibility. I am glad, therefore, they are worthless: such a weighty responsibility is not something I wish to bear. Life is better simplified into the day-to-day gratification of basic needs and petty desires.

A dark anonymous bird glides down from the pines to settle in the bauhinia. It does not sing but flits silently from bough to bough uttering a soft, almost inaudible weep. It knocks one of the blossoms, lilac-and-white petals fluttering down to the pavement.

I am not alone in the street. Where it joins another, wider road, is a gathering of twenty amahs wearing their customary uniforms of white smock tops and black, loose trousers. They chatter and laugh in high-pitched voices, their gestures stilted and unnatural as if their lives are a sham. Not one of them is over thirty-five and they look quite sexless: they might be eunuchs rather than spinsters.

Next to them is parked a tricycle on the saddle of which balances a man wearing a blazer besmirched by dust and worn through to the point of stripping into tatters. His machine consists of a single rear wheel with two forward, larger ones upon which is mounted a tall aluminium box. This had once been painted with a background of white with blue Chinese characters and the outline of a snow-capped mountain peak stencilled over it but it is now scratched, the peak having lost its summit. The corners are dented and the lid does not fit for a wisp of white mist is eking out of it. He has his feet up on the handle bars with his back resting on the wall behind him and is studying the back pages of a Chinese daily newspaper. I try to read the headlines, printed in red characters, but he is too far away.

From the other side of the concrete wall across the street, an electric bell sounds: it is not so much a ringing as a metallic tattoo of hammer on cracked steel.

Before it stops, the amahs fall silent, suddenly demure and the tricycle rider is seated upright in his saddle, the newspaper folded and tucked into the springs. The bird in the bauhinia squawks and zips away, jinxing in flight over a tangle of barbed wire.

The gates in the opposite wall open and Chinese children aged six or seven begin to issue from it. A few run or skip with the sudden freedom of their release, but most seem unperturbed by the fact school is over for the day. Each carries a satchel or a bundle of books held together by a canvas strap and they all wear a uniform of white shirts and blue trousers or skirts. The boys have short, tidy haircuts, the girls wearing little pony-tails or bobs tied with coloured twine. From the colour of their uniforms they might be somehow related to the company owning the tricycle.

A number of the children set off on their own or in pairs along the street, holding hands with a touching innocence, disappearing as they reach the next road. Others go to the group of amahs from which each steps in turn, says something and takes a child's books or satchel. Then they, too, walk out of sight. Others cross to the tricycle. The rider opens the lid, pushing aside blocks of fuming dry ice and selling them small cylindrical popsicles on sticks, stripping the paper wrappers off before handing them over and dropping the ten cent coins into a pouch tied to the cross-bar of his machine.

I watch and wait in the shade of the bauhinia. There are only four amahs left. Suddenly, a little girl appears at the gate on her own. Pausing for a moment, she surveys the street as if expecting to see someone waiting for her, visibly shrugs her shoulders and sets off in the direction of her schoolmates.

As soon as she has turned the corner, I follow, leaving the shade, my feet crunching on the gravel. As I pass the gate, I give a quick glance at a brass plate screwed onto the pillar. It reads *China Coast Catholic Mission Society – Kindergarten*. Above the lettering is etched a cross and a Sacred Heart.

Out of the protection of the tree the late sun's rays, low over the roof-tops, blind me and I shield my eyes with my hand.

The child passes through a number of streets of well-to-do residences until she reaches a very wide main road down the centre of which runs an open nullah. The breeze wafts the acidulous stink of sewage issuing from the putrid stream flowing in it.

Crossing the nullah by a stone bridge, the child heads north, towards the foothills of Kowloon. In the haze of late afternoon, the ragged outline of Lion Rock juts defiantly at the coming sunset.

After a quarter of an hour, the child reaches the end of the road by a bus stop at which is parked an empty bus. Here, she starts up a pathway towards the hills. I stop at the foot of the path and watch as the child climbs higher between scrubby bushes, disappearing at last into a gully. From higher up in the hills comes a drift of wood-smoke but it is too far away for me to pick up even a slight trace of its perfume.

For some moments I wait, my eyes set on the point where the child has vanished, then I retrace my steps to the bus stop and, checking it is a number 7 service, board the vehicle and sit heavily on the wooden slats of the seat by the door. As if he had been waiting for me, the driver starts up the engine and the conductor pulls the sliding bars of the gate closed across the entrance, tugging on a cord running along the ceiling. A bell chimes twice and the bus sets off.

As it drives along by the nullah, the bus passes the popsicle vendor pedalling slowly along, his back bent with effort and sweat streaming down his neck to soak into his vest and blazer collar.

'One day,' I say to myself, 'I'll buy her a popsy.'

Yet I know that is not possible. I shall never be able to approach the child for to do so would be to give too much away of myself.

The mission was not situated upon one of the town's main streets but in a *hutong* lined with buildings, many of which were as ancient as the mission nursery. Some were built of grey stone and others of dull red brick, but none was more than two floors tall. No windows faced the street except for a narrow grill or shuttered hole through which no passer-by could peer, its function being not so much to let light in as smoke out and to act as a spy-hole to study who might be at the door.

The *hutong* was dirty, with leaves, spilled rice and chewed sugar-cane stalks lying on the flat cobblestones. Down the centre ran an open sluice which, judging from its contents, served as the only provision for sanitation to the houses.

'It smells a bit,' Father Callaghan declared as he stepped over the drain. 'Especially now, in the hot months. In winter, it's nothing like so bad. These little nullahs are also a good reason for wearing native costume. One is forever picking up the hem of one's cassock otherwise. Nothing worse than discovering a damp hem on returning home.'

Had there been a window or casement of glass in any of the properties, I should have liked to have seen my reflection. At Father Callaghan's recommendation, I had given up my clerical dress and had attired myself in the costume of a Chinese gentleman, consisting of a jacket called a *sam* and baggy, loose trousers referred to as *fu*. These were not fitted with a tight buttoned waistband or belt, as were clothes of European cut, but by a wide strip of white material which Father Callaghan told me was called the *fu tau*, or head of the trousers.

'Sometimes,' he had said as he showed me how to fold this strip, tucking the loose ends in and tightening the material about my midriff, 'it is called the *baak tau do lo*. This means the white head and old sage. It implies the wearer wishes to live a long time.'

'Why do we dress in native fashion, Father?' I had enquired. 'Surely it is best to wear our cassocks. They will then know us as priests.'

'Don't you worry,' he had laughed, 'they know who we are and what we are. Whether we wear the black or the white habit of our calling, the smart suit of the merchant or the outfit of the shopkeeper, they know us. I wear Chinese clothes because they make me comfortable in the heat. Those long cassocks were made for a penance, I'm sure of it. Besides, if we wear their dress, they'll feel we are closer to them. And that's what we must be, if we're to do the Lord's work. Be closer to them. Be a man amongst their men, not a foreign devil in his weird get-up stalking the streets like a predator. They think we hunt for their souls as it is.'

The two garments were made of black gummed silk which was shiny and a little stiff to the touch and yet not abrasive against the skin. Upon our heads we sported black skull caps with matching buttons in the centre and, upon our feet, we wore white socks and black cotton shoes, through the thin soles of which I felt every bump and stone on the ground.

Just down the *hutong* from the mission entrance was a wooden building with carved beams and a balustraded balcony. I paused in front of the house to admire the carved flowers, leaves and, as I now realised, inevitable dragons. From the balcony hung prayer flags which moved gently in the warm breeze and by the door was a shrine, in front of which guttered a red wax candle on the end of a splint, looking somewhat like a bizarre fruit. The door into the building was made of wide planks studded with iron bolts, reminding me of the church doors one finds in rural Italy. There was no handle to turn but a wooden latch which was well-polished by what I assumed to be centuries of pressing fingers. The timber of the building was, like the roof of the nursery yard, blackened by age and smoke. Although the house looked rickety, I could tell it was solid and somewhat forbidding.

Father Callaghan, who had walked on unaware I had halted, came hurrying back and took me by the arm.

'Don't pause,' he advised. 'Look, by all means, but show no interest unless you are so invited to do. Some regard us as harmless dolts, some think of us with charity but there are many who believe we cast an evil eye.'

We walked on in silence. Although the sun was now hot upon our heads, I felt surprising cool in the Chinese clothing and the slipper-like shoes were not only comfortable but also gave me a good grip upon the steps descending at the far end of the *hutong* towards a main street. The stones were worn smooth, angled dangerously in places and I was glad for the confidence the footwear afforded me. My own leather-soled shoes would have sent me tumbling for there was no handrail.

So far, we had not seen a single living creature but, as we neared the street, the sounds of commerce and life grew louder. Ahead, I could see people passing and re-passing the *hutong* entrance, going by like figures in a magic lantern show.

'Now remember,' Father Callaghan said as we reached the street, 'don't stare. Look about you but don't linger on any one sight. Look back again a minute later but – well, don't stare. That's the cardinal rule.'

The street was very wide and paved with bricks and flags. The buildings were two or three storeys high with colonnaded arcades on the ground floor under which the pavement ran although most people were walking in the street. Upon the pillars of the arcades, six feet from the ground, were mounted stout iron rings.

'They tie their mule's heads up high,' I remarked.

Father Callaghan laughed and said, 'Those are not for mules. Nor even horses. You'll not find many mounts in southern China. They're for boats.'

'Boats?' I queried.

The street was at least several hundred yards from the river which I could see in the distance down a gentle incline.

'Boats,' Father Callaghan said again. 'Sampans mostly but I've seen bigger craft moored to them.'

'Why do they drag their boats all this way up from the river? Are there no mudbanks upon which to beach them?'

'They don't drag their craft up here. The river does it for them. You see, Father Stephen, in the summer months, the river floods something terrible. It can rise ten feet an hour and it's not unknown for it to flood three quarters of the town. You've come at a peculiar time for in a normal year the river is fifty feet higher than you see it now. The drought this year is exceptional. You might have arrived in a boat to the very end of the *hutong*. I've known the waters to come up so far.'

As we continued on our way I tried to imagine

what the town must look like inundated by the Si Kiang and pondered on whether or not the people believed that, when the river rose so far, the dragons entered their houses and shops.

The pedestrians mingled, crossed and re-crossed the street, weaving in and out of each other with the alacrity of fish whilst, within the shadows of the arcades, were stalls selling vegetables, kindling, charcoal and small clay pots, everything contained in rattan or wicker baskets of various sizes. The vendors squatted by their merchandise, calling out to attract custom or haggling vociferously with would-be clients.

Within a few minutes, I had seen two old crones with crooked spines arguing with an equally aged man over the price of living, grey-green fish flapping in a wet basket, young men in smart and intricately embroidered silk jackets walking together in animated conversation, coolies loping by with their poles bending under the weight of loads of sugar cane, stringy-looking cabbages and squealing piglets trussed up in rattan cylinders. Children ran by with hoops of bamboo. In the centre of a street, a solemn little boy stood holding a triangular paper kite made of brown rice-paper stretched over a bamboo frame. By a cobbler's stall, the air punctuated with the tap-tap of his hammer upon a wooden clog, I bumped into two young women strolling purposefully along. Each had a baby strapped to her back by a brightly dyed square of cotton secured in the front by straps, pushing the women's breasts apart. I smiled my apology, prompting giggles from them as they raised their hands to their mouths and averted their eyes.

'So, what do you think?' Father Callaghan enquired

as we reached a part of the street not lined with the stalls of peasant farmers and therefore not quite so crowded.

'I don't know,' I answered. 'It's all so . . .' I searched without success for an appropriate word, '. . . unusual.'

'Yes, it is,' Father Callaghan agreed. 'I've lived here – in China, that is – for nearly twenty years and I never cease to be astounded. Not one day passes when I don't see or hear something new.'

He turned into the shade of the arcade and I followed him. It was much cooler out of the sun.

'Where are we going?' I asked.

'You shall see. We shall take just a short perambulation so you might get to know the town. This is the Street of The Cranes and our alleyway goes between this and *Bei Shan*, the North Mountain – that's the hill behind the town. *Shan* is Cantonese for mountain. The next street we come to is the Street of Heavenly Happiness. You'll soon get to know them by their Chinese names and recognise the characters for them. You'll pick it up. I shall give you a few lessons. It's not as hard as it seems.'

'As it sounds,' I said.

'True, Father. The sounds are often more important than the words.'

We arrived at the junction between two streets and turned left, keeping to the arcade. The Street of Heavenly Happiness was wider than that which we had just quit yet not as busy.

As we passed, I glanced in the shop doorways observing what I could without slackening my pace: a rice shop with polished wooden barrels and hessian sacks, stone tubs and a cat asleep upon a bale of straw; a tea shop with its casks of different teas ranging in colour from light green to matt black; a herb shop, its ceiling hung with a dense array of roots and dried leaves. Some of the premises were workshops where craftsmen beat out copper cooking vessels, turned clay on foot-propelled wheels or cut planks with two-handed saws.

Not only the sights impressed themselves upon me: so too did the smells. The rice shop smelt merely of dryness and the incense burning in a shrine on the wall at the rear, but the tea shop was scented with a tart fragrance, the herb shop emitting such a confusing cascade of sweet perfumes and acrid odours they made me sneeze. Even the potter's shop had aroma all its own, of wet earth and linseed oil.

A few of the shop-keepers acknowleged my quick glances into their businesses. The herbalist, a crouched man wearing steel-rimmed spectacles with several strands of thin hair issuing from a mole on his lower jaw, looked up from a set of hand scales to leer at me. I smiled back and looked at the brass pan hung by small chains from the scale bar. The concoction in it consisted of dried bark, gnarled roots and flakes of what looked like crushed leaves.

'Snakeskin,' Father Callaghan said, as he saw my attention taken by the scales. 'Snakes have a powerful medicinal value to the Chinese.'

A little further on, the proprietor of an egg stall tucked into a doorway beckoned to me to make a purchase. I stopped for a moment to study his stock. The eggs were of three varieties: the first were ordinary eggs, their shells pallid and clean, the second were coated in what appeared to be chopped wheat straw bound with dried clay and the third were black with a soot-like covering. Several of the latter had been scraped with a blade so they appeared striped.

'This is Kung,' Father Callaghan said, adding a quick burst of Cantonese to the egg-seller. 'He's one of ours.'

Kung bowed and spoke to me for at least thirty seconds without taking a breath.

'What does he say?' I asked when the tirade was over. I was afraid I might have somehow offended the man.

'He says, broadly translating,' Father Callaghan replied, 'he welcomes you to his stall and the town of Wuchow. He wishes the Lord go with you in your business. He also asks you to buy his provender.'

'Are his eggs good?'

'Generally. He supplies the mission.'

'Then perhaps we could buy some?' I suggested.

'Ah Fong does all our buying,' Father Callaghan said. 'He's our compradore, our go-between with merchants and the like. I cannot go over his head. He'd lose face. But . . .'

He spoke briefly to the stallholder who picked up one of the black eggs and commenced scraping the covering off, which fell to his feet in lumps. Had I known Father Callaghan better, I might have been alerted by the quick, mischievous glint in his eye. When the egg was more or less clean, the vendor rapped it against the wall by his head and started to peel the shell away.

At the end of the street, two dogs were snapping and snarling at each other, arguing over a scrap of entrails thrown into the thoroughfare from a butcher's shop. No one attempted to separate them.

'Quite a delicacy, this,' Father Callaghan remarked,

looking down the street as if distracted by the dog fight. 'It's called a one- hundred-year-old egg.'

Kung dipped the egg in a small bowl of yellow sauce and held it out to me: I was not sure whether I should accept and eat it or admire its longevity. My uncertainty was allayed when the Chinese pushed his arm further outwards in a motion of offering and Father Callaghan felt in the pocket of his jacket for a coin which he placed on the stall.

'A hundred years old?' I mused.

'That's what they say,' Father Callaghan said, adding by way of assurance, 'but of course that's just a metaphor. It's no more than a few weeks old. I'd bet my belt on it. I'm sure it's the fashion of the preparation gives them their name and distinct colouration.'

I looked at the proffered egg. It was a dark translucent green, reminding me not so much of an egg as the bulbous indentation at the base of a wine bottle.

'You see,' Father Callaghan continued, 'to the Chinese, everything is either a hundred years old or a thousand years old. As a nation, they are somewhat given to hyperbole.'

I glanced at the egg. The colour made me feel slightly nauseous.

'The yellow sauce,' Father Callaghan concluded, 'is a variety of mustard but not as hot as our Colman's.'

I took the egg. It was firm yet pliable as if it had been hard-boiled. I held it up to my face and sniffed surreptitiously at it.

Anticipating my next concern, Father Callaghan said, 'It is cooked. Kung has prepared it in the manner of hay-box cookery. It is not so much hard-boiled as

101

hard-baked. One eats it in one mouthful,' he added, his face still averted in the direction of the dogs which had now ceased growling and taken to a tug-o'-war with the offal.

Considering it best to get this experience over with as quickly as possible, I placed the whole egg into my mouth, closed my lips and bit into it: it was as if every swamp east of Suez had been emptied into my throat. My nostrils burned with the stink of rotten egg and my tongue smarted from the sauce. The white of the egg, if it could be called such, slithered unpleasantly down my gullet whilst the yolk was dry and clung like ashes to the sides of my oesophagus.

'They are rather fine, aren't they?' Father Callaghan commented.

As quickly as I could I swallowed the egg and did my best to smile at Kung who grinned at the evident pleasure his egg had given.

'Well done!' Father Callaghan exclaimed as we walked on. 'A rare delicacy. However, I allow they are an acquired flavour.'

'Yes,' I replied, the taste still lingering strongly in my mouth and the smell at the back of my nose, 'they are.'

We arrived in the central square of the town. It was a broad area around the edge of which were market stalls. In the centre was a stone dais upon the plinth of which were pasted a number of public notices, written in black ink upon white or yellow paper.

'Edicts,' Father Callaghan explained, cursorily reading one. 'This one emanates from the Peacock Throne. It says foreigners may not trade in jade discs. Not something to affect mendicant friars like us, eh Father Stephen?'

'Is the platform where the town crier stands?' I asked as we moved across the square.

'No. They don't have town criers,' Father Callaghan replied. 'That's primarily used for public executions.'

We were still halfway across the main square when I felt the waistband of my trousers suddenly loosen. I stood stock still and spread my legs apart.

'What is the matter?' Father Callaghan asked. 'Are you not feeling well? The egg, perhaps?'

'It's not that,' I said, my voice somewhat hushed. 'I think my trousers are falling down.'

I looked around in despair for cover. There was none. The nearest side of the square was at least a hundred feet away.

Father Callaghan put his hands on his hips, threw back his head and roared with laughter. A number of passing coolies turned abruptly and stared at him.

'It's not in the least bit amusing,' I retorted peevishly.

My words made no impact. Father Callaghan continued to laugh, if a little less raucously, the tears streaming down his cheeks. He wiped them away with the broad sleeve of his jacket, the wet patches marking the silk. At last, his mirth subsiding, he beckoned to me to follow him. My hands in the pockets of my *sam*, gripping at the folded material at the sides of my trousers, I limped after him towards a tea-house behind a row of trees.

Once inside, Father Callaghan led me into a cubicle and, while the waiter fetched us tea, he unbuttoned my jacket and refolded my trousers, showing me again how to shape the *fu tau* so it would not work loose.

When the tea arrived, I took a long drink of it,

disregarding the fact it was piping hot. It burned my lips and scorched my tongue.

'You're suppose to sip it,' Father Callaghan said. 'That's the etiquette.'

'I'll obey it next time,' I promised, taking another pull and risking swilling it round my mouth.

'The egg?' Father Callaghan suggested.

I nodded.

'You'll learn, Father Stephen,' he declared, sipping at his own cup. 'In time. The east is not as inscrutable as they make out back home, you know. And I'm sure you'll enter into the spirit of China.'

'I will?' I wondered, sucking my lips and tugging nervously on the trousers to see if I could unravel the folds.

'Oh, for certain,' Father Callaghan said with utter conviction. 'You will. You will, Father, for sure.'

☯

I am a man of habit.

I do not live by a timetable but there is a certain round I follow, if not regularly then at least frequently. I am not adventurous, preferring that which I know and like to that which is new. It is better at my age to stay within the boundaries of the familiar than to investigate some other landscape. The times are passed for such indulgences: I did all that as a young and foolish man.

A man is not what he is because of what he does, but where he goes, whom he meets. Any police officer will tell you a criminal is judged not only by his crimes but also by his friends and the places in which he may be found. If I am to be assessed in such a fashion, I may be seen to be an ordinary man with quotidian desires and common vices. And this would be right, for I am an ordinary man, was always thus although, when younger and naive, I considered myself extraordinary, an arrogance within me born from blind ignorance: but that was long ago, before manhood put its fist down on my table, rattled my windows with its loud voice and told me to stop being a buffoon.

One of those whom I regularly meet is Sam Kwan. At least once a week, often twice, we happen to cross on our paths to oblivion. We do not talk much. He is often preoccupied with his work and cannot spare the time to chat. We are just in each other's company which gives me a sense of familiar well-being and him the idea he has an ally at hand, albeit one who, in a pinch, can do nothing more than lift the telephone and call for help.

It is always evening and I always approach our meeting in the same fashion, walking round the corner by the rice shop and looking up and down the street. My actions are a reflex. I am not afraid someone might see me, report my behaviour to higher authorities: besides, were there a snoop about seeking to muddy my pond, I am confident I could bluff my way out of trouble.

I do not feel ashamed of or regret my association with Sam nor of my going to his place. If I were, I would not look from side to side but upwards as was once my nature but is no longer.

Only last evening, I paid a visit to Sam. It was already dark. The bright bulbs hanging in the rice shop illuminated deep mahogany rice tubs with bands of polished brass. The red characters on the label boards jammed into the contents of each, denoting quality, variety and price per catty, glistened as if painted with fresh blood. A small brazier down the street guttered with flames lifting feathers of burnt paper into the air: someone was either burning garbage or lucky money to a dead relative, paying their rent in heaven.

At a fruit stall, the proprietor leaned against a pile of crates reading a Chinese comic whilst a young boy flicked a feather duster of orange cockerel plumes over the display. Under a neon light, his merchandise appeared more like artificial fruit than edible produce, the pomeloes sickly yellow as if curiously jaundiced, the near-ripe mangoes as red as if blushed by rouge, the guavas pink as cheap plastic dolls and the star-fruit inesculent. As I walked past, the furniture maker's shop was closed but through the stencil-cut holes in the steel shutters came diamonds of light, the pungent smell of French polish, varnish and camphorwood, the deep drone of conversation and the slap of mah-jong tiles on a table.

From the outside, Sam's — how shall I put it? — *establishment* looks little different from any of the other hundred or so joints scattered throughout Wanchai. The frontage contains no windows as a protection against brawling matelots. The wooden door, painted scarlet with a writhing golden dragon spitting yellow flames, looks like a panel stolen from a Taoist temple. It automatically swings shut but was propped open as I drew near, the entrance hung with a new curtain of red-and-blue plastic beads. On the pavement beside the door is the inevitable miniature shrine.

Projecting twenty feet into the street, vying for space with those of neighbouring shops, is the signboard. Sam is particularly proud of it for it cost several thousands of dollars and is an indication his business is doing well.

Fifteen feet long and eight high, it is suspended from a dubious steel framework bolted into the building. Shaped in neon strips, it portrays a large black cat in a top hat with a supercilious grin on its face, standing on its hind legs with a martini glass in one paw: the other is placed around the shoulders of a smaller, pink cat with long eye-lashes and a cheeky smile which is intended to be sexy. She is wearing a ballerina's tutu and is seated on a bar stool. The two figures ride a chariot of neon lettering which spells out the name of Sam's place – *The Black Pussy Bar & Nite Club*.

I looked up at these two felines. I always do for they seem not only loftily orgulous but also ridiculing and I like to feel I am the subject of their mockery. It does one good to be occasionally humbled. As I glanced up at them, the garish sign sputtered into life with a few pops of electricity, the explosion of light alarming sparrows which had been roosting on the framework. With twittering complaints, they took to the wing, darting into the sky, twisting in mid-flight to weave over the roof-tops. I drew aside the plastic beads and entered.

The bar is large with a set of stairs at the rear beside a green plastic sign reading *LA ATORY*: the *V* has dropped off and in its place some wit has scored in the letters *VD*. An internal toilet is not common: many bars direct clients to the gutter at the rear, despite the demands of the urban council inspectors. However they, like the police, can be persuaded to turn a blind eye to the finer vagaries of the by-laws. This indoor convenience is another object of Sam's pride.

Once within, I halted for a moment. My eyes smarted from the neon sign and the interior was dark, the only lights I could see being those in the winking jukebox, one behind the face of a wall clock advertising Johnnie Walker scotch whisky and an ultraviolet strip over the bar.

I feel vaguely uncomfortable whenever I am in that dimness, like a blind man coming into a place with which he is not familiar. I need fear nothing but, nevertheless, the feeling always persists for a moment. Perhaps it is some long-lost guilt trying to surface and not quite making it. I give it little thought and, as my eyesight adjusts and I notice more detail, it fades.

The room is slightly angled, the bar itself a curved counter at one end, not far from the entrance. Around the walls are cubicles of dark-stained wood, not unlike those of a traditional tea-house. They each contain a table and seating for four to six people. The cubicle walls are lined with padded benches of dark red leatherette: the individual chairs are of substantial construction. Just as a steak-house will fail with blunt knives so would a bar if the chairs are not capable of supporting two people, one on the other's lap. Lighting is provided by cast-iron Chinese-style lamps securely screwed onto the tables which, like the chairs, are bolted to the floor as insurance against serious injury in a brawl. Sam knows all this. He designed the place. He has been in the business man and boy and is *au fait* with all the tricks.

In the centre of the room is an area of polished planking fifteen feet square which serves as a dance floor, music provided by the jukebox. It is a bizarre contraption of yellow-and-red lights, rows of illuminated buttons and, protected by a perspex dome like the helmet of a space comic hero, the turntable and record selection equipment.

Behind the bar counter stood Sam. He is a middle-aged Chinese and always wears a white shirt which looks lilac under the ultraviolet strip. Upon his wrist he has a Japanese imitation of a Rolex watch whilst on the second finger of his right hand is a twenty-four carat gold ring set with an oval of bright green jade. The gold is so pure it looks like costume jewellery.

'Hi, *san foo!*' he called out, careful in his enunciation. 'How are you?'

He is fluent in English but as he frequently has to communicate with drunks he has developed the pedantic style of a schoolmaster.

I looked at him. He was, as always when someone entered his bar, smiling broadly.

If you did not know it, that smile could be construed as a sign of friendship. Where I am concerned it is. Yet it is also a vital aid to good business, as seminal as the smile a doctor makes to a patient, a teacher makes to a new pupil or a priest makes to a stranger entering his church.

It is a smile with which I have had acquaintance for six decades, being both a recipient of it and the source of its congenial benefaction. I am as expert at it as Sam. He knows this for he believes we are both members, if disparate ones, of the same fraternity and therefore accepts the smile as part of my bag of tricks just as it is his own.

'You know, *san foo*,' he once said to me, 'you and me alike. Two pea on one pod.'

At the time the bar was empty of customers: a typhoon was brewing so the warships had sailed to ride out the storm at sea, the soldiers confined to barracks.

'Why do you say that?' I asked him.

'You a priest: me, I own a girlie bar.'

'I was a priest,' I corrected him, 'but go on.'

'Both make a living the same way, make promise we cannot keep, earn our money selling dream and we both want salvation when we die. Both want to be forgiven for broken promise, bad dream . . .'

There is, he believes, very little basic difference between a priest and a pimp. I tend to agree with him: we are both peddlers of fantasies which do not last and I cannot fault his thesis, of which the smile is an integral aspect.

It is not a smile of invitation and certainly not of a man about to charge $8 for a bottle of San Miguel lager which may be purchased in a hotel lounge for $5.50 and a shop for $3. More, it is a smile to put any newcomer at his ease, to let him know he is amongst friends, to inform him, no matter what happens, he has a pal, someone on whom he can rely, with whom he may share petty confidences and private miseries. It is a smile of universal provision guaranteeing alcohol, sympathy and, for a side charge, companionship.

'Hello, Sam, how are you?' I replied.

I have never discovered if Sam is a diminutive of Samuel or an abbreviation of his Chinese names. Perhaps he chose Sam as it sounded good with Kwan. Sam Kwan. It has a ring to it.

'Okay,' he said carelessly. 'I getting older, like you. Soon, we be old man together.'

'You will need to hurry,' I said, 'if you are to catch me up.'

Sam laughed, 'You are a funny man, *san foo*. Should take a job in a bar. In a night club. Tell funny stories. Make good money.'

I lifted myself onto a stool at the end of the bar, leaning against the wall and hitching my heels behind the foot rest. The stool seems a fraction higher each time I come, proof perhaps of the statement one passes through life from childhood to childhood: chairs which were tall at eight are tall again at eighty.

'What you want to drink?' Sam asked. 'San Mig.? Whisky? Gin?'

'San Mig.,' I replied.

'Okay. No sweat! One San Mig. comin' up!' Sam exclaimed and he turned to a fridge under the counter.

From my elevated position on the stool, I surveyed the bar. Sam and I were not alone. In the farthest cubicle from the door sat six young Chinese women huddled in conversation, whispering and giggling. All were dressed in tightly tailored brocade *cheong sams* with the slits in the sides reaching far higher up their thighs than Chinese decorum would usually permit.

'One San Mig. Ice cold.' Sam lowered his voice as if afraid the girls might overhear him. 'Four dollars, *san foo*. But pay when you leave. Credit is good for you.' He followed my gaze. 'You looking for good time?' he enquired. 'Can do. No too much for you. Early evening . . .'

111

'No. Not tonight,' I answered, turning away from the girls. 'I don't feel up to it.'

Sam laughed again. This is an old joke we share between ourselves. He knows I am not interested in his girls — his little ladies, as he calls them — but he always asks. Perhaps he hopes one day to see me succumb, vanish up the stairs over the la-atory for half an hour of rented bliss, one of the fake fantasies he or I are able to arrange. Yet he is aware I forswore the carnal long ago.

After about a quarter of an hour, there came from the street a curt, raucous shout followed by loud laughter. No Chinese would make such a public display: it meant the evening's first clients were on their way.

When the bead curtain parted, five American sailors entered. Their uniforms were starched white and upon their heads they wore those hats which remind me of steamed *dim sum* dumplings. These they removed as they sauntered across the room, tucking them into their belts. They were suddenly silent after the noise in the street, each one of them surveying the bar, the lines of bottles and the girls.

Sam was smiling his proprietary smile.

'Hi, you guys!' he greeted them. 'Welcome to *The Black Pussy*. What's your poison?'

'Beers,' one of the sailors replied bluntly. 'Not that San Mig. shit. You got any good American beers?'

'Ah!' Sam chuckled. 'You been to Hong Kong before! Okay. I got Schlitz, Bud, Coors, Miller . . .'

'Five Buds.'

Sam began to prise the tops of the bottles. The sailors eyed the girls. I watched. There was an almost tangible atmosphere of expectancy in the air. How

112

often have I observed such a scene. It is as ritualised as the courtship of birds, as strictly adhered to as a catechism.

One of the girls stepped forward, putting her hand on the arm of the first sailor she came to. She did not say anything but looked up into his eyes, smiling: yet this was not a Sam-like friendly smile but a covetous, enticing, beautiful smile. It was exactly the same smile as Adam saw on the face of Eve, promising paradise but delivering only bleak earthly joys.

'Beers up!' Sam said jovially and he placed five tall glasses on the counter, one after the other, as if setting up targets in a coconut shy.

'Forty dollar,' he said.

'Put it on a tab,' said the sailor who had ordered the round.

'No tab. Pay as you drink.' Sam laughed lightly. 'Pay now, no angry later. All's fair in *The Black Pussy*.'

The sailors paid up and drifted away to the cubicles, each with a girl. One, who had not been forward enough to get herself a sailor, sat at the end of the counter from me. She sipped a glass of iced tea and, when the girls called for drinks, acted as waitress.

By nine o'clock, the *Black Pussy* was doing a brisk business. More American sailors had arrived and a number of new girls had walked in to accommodate them. The jukebox played continuously, sailors dancing with the girls. It was the last night the US fleet would be in port and the sailors, forbidden alcohol on board ship, were eager to make up for anticipated lost drinking time. Those with brief romances were keen to take them to

113

their limit, those with money anxious to spend it.

The air was fogged with cigarette smoke, the door propped open to give ventilation, the bead curtains never still from a coming and going of sailors on the lookout for friends or girls with whom they had struck up an acquaintance.

As Sam served the drinks, gave the girls their pass-out chits and collected the money, I sat quietly, in my usual fashion, surveying the machinations of the clientele and considering my motivation for being there.

I come to The *Black Pussy* because it is my place to do so, to be amongst the sinners and the fallen, those who have failed or are failing in their lives, the dispossessed and the disappointed. I am not here to offer them salvation, as once I might have been. I am here, as they are, to avoid looking truth in the eye.

Just along the bar from me stood a sailor. Perched beside him on a stool was one of the bar-girls. She was barely five feet tall and he was at least six: more a gangling youth not quite yet a man. It was obvious this was his first encounter with a tart. I can tell a virgin in the *Black Pussy* just as readily as I could a sinner in the pews. It is a matter of having the eye trained for the tell-tale signs which say *I am lost*, or *I am afraid*, or *I have sinned, father, forgive me*.

The sailor was drinking beer, the girl at his side having a Sam Special in a shorts glass. Sam's smile is not the only front-of-house con. He mixes cold tea with sherry at a ratio of five to one and when a girl asks a sailor to buy her a drink, she requests this noxious concoction. It costs Sam about seventy cents a glass.

114

Once I had asked Sam why he added sherry: surely, I reasoned, cold tea would be cheaper. He had frowned and said, 'Maybe, *san foo*. But if I put sherry in, it cover the tea taste.'

'So what?' I replied. 'The girls aren't going to complain.'

'No. But the sailor maybe complain. See, *san foo*, I charge five dollar. Good profit! The girl get twenty five per cent. She glad for this. Good money for her, too. The more she drink, the more she earn. Even if the sailor don't take her out. But if you were sailor . . .' He poured the rest of my beer into my glass and dropped the empty bottle into a waste bin where it broke '. . . what you do if you found out you buying shorts glass of tea for five bucks?'

'I wouldn't find out,' I said.

'You could, *san foo*. You could. You lean over and you say,' he put on a mock American accent. '"Hey, baby! Wot you drinkin', eh?" And you take a sip. If it's tea you get angry. You come to the bar. "Wotthehell, you ass hole!" you shout. Make trouble. Maybe hit me, maybe break some things. But, if you taste sherry mix with tea, you say to your friend, "Jesus, Mother of Mary, Hal! You taste the crap these girls got? Christ, I'm glad I don't drink this Chinese wine shit."'

I had laughed, had to admire Sam's artfulness, his sheer audacity. Sam had then passed me one of the little glasses.

'You try, *san foo*. Maybe you like.'

Putting the glass to my lips, I drank it in one, rolling it round in my mouth. It was dark brown, had a film upon the surface like oil on rain puddles and tasted like sweet acid.

'It's foul,' I remarked.

'I no like it,' Sam answered truthfully. 'But the girls don't complain. So . . .'

He had shrugged his shoulders, corked the sherry bottle and set about wiping the bar down.

The bar-girl's hand was on the young sailor's thigh, caressing it and creasing the material of his white uniform trousers but she did not let her fingers wander up to his groin. That next move would only come if he gave her a sign of his intentions to pay her out of the bar for a quarter of an hour.

After a minute or so of her palm massaging his leg, she took her hand away and said, 'You want buy me another drink, John?'

At first, they are always John: John or perhaps, sometimes, Joe.

'No, I . . . I don't think so,' the sailor replied. He stuttered slightly, looking obliquely at her and smiling a little sheepishly.

'My name Rosie,' she said, undeterred. 'What you name?'

'Gary. My name's Gary,' he replied, quietly.

'Okay!' she exclaimed enthusiastically. 'Is a good name. Ga-wy. Like Gah-wee US Bonds. You know him? Good singer. You know him song?'

She started loudly to hum the opening bars of *New Orleans*, a popular song on the jukebox.

'Yes,' the sailor said. 'I know him.'

He looked over her shoulder. In one of the cubicles sat a more experienced sailor, his companion's face buried in his neck, her fingers pushed well down the front of his pants.

Rosie ceased her humming, drained her tea and sherry cocktail and put her hand on Gary's arm.

'You buy me one drink, Gah-wee,' she wheedled. 'No' too much. Jus' one drink. Five dollar.'

I looked at Sam who was reaching for a tray of ready-filled glasses.

'No,' the sailor reiterated. 'Maybe later.'

'Why not now?' she cajoled. 'I can give you good time.'

The sailor shook his head yet he still smiled at her in a shy fashion. She became confused: willing punters smiled, dismissive clients bluntly told her to sod off. Her disconcertion made her angry.

'Why you smile if you no want fuck?' she demanded. 'You see something funny?'

'No,' the sailor said anxiously. 'I see nothing funny.'

He was afraid, an amalgamated fear of being seen to be a fool in front of his peers, of being embarrassed in front of a woman. It was also a fear of God, or the clap, or the ship's doctor and the rumour of his long needle, or simply not being able to do it. It was the fear of the unknown from which all men suffer.

'So! I no pretty girl?' Rosie suddenly exploded.

Sam, who was putting some coins in the till, slammed the cash drawer shut. The report drew Rosie's attention for a moment. She caught his reproving eye.

'You're a real pretty girl,' the sailor assured her.

'Maybe . . .' She spoke in a quiet undertone. 'Maybe you no can do.' She slid down from the stool. 'Maybe you think you cock drop off,' she added sarcastically and stomped off.

With her gone, the sailor hunched forward, concentrating on his beer. He cast a cautious glance at his shipmates but they were giving their undivided

117

attention to their own girls and had not noticed what had happened. After a few minutes, there was an outbreak of giggling from one of the cubicles where Rosie had joined a friend with another customer: her voice could be heard saying loudly, 'Maybe not drop off. Maybe him arse-bandit!'

The sailor stared at his beer, blushing.

'Bar-tender,' he addressed Sam who was looking disapprovingly in the girls' direction, 'give me a beer.'

Sam opened a bottle of San Miguel and poured it into the sailor's glass.

'How much?'

'Have this one on me,' I offered, leaning over and nodding to Sam. I felt sorry for this awkward youth and his clumsy attempts to accomplish what he thought would make him a man.

He did not know what it really takes to face up to the demands of manhood. Laying a whore is not even the most minute part of the process, not even a preliminary requirement for entry into the first stage of the initiation that will not be over in a day or a month, like admission to a select club or basic military training, but which evolves until the day life ceases. Manhood is not something one ever attains. It is an impossible goal like trying to resist temptation. One can dream of it but never achieve it.

I wished I could have told him this yet I knew I could not surrender the information. Even if I had had him in the confessional my words would have gone unheeded.

'Cheers!' I said, as the sailor raised his replenished glass.

'Thanks,' he said then, after a pause, added, 'but I don't need no sympathy.'

I replied, 'I'm not giving you sympathy. I'm giving you a beer.'

One of the girls thumbed a ten cent coin into the juke-box and walked straight across the dance-floor to him.

'Hi!' she said cheerily. 'You no listen Rosie. Rosie no good.' She lowered her voice, taking his hand in hers. 'You no upset. I know you cherry boy.'

The sailor took a long pull of his beer, looked at his reflection in the mirror behind the bottles and asked in soft voice, 'What's your name?'

'My name Lindy,' she answered. 'You like me.'

It was not a question but a statement.

The jukebox started to grind out a song by a singing duo called the Everly Brothers. It was entitled *Ebony Eyes*: I have heard it often in the past weeks for it is this girl's favourite. Intertwining her fingers in his, Lindy gently tugged at his arm.

'Come on, John. You dance, no buy me drink.'

He left the bar and the girl put her arms round him, hugging herself against him, her face level with his chest. As they began to move slowly over the planking, she began to sing along with the record.

'*My ebony eyes was coming to me, F'om out of d' skies on f'ight twel'e oh free . . .*' Her voice was reedy and thin, strangely sad. 'Is a good song?' she remarked as the singing became a spoken refrain. 'Is about a girl who die in plane crash.'

Nothing really changes. Sailors' uniforms alter and the ships in which they serve get larger and are better armed: fashions in drink shift from rum to scotch to beer: tastes in music move from jazz to rock and roll:

strains of venereal disease come to the fore before surrendering to a stronger antibiotic. Otherwise, things are as they have always been with young men afraid of the future and of losing their virginities, of stumbling clumsily into petty sin.

This is the way life is. I know it, accept it. It is a catalogue of experiences which makes the man. I have had a thousand of them, am accustomed to their hollow tauntings, petty triumphs and inconsequential failures.

The easel rocked slightly on the floor and the corners of the blackboard were no longer square. Decades of usage in a Jesuit school in Dublin had chipped and scarred them until they were now crudely rounded. The black surface had been freshly primed before shipping but was now beginning to wear thin so the chalk screeched jarringly. On the other hand, the pegs upon which the blackboard rested were brand new, but very unlike the originals, being hand-carved by a Wuchow carpenter with the bosses neatly fashioned into little birds.

Before the girls arrived, I had prepared my lesson on the board by drawing four simple pictures, filling them in with coloured chalk and hiding them under lengths of cloth draped over the top. On the desks I placed squares of card face downwards beside tablets of coarse rice paper, brush pens and ink pads. This done, I opened the shutters, decided the sunlight was too strong, closed them again then opened them halfway. I was as nervous as an apprentice fighter before his first bout in the bare-knuckle ring, fussing about the room until I heard the girls' footfalls in the corridor.

As they filed into the room, the girls did not look at me but went straight to their places, keeping their eyes lowered. Sister Margaret entered with them, standing next to me by the blackboard. When all were assembled, she clapped her hands once and the girls looked up, their hands at their sides.

Not sure what to do next, I said in what I hoped were unwavering tones, 'Let us think of the Lord and trust in His help with our work.'

I put my hands together. There was a soft rustle of cloth from the girls' sleeves as they followed suit.

'Lord,' I prayed, 'look down upon us, Your humble subjects, and guide us with Your strength and wisdom.'

The girls made no response until Sister Margaret said loudly, '*Ah-meng*!' which they imitated with gusto.

This preliminary over with, the old nun nodded briefly to me and walked towards the door. At her every step, I felt my spirits sinking, my fears rising pro rata. By the time her fingers grasped the door handle, I was near panic. With her outside the room, however, and the door closed, I sensed a surge of confidence which, at the same time, I knew was quite unjustified.

'My name,' I began very slowly, 'is Father Stephen. I have come from Ireland.'

The girls looked blankly at me, uncomprehending and docile. They did not fidget or attempt to look at the squares of cardboard, did not stare rudely yet nor did they seem to be giving me their attention. I was confused and nonplussed. If ever I had wanted an angel to materialise before me and give me divine inspiration, it was now: please God, I begged, give me some guidance but no light flashed in the sky and no revelation appeared. The sun continued to shine through the half-open shutters, dust dancing in the beam. From the *hutong* outside came the call not of a friendly God but of a street vendor.

I had no idea how to start to break through to them. I spoke only a few words in Cantonese which I had quickly tried to commit to memory all the previous night from a dog-eared booklet Father Callaghan had given me. It was called *A Merchant's Guide to The Language of Cantong-nese*. The publication date on the fly-leaf was 1846 and the booklet appeared to have been published in Macau. It contained little of use to me: words and phrases such as *fiscal, godown, compradore, held in bond* and *contractual obligation* were not relevant to priests or teenage girls destined to become sew-sew amahs in rich men's houses.

'I am your teacher of English,' I continued painfully slowly, mouthing each word with the exactness of the most expensive elocution mistress. 'I am your teacher,' I repeated. 'I will teach you to speak English.'

They still stared blankly at me.

'Me *sin shaang*,' I said, deciding to risk one of the useful words of Cantonese I had discovered in the glossary to the book. '*Sin shaang*, teacher.'

The girls tittered at my pronunciation. They quickly glanced at each other then, as if afraid I might be angry, stopped suddenly and looked in my direction again. I felt the panic returning.

'On the board,' I pointed to the blackboard, 'there

122

are some pictures. Today, we will look at some words.'

I was about to lift one of the pieces of cloth when a pupil in the front row stood up. She was one of the older girls, her hair not tied in a cue but gathered into little bunches behind each ear. Her white smock shone brightly with the sunlight.

'*Fuffer See Faat Han*,' she began.

The other girls tittered and she glanced round, smiling nervously at her classmates: then she seemed to pluck up her courage again.

'You come' – she pointed at me, – '*Eye-lun*. Me' – she pointed at herself, – 'come Wuchow.'

For a moment, she remained standing as if not sure what to do next then sat down, blushing and looking sideways at her companions for support. The other girls all looked apprehensively at me.

'Thank you,' I said, bowing slightly to her. '*Dor jay*.'

The girls broke into peals of light, happy laughter, their merriment infectious. I joined in with them which pleased them all the more. When, after a few minutes, the laughter died I was confronted with smiling, trusting faces. No planning on my part, I was sure, could have so reached through to the class and I thought how God had not abandoned me but answered my plea in his inimitable fashion. I gave him quick and silent thanks as I turned to the blackboard.

For over an hour, the lesson progressed with my feeling more at ease with my charges. I uncovered the drawings on the board one by one, each being greeted with surprised giggles and broad smiles. When the

123

chalk screeched on the board, the girls sucked their teeth and grimaced.

The pictures on the card squares produced as much hilarity as my chalk drawings. They had been prepared for a Catholic educational missionary society by a kindly lady whose knowledge of China was restricted to what she had gleaned from the pages of the *Illustrated London News*. Her drawings were artistically exact, her depictions accurate but she had no concept of the fact Chinese girls did not wear layered petticoats, Chinese housewives did not use saucepans and the European cow did not resemble, save in its number of legs and horns, a Chinese buffalo. When the girls turned over their sixth card to be confronted with a drawing of a black and white Friesian, they exploded into such laughter I was momentarily afraid I might lose control of the class.

By the time the lesson ended, the girls were convinced all Western dogs had patches over their eyes, all Western men had hairy faces and all Western houses must be very cold and full of evil spirits because they had so many windows. Yet they knew the words for cow, cat, mouse, dog and rat: and I also knew the equivalents in Cantonese.

When at last I released the class back into the charge of Sister Margaret and the girls filed out of the room, I leaned against the window sill with a feeling of intense exhaustion tempered by considerable joy. I had done it, survived my first lesson. Below me, in the courtyard, the girls passed by on the way to their sewing class. As they moved into the sunlight and it reflected off their smocks, I realised I had perhaps been visited by an angel after all, possibly by a whole assembly of them. They were wingless but had, I believed, invisible haloes and I felt an intense love for each and every one of them swell in me until it was so unbearably vast I had to look away, busy myself with wiping the blackboard clean and collecting up the cardboard squares to take my mind from its enormity.

'So how did it go, Stephen?' asked Father Callaghan as we strolled along the high bank of the river in the late afternoon.

'Well,' I reported, adding, 'I think.'

'Don't be modest. You were a great success. The girls spent the rest of the morning chattering about you. I overheard them and Sister told me you had made a great impression.'

'I think I may have made a bit of a fool of myself,' I confessed. 'I tried a bit of Cantonese.'

'And they loved it. You didn't pronounce it right, mind you. I won't tell you what you said. Just be sure it wasn't what you thought. But you broke the ice.'

'No, I didn't,' I quickly admitted. 'One of the girls did.'

'They're good little creatures,' Father Callaghan remarked as we stepped aside to allow two coolies pulling a large cart to pass. 'They mean and do well. You'll not have any trouble from them.'

We reached the confluence of the two rivers that joined at Wuchow, the Li Kiang which flowed from the north and the Si Kiang which ran from the west eastwards towards the sea at Canton. The river water was so brown with silt that the sun, now down in its afternoon descent, did not sparkle upon the surface. I gazed at the swirling and eddying where the currents vied with each other for dominance.

'A dangerous spot,' Father Callaghan remarked. 'That's where they say the river dragon lives. His tail causes the whirlpools. With the river this low, it doesn't look so bad but you wait until after the monsoon. Then it'll look like the maelstrom itself.'

'Always dragons,' I said, thinking aloud.

'Oh, yes! Always dragons. There are other evils in the Chinese bestiary but the dragon's the one to watch for. Yet they're not all bad, you know. Some are beneficial. China's a land of opposites, of checks and balances. The *yin* and the *yang*. Gods and devils.'

'Where do the dragons come from?' I asked.

'Everywhere. You get them living in hills, in forests, in rocks and rivers, in the sky . . .'

'I mean, where does the legend come from? What foundation has it? All legends are based upon some truth.'

'That's a fact.' Father Callaghan answered. 'Did you ever hear a banshee? Back in Ireland.'

'I did not,' I replied.

'I have heard it. In Galway, one winter, when I was a lad.' His eyes took on a brief far-away stare. 'But, you know, I didn't believe the old folk so I went to look for it.'

'Did you find it?'

'I did, for sure. It was the wind blowing off the Atlantic through a hole in a stone wall. And do you know, from that moment I wanted to be a priest. Dispel the myths of evil and show how they're all God's harmless work when you look closely at them.'

'And the dragons?'

'It's my theory, in ancient times, there dwelt along the coasts and rivers of China a breed of crocodile.

126

Sea-living ones such as they have in the Dutch East Indies. It's died out now, but the memory of its man-eating lingers in the collective consciousness of the people. They're simple folk so if a man's sucked under by the tow of the current why not say a crocodile – that is, a dragon – has him? The poor soul's dead whatever took him.'

We walked on in silence for a short way before Father Callaghan spoke again.

'We – you and I, Father Stephen – are in the myth business, you know. All those miracles Our Lord performed. Myths, really. It's our job to explain them, place them in context. They've all a basis in truth.'

'You sound like a heretic,' I said.

'Heresy's a frame of mind,' he replied. 'If you're true to God and seek the truth what difference does it make if you question a few things? Take the burning bush. A wonder, they said. But I've seen a bush catch fire of its own on a sweltering dry Chinese day. And if I had a silver dollar for every farmer hereabouts who's seen his hayrick catch alight of its own accord, I'd be richer than all the compradores from here to Shanghai.'

I looked across the river and up the wooded slope of a steep hill on the opposite bank.

'*Bak Hok Shan*,' Father Callaghan said following my gaze. 'White Crane Hill. Can you see the building through the trees? The British Resident's house, that is. A fine mansion built like a cross between a Chinese pavilion and an Indian *dak* bungalow. Trust him to arrange for his house to be built on a site with the best view of the town and river. You know, I think along with Latin and

127

Mathematics, they teach Strategics in English public schools.'

Towards us along the path came a figure dressed in a saffron gown slung over his shoulder toga-fashion, the material held in place by the strap of a brown cloth bag. His head was completely shaven, his feet shod in leather sandals. In his hand was a rice bowl.

'Buddhist monk,' Father Callaghan said. 'They're itinerant, like our mendicant brothers before us.'

He nodded to the monk who squinted vaguely at us, smiled distantly and raised his free hand in greeting. At that moment, a door opened in a building facing the river and a woman appeared with a cooking vessel. The monk abruptly held out his bowl, the woman ladling some rice into it. The monk muttered something, took a spoon from his bag and started to eat quickly. He made no attempt to squat down to enjoy his repast as any coolie might. Without speaking, the woman re-entered her house, firmly closing the door behind her.

'That's her duty for the day done,' my companion remarked. 'One step closer to a sure place in heaven.'

When the monk had finished his brief repast, he sucked his spoon clean, wiped the inside of his bowl with his finger and then, stooping to the ground, put a handful of grit into it which he scoured round the inside. This done and the grit discarded, he placed both articles in his bag and walked off, his eyes turned down at the ground before him.

'There's so very little difference between religions, when you come down to it,' observed Father Callaghan. 'All the world over, the clergy depend

128

upon charity and the congregations upon their consciences.'

Moored along the river were sampans and low barge-like vessels. We halted under the shade of a broad-leafed tree to watch the activity of the people, Father Callaghan hoisting up the legs of his *fu* and going down on his haunches like a native. I leaned against the smooth bark of the trunk, feeling its coolness through the cotton of my *sam*.

The bows of the vessels all faced the shore, coolies unloading them, carrying their cargoes up the steep bank on poles. Everyone was stripped to the waist and wearing a rattan hat with an oval crown and a down-turned brim which cast their faces in shadow. Stray dogs wandered about gleaning whatever they might whilst small children played at the water's edge.

Whereas the bows of the boats were theatres of frenzied mercantile activity, the sterns were calm, domestic areas. Women rinsed clothes in wooden buckets or prepared food over small braziers. Babies tottered about with a rope round their waists to prevent them falling overboard, the seats of their little pants cut out in a hole. Several men were engaged in fishing with lines. On one sampan, a man was plucking a hen, the feathers drifting down to the water to be snatched and whisked away by the current.

'The rivers are the life's blood of our town,' Father Callaghan observed, watching a line of coolies carrying tree-trunks up from one of the barges. 'If there were no rivers, there'd be nothing here but a few shacks and a tumble-down temple.'

I considered his words. He referred to it as our

town and, at that moment, I believed he was right: a strange place halfway round the world, filled with superstition and lost to God where he had found his home and where I hoped to establish mine. Beneath that shade tree overlooking the Li Kiang, I felt I had discovered what I wanted in life, a desire beyond even that to serve my God: it was to be with these people whose lives were so fascinating me, whose ways were so mysterious.

There was no revelation about my awareness. It was not a sudden realisation but the coming together of random, unspoken thoughts and feelings, a culmination of many factors — of the poverty of Ireland which I had left behind me and felt I could do nothing about, the misery of those without God who were doomed to damnation, the need to be a new man myself. Being in China, standing with the river flowing by and the coolies calling out to each other in their strange tongue, gave me the same feeling of rebirth and rejuvenation as I had experienced on the day of my ordination. It was as if a bright light had come into the darkness of my life and shone upon the path to a new future.

What I wanted more than anything else was to start again with new purpose in a new land which I could call my home and China afforded it to me.

'Do you know,' Father Callaghan interrupted my reverie, 'Wuchow was a city long before the Blessed Carpenter walked in Bethlehem? It received its present name in the Tang dynasty. In the year of Our Lord, 621. In the Sung dynasty, the poet Su-shi wrote of this place, *Every night, the moonlight on the river is beautiful: every dawn the cloudy hills look different.* Understand, of course, the poem loses a lot in the translation. But, you know Father Stephen, when I'm here and look across at *Bak Hok Shan*, I can imagine the poet sitting on this very spot and looking at just the same view. Save for the British Resident's bungalow . . .'

On the river bank, there erupted a commotion. Coolies dropped their loads to run pell-mell down to the sampans, shouting and bellowing. Women screamed, children started to cry with bewilderment at the pandemonium. The man who had been plucking the chicken had fallen into the river. He was already thirty or forty feet from his sampan, flailing his arms in the water and shouting in a high-pitched voice.

I started to run down the bank, struggling to unbutton my jacket as I went, Father Callaghan a few steps behind me. None of the coolies was making any attempt to save the man. They hollered and screamed: some of the women beat metal cooking utensils they had picked up from the sampans, yet no one made any effort to find a rope or jump in to the rescue.

Thrusting my way through the clamouring throng, I leapt onto a sampan, the deck heaving down under my weight and almost tipping me off balance. I was on the flat stern deck, pulling off my jacket when Father Callaghan gripped me so firmly by the arm it hurt.

'No, Father!' he said sharply.

'We've got to save him!' I shouted through gritted teeth. 'We can't just let him drown. And they're doing nothing.'

The man was now another ten yards away, his head turning this way and that as an undertow started to twist him around. He continued to shout, pointing at me.

'What's he shouting?' I demanded to know, still trying to get my arm free of both Father Callaghan's grip and my *sam*.

'He is saying, "Barbarian! Barbarian! Save me!"'

At that moment, the man's head disappeared under the surface. I watched the spot and prayed hard he would reappear. He did not. The crowd of coolies fell silent and then, as if nothing had occurred, returned to their labours.

'You should have let me . . .' I began angrily.

'. . . let you drown yourself?' Father Callaghan interrupted. 'You couldn't rescue him. None of us could.'

'I am a strong swimmer,' I complained, shrugging my *sam* back on.

'Not strong enough. The currents where the rivers meet are dangerous. You'd have gone under with him.'

'I should've tried.' I was irate, almost shouting. A small gathering of coolies and women looked on from the bank. 'What are we here for if not to save the likes of him?'

'We're here to save the living, my son,' Father Callaghan said coolly, 'not the dead. They've already gone to their gods and are beyond our touch. We're here for the abandoned, not the lost.'

His voice calmed my rage. I saw the reason behind his words but found them hard to reconcile. With my jacket back on, I started to make my way towards the prow of the sampan, stepping over some fishing nets and domestic utensils.

'Why didn't they do something?' I asked bitterly,

looking up at the little crowd which was dispersing and at the coolies along the bank raising their loads to their shoulders once more. 'Throw him a rope or at least a plank of wood. And quite what banging cooking pots would do to help him I cannot say. There was no need to raise the alarm. Everyone saw what was going on.'

'They didn't bang pots and pans to attract the attention of would-be rescuers but to drive away the evil spirits and the dragons.'

'I've heard enough of damned dragons already!' I retorted exasperatedly.

'And they dared not save him,' Father Callaghan continued. 'If they had, the spirits of the river might have taken one of them in his place.'

'That's ridiculous!' I exclaimed.

'It is,' he replied, 'superstitious, yet it's also logical. They know the treacherous waters. Why risk two men when one will do? Why orphan two sets of children? You must learn, Father Stephen, to be a realist. Temper your faith with practicalities. None of us can survive in China without pragmatism.'

I was shaken by the event and it was some minutes before I felt I wished to speak to my companion again. I found I was angry with him for preventing my actions and with myself for doing nothing. If I had jumped in and drowned, it would not have mattered: it would have been the will of God. I looked back at the spot in the river where the man had drowned. There was nothing to show for this tragedy but the vortex of brown water and, near his sampan, some white hen's feathers spinning around and around in a miniature whirlpool.

One of the scavenging dogs approached us, growling ferociously. Father Callaghan bent to the ground as if to pick up a stone and raised his arm. The dog, conditioned by years of experience, slunk quickly off.

'Beware of the dogs. They may be rabid,' he advised. 'So may some of the animals in the market. It's best not to touch them. Hydrophobia's not a pleasant way to die.'

We had walked on in silence for a quarter of a mile, each of us lost in our own thoughts. The river widened slightly, the bank below us no longer crowded with sampans or barges but with long, thin vessels resembling houseboats: whereas there had been a lot of bustle about the sampans, there was hardly a body to be seen here.

'These are flower boats,' Father Callaghan remarked.

'Flower boats?' I replied.

There was no sign of any flowers on their decks nor any coolies on the bank attempting to sell them.

'A colloquialism, Father. They're whorehouses. Floating brothels. If we did not save those girls we have, some of them would be down there now, plying their trade.'

As he spoke, a door on one of the houseboats opened and a young woman emerged onto a short length of deck. She was dressed in the lavish style of a Chinese lady, her full-length *cheong sam* embroidered in intricate detail with clouds and phoenix birds. Her black hair glistened and was worked into an extravagant coiffure piled upon her crown and hung with small pendants of pearls.

'She's heard our voices,' Father Callaghan commented, 'and come out to see if we might be her customers. In each of those benighted vessels there may be up to six or seven more like her. She's but the madam of the establishment.'

'Would she . . .' I paused, not sure of an appropriate verb to use, 'would she cater for us? For foreign devils?'

'For anyone, Father Stephen, who can pay the price. The Chinese may wish to keep our God and our customs at arm's length, but where the carnality of man is concerned, there are no racial barriers. Their natural xenophobia does not extend to the level of the courtesan.'

The woman looked up and down the bank. She could hear foreign voices but could not see us, expecting as she was men in tropical suits and tall hats rather than Chinese costume. When at last she realised which of the figures walking on the high bank were us, she turned away inside the boat, her footsteps short and unsteady.

'You see how she walks?' Father Callaghan said.

'Yes.'

'Do you know why?'

'She is a cripple?' I ventured.

'No, Father Stephen. Either she's in an advanced stage of syphilis which has attacked her nerves or her feet are bound.'

I knew of bound feet: infant girls had their feet from the toes to the ankles wrapped tightly in cloth bandages from an early age, misshaping the foot as it grew into a tiny, useless appendage which would bring pain and discomfort to its owner for as long as she lived. Yet I also knew this cruelty was exacted upon girls in wealthy families, not upon the poor: I assumed those who were whores came from poor families.

'I know what's in your mind, Father Stephen. But these whores — some of them — come from good backgrounds. They are not all waifs and strays, peasant girls with pretty faces. You see, when a man dies in China — a husband, that is — the chances of his widow remarrying are slim. Other men, the bachelors, regard her as sullied goods and will not seek to court her no matter how fair her features or her personality. She has only two real options open to her. The first is to remain in her husband's family where you can bet your very breath she'll be as like as not treated as a slave by her mother-in-law. The second is to leave, but to go where? Her own family will not take her back. She's an extra and unproductive mouth to feed. So she ends up as a tart in a boat.' There was a distinct hint of disgust in his voice. 'Mind you, there is a third option and those who are unable to resist take it.'

'A third?' I said.

'Suicide,' Father Callaghan answered bluntly. 'The Chinese are a sophisticated nation. They have some quite remarkably ingenious ways of killing themselves.'

We had by now reached almost to the outskirts of the town. The road along the bank petered out, becoming less of a highway and more a well-worn dusty track hardly more than a cart wide.

'Let us turn back,' Father Callaghan suggested. 'But I recommend you come this way yourself some time. Just beyond the trees, where the path bends, you'll find a place to interest you. And instruct you, I dare say, in more of the ways of China.'

Mr Chan's shop is halfway along Hankow Road, one of the thoroughfares traditionally and continually infested with tourists: only on Chinese New Year, when the shops close for four days, are they absent. His business is called the Hing Loon Curio and Jewellery Company and is announced, as are all the others, by a large wooden sign hanging in the forest of other, similar boards suspended over the roadway.

The shop is one of a kind that is gradually disappearing. It does not sell tourist garbage. The curios on offer are genuine antiques or antiquities, not fakes or fifty-year-old items dirtied up to look a good deal older than they are, and the jewellery is of a high standard. His rings do not wear through in months, the clasps of his brooches do not snap in weeks, his pearls do not lose their lustre nor the gemstones in his pendants drop free in hours. What is more he has not, as have many of his neighbours, concentrated his trade upon one area of activity. Most of the other shops in the street have become dedicated jewellers, watch-sellers, camera dealers, cultured pearl merchants or what I term kelter traffickers. He has not succumbed to the mid-twentieth century ailment of specialisation and the result is a shop of the kind that is truly Chinese, has existed for centuries and is a joy to enter.

I have known Mr Chan for many years and love him. He is a quietly humorous, gentle and generous man for whom the world is not just a place in which to make money but also to spread slivers of happiness.

The first time I went into his establishment, I was not seeking to purchase anything. Indeed, I was hunting out places where I might sell rather than buy. There are, of course, pawn shops aplenty in Hong Kong but the operators frown as soon as a *gweilo* enters: they are meant for the poor Chinese and a European face in front of the high counter raises suspicion, doubt and, on occasion, animosity.

Seated on a red leather stool before one of Mr Chan's glass-topped cabinets was an auburn-haired English woman. To her right was an expensive handbag resting against her foot whilst, to her left, there stood her son. He was about six years old, dressed in buckled sandals, white ankle socks, a pair of khaki shorts and a white short-sleeved shirt to which was attached by metal poppers a yellow and brown school badge. She was leaning forward, directing Mr Chan's finger under the glass.

'This one. No, next. Up one. No, other way. Yes!'

He removed from the display a sapphire ring set in rose gold. The strip lights under the glass top and the bare bulbs hanging from overhead split in the gemstone.

'Maybe.' She was undecided and pointed to another ring. 'What is that?'

'Alexand'ite,' Mr Chan informed her, removing a second ring from the cabinet.

I noticed he did not replace the sapphire ring but left it on the counter. This was most unusual. Shop-keepers, ever on the look-out for being cheated or robbed, rarely leave two items out simultaneously.

'This stone change colour,' Mr Chan remarked. 'If

you put in neon light, go one colour, but in plain go different.'

He handed it to the woman who moved the ring from side to side, to catch the various light sources, and I watched as the stone translated itself from a delicate mauve to a rich blue.

'I think . . . Let me see an aquamarine,' the woman requested, placing the alexandrite next to the sapphire.

Mr Chan, leaving the second ring on the counter also, started to rummage about in a drawer behind the counter, opening packages of folded paper, studying the contents then refolding them.

Apart from four glass counters and some stools, the shop is also furnished with tall, sombre cabinets made of dark-stained wood which give the place an air of solid if dusty history. This atmosphere of age is increased by the fact the cabinets are not illuminated and therefore contain an aura of mystery. They are crammed to overflowing with curios, the shelves so full it is almost impossible to see to the rear of them: I have known him to open a door and catch an item falling out.

Leaving him to continue serving the woman, I wandered towards one of the cabinets, peering into it. On the shelf just before my face were Buddhas carved of ivory or rosewood, ivory horses and elephants, soapstone still-lifes of karst mountains with little men climbing them on precipitous paths, glass snuff bottles with pictures painted on the inside, ancient pottery bowls, red-and-gold carved wooden temple tablets, cloisonné-handled paper-knives, black lacquerware boxes and cups, porcelain goddesses and a fifteen-inch high model of a sea-going fishing junk in full sail, complete in every detail down to the blocks through which the rigging ran. Upon the shelf below, surrounded by hand-painted eggshells in glass boxes and miniature fretwork landscapes cut from layers of cork, was a complete elephant's tusk intricately carved into a frieze of classical Chinese figures walking through a panorama of plum trees and pavilions.

'I can help you?' Mr Chan enquired, leaving the woman to decide upon her purchase.

His voice was soft, unhurried yet not unbusiness-like.

'Yes,' I replied in Cantonese. 'Do you only sell or will you also buy from individuals? I have some items I no longer wish to keep.'

For a very brief moment, he showed surprise at my fluency but this did not last.

'I do buy some things,' he said cautiously in his own language, 'but it depends upon the quality. If you bring the items to me I can see if we may do business. Are these Chinese items?' he asked as an afterthought. 'I do not usually buy Western things.'

'They are all Chinese,' I assured him, 'or of Chinese origin.'

'Are they made of gold?'

'No,' I said. 'Some are made of silver, others are jade but many are as you have in the cabi-nets.' I raised my hand to strengthen my point. 'Curios, antique items. Things I have picked up over the years.'

'Good,' he said warmly, 'I am sure I can do some business with you.'

He glanced in the direction of his lady customer. She was still trying to make her mind up, slipping the

140

rings one by one onto her fingers, comparing them at arm's length with her hand outstretched. The little boy was growing restless at his mother's indecision. He was of the age when to be still for more than a few minutes is the equivalent of a session of severe torture in adulthood.

Mr Chan excused himself from me and went across to the child, going down on his haunches so they might be face to face.

'Little boy,' he said in English, 'you come.' He beckoned to him.

'Can I?' the boy asked his mother.

Not turning round, she said testily, 'Of course you can. Mr Chan isn't going to eat you.'

Taking the boy's hand, Mr Chan stood and led him to the rear of the shop, unlocking one of the sombre cabinets, pushing the door wide and steadying a vase teetering on the edge of the third shelf up.

'When you born?' he enquired of the child.

'September,' he replied shyly.

'No, not this. What year you born?'

The boy considered this question then said a little doubtfully, 'Nineteen forty four.'

'You sure?'

'Yes.'

'Ah! Then I know you!' Mr Chan exclaimed. 'You a monkey.'

He laughed quietly and, reaching in to the cabinet, took out a two-inch high jade figurine of a monkey upon a small wooden base. The animal was depicted sitting with its hands before its face, holding a fruit of some kind.

'This for you.'

Mr Chan held it out to the boy who was not sure

141

whether to accept it. His face was filled with puerile doubt and unhappiness.

'He's giving it to you as a present,' I explained, sitting on a stool by the child.

'But he called me a monkey,' the boy stuttered, close to tears.

'No, he did not,' I said. 'He did not mean you were a monkey. He meant you were born in the Year of the Monkey. Each year in China has an animal to represent it.'

The child looked doubtful.

'I was born,' I went on, 'in the year of the Ox or Bull.'

The boy considered this. He was not at first sure if I was telling him the truth or spinning him some fantastic lie but, gradually, his doubt dissolved into the joy of being given the jade figure.

'You like it?' Mr Chan asked, sitting on another stool.

'I like it,' the boy admitted, holding it in both his hands. 'Thank you. Thank you very much.'

Unable to keep the fact of being given his own gift to himself, he ran across the shop to his mother.

'Mummy! Look what Mr Chan's given me. It's because I am a monkey boy.'

Whenever I pass the shop, I recall that act of simple kindness. It was not commissioned by a desire to close a deal with the boy's mother, or to impress, or to be some kind of advertisement, although it achieved all three. It was done simply because Mr Chan is a good man, one of those rare humans who, when he sees a petty suffering, tries to alleviate it. It is the likes of him who restore my faith in human nature, tell me there are good men in the world if only one is fortunate enough to discover them.

Over the years since that morning, I have sold perhaps two dozen items to Mr Chan. He is the only person with whom I have carried on such a trade; he has never once cheated me, has always given me a truthful evaluation of the object I have presented to him and not played upon my ignorance of its worth. Furthermore, he has always paid me in cash, in full and once, when he sold something obtained from me for considerably more than he expected, he insisted on giving me a percentage of the windfall profit.

This does not smack of bad business practice but basic honesty and such integrity is something I value more highly than any other human achievement. It is true, as one ancient maxim states, a display of honesty in any business is the surest way to prosper just as another apothegm declares the most certain way to remain poor is to be honest. Yet one does not grow rich in coin alone and poverty may take many forms.

The sun was not yet up, a vague grey light hanging in the room like a mist, slipping through the wooden slats of the shutters. It had been a muggy night and I had slept with the glass casement open but, on the recommendation of Father Callaghan, with the shutters firmly bolted, even though my room was on the third floor.

'They can be mighty wily devils!' Father Callaghan had remarked when he discovered at breakfast on the morning after my arrival that I went to bed with the window open. 'If they can't climb the walls or get themselves a ladder they'll as like throw up a grappling hook and shin in your room all the same. It amazes me,' he went on, breaking off a piece of bread and cramming it into his mouth, his next dozen or so words delivered with a light blizzard of crumbs falling upon the black cloth of his cassock, 'the further one travels East the more ingenious becomes the mind of the native pilferer.'

I swung my legs over the edge of the bed and scratched my shin. I had had a restless night, waking when an insect bit me just before dawn. I hoped it was not a mosquito: I was far more afraid of the malaria than a burglar. To combat the former threat, both Father Callaghan and I were sure to take a nightly dose of quinine disguised in a tumbler of gin and lime juice.

'Best drink in the world,' Father Callaghan declared when first introducing me to the bitter concoction. 'The quinine kills the parasites in your blood, the lime stops scurvy and the gin gives the evening a merry little glow.'

The drink was so sharp that, at first, I had found it hard to swallow.

'My advice,' Father Callaghan offered, 'is to wrinkle up your nose, praise God for the discovery of the drug and grit your teeth.'

Following his advice did not alleviate the bitterness: nor did the addition of sugar syrup which I tried at the suggestion of Ah Fong.

'Would it not be possible to take it with something else?' I enquired.

'I've tried,' Father Callaghan said. 'Rum does not

disguise the quinine. Rice wine and quinine turns the stomach and I'll not adulterate Irish whiskey with the stuff for any price. Or even Scotch. Gin's the only thing, but don't you worry, Father Stephen. You'll acquire the taste.'

'Like the eggs?' I replied.

'Exactly!' he retorted. 'Why, in a year you'll be asking, "Ah Fong, we've not had any of those ambrosial hundred-year-old eggs of late. How about a serving of them tomorrow?"'

I had to smile. He was a jolly man and doing his best to cheer me up.

'What's more,' he finished, 'if you were in Hong Kong, you'd be a man of society drinking this liquor. It's quite the thing to drink it thus – they call it gin and tonic.'

I unlatched the shutters. In the morning mist, the roofs of Wuchow looked like the scaly backs of reptiles. Slowly, I washed my face and upper torso in a basin of chilling water poured from a pitcher covered with a square of muslin on the night-stand. The leather-bound travelling clock on the bookshelf beside my Bible showed it was just after six.

I was nearly through with my ablutions when, over the splashing of the water, I heard a gentle knocking.

'Master? Master?' a voice muttered. 'You 'wakey, master.'

'I 'wakey,' I replied: speaking in pidgin English eased communication.

The door opened and Ah Fong entered carrying a steaming earthenware jug.

'For shafe,' he declared.

Before I could thank him, Ah Fong put the jug

down and, taking the basin, tossed the cold soapy water out of the window without so much as a glance to see who might be passing in the *hutong* below. He rinsed the bowl, threw that water after the dirty and filled the basin.

As I shaved, I heard a strange, brief sound from outside. It was a cross between a slurping, animal noise like a dog lapping and the rill of water over rocks. My face half lathered, I went to the window and peered down into the *hutong*. At first, I could see no one, the alley being in shadow, as if an hour of the night was lingering in it. It was not until a movement caught my eye I saw the source of the noise.

Below was a man with a hand cart. He was dressed in shabby clothes and walked with a stoop. Hanging down his back, over his cue, was a conical hat tied in place round his neck on a cord. Upon the cart were a number of barrels over several of which was placed a crude lid of split canes lashed together with bamboo strips. The man, bent in the shafts of his vehicle, was pulling the cart along the *hutong*, the wooden axles creaking and the wheels thumping on the cobbles. Just past the window, he stopped, lowered the shafts on uprights so the cart did not tip and hobbled to a doorway. I saw the man was either a hunchback or had been bent by years of labour.

From the doorway he carried a bucket which, having removed the lid, he poured into one of the barrels, making the sound I had heard. I was still pondering what on earth the man was doing when an atrocious and odious stench hit me. I reeled back from the window, almost knocking over the empty jug, pressing my hand to my mouth. Holding my breath, I closed the window and, before finishing my shave, rinsed my mouth out in case the stench carried some pestilence of which I was ignorant and to which, being a newly arrived foreigner, I could not hope to be immune. The stink seemed to linger in me as had the taste of the accursed egg.

When I was dressed in my cassock, I descended to the chapel and, after genuflecting before the altar, made my way to Father Callaghan's side. I must have looked white in the face for he commented, 'Are you well, Father Stephen?'

I recounted to him what I had seen, and smelled.

'That was what we call the honey-cart you saw,' Father Callaghan informed me. 'Old Quasimodo and his chums collect – how shall I put it? – family waste, including ours and take it out to the countryside. The polite phrase for this ordure is night-soil.'

'And then?' I asked.

'They spread it on the fields. There's few animals in China to manure the crops – not many horses or mules, few kine. And the droppings of chickens don't go far. All that leaves is the most plentiful animal – mankind.'

'Is this not a terrible source of pestilence?' I suggested.

'Indeed, it is,' Father Callaghan replied firmly. 'Especially of the cholera. And typhoid. This is the reason for thoroughly washing all vegetables before cooking. And perhaps why the Chinese have not invented the habit of eating a salad. You may like to know, Father Stephen, our annual expenditure of permangate of potash crystals is in excess of thirty pounds by weight. All you can trust to wash your greens in.'

The doors opened and the girls entered in silent

rows. It was a quarter to seven, the sun not yet visible through the mist yet their white smocks filled the room with light as if a holy presence had surreptitiously arrived. They filed into the pews and sat down, Sister Margaret chivvying a few along a bench with a flap of her hand.

Father Callaghan genuflected, faced the altar and began in a booming voice, '*In nomine Patris, et Filii, et Spiritus Sancti . . .*'

I looked up. The girls were kneeling with their heads bowed, their hands together at their breasts. Their hair was so black, so sleek where it was combed into short plaits. One or two, in the front row, wore little wooden crosses. Before them, on the tiled floor, were copies of their missals bound in black covers with gold Chinese characters embossed upon them.

In this room, I considered, lay my future. I had put Europe behind me, set my sail to the East and here I was, in a heathen land, doing the bidding of my calling. I wanted to feel proud I had made such a sacrifice. I might, I considered, in another age have been one of the ancient ascetics who wandered off into the desert to live as hermits in a life of contemplation. Yet my pride, which I knew was a vanity I should not allow myself, was in any case overcome by my feelings of humility.

I have given myself to God, I thought, surrendered myself to His mercy, to follow His path and bring His blessing to these poor, benighted heathens.

I had forgone the company of my own kind, the security of a parish living in Dublin or Cork, a caring congregation and a fine church, not to mention the chance to attend concerts, wander quietly through the art galleries or the park on a sunny afternoon.

Yet what, I considered, had these girls surrendered? Certainly, they had been cast out yet they had gone so much further. They had denied their own gods for my God, had taken to living in the company of foreign devils, of eating their food, relying upon their charity and doing their bidding. Theirs, I considered, was the greater sacrifice and I, for my part, must honour it by giving myself to them.

When they sang the *Gloria*, the musical score was familiar to me but the words were incomprehensible. Father Callaghan had translated them from Latin into Cantonese, another example of the unorthodoxy of which he had warned me. I tried to sing along in Latin but could not so took to humming the tune instead, the words passing in my head.

It was, I thought, like my first day as a child at the brothers' school when I had felt so completely alone, unknowing and afraid.

I remembered what I had done, as a small boy living in a village near Cork. My grandfather had recommended it to me on the morning I had left for school for the first time, riding in a dog-cart driven by Mr O'Hara, the butcher.

'When you're afraid, Stevie,' the old man had said to me, picking bits of pipe tobacco out of his whiskers, 'when you're truly afraid not of the sword or the fist but of the whole world, take my advice and ask for His help. You don't need to pray. No kneelin' and puttin' your palms together. Just look up for a moment and think, "God, will you not help me now I'm so scared?" And he will, Stevie, he will.'

I looked up. The ceiling of the chapel was bare to the rafters. I was, I think, about to ask for help with the incomprehensible *Gloria* when I saw something move. I narrowed my eyes. On one of the beams was what appeared to be a small dragon. I could clearly see its head. It was ten inches long with a broad, flat skull and yellow eyes. As I watched, it shifted onto the side of the beam clinging there with wide-toed feet, its tail hanging down. Its skin was grey with spotted markings which, even in the gloom, were brilliantly scarlet.

Suddenly, it vanished: one second it was there, the next it was not. All thought of Cantonesified Latin, prayer and fear was gone, replaced by a fascination in the creature.

The service continued under Father Callaghan. I played my part when it was required of me. Just as the final words were being spoken, from high in the rafters came a curt shrill call. *Tok-eye*, it went, then repeated itself twice. *Tok-eye*! *Tok-eye*! It was a penetrating sound like the metallic click of the tin frogs to be found as prizes in stalls at fairgrounds and it made me jump.

Father Callaghan, his back to the congregation, glanced upwards and, noticing my consternation, whispered over his shoulder to me, 'Gecko. Noisy as the devil but they keep the cockroaches down.'

With Mass over and my fast broken, I went around the town on my own, getting used to finding my way about. It was a daily routine that one of us should wander the streets, watching out for those who may need our help, be brought to Christ or just befriended. The sooner I had a grasp of my bearings the sooner I could take my share of the burden of God's calling.

For the whole morning I wandered the streets, mentally noting landmarks by which I might know

150

my specific location in the future until, at about noon, I reached a wide street in which there was a thriving animal market. The stallholders sat on low three-legged stools next to bamboo cages, some shaded by the buildings, others by umbrellas of wax paper.

The first stall I came upon was selling cats: a few were domestic cats but others were larger, spotted leopard-like cats with sleek coats and rounded ears which spat and hissed at the feet of passers-by. In one cage was a palm civet with a black-and-white striped face like a badger's and a long tail which hung out of the bars.

'Buy cat?' asked the vendor hopefully.

I was taken aback at his speaking English: it was the first words I had heard uttered all morning that were not in Cantonese. I should not have been surprised for there were over twenty Europeans living in Wuchow, merchants and their wives, expatriate officers working for Chinese customs authorities and the British Resident: the trader, I assumed, probably sold them pets.

'You speaky English?' I asked.

'Small small.'

I shook my head and replied, 'No buy cat.'

'*Ho sik*! *Ho sik*!' the cat-seller said, smiling broadly. He pointed to the cat and tapped his teeth with an inch-long fingernail.

It was then I realised the cats were on sale not as household pets or the hunters of vermin but as food. I looked down at a tabby in a bamboo basket. It was hunched up, its eyes half closed against the bright sun, its tail curled around its side. It might have been basking in front of a hearth.

Moving on, I passed cages of tusked, bristle-haired wild boar trussed with bamboo thongs, small ginger-pelted deer with short horns crammed into boxes with their forelegs broken to prevent escape, tubs of giant salamanders and golden-shelled turtles, buckets of frogs and leather or canvas sacks tied at the neck. The contents of the latter thrashed and writhed: I guessed they contained snakes. At the end of the street, I came upon two cages erected in the shade. Whereas most were on the ground, these were set up on trestles, protected from the sun by two umbrellas and a length of hessian.

Inside were a dozen monkeys. They sat at the rear of the cages, huddled together, several clutching each other. Every one of them had such a deep human sorrow in its face I was immediately affected. Reaching forward, momentarily forgetting Father Callaghan's warning about hydrophobia, I put a finger through the bars. One of the monkeys stared at it then grasped hold of me. Its own little fingers were like a child's, the palm cold. It was shivering despite the midday heat.

I wanted to buy them all, set them free in the hills and watch them swing into the branches, chattering excitedly at their unexpected liberty. Yet I knew this was impossible. I could not transport them and, besides, it would most likely be only a few days before they were recaptured, imprisoned and waiting once more for a fate of which I believed they were fully conscious.

As I left the animal market, thoroughly depressed and still wondering how I might rescue the primates, I met Father Callaghan in the company of Ah Fong.

They were doing their rounds, looking to follow Christ's bidding.

'So how are you finding Wuchow, Father Stephen?' asked Father Callaghan as I joined them.

'Interesting,' I replied thoughtfully.

'But disturbing?'

'Yes,' I allowed.

'It's the strangeness, Father Stephen. You'll become used to it. To the sights and sounds. Oh! And the smells,' he added. 'Not all as unpleasant as your early morning encounter.'

I made no response and he sensed there was more on my mind for, after a few minutes, he touched my arm and said, 'You've seen the animal market.'

'Yes, I have.'

'All for food, you know.'

'Yes,' I repeated.

'You'll come to understand it,' Father Callaghan remarked as we turned a corner. 'It's a cruel, hard world here but that's for the better. If it wasn't we should have no job to do. As for the Chinese, they're good folk. They mean well and they work hard. Industrious and pious in their own way. Respectful of . . .'

He stopped abruptly, took a firm hold of my arm, catching me off-balance and making me stumble. At the same time, he uttered a curt command to Ah Fong who was walking a few steps to our rear.

About a hundred yards down the street was a small crowd listening to a man standing on an up-turned wooden tub. He was tall for a Chinese, with his head half-shaved, his cue hanging down his spine. Around his forehead was wound a red scarf. He waved his arms as he spoke at the top of his voice, his head turning this way and that as he addressed the people before him.

'Well, most of them,' Father Callaghan added as a codicil to his praise and then he pushed me into a doorway. Ah Fong joined us but not quite so precipitously.

'What is it?' I asked.

'Bad man,' Ah Fong said. 'He no good for you, for me.'

'A revolutionary of sorts,' Father Callaghan added. 'And, as Ah Fong rightly says, potential trouble.'

'A revolutionary?' I questioned.

'*I Ho Ch'üan*,' Ah Fong declared.

Father Callaghan was listening intently at the corner of the doorway.

'A Righteous Harmony Fist,' he said.

I was none the wiser but I did not speak. Instead, I listened.

The Chinese was clearly a skilled orator, the tone of his voice at one turn haranguing the crowd, at the next cajoling, pleading or reasoning with it. He seemed to be able to talk without pausing to catch his breath, reminding me of one of my fellow noviciates in the seminary who had been able to recite the whole of the *Ordo Missæ* in just the same way, a feat he had performed as a party piece until one of the priests caught him doing it and severely reprimanded him.

'What is he saying?' I enquired after some minutes.

'He is saying,' Father Callaghan replied, 'it is time China was cleansed of the Pale Ghosts. And that, Father Stephen, is the likes of you and me. And when we go, be sure as hell is a hot place, the Holy Ghost'll come with us.'

154

We slipped from the doorway, making for a narrow passage-way. I glanced in the direction of the orator. His audience had swelled threefold since we had ducked out of sight.

Caution being the better part of valour, we returned to the mission and, on Father Callaghan's advice, I did not set foot from it again until, early in the evening, I left the gate, walked along the *hutong* and attempted to retrace my steps of the morning. Ah Fong accompanied me, at Father Callaghan's instigation: he would, my superior explained, know what he saw and would steer me safely from trouble.

It was a balmy end to the day. Birds sang in cages hanging from the eaves of the houses or the branches of trees under which their owners sipped tea, smoked and conversed. Although it was not yet dusk, lanterns had been lit in some of the tea-houses and shops, bathing the interiors with soft light as if the air was somehow bending the last of the sun in through the doors.

No one gave me a second glance. Sedan chairs passed by, their small doors or cloth hangings closed against the last of the day, the chair coolies shouting to clear the way of pedestrians. I was eager to see the sights of the city and felt supremely but unjustifiably confident no one would wish to do me harm.

There seemed to be more children playing in the streets than there were during the day. A toddler carrying a colourful paper fish on the end of a stick caused one chair to halt, the coolies bellowing at him and so scaring him that, rather than run, he stood his ground petrified. The child's mother appeared from

155

a doorway, shrieking abuse: when she saw the chair, she was instantly silent, kow-towed and lifted the little boy out of the way.

The games the children played fascinated me. They were quite unlike those of their counterparts in Europe. Here there was no hop-scotch or skipping. Instead of rolling hoops or playing tag, they kicked a feathered shuttlecock into the air with their heels or tossed coins against a wall. On a street corner, a group of older boys squatted in the last of the sunlight coming through a gap in the mountains, playing what Ah Fong informed me was *Hsiang-Ch'I* chess, the white counters embossed with black and red characters.

As we turned into a side street leading to the animal market, we found our way blocked by an angry crowd of some thirty people. I was immediately on edge, fearing an encounter with another of the revolutionaries.

'We go other way?' I asked Ah Fong.

'No. Can go here,' he assured me.

The crowd's ire was not directed at either myself or a revolutionary. Indeed, several people nodded respectfully to me as I went by. To them I made the obligatory return, a slight tilt of the head.

Reaching the front of the crowd I saw a young man squatting against a wall, his face a picture of misery and embarrassment, his clothing shoddy and his feet bare. His hair was not plaited into a cue but hung in dirty clumps from his head, although his crown had been shaved, whilst around his neck was fastened a cangue, a heavy platform of boards through holes in which projected his head and hands. About his ankles were thick iron manacles attached to a short length of chain which would allow him to walk only at a shuffle. Pinned to the upper surface of the cangue was a notice.

'What does it say?' I asked Ah Fong.

'He feef,' reported Ah Fong. 'Take no belong him.'

'How long he stay like this?'

'Long time, master.'

'How long? One week? One month?'

Ah Fong looked in my direction.

'I no know,' he whispered. 'He die.'

'They execute him?' I asked.

'What *ex-ee-koot*?'

'Kill him.'

'No, master. No kill him. People no give him food. He die.' He turned from the sight. 'Come, master. We go. No good stay long time. People no like you look see long time.'

For another hour, as we wandered through the city, I could not cease contemplating the living death I had witnessed. Finally, as the twilight began to deepen, we started back towards the mission.

In the town's main square, a sort-of small circus was performing by the light of pine torches mounted on poles. Their flames burned with a yellow light, sparks falling in showers to the ground. A large gathering had congregated around two acrobats who were leaping into the air, turning cartwheels and prancing about with mock Chinese swords flashing in the light. Peddlers mingled with the crowds selling toys. One had a tray of cup-and-ball games fashioned from wood, another offering ladder puzzles with the steps cut out of polished bone and the strings made of twisted silk yarn. A third displayed carved miniature

157

acrobats, imitations of the real thing nearby, which tumbled head over heels at the turn of a little wheel.

The centre of attraction, however, was a kiosk like a Punch-and-Judy show, the puppets operated by poles rather than strings. One was a mandarin in a fancy costume of red and gold: he appeared to me to be the hero of the pageant. Another was the fair maiden with a pretty costume from the head of which protruded the eye of a peacock feather. There was also a dragon. The theme of the play centred on the dragon wanting the girl for a meal and the mandarin wanting her for a bride. There was much jumping and fighting, to the accompaniment of a small gong and a high-pitched penny-whistle-like instrument played by two young boys at the side of the kiosk.

For fifteen minutes, Ah Fong and I watched the performance, the light of the torches throwing shadows from the puppets and giving the play an added drama. Subsidiary characters appeared — a peasant, a god, a ghost and an old crone — and the action became a little more heated. Suddenly the dragon, which had been on stage throughout the performance, vanished. In its place stood a figure dressed entirely in black with a round, dish-like hat on its head. The mandarin, the fair maiden, the god and the peasant started to shout at the black puppet. The gongs banged more frequently and the music rose an octave and quickened its pace. The black puppet was driven to the very edge of the stage by the peasant which hit it repeatedly on the head with a hoe. He beat it down until it hung over the front of the kiosk, struggling to regain its balance. Around its neck was a white circle and, painted on its front, was a cross. The audience was laughing.

No one had taken the least notice of me, but I suddenly knew I was in danger: then, before I could address this feeling, the gong bashed loudly, the mandarin puppet screamed and the entire gathering fell silent, turned as one and stared at me.

'We go, master,' Ah Fong whispered and touched my sleeve. 'Go now. No good.'

We turned and walked sedately away. I wanted to run but knew I dared not. For a moment, there was no reaction to our departure, then the audience began to shout. Some hurled what were plainly obscenities at Ah Fong who coloured up but ignored them.

'Mus' turn o'er cheek, master,' he said and walked stolidly ahead, not looking either to left or right.

We turned a corner into the Street of Heavenly Happiness and quickened our pace, but the crowd did not follow. I heard the gong begin to strike again and the penny whistles pick up their tune once more.

'I understand from Ah Fong you saw a criminal?' Father Callaghan remarked as we sat later together on the roof of the mission, watching the moon rise and sipping our gin and quinine.

'Yes. A thief, according to Ah Fong.'

'That's right. He was caught stealing a hen. From the house before which he was pilloried.'

'Just a hen?'

'A mere chicken. I saw him this morning. He's not a town-dweller but a countryman. You could tell from his clothes. He's just a hungry peasant. There's a degree of famine in the land. Because of the drought,' he added.

'Ah Fong says he'll starve to death.'

'That's right,' Father Callaghan said. 'Or they might execute him by strangulation.'

'They will hang him?' I asked incredulously.

'No. They'll strangle him by hand with a knotted rope. Only the worst criminals are beheaded. In the eyes of a Chinese, there is no worse fate than to die incomplete, as it were. This is why, when eunuchs leave the emperor's employ, they are given back their genitals which have been stored in special boxes. They may then be buried whole and be men once more in the after-life.'

'It's a barbaric land I have come to,' I said.

'It's a land where Our Lord's as much a stranger as we are,' Father Callaghan said, 'and it's our work to introduce Him to it and the people to His glory and His love.'

Hsiao has his pitch and, indeed, his home opposite the tea-house I occasionally frequent in Prince Edward Road. It is a wide street and the traffic invariably heavy so, unless there is an accident or roadworks, I only see him for a glimpse at a time as the buses and lorries zip by.

The tea-house is a modest establishment. The half a dozen tables are of the small round folding type, each of which can accommodate up to five people without becoming cramped. In the early morning, it is packed with workers on their way to the factories in Sham Shui Po or the offices in Central but when I visit it in late morning it is usually doing a slow trade of old men like myself taking their constitutionals or on their way to a mah-jong game.

There are four urns in the tea-house, each made of polished brass with Chinese characters set upon them in copper. They gleam like the statuary in the gold dealers next door but three: if this were a temple, they would be the most important idols for miles around. One of them hisses from a slight leak: it has done this for as long as I can remember. The air is aromatic with the competing scents of different teas and the counter is stacked with little green, red or yellow cartons and tins of tea.

Nowhere in the tea-house is there a single word of English except upon the tea packets and that is very small. This is one of the reasons I like the place. It is utterly Oriental without so much as the merest hint of the Occidental. One does not find tea-houses in Europe – cafés, bars, cantinas, bistros, coffee-shops and even tea-shops there are, but no tea-houses. This place does not serve little sandwiches or dainty cakes, or the Chinese equivalent thereof. It sells tea to refresh the mind, rejuvenate the body, enliven the parts that are failing and cure the others which are ailing. It is a serious place for thought and health, not gossip and banter.

My tipple is gunpowder tea. The name is not indicative of some punch hidden it in, such as lies in rice wine. It is a raw tea which comes looking like little grey pellets of seventeenth-century gunpowder, hence the name. I like to watch as the water is added to the pot, the pellets swirling and opening slightly, looking like tadpoles: then they quickly spread out into thick, dark leaves and a delicate perfume lifts from the surface. At that point, I put the lid on the pot to keep the heat and flavour in.

The tea is the colour of plasma, a straw-yellow which, when it is warm but not hot, slips down the throat like molten honey. It lifts my spirits and clears my head.

Sitting at the front table, I can see Hsiao. He is a wizened stick of a man with untidy, short grey hair and a pinched look who wears rimless pince-nez which lend his countenance a vaguely professorial appearance. Always dressed in what we term a Mao jacket, for it is like that worn by the arch tyrant of Peking (as Mr Wu calls him), he sits all day long on a stool by his wares at the mouth of an alley which he has made his own.

At the entrance is his stall selling magazines and paperback books. By the pavement the racks, which are nailed to the wall of a tenement, carry copies of *Mad* magazine, *Time* and *Newsweek*, *Life* and *Paris Match*, *Punch* and *Vogue*, *Vanity Fair* and the *New Yorker*, and American comics which retell the classics in abridged, picture form.

When I first discovered Hsiao's pitch, I could not for the life of me see how he could make a living from such publications. This is not an area often visited by Europeans, save those tourists who have lost their way or police officers doing the rounds with their Chinese constables. To understand Hsiao's business success and acumen, one has to quit the pavement and go into the alley.

Next to the international publications of repute, a little further from the street but not too far, are displayed copies of *Playboy* and *Men Only*, some Chinese girlie magazines with the titles or captions

162

carefully placed so as not to offend the eye of passers by and thin pamphlets with plain covers.

I remember very well my first call on Hsiao. Stopping at the rack nearest the pavement, I took down a comic entitled *A Tale of Two Cities*. The front cover showed a colour illustration of Sydney Carton riding in a hay wagon, hand in hand with the little seamstress: across the foot of the page was pasted a sticker in English and Chinese stating 'Air Mail Copy – $5'. From the grimy state of the cover and the faded colour of the label, I deduced it had not recently been flown in, although I was sure five dollars would still be the asking price. I opened the comic at random and read the bubble coming from the mouth of a pretty young woman in a poke bonnet, her blonde tresses showing under the small crown at the back of her head.

'As a wife and mother,' I read aloud, 'I implore you take pity on me, Madame Defarge. Oh, sister-woman, think of me.'

Hsiao left his stool and came to my side, looking up at me over the top of his pince-nez. His spine is curved by years of sitting on the stool in all weathers with nothing against which to rest his back. I am not a tall man any longer but I still tower over him.

'You wan' buy?' he hissed in English.

Looking up from the tragic face of Lucie Manette, I studied Hsiao at close range. His face was not only pinched but hard and I guessed he had not long to live: I was, of course, wrong. He is still going strong, like a buffalo in a paddy-field one thinks must long ago have lost the power to pull a plough through such cloying mud.

'No wan' buy,' I answered.

163

Before I could replace the comic on the rack, he snatched it from me and, straightening a crease on the cover which I had not made, said curtly, 'No buy, no read.'

I took a few steps down the alleyway and, reaching to the top rack, removed a magazine on the front cover of which were two lines of Chinese characters over the photograph of a naked Chinese girl smiling coyly at the camera, her arms crossed over her chest, which was also partially hidden by a strategically placed price label: a large Ming vase hid her body from her waist down. I opened the magazine at a page depicting two other Chinese girls, their backs to the camera, playing with a bright beach ball. Their bottoms were small, their buttocks clenched.

The old man, having been angered at my fingering the comic, was not so upset at my handling this merchandise.

'Make in Taiwan,' he stated. 'Chinese girl. Guruntee good pikchur. You want B'itish girl? Can do. Also can do Japonese. Black girl okay.'

'Maybe,' I said, more out of curiosity than a desire to purchase any of his trash, and returned the magazine to its slot on the rack.

'Got more,' Hsiao volunteered, pointing to the rear of the alley. 'You wan' see? No charge.'

I briefly nodded and he led the way down the alley to what any casual observer unused to the ways of Kowloon back-streets would have assumed was a pile of rubbish awaiting collection but which was, in fact – and remains to this day – Hsiao's residence.

He lives in a very large wooden crate which, according to the writing burned into the timber, had been used to transport a German loom from a factory in Stuttgart to another in Tsuen Wan. He has improved upon it by giving it a covering of tar-soaked canvas and fitting to it a heavy door with a brass Chubb padlock which would do credit to a bank vault. The electric light within has been wired to the public street lamp: a tap just by the door provides running water. Behind the crate, at the dead end of the alley, is a cubicle erected from corrugated iron which is Hsiao's personal convenience.

Unlocking the door, he swung it wide, banging it back against the crate wall.

'You go in. I come.'

The interior, in which I had to bow my head but Hsiao did not, was cramped yet surprisingly homely. Against the rear of the crate was a folding bed. Shelves nailed to the walls carried Chinese books, eating and cooking utensils and a few ornaments of the tacky tourist variety. A minuscule table for one stood under a calendar for the Chinese year, a pictorial map of South East Asia cut from a *National Geographic* and a colour portrait photograph of Her Majesty, Queen Elizabeth II in a cheap beaten-tin frame.

'Queen ve'y good,' Hsiao declared, tapping the picture with his knuckle. 'Look Hong Kong good. No Commooneest come if Queen.'

He pulled out a stool and a folding chair, inviting me to sit. I did so as he squatted on the stool and, from under the bed, pulled out three cardboard boxes, flicking on a bulb hanging by a flex from the centre of the ceiling.

'You wan' photo? Book?' he enquired. 'I got good books. Make in Holland. Make in Singapore. Hot stuff!'

Without waiting for my reply, he rummaged in one of the boxes, pulling out a lurid publication, on the cover of which was a totally naked European girl unadorned by price labels or Ming vases. She was bending backwards over a chair and looking between her breasts at the camera. Her legs were spread apart, one of her hands resting inside her thigh.

'Dis a good one. Ve'y popular. Plenty people buy. Fifty dollar. But for you,' Hsiao paused as if doing some mental arithmetic, 'thirty-five dollar.'

'I don't think so,' I replied.

'Okay. No sweat,' he answered lightly, undeterred by my negativity. 'Got more.'

From another box, he took out a thicker book, handing it to me. The photographs were interspersed with text printed in German. The early pages carried a series of photographs of a fornicating couple: after page twenty they were joined by another woman dressed in a military uniform.

'Come f'om Germany. Very good. Good pikchur.' He took the book back and flicked through the pages with his thumb. 'All colour pik-chur. No black-an'-white. Good story. Forty dollar for you. First sale for today. Good p'ice.'

'I don't want anything,' I said in Cantonese.

Hsiao was immediately cautious. My speaking Cantonese was what put him on his guard: I was no idle, elderly tourist but a *gweilo*.

'You policeman?'

I laughed briefly and, reverting to English to put him at his ease, said, 'I look like a *chaai yan*?'

'No . . .' he replied pensively, then added, 'What you wan'?'

'Nothing.'

He became cross with me, annoyed I had apparently wasted his time and he was not going to make a sale.

'So! You *chun chu*! Stupid man! Like pig!'

He began to wave his arms about.

'Okay! You go. No buy, no come.'

I rose to my feet and left the crate. He followed me to the street, muttering and swearing in Cantonese. As I reached the pavement, I suddenly stopped and removed a copy of *Time* from the rack. I turned round. Hsiao halted dead in his tracks: he reminded me of a dog that is brave when its quarry retreats but unsure of itself when confronted.

'*Kei toh*?' I asked.

'*Sze mun*,' he snapped.

I gave him four dollars, crossed the road, entered the tea-house and, sitting down, ordered a pot of gunpowder tea and read the magazine. Every so often, looking up, I saw him watching me.

Sometimes now, he looks out for me. When I pass his stall, he greets me and I buy a magazine from him about once a month. He also continues to study me from across the street. When I have read the magazine over my tea I always leave it on the table and I am told by the waiter that, as soon as I have disappeared, Hsiao scuttles through the traffic and takes it back again for resale. He has not told me this, but I know the waiter occasionally charges him a dollar for the buy-back which he begrudgingly pays.

At the moment, Hsiao is not glancing in my direction. He is sewing. Across his knees is a pair of trousers in which he appears to be repairing a rent. Possibly a previously undiscovered nail in the crate has snagged his clothing.

I feel sorry for Hsiao. Not in a moralistic sense. I declare no interest whatsoever in his soul. My days of worrying over another man's place in the immortal kingdom – heaven, nirvana, Zion, paradise or whatever – are long since ended. If he wishes to make his living purveying pictures of copulating couples and girls with their buttocks taut with embarrassment I care not a jot.

My sympathy for him is beyond definition. Perhaps it is his crate home that causes me to feel something for him, or his utterly hopeless situation, for he will never rise out of it. Pornographers make big money but their salesmen remain poor. It is the same in any business. As Americans say, the bosses strike rich and the bums strike out.

Perhaps I should have befriended him, my sympathy not for him but for myself for not doing so, for losing the opportunity of knowing another man whose friendship might have amused me.

The message reached me this morning just before eight o'clock. I have no idea who delivered it – as, indeed, I never have on these occasions – but it was contained in an envelope upon which was written the words *By Hand* in that particular cursive script taught as standard in Chinese schools. Above this was printed *Golden Phoenix Film Production Co. (HK) Ltd.* and the company's address some ten minutes' walk from my home. I slit the envelope open with my finger. The sheet of paper within was crisp and headed

Golden Phoenix Films: *from the Desk of Desmond Tan.*

I have known Desmond Tan for four years. He is a would be mogul in the movie world, his dream to be the equal of Run Run Shaw, with his own studios in the New Territories, a gold-painted Rolls Royce and a house in the countryside overlooking the sea. Whenever we meet, he tells me he is one step nearer to fame and fortune: always a little step, he assures me, but he qualifies this by saying that babies take little steps to practise for the bigger ones of adulthood.

The truth of the matter is he will never be the tycoon he wishes for he does not think big. Roughly translated, for much nuance and imagery is lost in the transposition from one language to another, there is an old Chinese saying: the sparrow would be an eagle but he does not stretch his wings.

Desmond is a sparrow. He picks up the crumbs from the rich men's tables. He does not produce films, nor does he direct them: he would like to, of course, but that takes talent, capital, ambition and vision. He lacks three of these seminal necessities. Instead of producing films, he dubs them. He is what is known in the parlance of his trade a facilities house, which is to say a pretty low but essential bird in the pecking order. In short, a sparrow.

I like him for he is a man not unlike myself, one who dreams. He has no real vision, and I have lost mine, so that sets us together. He takes life as it comes, harms no one deliberately or not, at least, maliciously and has a sense of justice. That is rare.

169

The note read,

Dear Stephen,
I am able to offer you some work today.
Can you be ready at ten o'clock for the rest of the
day? Usual rate but with overtime because no time
to stop for lunch. Sanwitchs will be provided with
tea and beer if you prefer.
If you can not come, let me know on receetp of
this note. Otherwise, see you at ten o'clock.

It was signed, *Your buddie, Desmond Tan.* His signature is large and full of flourishes: at least he has developed the handwriting for the job.

His studio, which is to grace the establishment with a grander word than it deserves, is on the seventh floor of a fairly modern tenement building in Mong Kok. It was intended as a light industrial factory unit but Desmond has reconstructed it as the start of his movie-making empire.

The entrance is through a glass door into which has been etched the name of the company under a stylised phoenix rising from flames and flecked with gold dust. Beyond this is a square of red carpet (with another phoenix woven into it) and a polished plywood desk which looks as if it was designed by the same person who made Sam's bar counter. Behind this sits the receptionist, a pretty Chinese girl who obviously shares Desmond's dream of making it big in the movies one day for she keeps her hair trimmed and cut in what she deems to be the latest Hollywood fashion (this month her mentor appears to be Doris Day) and makes sure her blouse is tight enough for even a casual observer to notice the curve of the top of her exceedingly small breasts. Her name is Audrey, after Hepburn.

I pushed open the door and stepped across the carpet. Audrey looked up and smiled at me as if I might be coming to offer her a first-class Pan-Am ticket to Los Angeles, Sunset Boulevard and stardom.

'Morning, sir,' she greeted me. 'Goo' to see you again, sir.'

She has developed a sort of American vocabulary and accent which makes her hard to understand in a sustained conversation. Earlier this year, I was present when an American producer, in Hong Kong to make a film on location, visited Desmond to discuss using his studio to look at unedited film. In what he believed to be Hollywood style, Desmond had laid on rather good quality *sanwitchs* and, from a friend in the hotel trade, had borrowed a cocktail waiter. I was asked to attend to lend, in Desmond's words, an air of sophisticated internationality to his business: in other words, I was to stand around, pretend I was one of his partners or a man of greater stature than I am in the world, and make small talk to the American's assistant. For this, I was paid $280.

All went well at first. The American was impressed by Desmond's equipment and apparent knowledge of operating it; the viewing studio was comfortable; the studio seemed efficient and, by Los Angeles standards, was not far from the producer's hotel. I made small talk with the producer's aide, a somewhat delicate young man in a lilac shirt and a pair of denim jeans that fitted him like a glove and had been permanently creased. At a lull in the conversation, one of those silences that occurs every now and then

171

when more than four people are talking together, Audrey saw her chance.

'Yall seen *Solijer of Forchoon*?' she piped up. 'Weal goot moowie. Cluck Gabul an' Soosun Haywoot. Soosun Haywoot weal goot actwess. You guys mus' see it.'

There was a stunned silence. The American producer stared at Audrey. So did his fey assistant. So did Desmond but whereas the others were somewhat bemused, he was plainly unamused. Audrey smiled delicately at the Americans then caught Desmond's eye and scuttled from the room.

'She one of your staff?' the American enquired.

'She make the tea,' Desmond lied.

The two Americans exchanged glances.

'She is a school girl,' I chipped in, hoping I was lying convincingly: it has never been part of my repertoire. I am truthful to the point of bluntness and generally don't give a damn what I say.

'School student?' the aide asked.

'Yes,' I said. 'We employ her when she has time off. To help her improve her English.'

'Been here long?' the producer wanted to know.

'Six month,' said Desmond.

'She's finding the language hard then,' the American observed and sipped at his cocktail.

Desmond was awarded the contract and, for eight weeks, his studio was one step nearer to the back lot of Metro-Goldwyn-Mayer and he was half an inch nearer his Rolls Royce.

'Morning, Audrey,' I replied, adding, 'which door today?'

'Stoo-dio B,' she said, pointing down to the left. 'They waiting for you.'

I could not get lost in Desmond's establishment for there is only one corridor and two studio suites, A and B. The light outside the door to A glowed red meaning a film was being worked upon inside. The light by the door to B was green. I pulled on the handle and entered the sound lock between the corridor and the studio. Through a glass pane in the door I could see Desmond and several other people standing together.

'Hi, Stephen,' he welcomed me as I entered, the door closing on a wheezing hydraulic hinge.

We shook hands. Desmond is tall for a Chinese, nearly six foot, and he always wears a pin-stripe suit, which gives him the illusion of being taller still. On his right wrist he has a gold-link bracelet, partly because this gives him a sense of status when in the company of other Chinese, indicating he is wealthy, and partly because the American producer wore one. He has a jade-and-gold ring on the little finger of his left hand for the same reason.

There were four other people present. One was a European woman in a tight black skirt and white blouse, two were European men in their twenties whom I took to be soldiers from one of the barracks earning a bit on the side and the fourth was a short, dapper Chinese man in a tweed jacket.

'Everybody. This is Stephen,' Desmond introduced me adding in his best Hollywoodese. 'He's an old pro at the dub game.'

I smiled distantly and we all exchanged nods.

Desmond left the studio and the European woman began to talk to me. I felt she believed she was obligated to do so, my being the last to arrive and not yet an integral member of the group. In this respect she was like those spinster women who linger at parochial church functions, eager to see no one is left without a cup of tea and a bun.

'Hello, I'm Barbara,' she said. 'So you've done this before?'

'Yes,' I told her, 'many times.'

'It's my first,' she confided. 'I'm a little nervous.'

'There's no need to be,' I reassured her, 'if you keep your wits about you.'

'I don't mean just the dubbing. It's – well, not the usual thing, is it? I am, I admit, beginning to have second thoughts.'

'The usual thing?' I replied.

'Well, the sort of thing . . . This is Hong Kong. As soon as my name appears in the credits . . . Bang goes invitations to Government House, for a start.'

She glanced at me for a moment, her eye running me up and down. I was wearing an old padded *sam* and she was nonplussed at seeing a European in semi-Chinese attire.

'Then don't use your real name,' I said. 'I seldom put my name on the films I dub. I use a fictitious one. A pseudonym. Sometimes, I am Peter Hansard, sometimes Bruce Carter, at other times Raymond Leung. What does it matter? I get paid.'

'But,' she began, then she paused.

'But?' I asked.

'Well, forgive me but you are a . . . I don't mean to be nasty, but you aren't one of us, are you? I mean, you've,' she paused and was plainly embarrassed but knew she had to finish her statement, 'rather – how can I say this? – gone native.'

I laughed and this put her a little at her ease. I

think she was expecting me to be either angry or distantly aloof.

'I can assure you,' I said, 'I am one of you. More or less. You're English and I'm Irish but that's the extent of our differences, gender apart. As for going native . . . Well, my dear, I have lived in China since the early summer of 1900 and I have not once, as you would put it, gone home. Indeed, China is my home.'

She stared at me almost in disbelief and asked, 'Have you never wanted to?'

'Not once,' I confirmed and it is the truth. 'I came out here leaving nothing behind me and I have stayed.'

'But how have you made a living?'

'This and that. Buying a little, selling a little. I taught English for many years, teach Cantonese and I dub Desmond's movies. I am, I admit, quite immodestly, a dab hand at kung fu fighting ones.'

'Were you in the forces when you came out?' she enquired. 'In 1900, I mean.'

'No,' I answered, relishing what was coming next, 'I was a Roman Catholic missionary.'

The look on her face was one of shock, her hand even going halfway up to her mouth. She may well have been the heroine of one of Desmond's corny romance films.

Just then, Desmond returned, clapped his hands and Audrey appeared carrying a pile of cardboard folders, handing us one each. She smiled sweetly at her boss and I wondered, just for a fleeting moment, if she was sleeping with him in the true Hollywood manner: I would not have been surprised. They might both have been practising for the future.

'Today just first twenty-six pages. Fifteen-minute read then we make a run-through. Each person marked for them,' Desmond declared officiously and he left, tailed by Audrey.

I sat on one of the tall stools in the centre of the room and pulled the reading shelf projecting upwards from one of the legs round in front of me, latching it in place with a little brass bolt. I placed the folder on the shelf and peered at it. On the cover was typed *Lord Yuan and The Merciful Lady*. I opened it, removed the script and began to read the outline.

The story was not out of the ordinary. Lord Yuan wanted to marry Lily Flower but she was betrothed to Hwang, an evil war-lord. She planned to elope with Lord Yuan and wed him in the mountains, where he had been forced to live in a fortress cave ever since Hwang had killed his father and usurped his lands. Hwang heard of Lily Flower's plan and kidnapped her. He was now holding her in his impregnable castle on the plains. Lord Yuan was bent on recovering his lands, eradicating the evil Hwang and marrying his true love. Where the Merciful Lady came into it I could not tell as we did not have pages relevant to her part but I am sure it was she who aided Lord Yuan in getting into Hwang's base, guiding him to Hwang's chambers, having drugged the guards either with a potion or with magic. Hwang, of course, would be awake being too strong or too evil to be affected by the poison or the spell.

I was to play two parts: an Old Sage who was Lord Yuan's adviser and Leaping K'uo, a character into which the Old Sage metamorphosed for a few minutes at a time when he touched a magic jewel he kept in a pouch around his neck.

My reading done, I sat and looked about the studio as a technician entered and began to position microphones, adjusted reading lamps on poles and placed vertical sheets of black cardboard here and there to deaden echoes.

Each dubbing suite is divided into two, the recording studio and the control room, separated by a double-glazed window. The walls are painted black but, here and there, the paint is peeling to display the last colour scheme, which seems to have been brilliant yellow. The ceiling is also painted black and is lined with an acoustic material consisting of irregular peaks and troughs of foam rubber. The floor is covered in a thick carpet which is worn threadbare by the door. The viewing screen is like those one sees in lecture theatres, mounted on the wall and capable of being rolled away into an oblong box.

Through the soundproof window I could see Desmond sitting at a table in the control room with Audrey standing behind him. He was reading and she was gazing vacantly into space. Two technicians, dressed in trousers and vests, busied themselves with a projector and a console of knobs and meters.

'All Okay?' came Desmond's voice through a crackling loudspeaker somewhere behind the screen.

We all nodded except for Barbara, who smiled nervously at me and whispered, 'I'm Peach Flower. The girl warrior in Lord Yuan's band.'

'Don't worry,' I answered. 'Next time, you may well be Lily Flower or the Merciful Lady.'

'I'm not sure I can do this,' she said quietly.

'You'll be all right,' I said. 'Just follow the counter on the film and relate your speeches to the character on the screen. You don't have to be too exact. Just so long as you don't speak when your character's mouth is shut.' She seemed unconvinced, so I added, 'This isn't Shakespeare, you know.'

She smiled wanly, the ceiling lights dimmed, the reading lamps came on and the film began to roll. Upon the screen appeared a number of warriors in seventeenth-century costume. Lord Yuan was young and handsome, Peach Flower young and beautiful, the five followers young and strong and the Old Sage wrinkled and hunch-backed. He was dressed in what looked like old military blankets and carried a staff: for a moment, I had a fleeting vision of Quasimodo, the honey-cart operator. Peach Flower wore baggy trousers, a tight bodice and had a sash tied around her head.

The action in the film consisted of brief bursts of conversation, followed by long, intense fights with Hwang's henchmen in which Peach Flower killed up to four men with one swing of her sword, Lord Yuan fought with two different types of weapon, one in each hand, and the Old Sage either grunted and ducked or metamorphosed and leapt over trees with his staff flailing. The dialogue consisted mostly of shouts of warning, curt commands and short lines of explanation to keep the plot, such as it was, evolving. One of my lines, addressed to a Hwang bandit, was *'Where is the Lady Lily Flower?'* to which he replied *'In my lord's castle, safe from the hands of scum like you'* which was the only indication to the audience as to where the maiden was being held.

As is usually the case, I became involved in this

puerile story. For three hours, apart from a twenty-minute interlude for Coca Cola and *sanwitchs*, I was the Old Sage and Leaping K'uo. I delivered my lines and saw myself not as an aged man on a stool before a microphone but as an ancient hero combating injustice and righting wrongs three hundred years old. When the work was done, the final dub made and the lights switched on once more, I felt exhausted as if I had not been the voice of the actor but the body as well. I might have done all that metamorphosing, leaping and staff-play, I was so tired.

As I left the building Barbara called out, walking quickly to catch up with me.

'Would you like a cup of tea?' she asked.

'I'm afraid I can't,' I lied. 'I've another appointment.'

I did not want to be with her. It was not a matter of dislike, just wanting to be on my own.

'I hope I didn't hurt your feelings,' she said. 'About going native and so on. It was impertinent of me and I'm sorry.'

'No, you did not hurt me,' I replied to put her at her ease. 'And your apology is not required. I'm not bothered by what you or anyone else might think of me. I am what I am.'

I carried on down the street thinking she might leave me but she kept up.

'May I ask you something?' she requested.

I nodded.

'In his office, I caught a glimpse of some pictures from one of Mr Tan's other films. They were quite,' she searched for an appropriate phrase, 'rude.'

'He does blue movies,' I confirmed.

'And do you — I mean, do you dub those, too?'

'Sometimes,' I admitted.

She thought for a moment then went on, 'The fighting films with mythological sorcerers and lords and so on I can understand but how can you, as a missionary – a priest – justify dubbing such immoral – such . . .?'

'Pornography?' I suggested. 'Quite easily. First, I'm not a retired priest. I'm a former priest. There is a distinct difference. You see, I gave up my vows. Second, I don't see such a film as either moral or immoral. If anything, it's beyond morality. A mere sequence of pictures to give pleasure to others. The pleasure may be dubious, but it is not for me to judge. Indeed, I'm not one to judge any man.'

'I do not understand,' she began but I cut her short. I had no intention of standing in a busy street justifying myself even to someone who had attempted to show me a kindness after inadvertently speaking their thoughts.

'To be a judge, one must be above others. I'm not. Even you consider me below you. An old man gone native. And I am below you. I'm on the lower levels of humanity but I do not worry about it. It's a condition in life to which I promoted – perhaps demoted might be more apt – myself and where I'm quite happy. As for morality, I don't believe in it. It's a man-made set of judgements, fashioned by each society to validate its own actions.'

'Surely morality comes from God?' she submitted.

'God,' I told her, 'is the most immoral of all. Or amoral, depending upon your point of view. And before you ask me why, I shall tell you. Because he disregards his creations.'

A coolie came between us pushing a low hand-cart

180

on rattling metal wheels. Upon it was a cylindrical wicker basket containing a live pig. Its ears and curling tail stuck out through the wickerwork against which its snout was pressed: the animal's feet were folded up under its belly and tied in place.

'You see,' I pointed out as the man passed with his load and we were able to move together again, 'even pigs are abandoned by their gods.'

'Shall I see you again?' Barbara inquired as we arrived at the bus stop.

'I am sure you will,' I replied, holding out my hand and shaking hers. 'Desmond will be calling upon our services again. And quite soon. We've yet to reach the Merciful Lady, who may well be you. So practise another voice before then.'

She smiled and hailed a taxi.

'Can I give you a lift?' she asked as a red Mercedes Benz slid to the curb.

'I shall take the bus,' I said, 'but thank you.'

The rear door of the taxi sprang open on the automatic lever operated by the driver and Barbara got in. I heard her tell the driver to go to the Star Ferry. As it drove off, I could see her glancing at me through the rear window. She was plainly puzzled. I was, for her, another enigmatic and paradoxical aspect of life in the Orient and would, I knew for certain, be the subject of cocktail party conversation before the week was out.

Now, back in my flat in the evening twilight, the glare of the street lights slicing through the venetian blinds and the last of the day glowing in the sky, the drone of traffic and voices in the street, I feel somehow disembodied as if I have returned from another life, where I was not old and moving towards death but old and in command of that magic gemstone.

I look around my room, my cell in the middle of the twentieth century and wonder what the Old Sage's corner of the fortress cave looked like. And I think how, when I was young, vibrant and eager like Lord Yuan and Leaping K'uo, like Luo the swordsman and Gong-sun the fire-master, I saw people like them. Not characters on a screen or actors on a stage but real, walking the streets.

I glance up at the bookshelves, at the thin black leather-bound notebook near the end which I never touch. As if I am outside myself, an actor escaped from Desmond's studio and alive in my flat, I rise from my chair, moving it to the bookshelves. Balancing upon it, I reach up and take hold of the book. It is jammed tightly between the others as if it does not want me to take it down. I pull a little harder and it suddenly gives way as if it has lost its grip upon its companions. I sit at the table and, not opening it, look at it in my hands.

The black leather is blotched by damp and mould: the spine is split where the leather has become brittle. I have never attempted to repair it just as I have never put an annual coating of dubbin on the leather to keep it supple: the Oriental climate is unkind to books.

I cannot account for my actions. There is no need for me to remove it from its place.

I open it at random.

The page is for a day in the early summer of my first year out East. The exact day is of no concern. The first part of the entry reads simply: *Vy. hot. Sun high and glaring. Air dry, no humidity. Town swelters. No*

*cloud. Drought severe. Will rain come? The land and
people need it.* That is all. Two dozen words with no
narrative. A telegrammatic statement best written on
a postcard sent to an ageing aunt. Anyone reading
this would judge nothing from it. Yet I remember it
all so well.

I had, I recall, written my entry in the early
afternoon and was lightly snoozing, dressed only
in baggy Chinese trousers. The sun beat down on
the roof and the air was sultry and oppressive. The
heat made me lethargic, causing my eyes to grow
heavy and my back ache. The entry on the page was
as banal as the day was acheronian.

It was one of those fulcrums in time upon which
my life tottered before swinging the way it has. It was
one of the days which began to shape me.

☯

The sun was just touching the hills when Father
Callaghan and I settled into our sedan chairs to
set off through the town in the direction of the Li
Kiang. Although it was not customary, I left my chair
open, confident that no passers by could see in for the
shadows were deepening.

Proceeding down a narrow street, we came upon
a group of some forty people standing silently before
the wooden façade of a building. Father Callaghan's
chair continued past but my bearers halted, lowering
my chair to the ground. The one in front started to
gesticulate and I, assuming he wanted me to dis-
mount, began to clamber out. This greatly agitated
him and, muttering what might have been curses,

183

he thrust me roughly back into my seat, tearing the curtain across. He muttered something again under his breath, the chair rose and we set off once more.

Needless to say, I was curious to see what it was the bearer would rather I did not and, as we passed the gathering, slowed to less than walking pace by the crush, I reached forward to edge the curtain aside.

Before the semi-circle of people was a tall, T-shaped perch, upon which balanced a common monkey with greyish fur, a pink face and staring eyes of the same species I had observed in the animal market. Beside it stood what I took to be the owner. He was a sturdy young man, his head wrapped in a flaming red turban which held his cue in place, coiled like a ship's rope upon his crown. Red ribbons were tied around his bare ankles and wrists and around his waist was a brilliant red sash, all the brighter for being set against the white cloth of his jacket. In his hands he nonchalantly swung a curved sword which reminded me of a paper-knife owned by the priest in charge of noviciates in the Dublin seminary I had attended: there, however, the similarity ended for Father Ciano's knife was so blunt he had to slash at envelopes whilst this weapon was razored so finely I could almost feel its sharpness upon my flesh.

The monkey was dressed in clothing as well. At first, I did not take these in but then realised its garb was an approximation of a European suit, with a jacket, trousers and waistcoat.

As I watched, the young man flung back his head and bellowed a single word into the sky: I could not understand it yet I knew it to be terrible. His lips contorted like those of a snarling cur, his eyes wide and empty. Then, with a movement so lithe he could have learned it in a dancing academy, he spun on his heels and sliced the monkey's head off as neatly as a man picking off the top of a boiled egg. The little body remained for a few seconds upright on the perch, blood fountaining from its shoulders: then it dropped to the ground. The head smashed against a nearby wall.

The crowd made no move nor did a sound rise from it. I let the curtain drop, my hand shaking and my cheeks turning cold with the drainage of blood. The chair gathered speed as the bearers worked clear of the crowd.

At the river bank, my chair was lowered to the ground and I joined Father Callaghan already seated in a sampan. A woman in a broad rattan hat started to row us across the river, standing up to work a pair of long oars projecting over the sides near the stern. Towards the centre of the river, she began to row harder and I recalled with a chill running down my back the sight of the drowning man. We were not a hundred yards from the point where he was sucked under.

'You'd not be thinking of dragons, would you, Father Stephen?' Father Callaghan asked.

'Yes,' I admitted, 'in part, I would.'

'Well, you need not,' he replied. 'We've the good Lord looking down upon us and if His efficacy isn't sufficient, which I'm sure it is, we've this good lady's little god to guard us, too.'

He nodded towards the prow of the sampan where, tucked under the gunwale, was a shrine no bigger than a pocket missal containing a wooden idol painted in red and gold and some little paper flags.

'I'd say that was blasphemous, Father,' I remarked.

'What is?'

'Saying if the Lord Jesus doesn't do a good enough job then that little effigy will do the rest.'

Father Callaghan laughed and said, 'Father Stephen, I'm sure the Lord knows when I'm joking and when I'm serious. Regardless of what monsignors and cardinals might tell us, I'm sure God has as good a sense of humour as the rest of us.'

I wanted to mention what I had witnessed in the town but felt I could not for, somehow, the sight was an intensely personal one. I believed – I cannot say why – fate had deliberately staged the murder of the little primate so I might understand something of which I was still ignorant, something about China, the Chinese and, maybe, also about myself.

On the far bank another pair of chairs was waiting which took us up the hill to the British Resident's house, our names being called out by the bearers as we passed the sentry at the gate, who made a curt response. I saw the guard was not a British soldier but a Chinese wearing felt slippers, puttees, baggy trousers and a wide waistband under an embroidered jacket. He held a carbine to his side and stood to attention.

The building was a large stone bungalow with a veranda running all the way round it, its walls painted imperial yellow with scarlet footings. The gardens were neat with trimmed bushes, paper lanterns hanging from the trees. A light breeze, rising from the town, swayed them gently. From the veranda, a European man in his mid-thirties appeared, walking towards us as we alighted from the chairs.

'Fathers! Good evening!' he said, extending his hand. 'And how are you, Father Michael?'

'Tolerable, tolerable,' said Father Callaghan.

'And so you are Father Stephen,' the European went on turning to me. 'Robert Morrisby, I'm the Resident. And I'll bet,' he continued as we shook hands, 'you're already known as *See Faat Han*. That'll be the nearest in Cantonese I think they can get.'

'I am,' I replied, 'and I have been apprised of the meaning.'

Morrisby laughed and gave my hand a final shake.

'A sign of respect, Father. Endearment. I always say, never trust a schoolmaster who doesn't have a nickname, eh? No moniker, no character. Now, come and join the others. We're not a large community in Wuchow, Father Stephen. Indeed, you see half of our number before you.'

Upon the veranda, sitting under a string of lanterns, were a dozen Europeans, only three of the assembly being women. Some of the men stood in a group looking out over the garden whilst the women, dressed in long skirts and blouses, with lace collars and cuffs, sat together. A Chinese servant in black trousers and a white jacket handed me a drink. I knew before putting it to my lips it would be the same gin and quinine concoction Father Callaghan and I drank each evening.

'Sit next to us, Father,' one of the women said, beckoning to me. 'I am Mrs Elizabeth Tremlett — but do call me Betty. And this,' her hand waved over her compatriots, 'is Mrs Harriet Blair and Miss Alice Trowell.'

187

Looking from one to other, I took in the details of each as I remembered, a little balefully, the warning I had received from Father Piazzoli, the Vicar Apostolic in Hong Kong. The night before I set sail in the *Lucky Moon*, he had taken me aside in his house and, after praying with me for a short while, gave me several pieces of advice.

'Remember, my son,' he had said in his rich Italian accent, his hand upon my shoulder, his full beard twitching as he spoke, 'three important things in China. First: take care of your feet. There is much walking to do in China, in the path of Jesus Christ. If your feet are hot they will grow big and sore. Keep them cool. Second: take care of your soul. There are many temptations in China for a young man. Our greatest enemy, Satan himself, works his black wonders there on the most staunch of souls. And third: beware of colonial women. I do not mean this in a carnal sense. But you should know they are like society ladies where there is no society. They will commandeer you. A priest is of fascination to them.' He rubbed his long nose. 'Why, I cannot tell. It is a mystery God has not yet shown to me.'

Mrs Tremlett was a small woman with the angled features of a bird. Her chin and nose were sharp, her eyes small and porcine and her hands, where they projected from the lace of her cuff, thin-fingered and active. On the other extreme, Mrs Blair was a formidable and buxom woman, broad-hipped and looking better suited to a shooting party in the English countryside than a sundown party in the wilds of the Orient, whilst Miss Trowell was petite and delicate yet singularly unattractive. Indeed, all three of them held little I felt would have encouraged carnal desire in any man: were I not celibate, I was sure I should not have been tempted by any one of them and would rather have talked to the men than associated with what I was afraid might be mindless prattle, yet convention controlled me and, heedful of the Vicar Apostolic's warning, I joined them.

'You are the new Catholic father,' Mrs Blair remarked unnecessarily, adding to my first introduction, 'Mrs Tremlett's husband is a merchant here in Wuchow whilst my husband is in the Chinese Customs Service.'

'And I am Betty's sister,' Miss Trowell chipped in. 'I'm on my way to Japan. To be married.'

Mrs Tremlett frowned at her sister and said, 'I am sure the Father is not at all interested in that, my dear.' She turned to me. 'Her beau is a missionary in Honshu. A Protestant, I fear, Father . . .' She was clearly embarrassed to make this declaration and, taking her glass from the table beside her to cover her discomfort, went on, 'But enough of that! Now, you must tell us all about what is going on in the big, wide world. We are quite out of touch here.'

'I'm afraid,' I responded, 'I know as little as you. I'm not one for reading the newspapers.'

'You priests are too unwordly, Father,' declared Mrs Tremlett, straightening her back and rearranging a cushion in her chair. 'So! You will have to entertain us. But first, did you see the criminal near the ferry?'

'I saw a man in red and white with a monkey,' I said.

'That was a Boxer,' Mrs Blair informed me. 'Just a troublemaker. I think what we are referring to is the man in the cangue. A nasty piece of work. Dirty as the soles of your shoes. You know,' she continued, 'I feel we should still treat our criminals so. It's no use imprisoning them. A drain on the exchequer. We should bring back the village stocks. I'm sure it would be cheaper and more effective.'

'The criminal in the cangue,' I said quietly, 'I saw near the animal market. He is going to die.'

'No, no. That board thing they put on him doesn't kill him,' Mrs Blair interrupted. 'It merely hampers him.'

'He cannot feed himself,' I said patiently, putting on my best priestly tone, 'and the people will not feed him. He will die of starvation.'

The three women exchanged glances.

'I'm sure you can't be right, Father,' said Mrs Tremlett.

'I assure you I am,' I answered and there was a long pause.

'Do you know,' said Mrs Blair, changing the subject, 'what the Chinese call Bruce?'

'Who is Bruce?' I asked.

'Bruce is my Jack Russell terrier,' Mrs Blair informed me. 'I had him sent out from England.' Her voice softened. 'He's such a jolly little chap! Anyway,' her tone became brusque, 'do you know what they call him? They call him a rat. Because he's small, you see,' she went on as if an explanation was needed. 'They don't seem to grasp the fact that anything other than their damnable Esquimaux chow-chows can be a real dog.'

After a quarter of an hour of listening to almost continuous feminine babble, I excused myself and stood on my own at the edge of the veranda. The last of the day's light was pencilled along the mountains, a bat flying silently in and out of the lanterns, picking off insects attracted to the flames.

'Father Stephen?'

I turned to discover an elderly man in a black suit with a pair of bifocals pinned to his nose.

'Arthur Doble,' the man said, offering me his hand. 'I'm a merchant here in Wuchow.' He cast a quick glance at the women. 'You seem to have mercifully escaped the tirades of banality.'

'That I have,' I agreed, 'and feel I've done my Christian duty by them.'

'Forgive my lack of charity, but I'm sure Our Lord would consider five minutes with the ladies to be sufficient penance for all but the most heinous of sins.' He looked through the trees and suggested, 'Shall we take a walk? The Resident has a fine garden and the view can be quite beautiful on a calm evening such as this.'

We set off through the bungalow grounds, passing neatly manicured bushes and stately trees.

'A pity you can't grow real grass in China,' Doble remarked as we went by an area of beaten earth in the centre of which was a boulder, the crannies planted with miniature trees, giving the appearance of a mountain in classical Chinese paintings. 'I do so miss lawns. And croquet. One cannot play croquet on earth. Or anything except that game of French bowls and horseshoe throwing. But where can one get a horseshoe in southern China?'

'Perhaps,' I suggested, 'Mrs Blair could be persuaded to import some with her next pet, perhaps?'

Doble laughed and said, 'You've a wicked mind, Father. A devious, wicked mind!'

At the end of the garden, we reached a steep drop

to the river at the top of which was a small pavilion. We entered it to look across at the town on the opposite bank.

'China's a fascinating land,' Doble said, sipping at his gin. 'Just look at that.'

The town was a mass of pinpricks of lantern light, the haze in the warm air making them glitter and wink. Smoke rose in vertical columns, not disseminating for perhaps a hundred feet. The occasional call of street traders and the buzz of human commerce drifted over the river to us whilst far out in the dark mid-stream bobbed fishing lanterns.

'That's a scene unchanged for a thousand years,' Doble remarked. 'Perhaps two. Who can tell? But it will change. Oh, yes, it will all change.' There was a sadness in his voice. 'The railways and steamboats will alter it irretrievably. We shall change it, the pale ghosts from the west. And it is our job — yours and mine — to see change is done in a Christian way, the barbarism of the Orient replaced by the Love of God.'

I nodded and looked up the Li Kiang to the flower boats moored upstream from the cargo sampans and barges and thought again of the drowned man.

'I love China,' Doble said, interrupting my thoughts. 'Been out here for twenty-two years next month. Traded first in silk then shifted to tea, cotton and porcelain. Dabbled in opium.'

I looked at his face. He was gazing down on the town but I could tell he was not seeing it. Like a man making a confession, his thoughts were far away in the history of his life, of his sins and sinning.

'That was long ago,' he went on. 'Bought it in India, sold it in Whampoa. Had a little godown there in partnership with a Scotsman. Sold some of it back to London. Medicinal purposes. Useful to promote the literature of our land. Ah,' he paused, 'I apologise, Father. You're Irish. I mean, of my land.'

'Promote literature?' I asked, wondering if he used the profits from his opium trading to patronise writers.

'Oh, yes. Keats, Shelley, Coleridge, Wilkie Collins. All took laudanum. All had the dreams that made good writing. Xanadu where Kublai Khan his stately pleasure domes decreed is not in China, it is in the misty countryside of the narcotic.'

'Do you take opium yourself?' I ventured.

'Not the done thing, Father,' he said quickly. '*Gweilos* do not imbibe of native vices. Yet, as you are a priest, I confess to you that I do, from time to time. But you are beholden to keeping the secret. Oath of the confessional, or whatever it is called. I am not, Father, a Catholic.'

I laughed to put him at his ease, assuring him his secret was safe.

'You should try it once in a while. Taken in moderation, it's not addictive. And it does less harm than alcohol.'

I drained my drink, sucking my cheeks in at the tartness of the quinine. I had not agitated my glass whilst standing talking and a residue had collected near the bottom.

'Have you been back to England since you came to China?' I enquired.

'Once, eight years ago. I found it — how shall I put it? — bland. There was nothing to it. In London, you know what you will find around the next corner. And, I dare say, it is the same in

193

Dublin. Or Paris. Here, each turn of the path has a surprise.'

'Father Callaghan told me as much,' I remarked. 'He said he never ceases to be astounded, not for one day.'

'He's right. Even after nearly a quarter of a century, China still holds surprises for me.'

'And is that why you love China?' I asked.

'Yes. And also because it fascinates me. In China is all of humanity, all we, as a species, are. The people are . . . Well, beyond description. There are depths to them, Father, our race has yet to devise. It comes from thousands of years of civilisation. When the Romans were building their first road, the Chinese had mapped the heavens. And as for us, in the British Isles!' He shrugged his shoulders and emptied the remains of his drink into a bush by the pavilion steps. 'We were dressed in fatty animal hides when the Chinese hung themselves about with silk.'

'I am beginning to feel as you do,' I admitted.

My reason for coming East was not to fall in love with the people but to bring them to Christ, to the ways of humans in which I believed lay not only religious but also social salvation. Yet, at that moment, standing in the pavilion with the lights of Wuchow coruscating before me, I felt God to be almost a side issue in my life: I had not sailed half way around the world merely to do His bidding but to discover new horizons for myself. In short, I was not seeking to save the Chinese, to alter their way of life thousands of years old, but to save something in myself which I knew existed but which I could not name.

This self-revelation, if such it was, made me

profoundly afraid, a fear so deep-rooted my skin contracted as if I were suddenly transported from a balmy South China evening to one of the frozen poles. I was not ready to deny my mission and my Saviour: yet something deep within me was touched, something I could not reach down and undo.

An intuition, it can have been nothing more, told me it was not Satan at play in that dark corner of my being but another power, neither good nor evil, one beyond morality or religion. It had no rigid doctrines, inflexible dogmas. It was devoid of ideology and theology. I struggled to know what it was and then, as if it had been waiting for the right instant to introduce itself, it did so. It was reason, reality, the cold rationale of intellect, the same power which told me there were no dragons living in the river, no spirits existing in the rocks and, consequently, possibly no God in heaven.

In a fleeting instant, I saw an awesome question loom within me, offering no solution but doubting the premise of my God, challenging the very fundamentals upon which I had based my life. That I wanted to do good for my fellow creatures was as firm a purpose within me as my desire to draw my next breath: what was different now was that I wanted to do this in my own name, for my own reasons.

'I'm not in the least surprised, Father,' Doble said quietly, stopping my confused race of thoughts, 'China works upon a man such as no other country.'

Above the mountains briefly flickered a flash of lightning. It might have been a charge set off in my soul and seeking release in the heavens.

'There's a storm coming,' I observed.

'On the contrary, Father,' Doble replied, smiling, 'there is no storm coming. You won't have seen this before. It is heat lightning, presaging not rain but heat. We are, I fear, in for more rainless weeks.'

There was another flash but no accompanying thunder.

'Have you yet travelled to the north?' Doble asked.

'This is my only experience of China,' I said.

'Not the north of China, Father. The north of the world. Many years ago, before coming East, I went to Russia. Beyond St Petersburg, into the far bleak north. There I saw one of the wonders of the world. It was as if a vast hand was painting the sky. They call it the aurora borealis. The sky is hung with curtains of the most delicate nature — blues and greens and reds — which shimmer as if they were a heavenly veil of chiffon. Have you ever seen this?'

'I have not,' I said.

'I think,' Doble went on as another flicker of lightning appeared, 'that if the Northern Lights may be the gift of gods then this heat lightning is the doing of devils.'

Somewhere far off in the trees, a night bird called with a strange, melodic music. Another bat flitted through the pavilion and out into the air above the river, weaving this way and that in its crazy flight.

'Hot summers here spell drought,' Doble said at length. 'The rivers are already much lower than usual. And, in China, drought means starvation.'

I thought of the thief in the cangue. Such a sight would become a commonplace, I considered, if Doble's prediction came true.

'If there's a flood or a drought,' he continued, 'it is

196

thought by the people the Emperor has done wrong, displeased the gods and jeopardised the Throne of Heaven. In that event, the people must overthrow him or he must appease the spirits to avert their wrath being visited upon the nation. Yet, should such a turn of events come to pass this year, I do not see the Emperor or the Old Buddha being de-throned'.

'The Old Buddha?' I queried.

'Tzu-hsi, the Dowager Empress,' he explained. 'An evil woman, that one. You mark my words Father: it is my belief the tables will turn not on the Emperor or her but upon us. There is already much feeling against foreigners. Being whipped up by ne'er-do-goods.'

'I saw a street entertainment the other day,' I replied. 'In it a Catholic priest was beaten by a Chinese Mr Punch.'

'Or Anglican, Father. Or Anglican. You Catholics do not have a monopoly on martyrdom.'

From the town came the sudden rattle of exploding firecrackers. A street near the waterfront was illuminated with a series of brilliant flashes. In the last of the twilight, a dense column of smoke rose into the sky, blotting out the lanterns behind and spreading as it climbed higher. As the echoes died away, dogs could be heard barking hysterically, through which din came the muffled dull boom of a gong.

'Fireworks and gongs tonight,' Doble said, 'I fear it may be gunfire or grenadoes tomorrow.'

In the rock-strewn, scrubby foothills of the Nine

Dragons, north of Kowloon, tucked between the city and the uninhabitable slopes, tens of thousands of people live in anticipation and hope. Known as squatters, they have erected shacks and lean-tos wherever the gradient is sufficiently short of the perpendicular to allow construction. Their towns are illegal, regarded as dangerous by the fire brigade, unsanitary and disease-ridden by the health authorities, corrupt by the police — even the education department lists them as places of ignorance and low literacy: yet this is to misconceive the situation, to fail to appreciate the tenacity of the Chinese.

The buildings in the squatter areas are made of the detritus of the city, much like Hsiao's shack or that of the old woman on the roof of my tenement, but often with considerably greater ingenuity. Hsiao, after all, only lives in a converted crate. The hill squatters do not adapt, they construct. Their buildings are fashioned from rough timber, sheets of corrugated iron, tin or aluminium: the windows contain glass or waxed paper and the doors ride on hinges of iron or leather. Between them run a maze of passages, alleys, and narrow streets, a few crudely paved but most bare earth trodden hard by feet. Dogs lie in corners, chained to the walls which look so flimsy one might assume the dog, taking umbrage at a passer-by and straining on its leash, might cave the wall in or tug the building with it. In addition to dogs there are innumerable cats and, here and there, hens, ducks and even pigs in minute pokes.

Between the ramshackle buildings run ditches serving as sewers: these are noxious little nullahs, foul-smelling even on the coolest of days, jammed with garbage and effluence which are only flushed when there is a rainstorm. The chickens scratch on the banks of these filthy drains but the ducks and dogs know better and keep away.

These derelictions are sturdy. They withstand the high winds of typhoons, the chilly blasts of winter. Many are cosy within, snug hovels which are the homes of extended families of up to ten folk, each with a job to do and a purpose in life.

The grandparents mind the shack, sweep the floor and hang out the laundry, feed the dog its daily bowl of rice and watch its spine gradually arch like their own for want of a proper diet. The women cook, mind the children, wash clothes and sometimes labour as coolies on the building sites of the city. The men also do hard labour or work in the factories of Tsuen Wan dyeing cloth, rolling material, setting looms or driving trucks. The teenagers attend school, the toddlers sit on their grandparents' knees and hear of what it was like in China in the old days, when the Kuomintang held sway and the Communists were just a rabble army in the far north.

I could tell them of those times.

Not all the buildings are hovels. Some are large, with a second storey, divided into two or three rooms, have kitchens and storerooms, lined with metal to protect against the weather and vermin rather than thieves: few rob each other in these places. Some of the buildings are thriving industries devoid of safety regulations, unregistered and untaxed, unknown to the factories inspectorate. I have seen men rendering fat collected from the meat markets and turning it into cooking oil, hair cream, soap or temple candles: other businesses I have

199

come across make plastic flowers, metal washers, fish-balls, biscuits and egg rolls, boiled sweets, paper kites and latex rubber penises for export to sex-shops in Japan. Other shacks are cinemas, shops, restaurants, gambling and opium dens, whorehouses for coolies and unlicensed schools.

Once or twice a month, I make my way to the squatter area north of the airport called Tsuen Shek Shan, or Diamond Hill. The residents know me by sight and I no longer draw anxious looks for they appreciate I am not a resettlement officer, health inspector, charity worker or policeman. Quite what my motives are they must wonder at but they are too polite to ask and I do not tell them when I stop to chat, buying a glass of tea or a sticky, sweet cake.

I have a number of contacts in Tsuen Shek Shan whom I would not class as friends and yet they are more than mere acquaintances.

One of these is Mr Yee, to whom I was first introduced by Mr Wu: he is our opium supplier. A portly man of about fifty, he is the chairman of the Tsuen Shek Shan *kai fong* association, the committee of residents which governs the shanty town, elects representatives to speak on their behalf to the authorities and decides matters of social interest. As Mr Yee is also the Dragon Head of a local triad society he is in a good position to wield power over the locality. He controls the water standpipes, the illegal electricity supply and the network of coolies which the assorted factories are obliged to employ to transport their goods to the nearest highway. In addition, he owns a barber's shop, two eating-houses and a general store, none of them licensed, which front for an opium den he operates at the farthest point in the squatter area from the road. To assist him, he has a band of some one hundred followers in different ranks of the triad hierarchy: of these, seventy-seven are always Red Poles, the soldier rank. He maintains this number for it is not only militarily sufficient but also very lucky. He was, he has informed me, born on the seventh day of the seventh moon, which is why he has done well in life.

In short, he is a powerful, well-connected man to whom the squatters are bound by fear or allegiance and upon whom they rely.

Do not assume he is an arrogant or selfish man. He takes his responsibilities very seriously. An electricity failure is repaired more quickly than it might be by the China Light and Power Company. If the water ceases to flow, he is quickly onto discovering the leak and having it repaired. He is also in charge of the town plan of the area: he decides where huts will be erected, factories opened up and the sewage ditches dug. He is no expert in town planning but he is logical and does his best. In other words, he is part master criminal, part businessman and part mayor: in this respect he is no different from any other local politician the world over.

It is to his barber's shop that I go to get my hair cut. It operates in a larger than average shack made of one-inch sawn planks under a roof of beaten aluminium. Some years ago, an aircraft missed the airport approach, crashing on the mountains. By the time the rescue services reached the site, the dead crew had been respectfully removed from the wreckage, their bodies covered by sheets and the cargo – rumoured to be gold bullion – had vanished. A section of the aircraft was also missing: that is now the barber's shop roof.

Within are seven barber's chairs in shining chrome and white enamel, seven stainless steel basins and taps, seven mirrors and shelves lined with ranks of bottles of hair oils, perfumes and other impugnable unguents. His staff are equipped with the latest German electric trimmers and a comprehensive range of scissors, combs or cut-throat razors which they strop in turns on a length of wet leather attached to the wall. A haircut, shampoo and curl costs one dollar and fifteen cents. Not being a young Chinese man-about-town, I forego the curling and pay ninety-five cents.

If Mr Yee is not in his opium den, he is in the barber's behind which he has a little office. When my hair is trimmed, he usually invites me to take tea with him. So it was today.

'How you?' he asked as I got out of the chair and paid for my haircut with a dollar bill, dismissing the change as a tip, something which always pleases the staff: the local Chinese seldom offer gratuities.

'I am well,' I replied in Cantonese. 'And you? How is business?'

'Business is good. Will you take some tea with me? Or are you, perhaps, in a hurry?'

He always says this: he does not wish to intrude upon my time. I always accept.

His office is a room about ten feet square containing a steel desk, a filing cabinet and three upright chairs. Upon the shelves are file boxes and upon the desk is a shining black telephone. It is, I am sure, the only room in the entire squatter area that has a smooth concrete floor.

'Come! Sit down!' He indicated a chair and called through the door for tea. 'Or would you prefer a Coke?' he enquired as an afterthought.

'Tea,' I assured him, sitting by his desk, out of the beam of sunlight coming in through the window which was open but covered by a fine mesh of the sort one saw in the old days lining meat safes.

'Good!' He smiled beneficially and sat down behind the desk. 'Cola is for the young. We are not young. We are older and wise.' He leaned forward conspiratorially. 'Let me tell you something. You, I can trust. You will not run to the police. Near to Shek Kip Mei, I have heard of a man who is a counterfeiter. He makes fifty-cent coins. They look very real until you drop them – then they do not chime. When they come from the press they are dull. So do you know what he does? He puts them in a *kong* of Coca Cola. This polishes the coins so they look new. Then he rubs them in a little graphite – from pencils. The finished article – perfect! Unless you drop it.'

'Has he made many?' I enquired.

'Over twelve thousand. That is six thousand dollars.'

The tea arrived, brought in by the man who had cut my hair. I wondered, as he poured it from a rice-pattern teapot into my glass, if Mr Yee had invested in the coining operation.

'How is our mutual friend, Mr Wu?' Mr Yee asked. 'I have not seen him for ten days.'

'Well, he is well.'

'And have you and he chased dragons lately?'

'Not for some days,' I replied, smiling and slurping at my tea in the best fashion.

Mr Yee drank from his glass. He looked at me over

the rim and I wondered if he was looking for a way to get some kind of a hold over me. Yet no sooner had the thought occurred to me than I dismissed it as preposterous. I had nothing he wanted and, besides, I know more about him than he will ever know about me. Maybe this lay at the root of his comment: he wished to redress the situation somewhat.

When we had finished our tea Mr Yee offered to walk with me to the road and we set off, walking down the hillside through the densest areas of occupation. On the way, we halted at Mr Yee's shop, where he spoke for some minutes with the shop-keeper. I stood in the doorway, glancing over the well-stocked shelves laden with boxes of matches, packets of needles, cakes of soap and tubes of Palmolive toothpaste, tins of lychees in syrup and, incongruously, corned beef and Irish stew. Elsewhere were wooden tubs of rice and beans, bags of brown raw sugar, bundles of sugar cane and piles of cabbages, whilst from the ceiling hung Chinese sausages, shiny flattened ducks and dried fish. A counter carried bottles of *mai tai*, San Miguel beer, *sam she chiu* snake wine and the ubiquitous Coca Cola.

Mr Yee's business concluded, we made our way down a path stepped with wooden boards zig-zagging back and forth upon itself.

'How is the girl?' I asked.

'You always enquire about the girl,' he replied. 'Why?'

'As you know, I have my interest,' I said.

Mr Yee halted by a lean-to selling fruit, absent-mindedly helping himself to two oranges, one of which he passed to me. The vendor made no attempt to elicit payment: such is Mr Yee's position in the community.

'Tell me, why do you have this interest? The family can be nothing to you. You do not know them. You cannot benefit. Or perhaps,' he scratched his ear and peeled his orange, 'you maybe knew the mother.'

I was not insulted: it was natural for him to assume there might have been another reason for my actions.

'No,' I assured him, 'I never knew the mother. Indeed, I have never known any woman. That is, in the way you imply.'

'Then you are either a very foolish man or a very guilty one.'

I did not reply immediately. Like all successful men of business, Mr Yee is a good judge of character. He knows I am not foolish and his comment was not intended as a sleight but a probe.

'Guilty, I expect,' I admitted.

'What have you to be guilty of?' he retorted. 'You were a priest.'

'A priest is not excluded from the luxury of sinning,' I said, 'and I have lived a long life. There has been plenty of time for me to do wrong.'

'That is so,' he agreed, 'but usually the sins of a priest are surely small. Little indiscretions. Nothing big.'

I did not answer but let him guess the magnitude of the errors of my ways, what it must have been which made me, in his opinion, so guilty.

'Maybe you would like me to find you another little girl? There are many here who would benefit from your interest.'

'Perhaps, but not yet. I am not a rich man.'

He dropped his orange peelings on the ground and a scrawny hen made a rush at them.

'Is there not a saying in the Bible,' Mr Yee remarked, 'it is easier for a poor man to pass through a needle hole than a rich man to enter heaven?'

I nodded and said, 'Yes, there is. Have you read the Bible?'

'No. I am not a Christian. But I went to a Methodist school in Shanghai. The masters taught us such things. Maybe,' he continued, 'you want to be poor so you can go to heaven and, by spending your money in this fashion, you will make it easier.'

'I do not wish to go to heaven,' I said.

'Then you will go to hell.'

'Nor shall I go there,' I responded. 'There is neither heaven nor hell. I shall simply pass into the void.'

'Become an ancestor?'

'Quite possibly.'

'Ah!' Mr Yee said, putting an orange segment in his mouth. 'Then you do this so there will be someone to burn gifts for you at Ching Ming.'

'As I do not know the girl except by sight and as she has no idea about me, how can she make offerings for me? Besides, those gifts go to heaven, do they not? And I shall not be there.'

'You puzzle me,' Mr Yee admitted, spitting out the pips and attracting the attention of two more chickens. 'You are not like men I know. You act without reason.'

'I do not. I have a very good reason, but you have not yet found it.' I smiled at him and added, 'You have still not told me how she is.'

'She is well.'

'Her mother?'

'Her mother is well. Her father is working with the company clearing the hills in Ho Man Tin. He was a general coolie but now he is in charge of the dynamite charges. He is the one you will see on Waterloo Road, beating the gong as the time draws close to press the detonator.'

'And the other child?' I asked.

'The elder daughter works in a factory in Sai Ying Pun.'

'And the baby?'

'Born last month. Another girl,' he replied. 'They are not lucky people. No sons.'

As I approached the door to Father Callaghan's room, I could hear him talking. At first, I thought he was praying, but the tone of his words seemed not to be that of a priest talking to God but of a man angry with a child he was reprimanding. I knocked on the panelling and he fell silent. I knocked again, less loudly, for fear of interrupting him. It occured to me perhaps he had someone in the room with him.

'*Pin kòh-ah*?' I heard his voice enquire.

'Father Stephen,' I said in reply, assuming he was asking after who was visiting him.

There was a shuffling, followed by soft footfalls. The door opened. Father Callaghan was dressed in his cassock but it was unbuttoned to the waist. His chest was shiny with perspiration.

'I wondered if I could see you a moment, Father?' I asked. 'But not if I disturb you.'

'No,' he said quickly, 'no, you're not disturbing me. Come along in.'

He pushed the door wider and I entered his room for the first time. I was surprised how bleak it was. My own quarters were hardly lavish but his were positively ascetic. His bed bore no thin quilt, the only covering being a straw mat with no pillow block. There were two upright chairs made in the square style of Chinese furniture and a table with a wooden crucifix, Christ's figure cast in steel, and an open missal. The bookshelf, above a brass-bound sea chest, carried a number of small indeterminate ornaments and not more than a dozen books bound in black leather. Beneath the shelf hung two sets of ecclesiastical clothes and four Chinese-style suits. Beside the window was a small Madonna, carved in wood and painted in subdued colours. Upon the floorboards by the table were two dark stains which I realised were damp marks where he must have been kneeling for some time, the sweat running down his legs.

'Please, sit down,' he suggested, indicating one of the chairs.

I sat as he bade and he perched on the edge of his bed.

'I thought,' I began, glancing round the room, 'that you might . . .'

'. . . that I was holding a discussion with someone. Well, in a manner of speaking, I was. With myself.'

'I see,' I said, not quite sure how to respond to his revelation.

'Let me tell you something, Father Stephen,' he went on. 'As you know, you're the first priest to join me in a number of years. I've been ministering on my own since '94. Not just here in Wuchow but also to the north, far to the north. Anshun, Kwei Yang and a God-forsaken spot called Hsüyung. No one to talk to up there, not in my own mother tongue. So I took to talking to myself.'

'I see,' I said again, finding his admission a little embarrassing.

'There's nothing wrong with it,' he continued, looking at me sharply. 'Indeed, I'd say it was a prerequisite of being a priest and I recommend the habit to you. The only people you can really talk to, other than a brother or sister in God, is yourself or The Lord. Quite often, I talk to myself not because I'm going mad but because, by making what I'm thinking into a dialogue instead of a soliloquy, I can reason all the better. After all, what's prayer if it's not just that?'

'Were you never lonely?' I asked.

'To be sure,' he began but then paused a moment. 'Well, no,' he mused, 'not lonely. I always had Christ as a companion. But I did sometimes yearn to hear a Western voice. Yet now, in Wuchow, where there are others of my own kind, so to speak, I still like to talk to myself for a few minutes every day. It gets things straight in my mind.'

'You may always talk to me,' I offered.

Father Callaghan laughed quietly and replied, 'I know Father Stephen. And I will, I will. But you must still allow me my little indulgence. Just so long as you don't think I'm losing my mind. If that was to have happened, believe me, it would have happened in that accursed Hsüyung.'

'May I ask what you were talking about?'

'You may. We have no secrets, you and I, Father Stephen. I was confessing to myself.'

I stared at him in surprise.

'Well, what do you expect?' he continued. 'Up there in the north, I had no one to hear my confession. I couldn't call around the next village, knock on the priest's door and say, "Father O'Brien" or "Father Kelly, will you pause for a moment to hear my confession?" The nearest Catholic father to me was over two hundred miles away. But now you are here, Father Stephen, I'll come to you. When you're not busy. But I may still confess to myself, if you don't mind. It's nothing against you, of course. But when I confess to myself, I sense I'm doing it directly to God.'

He put out his hand, briefly touching mine where it was resting on the arm of the chair. It was an action of neither friendship nor love but one of compassion, of companionship perhaps, and I sensed he did it more for his own benefit than for mine.

'Surely,' I said, 'we are instructed that just the desire to repent is sufficient.'

'That's true,' he agreed, 'just as it's also true I cannot give myself absolution. But you know, I gain a strength from putting it all into words. A thought is such an easy thing to accomplish. The voicing of it takes a bit more determination. Anyway, I've no great sins to confess. Only the usual little ones every man has and cannot seem to rid himself of. Unless he's a saint. Now,' he straightened his back, pressing his hands down upon the mat on his bed, 'what is it you want of me?'

'I have a need to confess.'

'I see.' He grinned at me. 'And you've not been here

210

long enough to hear your own. Shall we go down to the alter?'

He began to button up his cassock.

'Would it be possible for you to hear it here?'

'Of course. God does not listen only in the confessional.'

I knelt on the floor before Father Callaghan and admitted to him and Our Lord that I had sinned.

'Tell me of your sin, my son,' Father Callaghan ordered.

Settling my knees again, for the floor was hard and there were knots in the boards, I told him of my stupidity on the night of my journey up the river, of how I had gone ashore to satisfy my own indulgence and how I had eavesdropped upon the occupants of the house and had fled for my own safety rather than their privacy, how I had startled the dog and how a search party had been sent out to find me and the captain had killed the villager.

'Is there something more?' Father Callaghan enquired when I eventually fell silent.

'No, Father,' I replied but he sensed I was lying.

'Are you sure? Quite sure?'

'Yes,' I said. 'Quite sure.'

I should perhaps have admitted my doubts to him, the confused thoughts I had experienced in the pavilion of the Resident's garden which had so logically resolved themselves in a way contrary to the well-being of my faith yet I believed I need not. Kneeling before my confessor, I did not view them to be a sin. They were, I considered, perhaps a failure of my character, a perverse twist in my mind but not a sin: for I was not casting God out of my presence, denying His existence or slighting Him but casting myself away from Him.

'Very well,' Father Callaghan said.

I felt his eyes looking hard upon the top of my head as if willing me to confess further but I resisted him. Reason took control of me, overriding emotion and theology. If there was a wrong involved, I thought, it was against myself and not Jesus Christ: that I could and would bear.

For a few minutes, Father Callaghan did not speak again. At length, he stood up from his bed and went to one of the windows, looking across the town bleached by a high sun. He remained there for several minutes, a black silhouette against the scorching day. When he turned back to the room, he sat in one of the chairs behind where I was still kneeling awaiting his – or perhaps God's – criticism or forgiveness.

'Get up, Father Stephen.' When he finally spoke, his voice was quiet and gentle. 'Sit with me a moment here.'

I took the other chair, wondering when or if he was going to absolve me, forgive me. I was repentant. The death of the man had weighed upon me. What I needed was to be given a penance and absolution for this terrible wrongdoing.

'Father Stephen,' Father Callaghan said, 'I know your feelings and, for whatever sin you've done, you're forgiven if you are truly remorseful. And I know you are, so that's all there is to it. But . . .'

He was not looking at me but at the window again. A small bird had landed upon the sill and was watching us. It was a dull-coloured little creature with a short, black beak and a bead of an eye catching the sunlight, sparkling like a pebble of jet.

'There's something you must learn now you're in China,' Father Callaghan resumed. 'Here, the value of life is much cheaper than we consider it. A man's death is not regarded as important as, indeed, we saw with the poor soul who drowned. For us, life's precious even if we are in expectation of the glories of heaven. We seek to nurture it, encourage it. But the Chinese do not share this concern. Death and life are but parts of the turning of fortune's wheel. For them, life's not unique. Today they are men, tonight they die and become either revered ancestors in heaven or are resurrected, according to their faith.'

The bird piped a single, shrill note as if to lend its weight of native opinion to Father Callaghan's statement.

'But I was the cause of the man's murder,' I said. 'If I had not been so proud as to take an evening walk . . .'

'Fate, Father Stephen. Nothing more. You did not kill the man. Nor did your pride. He was a victim of circumstance.'

I could not believe Father Callaghan, a guardian of discarded girls and a Christian priest who had forgone the company of his own kind in order to dedicate himself to bringing the Catholic faith to heathens, could be so callous.

'Father,' he said, interrupting my thoughts and once more touching my hand, 'I know what you're thinking. Yet consider this: we are here to show the Chinese the word of God but we cannot change their ways nor, I think, should we. In time, they may follow our example but, until then, the Chinese must live as they do and we must relieve their suffering where we may.'

He then gave me absolution, his voice soft and low. '*Ego te absolve in nomine Patris . . .*' I heard him say, but my attention was captured by the bird.

It remained on the sill watching us until, just as Father Callaghan completed his absolution, it imparted its brief whistle again and flitted from sight. I wondered if it had been a deliberate witness sent by Our Lord to check up on us, an insignificant brown angel already flying high on the thermals above Wuchow, preparing his report.

'Would you kill a man?' I asked as I rose from my knees.

'I would not!' he exclaimed. 'But nor would I prevent another's hand. Not here. Not in China. If I were in Dublin it would be different but I am not. I am in Wuchow. Every day the opportunity arises for me to save a man from another's hand: consider the thief in the cangue. It would be nothing to step forward, cut free the wood, bless him and preach brotherly love on the spot to the onlookers. Teach them compassion and mercy. But, I ask you, is it worse to starve a man to death in the cangue than to steal him from his loved ones and transport him to the Australian colonies, send him and his family to the poor house for the theft of a silk kerchief which, to its owner, is a mere bauble? It is a matter of priorities, customs and attitudes. No, Father Stephen, I believe we may observe and relieve suffering, teach by example, but we may not go beyond. We may not interfere.'

There came a tapping on the door.

'*Pin kòh-ah?*' Father Callaghan said again.

'What does that mean?' I asked.

'It means *who*. It implies *who is there?*' He smiled kindly. 'You are learning, Father Stephen. That's the way to be. Curious, inquisitive. Find out all you can. Of language and life and death. And if you live a hundred years you will still not know more than a smidgin of this land and its people.'

A voice outside the door called, 'Master. Ah Fong here. Food on table.'

'Come,' Father Callaghan suggested, 'it's time for us to eat.'

He completed the buttoning of his cassock, stood up and held the door open for me. As we descended the stairs, I could hear the shuffling of feet as the girls made their way towards the refectory.

'You've not given me a penance,' I said as we reached the refectory entrance.

'I've not,' he replied, 'and it's remiss of me. Well, I'll give you one shortly.'

We made our way to our places at the head of the long table. After Father Callaghan had said grace, he beckoned to Ah Fong, speaking in a louder than necessary voice, considering his proximity. The Chinese left the room to return with a small box which he opened and placed on the table. Had we been gentlemen in the smoking room of our club, sitting together with a decanter of port, the box might have contained cigars. Instead it appeared to hold a number of shrivelled grey-brown pebbles.

'What are these?' I enquired.

'*Wah mui*,' Father Callaghan replied but offered no translation. 'Try one, but beware for it contains a large pip.'

'Try it?' I said.

'Eat it, Father, eat it.'

'What is it?'

'Have faith, Father. Pick one up and eat it.'

Thoughts of the execrable egg returned to me but I did as he instructed. The *wah mui* was hard and rough to the touch. I placed it cautiously in my mouth. Instantly, there was a slight sensation of sweetness upon my tongue.

'Put it in your cheek and suck it,' Father Callaghan advised, 'as you would a cough lozenge.'

All down the table, the girls were craning their necks, watching me avidly. Sister Margaret, at the far end, was leaning forward, so intense was her attention. Ah Fong stood close by with a deadpan expression.

I sucked. A peculiar sweetness came off from the thing: then, suddenly, the back of my mouth was hit by a terrible saltiness. I felt my throat muscles contract under the shock. I wanted to spit the thing out. Instead, I sucked harder. Now the sweet and the salt were mingled and the flavour, though tart, became bearable, even slightly pleasant.

'So?' Father Callaghan enquired.

'It is . . .' I was lost for words to describe the taste.

'Now, I'll tell you what it is. A *wah mui* is a salted plum,' Father Callaghan informed me, 'a favourite sweet of the Chinese. The plums are picked when ripe then pickled in salt water for some days. When shrivelled by their immersion, and the salt permeated into them, they are spread out to dry in the sun. Usually', he added, 'on the pavements of the town.'

I chewed the flesh of the sweet and swallowed it, removing the large stone from my mouth with my fingers and placing it on the table beside my rice bowl. I smiled at the girls who all broke into giggles. Sister Margaret clapped her hands, not to halt their mirth but in applause at my having eaten the thing.

'That was your penance,' Father Callaghan said, 'and you must be truly repentant for you were not nauseous. I have known others rush from the room on their first encounter with a *wah mui*.'

'It was not as bad as the egg,' I replied.

'No. You're right,' Father Callaghan declared. 'That was my mistake. I should have saved the egg for your first confession in China.'

Mrs van der Poehl is a short, etiolated woman who wears just too much make-up to be decent. She has no disfigurement to hide, nor is she trying to retain her youth: she likes to stretch the bounds of propriety to their limits. In colonial society, she would be regarded as outrageous, one of the select company whom it was fun to invite to a dinner party if one wished to shock the other guests, but whom one decidedly did not invite to a cocktail party where there might be children under fifteen years of age. She is the sort who would have been known, in the years preceding the Second World War, as NBHE – Not Before His Excellency.

In Chinese society, however, the community of the back streets, the fellowship of the tenements, she is regarded not as a semi-pariah but as an eccentric who, being elderly, commands respect.

I see her almost every day, although not necessarily to speak to: I spy her walking in the streets, taking her pug dog, Pu Yi, across Nathan Road and up the path to King's Park where she lets it off its lead to defaecate upon the grass around the blocks of government quarters there. She dresses in the style of the 1940s, disdains hats and sun creams with the result that the backs of her hands, and possibly her face under the just-too-liberal coating of cosmetics, are dried, the skin having a papery texture, like that of brown manila envelopes. Her hair was once, I guess, ash blonde but is now a sort-of ash grey and she wears it wound into a bun. I have never seen her without a string of pearls at her neck which, like her face, is also well besmirched with powder.

To sum her up, she is a character and for this I admire her. She fights convention. In a society such as that of a British colony, she is brave – courageous, even – to be the way she is. Many women better than her have been destroyed, and their husband's careers terminated or stagnated, by the vindictiveness of tennis court chitter-chatter in the Ladies Recreation Club, the censure of tight corsets in the tropical sun and the sneering snobbery of those for whom individuality is a threat and a sense of independence a trait unbecoming in a female.

She has done just as I did many years ago: she has assessed the mundane, found it not to her liking and rebelled against it. She has not won, and she cannot win just as I have not, but she fights on with the dogged determination that would have earned a soldier accolades but has afforded her acrimony.

Furthermore, like myself, she is in love with the East. This is not a rational love nor one based upon emotion. It is a fact, built upon necessity. Mrs van der Poehl has abandoned her past, all that history and birth have given her and chosen to live as she does. And she is trapped, as inescapably as I am, in this place.

Both of us, I am sure, could buy ourselves a ticket to leave: we could go to the airline desk in the Peninsula Hotel, hand over sufficient in cash and take a taxi to Kai Tak. There, we would present our docket to the hostess, place our bags upon the conveyor belt and, at the appointed hour, step onto the concrete, mount the steps of a BOAC airliner and vanish.

Yet we do not. There is something in us which prevents us going, something we love and yet which we hate, something it is better to live with than to escape from, something with which we have come to terms. We have deemed it desirable to maintain the status quo rather than stir things up. Perhaps it is something we hate in ourselves.

Be that as it may, in the case of Mrs van der Poehl, she has not only abjured her past and her own kind but has positively taken on the side of the Chinese against the European.

Once, some years ago when I was getting to know her, I met her in a market on the praya of the Yau Ma Tei typhoon shelter. This is an artificial harbour behind a high breakwater which, in times of impending inclement weather, is packed with the smaller, fragile craft the storm would destroy like matchwood. When the weather is fair, it is the haven for these craft when they are not out in the harbour, or the South China Sea, plying their various trades. It is like a floating city of fishing and cargo junks, sampans, wallah-wallah boats, lighters and the smallest of the coastal traders. The whole ragamuffin fleet, with the exception of the lighters, has one thing in common – every vessel is made of wood.

On the praya, when the authorities are not about, there exists an impromptu market in which a number of commodities may be purchased without let or hindrance from the street trading laws, the hawker legislation and the strictures of public hygiene. Seafood is landed without going through the fish markets: goods brought down the coast from China, regardless of border regulations, are also traded – I have done business there over the years in raw silk, white and green tea, unrefined opium, poor quality firecrackers, matches with too high a phosphorus content, antiques and old jade and fake copies of Sheaffer fountain pens which may all be bought if the price is right and the dealer knows the customer well enough to appreciate they are not in the pay of the police, the triad cartels that operate the street markets or the health authorities.

Mrs van der Poehl and myself are the only Europeans who visit the place. Our faces are known. We are *gweilo* folk but we may be trusted.

On this occasion I was there buying fish. The prices are much lower than in the organised markets or the streets. There are no middlemen involved: the man who hauls the nets offers his catch for sale from buckets and tin-lined trays. My aim was to purchase shrimps and I was walking along the quay looking into the assortment of plastic and tin buckets when I saw Mrs van der Poehl ahead of me waving her arms at what I took to be a fisherman. She was speaking in rapid, fluent and colloquial Cantonese, her voice raised and her ire clearly up.

'What are you doing? What *are* you doing? You blockhead! You utter blockhead!'

I remember quite clearly she used the phrase *mok tau* several times.

She took no notice of me as I drew closer, so intense was her attention to the object of her tirade, a Chinese man crouched by a large wooden tub of live squid. The animals were swimming round in the water, delicately changing colour from brown to an off-pink as if occasionally feeling intense embarrassment at her pronouncements. A crowd began to gather, consisting of fishermen, children from the sampans, women in wide-brimmed Hakka hats, stevedores and coolies. They all stood by in a respectful silence, bemused at this elderly European woman creating hell.

Whenever the Chinese began to speak he was drowned out by her.

'You fool! What right have you to do this? These squid . . .'

At that point I wondered if she was one of those kind- yet ignorant-hearted people who will not see an animal treated in a manner which they believe to be cruel and who, if they lived in China, would exist in a permanent state of angst. Glancing into the tub, I could see nothing wrong with the squid at all save that they were bound for the *wok*.

'These squid . . .' the man began, rising to his feet, but it was as far as he got.

'These squid . . .' Mrs van der Poehl erupted at him. 'One and a half catties of these squid are going to be sold to me. You cannot prevent me from buying them and you will not prevent him from selling them to me.'

221

She waved her hand cursorily in the direction of a second, barefoot man standing nearby, dressed in trousers rolled up above his knees and bare to the waist, his front besmirched with fish blood and scales, his hands clutching a thin, much-sharpened shiv.

'It is his right to sell these to me. To me! To me or to any of these people here.'

She swung her arm around the crowd, some of whom edged a little backwards as if she was about to strike them.

'Hong Kong is a free trade port. An entrepôt port.' She spoke the word *entrepôt* in English. 'You will not – I repeat, *not* – interfere.'

It was at this point I noticed that the Chinese man who was the object of her attack was holding a clipboard. A plastic ball-point pen dangled from a piece of string tied to a hole drilled in the board.

He reached for the pen and caught it.

'You can forget that! Don't you dare write a single word. Not so much as one character!'

The man let go of the pen and attempted once more to speak.

'Go!' Mrs van der Poehl shouted regally, pointing to the distant hills. 'Go! Do not interfere here again. I shall have words with your superiors. You may count on this.'

At this juncture, the people parted suddenly and a European man dressed in a white shirt, white shorts, long white socks and brown brogues appeared. He was tall and tanned: his hair was blonde, cut short and he wore a pair of American-style sunglasses which he removed as he approached the centre of the crowd, tucking them into his breast pocket.

'What's going on here?' he shouted in Cantonese: then he spied Mrs van der Poehl and reverted to English. 'May I help you, madam?'

'Yes,' snapped Mrs van der Poehl. 'This upstart here has had the temerity to prevent me from purchasing these squid.'

'I see. If you'll wait a moment?'

He went to the Chinese with the clipboard and they spoke in hushed tones for some minutes: there was much gesticulating upon the part of the Chinese whom the European tried to calm down. At last, he returned to Mrs van der Poehl who, in the meantime, had chosen the squid she wished to buy, had had them caught by the man with the scaly chest and had paid for them. The fisherman had placed the animals in a plastic bag of water.

'Madam,' the European began, 'may I explain? This fisherman is contravening the law by selling his produce on the praya. He has . . .'

'I'm not interested . . .' Mrs van der Poehl started but the European raised his hand.

'If you would be so kind as to let me finish, madam,' he said tersely. 'This fisherman, and indeed all these traders, are operating without licences. They are therefore committing an offence by trading on the praya and it is the duty of my inspector here to prevent them from so doing.'

'I don't give a jot,' Mrs van der Poehl returned, her fingers tightening on her plastic bag of squirming squid.

'Madam,' the European continued, 'these laws are here to protect you. Those squid,' he nodded in the direction of the bag, 'may not comply with the hygiene regulations.'

'Dear God!' Mrs van der Poehl said, raising her eyes momentarily to the skies as if for divine encouragement. 'Do you think I give a sod about that? Let me tell you, young man,' she went on, a certain irony in her words, 'when I was a prisoner-of-war in Hong Kong, I ate rats roasted on a shovel over a fire of driftwood, seaweed and dried shit. And I am still here. What is more, there were young children in the camp who shared the same *menu de la maison japonaise* and they are still with us, hale and hearty. So . . .'

'That notwithstanding,' the European butted in, 'my inspector has rules to apply and apply them he will. These traders are operating without licences. They are therefore committing an offence . . .'

'*Diu lei lo mo!*' Mrs van der Poehl hollered.

An approximate translation for this common colloquialism might be fuck your mother. An American might use it to imply the object of the abuse was a mother-fucker. The crowd, now at least an hundred strong and for the best part ignorant of what had been said since Cantonese had been abandoned as the language of the contretemps, hissed with amazement. A few of the coolies and stevedores laughed. I sensed their humour was almost nervous.

Somewhat nonplussed, the European took a step back and sideways but Mrs van der Poehl was not to be stopped. She dropped her bag of squid onto the stone flags of the quay and went for him, her arms flailing. She hit him hard in the middle of his chest and he attempted to grasp her wrists but without success. To avoid her, he next stepped backwards again and Mrs van der Poehl, seeing her chance, rammed into him with her shoulder. The European

224

arched over backwards and disappeared. There was a muted splash. The crowd surged forwards, leaving a respectful space around Mrs van der Poehl: one of the coolies retrieved her bag of squid and almost reverentially handed it to her. She was breathless with indignation and exertion.

Gazing over the side of the praya, I saw the European in the water, floundering about in a thick wadge of flotsam in which I could see floating some offcuts of wood, rice straw, a discarded plastic sandal, a broken rattan basket, some sheets of paper, a small drowned rodent and several anonymous brown lumps I took to be human excreta. A man on one of the sampans was pushing a thick bamboo pole out towards the European, who began to swim clumsily towards it.

'Are you all right, Mrs van der Poehl?' I asked, moving to her side.

'Quite!' she replied, adding in the direction of the swimmer, 'Bumptious little bugger!'

I was out following Father Callaghan's suggestion, that I should go north along the river past the clump of trees: I was eager to discover the place he had said would interest and instruct me in the ways of China.

The road along the waterfront was crowded with coolies. Upstream from the flowerboats, a larger than average barge was moored side on to the bank, unloading a cargo of stone. The blocks were several feet square and each took two men with a substantial bamboo pole slung between their shoulders to lift it.

225

These pairs of men struggled up the steep bank with the blocks, their breath coming in starved gasps by the time they reached the road, their horny bare feet kicking up dust as they staggered off into the town.

Pausing for some minutes, I watched the procession, wondering what the life expectancy might be of these near-slaves. They could not be able to look forward to long lives and it was of no surprise to me the British had found it so easy to addict the Chinese to opium. Anyone with such an existence would want frequent release into a better world.

The copse stood out from a tall, rock-strewn bank which over-hung the road at the point where it deteriorated into a wide path, on the left of which was a precipitous drop of sixty feet to the river below. Conscious of the currents and afraid of the state of the pathway on the edge of the brink, I kept well in to the rocks, in the crannies of which scuttled lizards. For a moment, I stopped and studied one of the creatures. It was not a big-headed, awkward looking reptile like the lizard I had seen during Mass but lithe and streamlined with a black body decorated by yellow stripes and a bright blue tail. It rustled the leaf litter as it scampered away from my presence.

Once past the trees, the path ran in a straight line along the river bank with groves of dense bamboo growing on the right, behind which were scattered some houses and terraced fields rising up a low hill. None of the buildings was situated on the pathway save one, around which was built a six-foot-high stone wall painted dark red and topped off with green glazed tiles. In the centre of the wall, facing the river, was a wide roofed gateway with two smaller ones to either side, one of which was open.

As I approached, I caught the perfume of incense on the wind.

Above the central gate was a carved wooden plaque of several characters surrounded by a curling dragon. It meant nothing to me, but by the open gate was a square of board hanging from a nail, upon which someone had written, presumably for the benefit of the *gweilo* residents of Wuchow, *Lung Mo Dagon Mothr tempul*. I smiled at this enterprise: clearly, the temple priest realised foreigners visited temples and, out of a felt obligation if nothing else, left offerings of money just as trippers in Europe did when visiting holy shrines or cathedrals.

I looked through the gate. There was no one about and, as the gate was open and the notice a virtual invitation, I mounted the raised step and entered.

In the centre of a beaten-earth courtyard, between the main gate and the equally large front door of the temple, which was also closed, there stood a massive bronze urn a foot taller than myself. The legs were bowed like those on Jacobean tables and cast as the shins and feet of a dragon. From the top of the vessel projected a few dozen smouldering joss sticks casting a bluish mist into the sunlight. On either side of the main door, as in the case of the gates, were two smaller entrances. I walked past the urn and entered the building.

I found myself before a side altar: had this been a Christian place of worship, the room might have been a lady chapel. The altar was a simple affair consisting of a table draped in scarlet-and-gold cloth upon which was standing a number of brass open-flame oil lamps of the sort one saw in children's picture-books, illustrating the story of Aladdin. They

227

were all lit and guttered fitfully. Some fruit and little cakes were piled on dishes before the idol, which was a small, unimpressive statue of a nondescript figure of a woman positioned under a canopy of similar material to the altar cloth.

There were no pews, but before the altar were a number of low wooden stools to assist kneeling worshippers. Apart from these the only other furniture was a large bronze bowl on a stand in the middle of the room. It was filled with water, the metal sides tarnished but the rim highly polished. Another little notice hung from the stand. I raised it and read, *Empuroar Good Luk Boll. Puss fingr on edge, make noise in watr. If round good you got good luk.*

Following the instructions, I placed my finger on the rim and began to slide it round the bowl. Nothing happened so I pushed a little faster. Suddenly, the metal began to hum then whistle an incessant whine. In the water, ripples appeared in perfect circles radiating out from a point in the very centre of the bowl where the liquid danced and bubbled as if boiling. I stopped abruptly, the ripples vanishing and leaving no waves but just a mirror-flat surface.

The main part of the temple was reached through an archway, from the other side of which I could hear noises. I wondered if I should pass through, encroach upon someone at prayer, yet I knew temples were not like churches. There were no set services at specified times and visitors could come and go as they pleased: in a Hong Kong temple, I had watched two men praying whilst a sweeper flicked a duster over the altar before their very faces.

Casting my concern aside, I passed through to discover myself in a far more opulent and colourful shrine. Incense coils were suspended from the roof with bright red prayer flags, curtains and triangular banners hanging down to the floor: joss sticks burned in profusion from two urns filled with dusty earth and, on either side of the altar, were positioned two seven-foot statues of fiercesome-looking gods with scimitars and ornate spears. The walls were decorated from roof to floor with embroidered tapestries depicting clouds and mountains, writhing snakes and dragons, delicate cranes and squat phoenixes, snarling lion-dogs and ferocious tigers. In front of the tapestries were a large gong and a massive drum shaped like a beer barrel but half as big again, both suspended in black wooden frames. At the rear, behind the altar, stood a flamboyant palanquin which, I assumed, was used to parade the effigy of the god round the town at festivals, in the same manner we processed saints through the streets.

Where the side chapel had contained the *good luk boll*, the main shrine displayed a table draped in an imperial-yellow silk cloth laden with offerings – fruit, cakes, bowls of rice and even coagulated dishes of stew. One platter held a complete, cooked fish. All these comestibles were beyond the point of consumption and only the thick incense smoke killed the stench of the rotten fish and kept the flies at bay. All the rice was spotted with either mould or ash from the overhead coils.

I had to rub my eyes for they were smarting from the smoke, my cheeks damp from tears of discomfort: my nostrils prickled as if I was on the verge of contracting influenza.

The main altar was magnificently arrayed with red

and gold brocades, more Aladdin's lamps and scarlet wax candles. The effigy was life-size, a goddess with a wooden face immaculately painted but not aloof or vacant in her expression. She was made not to look down upon her worshippers but out through the main door. Upon her head was a crown of gilded metal and she wore the silk gowns and robes of a wealthy dowager.

In front of the altar knelt an old woman. Her short grey hair cropped at her nape was swept back and her feet, although not bound, were small in black cotton slippers. She was otherwise dressed as a peasant in a dark blue woman's *sam* and black *fu*.

I did not wish to disturb her devotions and stepped back, half hidden by two of the prayer banners. She kept her head bowed, kow-towing several times to the idol, all the while muttering a low incantation in a monotonous tone. Her hands were placed together in the fashion of a Christian but, between her fingers, she held two or three joss sticks and she moved her hands up and down in front of her breast in supplication.

Just as I was about to leave to explore the third section of the temple, through yet another archway, the old woman completed her worship and rose unsteadily to her feet. She stuck her joss sticks in a small container on the altar and turned to go.

It was Sister Margaret. For a moment, I stared at her then hid myself behind the banner. She passed within a yard of me, oblivious of my presence. When she was gone, I just stood in the smoke-filled twilight and considered her actions. It was blasphemy. She, a nun in holy orders, was paying service to a heathen deity.

After a period of time and deeming it to be safe, I left the temple and, in the courtyard, sat upon a step to consider what my next actions should be. Obviously, I had to tell Father Callaghan. He would, in turn, have to notify the Vicar Apostolic in Hong Kong, and he in due course, would have to notify Rome. Sister Margaret would then be excommunicated.

And yet, I realised, the due process would take months. In the meantime, she could hardly return to the society of her countrymen which she had long since given up and, furthermore, she was needed in the mission to look after the girls.

I set off towards the town, keeping to the land side of the path and walking slowly so as not to catch her up and to give myself time to ponder further on the situation. When I reached the mission, I went directly to Father Callaghan's room.

'Where've you been, Father Stephen?' he enquired. 'You look as if you've taken a bit of the sun.'

'I've been to the temple by the river,' I replied. 'When I was there . . .'

'The Dragon Mother temple,' Father Callaghan replied. 'The story is there was a mother and her son who lived here a thousand years ago — well, what other time span would there be in a Chinese story! — and fought the dragon that made the river flood. Whether they won or not, I cannot say. The river still floods. Anyway, they were deified and the temple was erected to them by a pious general whose name I forget. Did you go in?'

'I did,' I said, 'and . . .'

'And did you try your luck on the bowl?'

'I did but there is something else I must tell you,'

I answered, all in one breath to try and halt his garrulity.

'What's that, Father?'

'When I was there, there was a worshipper . . .'

Father Callaghan raised his hand to silence me.

'I know what you're about to say.'

'You do?' I rejoined, annoyed he had, once again, interrupted me.

'For sure I do. You saw Sister Margaret there.'

I was speechless and stood before him open mouthed.

'You look like a fish,' he said. 'A carp,' he added.

'I don't know what to say . . .' I began.

'Then say nothing.'

'But you knew!'

'I've known for years. She visits the Dragon Mother once a month.'

'Why? She's a Christian.'

'She's also a Chinese,' Father Callaghan said, 'and she's covering her bets just as any pragmatic Chinese would. I don't blame her. I don't condone her actions, mind, but I'll not chastise her nor will I inform on her. She may not have given her soul entirely to Jesus Christ, but she has her life and that's good enough for me. If she wants to back two horses, then let her. The time will come for her to make her peace with God and that's her affair, as far as I'm concerned. And as far as you are, too. The matter is between us, her and Our Lord. Let it rest there.'

He closed a book on the table which he had been reading, his action emphasising his words.

'I told you,' he said quietly, 'you would see some unorthodoxies here in China and a few of her

232

mysteries if you went to the temple. Now, I think, you understand a little more?'

'I do,' I admitted and I left his room.

I learned an important lesson that morning and it had been taught me by Sister Margaret: it is not necessarily what one believes in but what one does with one's life that is important.

All day, I have been following the little girl, who is on a school outing with classmates, travelling by bus from Sham Shui Po in the company of a young Chinese lady teacher and a not-so-young Chinese nun in a white wimple and grey habit.

Their destination was the beach at the 11½ milepost on the Castle Peak road, where they congregated by the bus stop, chattering loudly, eager to get onto the pale sand and discover another corner of the world. The teacher and the nun, after taking a register, ordered them into a crocodile and marched them down the steps to the sand.

I had dismounted from the bus ahead of them and was already settled on the beach with the daily edition of a Chinese newspaper, my shoes off and my toes dug into the sand which, although it was only ten o'clock, was warm from the sun.

The children sat in a circle at the far end of the beach, the nun in the centre and the teacher on the outside. They removed their shoes and socks, as I had done, and lined them up in neat rows.

I was not close enough to hear what was said but it seemed they were listening to some kind of religious instruction, for the nun frequently paused in her diatribe, the children bowing their heads. This went on for fifteen minutes, ending in a prayer and a hymn in Cantonese which sounded distant and ethereal when sung in the open air by their tiny flute-like voices. After the prayer session, the nun quit the circle and, walking off a little distance in my direction, sat under the shade of a bush to engross herself in a book. Judging by the cover it was not a religious volume: the front was decorated by a lurid picture, although I could not quite make out what it was. Perhaps she was looking for the realities of life the nunnery had forbidden her. If this was the case, her confessor would have some interesting listening and she would be busy with a number of Ave Marias.

It is strange how even the most devout Christian must sin. It is not a matter of slipping into evil, for they do not sin to be wicked, but to show their goodness. If they deliberately sin they can deliberately repent and, in recanting, display their fealty to God. It is the responsibility of the pious to be sinful in order to maintain fidelity: no religion survives upon prayers but upon heresies.

The nun's book may well have been salacious. She sat with her back half-turned towards the children, shielding the cover illustration with her hand, her palm spread across it to form a little lectern of flesh.

With the nun engaged in her dubious recreation, the teacher took charge of the class, the little girls sitting on the shore side of the circle, the boys with their backs to the sea. For some minutes, she gave out instructions and asked questions, to which a forest of arms shot up. This phase of the lesson completed, the children jumped to their feet, formed lines then, at a clap of the teacher's hands, broke off into pairs and sped to a cardboard box from which they took plastic jars and toy nets. Thus equipped, they ran to the far end of the beach to paddle in a stream emptying from the hills into a series of sandy rock pools. At their departure, the nun closed her book, walked to the lines of shoes and socks and sat by them, guarding them like a hunched bird of prey. Once settled, she opened her book again.

The nature-study class continued for an hour, the children gathering specimens, shouting with glee at their discoveries. The teacher encouraged and laughed with them, wading through the pools, helping them catch elusive fish. One of the little boys, straying away from the pools with his partner and coming along the water's edge towards me, found a crab with a leg span of five inches and, egged on by his companion, succeeded in picking it up, its legs and pincers flailing infuriation, its mouth blowing bubbles and its swimmerets paddling hard against the boy's arm.

The child was terrified, his face screwed up with fear, tears running down his cheeks. Yet he was afraid to let it go. Perhaps he thought it might turn and attack him, drag him into the sea and under the waves, storing him forever in its submarine caverns.

The teacher did not see this little drama being played out and the nun was ignorant of it for she was still, even after an hour, engrossed in her sinning, which she had not ceased with the exception of one occasion when a child returned to the cardboard box.

I got to my feet, placed my shoes on the newspaper

to prevent it blowing away and walked towards the boys. The one with the crab was petrified and sobbing quietly, not moving for fear of enraging the crab further. His comrade was casting scared looks in the direction of the pools: they had evidently been told not to wander away and he was considering which might be worse, the teacher's wrath or the crab's fury.

'Are you in trouble?' I enquired in Cantonese.

They gazed at me in silence.

'Do you want to let the crab go?' I asked.

The boy holding it made no move but his friend said, in a small voice, 'Yes. It is a dangerous animal.'

'I will take it from you,' I said and, sliding my hand over the boy's, gripped the crab's carapace between my finger and thumb, instructing the boy to let go and remove his hand backwards.

'Do not let it go near the claws,' I told him, 'or the crab will bite you and we shall have to kill it.'

He did as he was told, his hand moving slowly so as not to alarm the crab.

'There!' I exclaimed. 'You are free of the crab and all is well.'

'Now you have it,' said the boy.

'But I am not afraid of it. And you should not be. Now,' I said, kneeling on the sand, 'let us look at him. Or her. For,' and I pointed to the rear of crab, turning it upside down, 'this is a lady crab. This mass of orange pips are her eggs.'

There was a shout from along the beach and the second of the two standing in front of me shouted, 'Look! Look!'

All the children came running, their teacher taking

236

up the rear. Only the nun did not rush in my direction, but she did put down her book.

With the children gathered, I said, 'This is a crab. It's Latin name is *Ocypode* but in English they call it,' – and I momentarily reverted to that language – 'the large ghost crab. This is not because it is a ghost but because it is white. Like a ghost. And, like a ghost, it comes out at night but, if there are not too many people on the beach, they also come out in the day.'

'What do they eat?' enquired a child standing beside me.

'They eat dead fish, little sea animals and other crabs.'

'Where do they live?' asked another.

'They live in sand holes,' I replied, looking up.

It was the little girl. She was staring straight into my face. For a moment, I was silent, awed by her attention. Her proximity seemed so strange, so dangerous. I had never been so close to her and wanted to say something more to her, tell her how glad I was that she was doing well in school, to inquire after her sister in the factory, request she give my regards to her family. Yet I knew none of this was possible: I must stay as a distant observer.

Mercifully, at this moment, another child spoke up.

'Where are its eyes?'

The spell was broken and I embarked upon a quick tour of the creature's anatomy, pointing out its eyes and mouth-parts, the clever hinges of its limbs and, with the aid of the teacher's pencil, its powerful claws.

The questions over, I put the crab close to the sand and let go of it. It stood stock-still for a second then fled, running sideways into the water where it started fidgeting with its legs to bury itself.

'Thank you, sir,' the teacher said in English, the children crowding the water's edge to see the little pit in the sand under which the crab was cowering.

'Not at all, it was a pleasure,' I told her.

She smiled and called all the children away and into a circle once more. The nun joined them and there followed a session of note-taking and drawing, the children silently concentrating on their work.

I collected my newspaper, put on my shoes and walked up the steps towards the road, turning right and setting off along the verge. Glancing down, I saw the children engrossed in their work, the teacher moving from one to another giving advice. Only the nun glanced up, watching me with that look one sees in sinners who know they have been found out.

It is not long to go until four o'clock. The warm sun is glinting off the harbour: one window in a house on The Peak is glimmering, giving the impression of someone hiding in the lush greenery with a heliograph.

The rickshaw coolies are hunkered down in the shafts of their vehicles by the Star Ferry, smoking and talking or sleeping uneasily in the contorted positions only the poor in tropical lands can achieve, their spines made supple by poverty and heat. A few squat on the pavement playing *tien kow* with strips of card. The exhaust fumes from the red-and-cream painted buses hang poisonously in the air and the taxis, swinging round to join the rank, screech and rattle.

Although I cannot see them I know that, in a doorway or dock gateway down Canton Road, there will be other rickshaw pullers sitting in the shade, not to escape the high sun but to hunt out some privacy in which they can chase the dragon, lighting small balls of opium in tea spoons or squares of silver paper gleaned from discarded cigarette packets, sucking the fumes hungrily, waiting as the drug soothes their lives, irons the wrinkles of their worries away.

It is still comparatively early in the year but the afternoon sky is already harsh and iron-like with heat as I stride out from the shade of the ferry pier: according to the necromancers in the Chinese press, it promises to be a hotter than usual summer.

Wiping my brow with a damp handkerchief, I set off along Salisbury Road, dodging the traffic of lorries, taxis and hand-carts heading up Canton Road towards the docks. I welcome the arrival of the next area of shade opposite the general post office, cast by overhanging creepers and trees growing along the top of a rock-face halfway between the driveway to the marine police headquarters and the fire station, but I do not slow my pace. I have never been one to saunter.

By the fire station, under the last tree, an old man with a shaved head and wearing thick tortoiseshell-framed spectacles has stationed himself on a storm culvert under a black umbrella. The rock behind him, faced with concrete to prevent erosion, is scrawled with a disorderly pattern of characters drawn in charcoal varnished in a feeble attempt to extend their life. One inscription is in English.

It reads, *Buy Grashoper Make by Hand with Leaf Good Luck Good Fortune Grashoper $1*.

The old man is weaving coarse grass leaves and strips of green bamboo bark, his fingers crooked but agile as they twist and fold, bend and tuck in corners. Beside him on the culvert is a row of variously sized green grasshoppers, whilst others are pinned to the surface of his umbrella.

'You buy?' the old man asks me as I pass by.

'*M'hai*,' I say, shaking my head, '*Mo cheen*. No money.'

It is a universal phrase used to dismiss persevering street peddlers and insistent beggars.

'You go' money. Pleng-ty money,' the grasshopper-maker replies adding, '*Jah maang*. G'asshopper. *Wan lai-ga*. For luck. *Ho wan ah-ma*.'

Yet he does not press the matter. It is hot and there will be tourists along soon. A large white cruise ship has berthed in the docks around the corner. The first battalion of passengers has already come ashore, trodden the streets and returned laden with packages: now lunch has been served on board, another wave will soon disembark and head for the camera shops and jewellers, the curio houses and the tailors, most of them passing this way.

Once more, I look at the sign on the concrete. There is no need for me to feel in my pocket. I know how much I have on me — thirteen dollars and eighty cents. But I have lived in China for so long the introspective caution of the European is reduced to a few seconds' inconsequential nag. Like every Chinese, I am inured to the acceptance of fate and the grasshoppers might be, in some oblique and unfathomable way, an omen I should not dismiss lightly.

Reaching forward, I pick up the smallest grass-hopper. It is cleverly crafted, the emerald leaves lending a lifelike appearance and the intertwining of the various constituents so fashioned they might almost be the casings of an actual insect's carapace. Only the eyes are not made of vegetable matter, but red glass-headed pins.

'Sixty-five cents,' I suggest.

The old man ignores me. This is a ploy and I know it – and he knows I know it.

'Seventy cents.'

'Sevung-ty-fi'e,' the old man says.' Small wung. Small g'ashopper, small luck.'

I take a dollar bill out of my pocket and hand it to him.

'One dollar. You buy big one.'

'No. Jus' small one. Small luck good for me. Got no luck now,' I tell him.

The old man shrugs, removes twenty-five cents from a leather pouch on his belt and drops the coins into my hand.

'Okay. You get luck, come back, buy big one.'

The grasshopper nestling in my hand as if it is a living creature which might take flight, I cross Hankow Road and enter the main lobby of the Peninsula Hotel, a bell-boy in a pork-pie hat holding the door open for me.

From time to time, I like to come in here. The ornate ceiling is thirty feet high, supported on pillars decorated in gold leaf. It is as much like the interior of a baroque Catholic cathedral as it is the lobby of an hotel. To left and right are comfortable chairs and polished tables standing on carpets with a rich pile and sombre pattern. Waiters in Chinese-style white jackets and black trousers move silently on slippered feet between the furniture, carrying silver trays laden with tea pots and bone china. Above, in one corner of the ceiling, a chamber quartet ensconced in a little gallery plays subtle music. At this moment, they are playing Bach.

Choosing a table, I order afternoon tea and request a newspaper, which arrives held between a pair of wooden strips screwed tightly together by butterfly nuts. Printed upon the gleaming wood in gold, cursive lettering are the words *Peninsula Hotel: Hong Kong – Do Not Remove*.

I cursorily start to scan the paper. I do not read it: I am not in the least bit interested in the news. It is just that the newspaper gives me something with which to occupy my hands and disguise my eyes as I wait for my tea to arrive. Long ago, I learnt that a man doing nothing attracts attention, but he who is seemingly busy is ignored.

From my vantage point behind the paper, I observe.

There are three types of people present, the Chinese staff excepted. I do not use the word class for Hong Kong is a classless society: there are no lords and lackeys but only the rich, the not-so-rich and the poor. In the lobby of the Pen, as the hotel is colloquially known only the former are present yet there is on view all three varieties of the sub-species.

At the next-but-one table are gathered three European ladies wearing neat dresses and jackets with low-heeled shoes. They are not adorned with lavish jewellery but the one nearest me has on her left wrist a solid gold lady's Rolex. Although they drink their tea and have eaten some of the sandwiches on a tiered rack, they have not touched the dainty cakes in frilled paper cups.

I do not look at them, but I listen to their conversation. They are discussing their servants, the merits of Ah Wong against those of Ah To, the advantages of having one's own sew-sew amah versus employing a freelance when there is darning to be done or a child's fancy dress costume to be made.

Scattered about the lobby are a number of other little cliques of European women no doubt discussing similar topics, the latest fashions out from Paris, the information about who is sleeping with whom and which marriages are on the rocks. These women are remainders from the old days when it was common to ask each other to tiffin and spend winter afternoons chasing native Chinese foxes in the Lam Tsuen valley with imported English hounds.

Six tables away is an example of the second group of wealthy folk. These are Chinese women. They wear tight skirts and high heels and are hung about with jewellery: one wears a diamond the size of a pea which shards the sunlight into a tiny prismatic explosion. I cannot tell of what they are speaking; even were I sitting closer I should not know for they lean together conspiratorially. Their faces are immaculately made up, their eyes outlined in mascara, their cheeks smooth as porcelain. They have eaten all their cakes but not touched the sandwiches.

The third variety of the rich are represented by just one table: there, sitting close together but not so close as the Chinese women, are four Chinese men. Their suits are made of shiny grey silk, their socks are black with embroidered motifs at the ankles and their ties are dark blue or green. Their wristwatches are heavy,

243

ostentatious and gold. They sip their tea but ignore the sandwiches and the cakes. They too are out of earshot yet I know they are talking of money, of how to increase their wealth, of what the day's rate is of the Hong Kong dollar *vis à vis* the pound, the yen, the American dollar.

The waiter brings my tea. I fold the newspaper and, when he has unloaded his tray, thank him in Cantonese, which takes him aback. He is not sure how to respond and says in English, 'You are welcome, sir.'

I pour out my tea into the bone china cup with the hotel crest printed upon it, stirring it with a silver spoon. I eat one of the sandwiches: it is almost as thin as a communion wafer and has a filling of anchovy paste.

The reason I visit this lobby is not because I wish to return to the world of European mores and fashions, nor is it because I wish to indulge myself in luxury. I come for the same reason that I visit *The Black Pussy* – to be amongst the sinners and the lost, to know that I am not alone.

For, as I chew on the fine white bread and sip the Earl Grey tea, I consider how, not a mile away from the oblivious and unforgiving rich, my tenement flat awaits my return, One-eye is selling chickens to pay off his extortionist's debt and how, two miles beyond that, there are shacks on the hillsides the residents of which pay homage – and tithes – to Mr Yee.

This irony is something I savour. It is the paradox of the human condition, the enigma some call justice and others injustice but which I refer to as fate, as destiny.

Here, genteel folk take afternoon tea to the strains

of Bach. Two hundred yards away, men sit in the shadows and chase dragons.

Arthur Doble's house was on the outskirts of the town, built on the side of a steep hill overlooking the river directly opposite Dragon Island. It was a Chinese house with heavy wooden double doors set in a windowless wall of dark grey stone and, from the pathway up from the river, appeared no different from the home of any well-to-do Chinese trader. The doorway gave on to a flagged courtyard and it was here that he welcomed Father Callaghan and me on the evening of 13 June 1900.

'I'm so glad you could both make it,' he said, as we alighted from our sedan chairs. 'I've two friends from Hong Kong whom you must see. Come,' he beckoned to us with an open hand, palm downwards in the Chinese fashion, 'and meet them.'

The reception room, which in a European home might be the drawing room, was large and lit by oil lanterns, the furniture traditionally Chinese but, as a concession to European comfort, the seats were lined with brocade cushions. The tables were low and in one corner was a massive wooden trunk carved with a view of Hong Kong Island in bas-relief. The only item not of Chinese manufacture was an enamel-faced carriage clock standing upon one of the tables under a scroll showing an intricate landscape devoid of perspective. We passed through to a second, larger room, in the centre of the ceiling of which was a square hole. Directly beneath this was a hearth in which a fire was burning without flames but giving off a column of smoke rising to eddy along the ceiling towards the hole.

'Sandalwood,' Mr Doble said as I sniffed the smoke-scented air. 'A pleasant aroma but, best of all, it keeps mosquitoes at bay. The little beggars tend only to feed between four and eight o'clock, so if we keep the embers glowing and the smoke billowing until eight-thirty it will greatly reduce our chances of being consumed by itching. Now,' he guided us around the hearth, 'let me introduce Mr Ronald Pearsall and Mr Eric Nicol.'

We all shook hands, exchanging pleasantries. Mr Pearsall was a tall man with very long limbs and a small, pinched face whilst Mr Nicol was shorter, more rotund and with fat hands. The former worked for W. Powell & Co., a trading firm in Hong Kong, whilst the latter owned a small printery. All three were dressed in dinner suits, as if they were not in the heart of Southern China but in the smoking-room of a London club, whilst both myself and Father Callaghan were in our clerical clothes. It was only the second time I had worn ecclesiastical garb outside the mission since my arrival in Wuchow.

'Arthur informs us you are new to China, Father Stephen,' Mr Pearsall remarked as we relaxed on wide settles around the fire.

'Just a few weeks and still wet behind the ears,' Father Callaghan said before I could reply. 'But you're learning fast,' he added, looking at me through the smoke. 'Already, he can fix his own *fu* so that they don't fall down and he's had his first thousand-year-old egg.'

The others laughed, Nicol asking, 'And have you had your first salt plum?'

'Indeed, I have,' I admitted.

A young Chinese lad entered and handed me a glass of whiskey.

'This is Ah Ping,' Mr Doble explained. 'He is my makee-learnee house-boy. An orphan picked up in the gutters of Whampoa when he was eight. Or so. He's been with me for four years. You see,' he went on, 'you holy men don't have a monopoly on the waifs and strays of China.'

'The Lord will look down kindly on you,' Father Callaghan responded, sipping at his whiskey in the savouring, luxurious way only an Irishman can.

'He may, Father,' Mr Doble replied, 'but I'm not looking to score points with the Almighty. I am merely doing another poor, benighted human a favour and gaining, I hope, a lifelong servant into the bargain.'

Mr Pearsall continued, talking to me, 'I'll not ask you what you think of Wuchow, or China come to that, for I'll bet every white man and woman you've met has sought the same information. But I will ask you if you think you will make it your home.'

'My home?' I said.

'When I first came to the Orient in '86, that was the question posed to me by the manager of Powell's. He didn't quite phrase it that way, mind you. He actually said, "Well, my boy, you're stuck out here for six years without sight of the White Cliffs of Anywhere. Do you think you'll be able to stand it?"'

'I think I shall,' I replied.

'Understandable,' Mr Nicol observed. 'Unlike us

mere business wallahs, you've the strength of your convictions to give you backbone.'

'On the contrary,' I responded. 'It may be true that the Lord Jesus will give me the courage I need to persevere but that is not to say it will make me happy and settled. It is one thing to be at home in a place and quite another to want to be in it. Yet I believe I shall make my home here. Happily and willingly.'

'You sound confident,' Mr Doble said.

'I am,' I replied firmly. 'Quite confident.'

And I believed myself. The realisations I had experienced when we first met were firming to resolute intention as the days passed.

Our conversation drifted into the realm of inconsequentials, topics such as expatriate men anywhere in the world might discuss – trade, colonial politics and the petty vagaries of colonial administrators, news from Europe that was weeks old. At precisely eight o'clock, as the delicate chimes of the carriage clock rang out, Ah Ping returned and, with a small gong in his hand, struck it once with a leather-padded hammer.

'Supper is ser-wed,' he announced.

We were led through a door onto a terrace where a circular table was set as for a Chinese meal under a number of red and gold paper lanterns hanging from beams entwined with creepers. Beyond was a small garden sloping towards the river and Dragon Island with its bright light shining upon the water.

'You've a fine place here,' Pearsall congratulated our host. 'Quite the best house I know in China outside Hong Kong.'

'I am fortunate,' Doble acknowledged, 'though for how much longer I cannot say.'

'Are you leaving Wuchow?' I enquired, sitting down as indicated by an elderly manservant who held the chair for me.

'I would not doubt it if we aren't all going to leave Wuchow in the not-too-distant future,' Pearsall said. 'There's trouble brewing.'

'The *I Ho Ch'üan*,' Father Callaghan commented, lifting his chopsticks and taking a small piece of chilli-pickled cabbage from a dish before him.

'Those are the fellows,' Doble said. 'Righteous Harmony Fists. Boxers. Causing a lot of problems in the north and there's a few down around here.'

The elderly manservant re-entered and placed an oval iron platter of meat on the table, resting it on a block of wood. From the dish rose a cloud of steam which smelled of ginger.

'They've the tacit permission of the Empress Dowager,' Nicol remarked. 'They refer to themselves as the Buddhist Patriotic Society. I saw one of their banners in Hong Kong, brought down from Shantung by an army chap. It was, of course, scarlet and had written upon it *Feng Chi Mieh Kiao*.'

The others nodded sagely, Father Callaghan frowning.

'What does it mean?' I queried.

'By Imperial Command exterminate the Christian religion,' Father Callaghan said.

There was silence about the table. The steam rising from the platter had decreased and Doble, picking up his chopsticks, leaned forwards.

'Let us eat,' he suggested, 'or else the food will spoil. We've fourteen courses ahead of us . . .'

We began to help ourselves in the Chinese fashion, the meat tasting unlike anything I had ever known, the manservant going round the table filling small cups with rice wine.

'I was at a ball in Weihaiwei last December,' Pearsall said after we had started eating, 'and there were a number of Chinese present affecting European dress. It's becoming a bit of a fad amongst some of them, when they mix with foreigners. They manage the swallow-tail coats and black trousers without much difficulty although some have theirs tailored with fur linings. Traditional Chinese winter clothes in the north are always fur-lined, the houses seldom being heated with more than a brazier. Must be hellish hot to wear such an evening suit at a legation party. Anyhow, as I was saying, they have no trouble with the coat and pants but the shirt confounds them. The studs and collars are a bit unusual for them. One old boy was having an awful time with his. It was several sizes too big for him and kept sticking out of his waistcoat. I noticed this — and so did the French consul. After about half an hour, the Frenchie said to me out of the blue, "When I return home, I shall sack my laundryman." "Why?" I asked. It was so sudden a statement and bore no relation to what we had been talking about. *"Cet homme,"* he started in French, so angry was he, *"il* . . . The man there is wearing my shirt. My crest is sewn into it, under the starched front. Now I know why my shirts stay so long in the laundry. My servant is hiring them out!"'

We all laughed, a little over-zealously: the story expunged our sombre thoughts of the *I Ho Ch'üan*, setting the evening on a pleasant course once more.

The meal continued for about three-quarters of an hour when, as we began on the eighth or ninth course, the manservant returned and whispered something to Mr Doble.

'Gentlemen,' he announced as the Chinese stood back, 'Ah Ching informs me we must go to the end of the terrace and observe something. He does not say what.'

We left the table, guided along the terrace by the elderly manservant and his master. The view down to the river, through some sparse conifer and willow trees, was as clear as if it had just rained, although not a drop had fallen for several months. At a low wall was gathered Ah Ping, two house amahs and the cook-boy with a white apron around his waist. They were standing in a silent and apprehensive huddle.

A full moon was rising along the course of the Si Kiang, about a third of its orb having appeared over the mountains. It was huge, filling a quarter of the lower quadrant of the sky, every crater and mark upon its face etched with an awesome clarity: and this was no ordinary grey, cool moon for it was as blood red as a setting sun.

No one spoke. Mr Doble put his hand upon Ah Ping's shoulder and one of the amahs took the boy's hand. I noticed the child was silently sobbing and the cook was shivering with fright.

Father Callaghan, standing next to me, crossed himself and muttered something in Latin under his breath which I could not comprehend.

'A bad omen,' Mr Doble murmured. 'Most inauspicious for us all I fear.'

251

'*Yat nin yau shâp yêe kôh yûet.*'

The boy was leaning forward, his shoulders hunched, his arms crossed on the edge of my table. The quiff of hair had fallen over his brow and, from time to time, he ran his fingers through it to push it clear of his eyes. He struggled with the tones again and with his accent.

'*Kòh yùet,*' I said, 'not *kôh yûet*. Try the next sentence.'

He took a deep breath as if about to submerge himself in freezing water.

'*Yat kòh yùet yau saam shâp yât.*'

He stressed the first three words, desperately trying to get them right, to gain my approbation.

'Good,' I said.

He smiled faintly at me. We were reaching the end of our hour's tutoring and he was flagging. So was I. Yet he was trying today, striving hard and this did not raise my ire, frustrate me as has been the case on occasions in the past.

'Now the next.'

'*Yat yat yau yêe shâp sày tún chung.*'

'Not quite. Not *Yat yat* but *yat yât.*'

I closed my copy of our textbook.

'Enough for today. You have worked hard and progressed. Practise on your own. Don't talk to your house servants in the kitchen Cantonese they expect of you. Communicate with them precisely. Tell them to correct you if you are wrong. You don't lose face

252

and they, being servants, will not gain any. Indeed, you will gain face.'

'Yes, sir,' he replied.

I pushed my book to one side and, from the drawer, removed my invoice pad. I opened it at the bookmark, a strip of bark fallen from my grasshopper.

For several days, I have had the air conditioner on the whole day: we have been having an unusually warm, humid spell for this time of year. The result is that the fabric of the grasshopper has dried out and begun to shrivel. First to go was a foreleg, then a piece of its carapace. Yesterday, a section of wingcase came free and it is this I am using as a marker.

'A receipt is not necessary, sir,' the boy said.

'I beg your pardon?'

'A receipt, sir. It's not necessary.'

'I am sure,' I answered, 'your father will require some proof of payment and I feel I must have the security.'

'But I trust you, sir. And as for my father, this has nothing to do with him. He does not pay for my lessons. I pay for these from my own money. My spending money, sir,' he added as if an explanation might be required.

I did not know what to say. I closed the receipt pad and pressed the little plastic nipple on the end of my biro, retracting the point. For some reason, I had assumed the boy was taking Cantonese lessons at the insistence of his parents. It was not unknown for colonial fathers to press such instruction upon their offspring: it assured a higher entry level into business or the colonial adminis-tration.

'I see. In other words, you have chosen of your own volition to learn Cantonese.'

'Yes, sir.'

'May I ask why?'

For a quick moment, I ran over the possibilities: he has a Chinese girlfriend, he wants to pre-empt his father's intentions, have another qualification to stand him in good stead with a prospective employer, he wishes to know what is being said about him when walking in the street. These have been reasons others of my former students have held.

'So I might speak to the Chinese, sir.'

His reply was put in the matter-of-fact fashion of a person as yet to learn of the guile and deceit of men.

'Why should you want to speak to them?'

He paused. I sensed my question was unexpected.

'Well, sir . . .' he began. 'I . . . Well, how else can one communicate? If I can't speak Cantonese, how can I learn from them?'

'Learn from them?' I asked. 'Learn what from them?'

Again, he was momentarily at a loss.

'But . . . Well, everything, sir.'

It occurred to me this boy did have more to him than I had appreciated after all. I looked at him, with his Tony Curtis film-star quiff and his tanned young skin, his blue eyes, his expensive gold fountain pen, his starched white shirt and I did not see a young boy living towards the middle of the millennium but another in a heavy cassock walking through history at the turn of the nineteenth century.

From his wallet, which he tugged from his tight hip pocket, he removed my fee, which he placed on my receipt pad. I could see he had more money in the wallet, a season ticket for the Kowloon Motor Bus Company and impressed into the leather of one of the inner compartments was a narrow oval. This, I knew from occasional glances at the contents of sailors' wallets in *The Black Pussy*, was a condom.

'May I ask you a question, sir?'

Now it was my turn to be taken aback. We have never spoken in this fashion before. He has always arrived, been polite, attended to his studies with more or less application and then, having settled the bill, left as politely as he arrived. Save for his occasional glance at my face, he has never sought to discuss anything other than the finer points of Cantonese tones.

'Yes, you may.'

'Why does the man who lives downstairs call you *san foo?*'

He pronounced the words correctly. I should have been mildly pleased: we had never gone over them.

'How do you know that?' I snapped.

'It's in my vocabulary book,' he replied.

'I mean,' I said, brusquely, 'how do you know what he calls me?'

'I met him once. In the lift. He wears round glasses . . .'

'And? Get on with it, boy,' I demanded.

He blushed and blustered.

'He asked me if I was going to see *lung wong hau*. I said I was visiting you. He then smiled and said you were *san foo*.'

'His name is Mr Wu,' I informed the boy. 'He is . . .' I was going to say friend but decided otherwise. '. . . an acquaintance of mine.'

I was hoping this would be the end of the conversation but it was not: the boy was determined to get the answer he wanted.

'So may I ask, sir, why he calls you that?'

'Do you know what it means?'

'It is the noun for a priest.'

'I was a missionary in China,' I replied, adding in the hope this would silence the boy, 'at the Catholic mission at Wuchow. On the West River.'

'Why are you not a priest now, sir?' he asked. 'I thought if you were once a priest . . .'

'That's none of your business,' I retorted sharply.

He blushed again and I felt sorry for him, regretted my curtness.

'I am not embarrassed by your prying,' I went on, 'but you must learn there are some things you do not ask of another man. If someone wants you to know something, they will tell you.'

'Yes, sir. I'm sorry.'

'There is no need for you to apologise.'

He stood and placed his books in his rattan briefcase.

'When were you at Wuchow, sir?' he enquired, his voice quiet as if, by not speaking loudly, he might not offend with his continued interrogation.

'A long time ago. A very long time ago. A considerable length of time before you were born. Or your parents, I doubt not.'

'Would you . . .?' he began but I cut him short.

'I don't talk about it. Indeed,' I lied, 'I seldom think about it. It is in the past and that's an end to it.'

I do not know what it was told me this but I knew he was not only not satisfied but would, given the chance, return to his delving into my life when he felt the moment opportune.

He finished putting away his books, pressing them down on top of some sports clothing in his basket, shifting aside a pair of tennis shoes to make room.

I did not want to alienate him. He is, after all, a source of my income and I admit to preferring to teach him than to coaching colonial civil servants striving to gain promotion.

'Do you play much tennis?' I enquired.

'Yes, sir. At the Kowloon Bowls Club.'

An uneasy silence fell then he was ready to leave. I accompanied him to the door of my flat.

'Before I go, sir . . .' he started again.

'Yes?' I responded.

I wondered what he was going to come out with next: ask me if I had fallen from grace with a woman and been excommunicated, been caught with a choir-boy behind the vestry cup-board.

'What does *lung wong hau* mean?'

His pronunciation was weak but I decided not to make a point of it for I understood him.

'Queen of the Dragons,' I told him. 'I believe Mr Wu was referring to the other European resident of this tenement.'

'There is someone else?' the boy said with amaze-ment.

'An elderly woman. But not as old as myself.'

He asked no more questions and I watched him walk to the lift, pressing the black call button. A green light behind a cracked perspex disc came on and I could hear the mechanism start to grind high up the lift shaft.

'Good afternoon, sir,' he said as the lift doors slid gratingly open.

I made no reply and closed my flat door.

That was over two hours ago. It is now late evening and I am sitting alone at the table. I have not put my Cantonese book away, nor even the receipt book, which remains with the boy's money untouched upon it. I am thirsty but I have not risen from the table to fetch myself a drink of water from the flat-sided Gordon's gin bottle in my little refrigerator.

Ever since the boy left, I have thought about him. He is so like me. I hate to admit it but the fact is plain. He is not learning Cantonese for any other reason than he has committed himself to China. Just as I did. He has found his home and wants to settle into it, merge with it so he can be a part of it, be accepted by it despite his blond hair and blue eyes.

What is more, he is burning to question me about China, knows I have a lifetime's knowledge of its geography, its people: he also appreciates I have experienced it, have come across its every mood and mannerism, have seen, he thinks, all it can show.

As I realise this, I simultaneously understand I should tell him nothing, should not risk colouring his judgement, giving him preconceptions he will use to formulate responses, assess his own experiences, come to terms with his own excitements and disappointments. He should discover the future and its landscape for himself, learning of it the hard way, the painful way.

It occurs to me, sitting in the last of the evening with the glow of the street lights and shop signs cutting coloured bars on my ceiling through the plastic venetian blinds, that he is my successor, the next generation of old China hands.

I do a little mental arithmetic. If he is seventeen now, which assumption must be fairly accurate give or take a year, he will be fifty-five years old when the century turns, my age in the year two thousand and twenty-eight.

By then, China will be a different land, as radically altered from what it is today as the present is from how I found it when I stepped off the *Lucky Moon* onto the pontoon at Wuchow.

A pang of terrible sadness strikes me through. How I wish, at this moment, for immortality. I should like to be here to see what the future holds in store, to share in its fortunes and vicissitudes. However, there are no deals for immortality, no devils with whom to make a pact: that is the stuff of fancies, literature and miracles.

There are no such things as miracles.

Yet, when the Dalai Lama dies, the exact moment of his last breath is recorded and monks are sent throughout the Buddhist world to find a boy child born at that exact moment in time and he is taken to Lhasa to be declared the new leader of his faith. In a similar fashion, my boy pupil is to be my successor. I am certain of it. He must inherit my past even though he knows nothing of it.

I cannot justify my certainty. It is one of those thoughts, those realisations that come to a man which he knows to be incontrovertibly right without having any logical basis whatsoever for his assumption. In this respect, it is not unlike belief and I am familiar with that and its dangers.

Standing upon my chair, I take down the thin

volume of my life, looking at the cover, at the gold leaf lettering – *1900*. Some men give their heirs fortunes in money or stocks, estates, wealth counted in precious stones and rare metals. I have none of these. My estates are the passing of time, my wealth is counted in pebbles.

I do not open the diary. Instead, from the drawer in which resides the receipt book I remove a brown manila envelope. The flap bears no gummed strip: instead there is a length of twine tied to an eye, a replica of which is attached to the back of the envelope. I slip the diary in, twisting the twine around the second eye, sealing the flap.

Although I know I should not do it, on the front of the envelope I write with my biro *Gerald Nelson – by hand* and, with the receipt book and the cheap pen, place it back in the drawer.

Through my dozing, I heard what I fancied was the slap of wet fish on marble slabs: it might have been the striking of sopping clothing against a laundry stone. It was at first a cool sound but it developed into the frantic drumming of a fist upon my door. I sat bolt upright, instantly awake with sweat dripping down my forehead and the small of my back. A voice began to shout.

'Mas-ter! Mas-ter!'

It was Ah Fong's voice.

'What do you want, Ah Fong?' I called out, suppressing my irritation at being abruptly woken.

'Big t'ouble! Big t'ouble! You come quick chapel-
side.'

The patter of his feet receded down the passageway
and I heard him descending the stairs, several steps
at a time.

I struggled into my clothing, the material sticking
to my damp skin, thrust my feet into my cloth slippers
and went after him.

From the chapel came the sound of a woman crying. It was not the soft, pitiful sobbing of a Chinese
woman, such as I had heard by the baby posting
box, but a strident, breath-catching weeping between
gusts of strangled words trying to form themselves.

Pushing open the chapel door, I discovered Father
Callaghan standing over a huddled form in the front
pew, his hand resting gently upon it. He was bent
slightly forward. At my entrance, he looked up.

'Father Stephen,' he greeted me, 'it's a terrible
thing has happened.'

At that moment, the person in the pew looked
up. It was Mrs Blair. Her hair was awry, her
face streaked with tears which had run in eddies
through a light coating of dust on her cheeks.
She put her hand up to try to bring some order
to her coiffure but all she did was make it more
bedraggled. The sun, coming through one of the
windows, glinted in the gemstones of her necklace.

'Mrs Blair,' I said, nodding politely to her.

I seemed incapable of any other response. I could
feel no rapport nor sorrow for this meretricious
woman in her bejewelled if dusty condition.

She began to sob again, her face in her hands, her
body wracked with sorrow.

'It's a tragedy,' Father Callaghan declared, quietly. 'An awful tragedy.'

'Yes,' I replied. Having yet to be appraised of the situation I could not think what else to say.

'He's been shot,' Father Callaghan went on. 'By one of the Residency guards. Just an hour ago.'

The muscles about my spine tightened. If Mr Blair had been injured in a shooting incident it could bring about serious political consequences. Even now one of the ships moored along the southern praya could be slipping her lines and sailing for Hong Kong. She could be there in a day and a half with the currents behind her, sooner with a westerly wind to fill her sails. After that, a week at the most would have a British man-o'-war anchored off Wuchow, her cannon aimed at the town. There was no telling then where it might end.

'Was it an accident?' I wondered aloud.

'No,' Mrs Blair whimpered. 'It was not. It was cold-blooded, deliberate murder . . .'

'He's dead?' I asked: in my mind, Mr Doble's foreboding and remarks at the bloody moonrise echoed hollowly.

'Dead,' Father Callaghan said dully.

Mrs Blair sobbed more loudly, blowing her nose in her handkerchief, which was already sodden.

'Where is he now?' I asked, assuming Father Callaghan wanted me to attend to the body whilst he comforted the widow.

'We don't know,' Father Callaghan explained. 'As soon as he was shot, the guard grabbed him and carried him off. Harriet,' he squeezed Mrs Blair's shoulder gently as she broke into another bout of sobbing, 'is afraid the guard will . . .'

Behind Mrs Blair's back, Father Callaghan mimicked with his free hand the picking up of something with chopsticks and transporting it to his mouth.

'Eat him?' I said incredulously, staring at my companion.

'Eat him,' Mrs Blair wailed in confirmation.

I put my hand on the back of a pew to steady myself. I could think of nothing more horrific.

'Do they do that? The Chinese?' I asked disbelievingly.

'They do,' Father Callaghan replied, 'but usually only in the winter months. For this reason, I am sure the guard will not do so now. In this weather . . .'

'My poor Bruce!' Mrs Blair howled.

'Bruce?' I said, puzzled. 'I thought Mr Blair . . .'

'You dolt!'

Mrs Blair was standing in the pew. She had got to her feet with such alacrity I had not seen her move. A snake could not have struck more rapidly.

'I'm sorry . . .' I began but she cut me short.

'You bloody fool! Not my husband, you dunderhead! My Jack Russell. That bloody Chink has shot my dog.' Her rage suddenly collapsed and she dropped back into the pew as if she had been a puppet of which the strings had been cut. 'Now he'll eat him.'

'I'm sure he will not,' Father Callaghan comforted her. 'I'm sure we shall find him. Now, come along, dear lady. Come and rest. Let us see what we might do.'

He helped her to her feet. After her sorrow and rage she quickly became meek and apologetic.

'I'm sorry to come to you,' she said in a near whisper. 'My husband . . .'

263

She looked from Father Callaghan to me then lowered her eyes.

'It doesn't matter,' Father Callaghan said softly. 'Now you come along with me.'

We assisted Mrs Blair to Sister Margaret's room, Ah Fong was sent to fetch tea and rice cakes to revive her and Father Callaghan lent her his smelling salts in case she should feel faint. When at last she was lying on the bed, her face turned to the wall and her soul lost in grief, we left her and climbed to the mission roof. The sun was fierce so we sat in the shade of the bell.

'There'll be hell to pay,' Father Callaghan remarked as he settled himself on the stone steps under the bell pergola. 'Tell me, did Ah Fong not tell you what had happened?'

I sat next to him. The stones were remarkably cool in the shadow.

'He just hammered on my door shouting, *Big t'ouble*!'

Father Callaghan chuckled.

'And you thought the old man had bought it?'

I nodded.

'Well, that's a rare one, that is!' he laughed quietly. 'If it had been Mr Blair, I doubt there would have been so many tears shed. Save in the name of decorum.' He tapped his nose with his finger. 'I'll not break the secrecy of the confessional but Mr and Mrs Blair do not see eye to eye on a number of subjects. Religion and dogs are but two of them.'

'What shall we do?' I asked.

'Nothing, Father. We shall do nothing. We can only wait.'

'Wait for what?' I asked. 'Surely, at the end of

the day, it's only a dog. The guard'll get fined or something. Did he shoot it for no reason?'

'He had a reason, to be sure,' Father Callaghan said, 'and in my mind a good one. Apparently, and Ah Fong's told me so it can't be far from the truth, the dog had been barking at the guard off and on for days. His comrades had teased him about it. You know they called the dog a rat?'

'Yes,' I remembered, 'she had mentioned it.'

'Well, the other guards took the rise out of him. Chinese are afraid of dogs. Hardly surprising, so many of their own curs being rabid. But this one – why be afraid of a rat? Anyway, the man had had enough of this teasing. He was losing face, so he took his gun to the creature.'

The sun was shifting and my foot was out of the shadow, my toes beginning to itch in the heat. I pulled my foot in, repositioning myself on the stone step. Looking out over the rooftops, the wood smoke of cooking fires rose in columns through the hot air before breaking to hang in a haze high above the town.

'If we can do nothing, what will happen next?'

From the *hutong* came the delicate sound of a hand-gong, its chime dulled by the heat. Father Callaghan nodded in the direction of the sound.

'We're about to find out,' he said, pushing his hands down on his knees to assist himself in standing: he might have been endeavouring to push his frame up through the day's dense heat. 'That's the mandarin paying us a house call.'

We went quickly downstairs, arriving in the yard as Ah Fong swung the doors open to allow the entry of a grand, four-bearer palanquin preceded by two men carrying a gong and a flag, four men holding coiled bull-whips and ten others carrying oblong plaques painted red with gold characters drawn upon them.

'He's the *fu tai*,' Father Callaghan whispered as we bowed low. 'The governor of the district. We're to be on our best behaviour. And,' he added, 'he speaks some English so be discreet.'

The palanquin was constructed of highly polished rosewood, the shafts smooth bamboo and the curtains red and gold brocade embroidered with chrysanthemums. The roof was made of lacquered rattan, domed with a wooden spire at the apogee, the corners curled upwards, the supporting pillars carved with dragons and mythical animals.

As the bearers lowered it to the ground, a short, tubby Chinese ran round from behind and hurriedly parted the curtains. He was joined by two other minions, one carrying a fan of black cloth and bamboo, the other an ornate umbrella. Just inside the gates two guards armed with long-bladed swords positioned themselves, their weapons unsheathed. From outside came the sound of feet shifting about. Looking to my left, I could see Ah Fong bending so far over I was surprised he did not topple forward.

'Welcome to the Catholic Mission of Wuchow, Your Excellency,' Father Callaghan greeted the mandarin in English. 'We apologise for our humble abode and hope you will forgive our unpreparedness.'

'*M'gan yiu*,' the mandarin said peremptorily. '*Dui ngoh mo m'fong been-ah.*'

Father Callaghan and I straightened ourselves.

'What did he say?' I whispered.

'He said,' Father Callaghan muttered, 'it is of no

consequence and does not inconvenience him. He's a very formal person. They all are at his rank.'

Carefully, but not obviously, I studied my first mandarin. He looked very much as I expected from the illustrations I had seen in a volume on Chinese costume. About five feet six inches tall, he was approximately forty years old with a smooth, expressionless face and dressed in a blue silk *ch'I fu* richly embroidered with gold dragons and swirling clouds. The base of the garment, reaching to his cloth shoes, was decorated with diagonal gold and blue bands under a border of rounded billows. Around his waist was a tight girdle, held in place with a mother-of-pearl clasp from which hung a rosewood fan case, an ivory snuff bottle, a thin bamboo tube which I knew from my reading on Chinese costume contained a pair of chopsticks and, incongruously, a silver pocket watch on a chain with an onyx fob. Across his shoulders was a *pi ling*, a stiff flared collar attached to the top front button of the *ch'I fu*. It, too, was adorned with woven dragons and a two-inch border of gold thread. His hat was a small cone of split bamboo held in place by a red cotton string under his chin. From the finial on the apex, a button of opaque jade, hung two peacock feathers attached to the hat by a small jade cylinder.

'You do not know our new priest, Excellency,' Father Callaghan said. 'May I introduce you? This is Father Stephen.'

The mandarin, who had been busying himself with one of his entourage, stared myopically at me. I kow-towed as low as I dared.

'I know 'bout you,' the mandarin remarked in

English, adding noncommittally, 'People tell me 'bout you in Wuchow.'

'To what do we humble priests owe the unexpected pleasure of your company, Excellency?' Father Callaghan said, continuing, 'I hope we have not unwittingly transgressed a law. It is not our intention to break the peaceful, law-abiding nature of the town of Wuchow.'

'You have Miss-us Bwair?' the mandarin enquired.

'She is indeed here, sir. She is resting in our quarters.'

'Fetch her,' the mandarin ordered. 'I wan' talk her.'

Father Callaghan signalled to Ah Fong, who bent low yet again then ran into the mission.

'May we offer you refreshment, Excellency?' Father Callaghan suggested. 'Our food and drink is humble but we have tea.'

The mandarin shook his head very slightly and, with a show of reaching down and stretching out the loose sleeve of his *ch'I fu* to its fullest extent, studied his watch. I sensed he was not doing this to discover the time so much as to pass it. The watch was less a timepiece and more an ornate piece of jewellery.

Ah Fong returned, Mrs Blair walking behind him. She had tidied her hair but her face, without make-up, looked ethereally white. She stepped towards the mandarin then, at a discreet distance from him, bowed as we had done. I had somehow expected her to curtsey.

'Miss-us Bwair,' the mandarin began, taking his fan out of its case, 'a message come say you dog shot by guard.'

268

'Yes, Your Excellency,' Mrs Blair replied softly, 'this morning.'

'The dog small dog,' the mandarin went on, toying with his fan, opening and closing it. 'The dog call *lou siu gau.*'

Mrs Blair nodded bleakly.

'You dog good dog,' the mandarin declared. 'Do his job good. Must guard also. Like tiger. Guard also like man for you. So! Dog must be gife honour. You come East Side . . .' He studied his watch again. '. . . one hour, one half hour.'

'Yes, Your Excellency,' Mrs Blair said.

'You come, *san foo,*' the mandarin added, pointing to Father Callaghan and myself with his fan. 'Must come. Important you come. I leave solijer help you.'

He motioned to one of his men and an order was barked out. Two of his personal guards stepped away from the palanquin, stationing themselves outside the mission gate. They were joined by a third liveried Chinese carrying a whip.

'One hour, one half hour,' the mandarin repeated, snapped his fan shut in the palm of his hand with an act of finality and turned to get into his palanquin.

Everyone quickly kow-towed and the procession, preceded by the gong, flag and whip bearers, marched down the *hutong*, scattering the crowd gathered there, children fleeing and adults hastily kow-towing in the dirt. Those who were slow to show their obeisance were cracked with the whip.

'What does he mean by the East Side?' I enquired as Ah Fong closed the gates.

'He means the cemetery,' Father Callaghan replied.

'Cemetery?' I queried.

'When we came here – the Europeans – we were

given a plot of land outside the town. On the hillside overlooking the river. They don't want us buried in their places. Where we have our final resting place does not have good *fung shui*. In other words, it's not a propitious spot. The balance of nature is out of kilter there. The wind and water – the *fung* and the *shui* – are not quite right.'

'Why does he want us there?'

'Only the Lord knows. But be sure it's not an invitation we can ignore. And we'll have to don our best robes. This is going to be an official afternoon.'

Exactly an hour and a half later, I stepped out of my chair to see the mandarin's party gathered on a hillside terrace lined with low stone graves and wooden crosses, some of them askew, others bleached by the sun. There must have been nearly a hundred Chinese present, many wearing the mandarin's livery. Some were guards, others I assumed to be secretaries, household staff or local Chinese dignitaries who had been obliged to attend. All were attired in formal finery regardless of the beating sun.

Our small group of the Blairs, Mr Morrisby, Father Callaghan and myself made its way slowly towards the assembly up the earth steps cut in the hillside, the mandarin impassively awaiting our arrival under an ornate umbrella. Before him had been dug a small square hole. As we drew near, there was a succession of kow-towing before the mandarin made it known, with a flick of his fan, he wished the proceedings to commence.

The throng parted and a servant appeared carrying the corpse of the Jack Russell on a lacquer tray. He laid it at the feet of Mrs Blair, bowed to her and stepped back. The dog was already semi-rigid, its legs stuck out at right angles, its jaws slightly apart showing a pink tongue and its eyes open but glazed. In its shoulder was a small black hole, the only sign of blood upon the little corpse a dark stain in the leather collar.

Mrs Blair looked down upon the dog and began to sob. Father Callaghan put his hand on her arm, whispering something to her whilst her husband took her other hand. A large fly buzzed over the wound. I flicked it away with my hand. It seemed the least I could do in the circumstances. The motion of my hand wafted a slight, sickly perfume of putrefaction towards my face.

At a signal from the mandarin, the servant stepped forward again, lifting the tray and taking it to a diminutive old man who produced a small pine box from within the crowd. With some ceremony, the dog's legs were folded and held in place with red silken cords. This done, it was wrapped in a sheet of white silk and placed in its coffin which was lowered into the hole. A Chinese in working men's clothes carrying a shovel was ushered forward and, after kow-towing, commenced to fill in the hole.

I watched all this in a detached way, wondering what Father Callaghan was thinking. It was not right that a dog should be buried in the Christian cemetery and it occurred to me the mandarin might have ordered this ceremony by way of a slight against the foreigners. And yet, I considered, he had praised the dog's good qualities.

Throughout the ceremony, the mandarin neither looked at the dog, the grave nor the people around him. With a stolid stare, he gazed into the distance,

271

at a pagoda on the far bank of the river and the hills behind, vague in the haze.

The dog buried, I assumed that would be end of the matter but it was not. With the earth mound above its coffin smoothed over, the mandarin stepped back, giving a brief sign with a flick of his hand. The crowd opened to allow two guards to push another man forward. Mrs Blair gasped and put her hand to her mouth.

'What is it?' I muttered to Father Callaghan under my breath.

'The Residency guard,' Father Callaghan whispered.

Stripped to the waist, the guard looked dejected and ashamed. He was a young man with firm muscles, his cue tied in a circle around his brow. He was thrust in front of the mandarin, to whom he kow-towed deeply, going down on his knees and pressing his forehead to the ground. The mandarin let him do this for several minutes before giving a curt speech in rapid Cantonese.

'What is he saying?' I asked softly.

'He's saying the guard did not do his duty and brought shame upon himself and his master,' Father Callaghan translated. 'By that, he means himself, not Mr Morrisby. He says he must now pay his respects to the dog. It's about the most insulting thing he could order him to do. He'll lose a lot of face.'

The guard shifted round on the ground until he was kneeling before the dog's grave. He looked quickly about then began to kow-tow to the mound of earth, bobbing his head up and down.

I did not see what signal was made, nor by whom, but as the miscreant bobbed up for the sixth or seventh time, one of his erstwhile comrades stepped abruptly forward and, with a swift single swing of his sword, decapitated him.

Mrs Blair screamed once, turning into her husband's shoulder. The Chinese crowd did not flinch. The mandarin continued to gaze distractedly at the faraway hills. Father Callaghan muttered what I assumed was a brief blessing for the dead man.

As for myself, I could think of nothing. I know I should have reacted somehow, joined my fellow priest in prayer, felt pity or horror. Even fascination, in the circumstances, might have been acceptable. Manic laughter would not have been amiss, would later have been forgiven. Yet I did nothing. I just stared, my mind a total blank, at the severed head lying on its cheek next to the dog's grave, the man's cue unravelled and his neck pumping the last of his blood into the freshly dug soil.

Last week, I had an accident. Of sorts. I have tried to ignore it but it nags, which I find most annoying.

It was a hot night and I could not sleep. I had lain for hours, tossing and turning with the sighing, rattling air conditioner turned off. Finally, in a restless fidget, I dressed in my pyjama trousers and went up to the roof.

Stepping carefully through rows of shrubs and flowers growing in pots tended by Tsoi, and ducking the washing lines strung between metal Y-shaped poles, I sat on the low wall surrounding the roof top. Glancing down into Nanking Street, all the cooked food stalls but one were shut and it was doing a brisk trade, steam billowing from the cooking range on the pavement, the sound of shallow frying exploding over the rise and fall of conversation at the makeshift tables.

There were a few clouds overhead upon which the lights of the city reflected but no moon, the stars invisible so the night sky seemed foreboding and sullen. The Kowloon hills were indiscernible against the darkness, but, as I peered into the night, I became aware of a band of orange hanging along their upper slopes.

'They are burning the hills again,' I remarked to myself.

I moved from the wall to a wooden tea chest in the middle of the roof in which Tsoi keeps his gardening tools and propagates cuttings to sell for a few cents in the markets. It is not that he needs the money: he needs the work rather than the income for, like me, if he stopped being active he would stop living.

A dark gap appeared in the line of fire. I watched it intently for some minutes: the fire brigade had arrived or the flames met with a rocky outcrop. Yet, in a short time, the flames had joined hands again, inexorably climbing higher.

'They're burning out the dragons!' I exclaimed, as if I had suddenly stumbled upon the *raison d'être* for the fire-raising. 'They're burning out the mountain spirits. Chasing the ghosts away.'

Unsteadily, I climbed onto the tea chest to get a better view. The wood creaked under my weight, but I was somehow unaware of my precarious position and became light-headed with a kind of exhilaration I had not experienced before.

'Go on!' I heard a voice mutter from somewhere in the sky. 'Get the bastards! Burn them out! Drive them away into the sky to be frozen by the clouds. Freeze their pointed tails off. Put their murderous eyes out.'

I shook my fists at the hills, but they were no longer fists but cudgels. My body seemed not to belong to me. Some kind of divine divorce had occurred and I was another entity, an observer watching an old fool totter on a tea chest in the middle of a flat roof on a hot night, surrounded by pots of mute flowers.

I assume I lost my balance.

One moment I was secure, the next I was falling. I seem to recall a dragon pushing me. Bars of fire seared across my ribs, a terrible pain running through my arms. I thought I was dying, that this was what it was like. When life left the body, it was drawn out like cords of twine being pulled through the flesh.

The next sensation I felt was an intense warmth. I opened my eyes to be confronted by a brilliant light. Trying to shield my eyes was useless: something was holding my right arm. I squinted and slowly became aware of my surroundings. Three feet beneath me were rows of chrysanthemums. Somehow, I was floating over them as if in a flying dream when a motion of the arms sets one swimming, soaring and gliding through the air.

It was a minute before I realised I was suspended above the plants on a mesh of washing lines. The warmth was the early sun. I tried to free my right arm but found I was well and truly hog-tied. Then I heard a voice from somewhere out of sight over the top of my head.

'So! Look at you, you old sod! How on earth did

you get into such a bloody pickle, eh! My god! The ways and whims of ancient fools.'

It was a woman's voice, rich not with mockery but laughter.

I screwed my head round. Standing by the edge of the garden of pots, the sun behind her, was a woman. I seemed to know her and yet I seemed not to. My mind was confused. I remember thinking if I was dead then this was no angel. She was short, slightly bent, with grey hair tied into a straggling bun, her face lined not so much by exposure to the passage of years as to the rigours of harsh sunlight. Her nose was prominent, Jewish and her eyes small, dark and shrewd like those of a clever rodent.

'Who's that?' I asked with alarm. I became aware my genitals were in full view, my pyjama trousers having twisted themselves around me so the button-less fly was wide open.

'Who do you think it is, you old buffoon!'

'I don't know,' I said, discovering my left arm was free after all and struggling to reposition my clothing.

'Stella!' the woman retorted.

I thought for a moment, my mind still befuddled. 'Stella what?'

'What do you mean, Stella what?' the woman replied in the impatient tones of a crabby school-mistress. 'Stella who! Stella van der Poehl! Christ almighty, man! Who the hell do you think it is? You've so many old women in your life?' She paused, then added, 'Plenty of young tarts perhaps, but no old harridans. Now,' she stood with her arms akimbo, 'what shall we do with you?'

'Cut me down,' I suggested, gathering my wits.

'We could leave you there.'

'We?' I exclaimed.

I turned my head further. Standing behind the woman were Mr Wu, Tsoi and a young man stripped to the waist holding a long knife which glinted in the sunlight. I recognised him as one of the workers from the butcher's shop along the street.

'What you doin'?' Mr Wu enquired.

'I fell,' I said lamely. 'At least, that's what I think happened.'

'So we see,' Mrs van der Poehl observed sarcastically, 'although God alone knows what you were up to.'

'I was watching them fighting dragons,' I answered, my memory clearing.

Mrs van der Poehl grimaced impatiently and nodded to the others. Tsoi moved all the pots away from beneath me then, with Mr Wu's help, they lowered me as the butcher's boy cut the washing lines, one by one. At last, I was standing vertically once more upon the roof top.

'You were bloody lucky,' Mrs van der Poehl said, pointing to the chrysanthemums. 'Another foot and you'd've been impaled upon Tsoi's garden.'

I looked at the pots: every plant was tied to a length of bamboo thicker than a pencil. The sight of the stakes weakened me and I felt my legs giving way. The butcher's boy caught me and assisted me to the lift and down to Mrs van der Poehl's flat.

'I can look after myself,' I protested as he lowered me into a worn leather armchair positioned directly in front of a television set. 'I don't need molly-coddling.'

'Nonsense!' Mrs van der Poehl snapped. 'Be quiet,

you old goat, and say thank you to the good souls who not only found you but cut you free. I couldn't have done it.'

I meekly obeyed, nodding my thanks to the butcher's boy who, smiling profusely but saying nothing, left. I noticed he had a curling dragon tattooed on his right shoulder-blade. It was not a crude picture such as sailors have but an intricate portrait drawn with careful artistry, not the result of a twenty-minute needle session but of hours of painful craftsmanship. The creature's eyes were incredibly evil, its claws and scales, the pointed edges to its spinal fins outlined in the finest detail. I wondered vaguely to which of the local triad gangs the boy owed allegiance.

Mrs van der Poehl draped a towel around my shoulders and began vigorously to massage my neck.

'They thought you were dead, you know,' she remarked as she manipulated my muscles, twisting my head in a circular motion. 'A goner. You weren't moving. Just hanging there. How long had you been there?'

'Since about two, I think,' I answered, 'and you're hurting my neck.'

'It'll do you good. Nothing worthwhile comes of lethargy. The best things in life are borne of pain. You're a priest. You should know that.'

'I *was* a priest,' I remonstrated.

'Once a good man always a good man. Or bad. Men don't change. Mr van der Poehl,' she spoke as if he was not a relative but a passing acquaintance, 'was just the same. Started life as a little shit and ended it as a bigger turd. Only size alters, not character.'

I put my hand up, grabbing her wrist.

'That's enough! I want to be able to hold my head up without having a brace on my neck. If you must massage something, do my legs. They've got pins and needles.'

Mrs van der Poehl pulled a low stool from under the table upon which the television stood and knelt before me. She rolled my pyjamas up and began manipulating my toes as if they were not part of a living man but of an inanimate doll.

I looked around the room. I had not entered Mrs van der Poehl's flat before although I had been afforded a glimpse of the interior from time to time through the door. The rows of books she kept on a set of shelves by the television leaned against each other as if exhausted from being read, the gaps between them indications of where she had sold volumes to raise money. The curtains were faded to a uniform khaki. Under a day bed slept a tabby cat, oblivious to a blue budgerigar in a bamboo cage suspended from a hook in the ceiling which had once held up a ceiling fan. A vase of daisies on a sideboard might have been newly picked, had they not been plastic: I guessed they had been rinsed to shift the dust forever ekeing through the windows.

On the day bed above the cat was the pug dog, Pu Yi. It was an even uglier sight at close range than it was from a distance in the street. The animal was asleep on its side, its feet jutting out and the folds of skin on its face all the more contorted for being wedged up against a cushion. Its pose reminded me of the terrier's corpse from long ago.

In the stillness of the room, the scent of the obnoxious beast and the cat mingled with that of Mrs van der Poehl's perfume, which rose from where she knelt before me, bringing back an uneasy memory of supplicants, psalms and the stifling fumes of censers. Had I not been used to the street smells of the Orient, the waft of different effluvia from shops, drains and obscure foods, I am sure I would have recoiled from the curious odour.

Hanging upon the wall was a red lacquer frame containing the photograph of a dashing man in uniform. About thirty years old, he had a bushy moustache and his cap was tilted, giving him a debonair rather than raffish look. The portrait was faded from exposure to sunlight, the bottom so deteriorated that a dedication in black ink stood out starkly. The writing was cursive and effeminate. Under the photograph was a small glass-fronted box in which hung five medals, the metal tarnished and the ribbons, like the photograph, faded from sunlight.

'My husband,' Mrs van der Poehl said, following the direction of my gaze.

'Yes, I guessed it was.'

'He was a little prick!' she replied, not looking up from my foot.

I squinted at the photograph. The figure seemed to be wearing a Sam Brown belt.

'Was he in the British Army?'

'HKVDF,' she said adding, 'Hong Kong Volunteer Defence Force. Not a real soldier. He was Dutch, you know. From Java.'

'You've kept his photo,' I remarked. I might have added, despite what you think of him, but I did not: my bluntness does not extend to cruelty.

'Yes, I've kept it,' she answered glumly. 'God knows why.'

I knew why. Just as I have not destroyed my diary or those few possessions I have in the bank, so has she not discarded her husband's photograph. I suspect she feels as I do about memory. A vision of him will remain in her mind until the moment of death so the photograph is superfluous: why chuck it out with life's other trash? And yet photographs are such handy items for they refresh vision, keep alive memories in the mind's eye. Perhaps, I thought as I looked at him, she was keeping this picture because she preferred to think of him as a little shit rather than what he became. There again, it might have been love.

The budgerigar came to life, hopping from perch to cage bars and whistling. The cat raised its head languorously then went back to sleep.

Her flat is not unlike my own. It is untidy, filled with the petty detritus of a long life in a foreign land. The furniture is plain and cheap, such as one might find in the down-market shops in Mong Kok, the only Oriental piece positioned away from the window. It is a temple table, a narrow wooden trestle supported by curved legs which end in balls gripped by carved talons. It was originally painted in deep scarlet and gold but time has darkened it the colour of plum juice. Upon it, amidst a debris of old letters, a tea cup stuffed with pencils, a brown glass San Miguel beer ashtray containing loose change and a paperback book, there stood a head of Buddha carved from a light, rich wood.

It was not a Chinese Buddha with a sublime smile on its round chubby face, which I take to be the grin of an imbecile rather than a deity, but an Indian or Burmese one. At least a foot tall, the eyes were hooded so the bust looked demurely downwards. It might have been reading the letters or casting a disapproving glance at the mess strewn around it. The god's chin was slightly pointed, the nose thin and the mouth like a young girl's with the hint of a pout. In the middle of the figure's forehead was a tiny spot.

'The third eye,' I said without thinking.

'I'm sorry? What did you say?'

I stared for a moment at Mrs van der Poehl. Despite her having left my feet to work upon my shins, her fingers tugging my flesh, I had forgotten her presence. Once again, this time only briefly, I had wandered away from myself.

'Your Buddha . . .' I began.

'My husband's Buddha,' she corrected me. 'What about it?'

'It's a fine piece,' I said. 'Made of sandalwood?'

'It is. Rub it and the fragrance comes off to this day. Over a hundred years old. I don't know where he bought it. Or won it. Or stole it.'

'The mark in the forehead is where the third eye hides,' I said.

'Who needs a third eye!' Mrs van der Poehl exclaimed. 'I see too bloody much with a pair of the damned things. If god had intended us to see more, he'd have arranged it. You should know. You're a priest.'

'I *was* a priest,' I corrected her again. '*Was*, not *is*.'

We fell silent. I listened to the sounds drifting in from outside. A hawker was calling out his wares. The horn of a passing lorry wheezed asthmatically. A coolie carrying a heavy load shouted '*Wei! Wei!*'

as he pushed through the pedestrians, his shouting punctuated by the rattle of the steel shutters going up in the butcher's shop.

Closing my eyes, I imagined the people passing below. By doing so, focusing on specific realities, I hoped to cease my mental drifting.

The coolie with the load would be dressed in ragged shorts, bare to the waist with his muscles bunched under the weight of his pole and load. The hawker would be similarly dressed, but instead of having bare feet would be wearing a pair of old tennis shoes or flip-flop plastic sandals made to look like leather. Down the street, towards the junction with Ning Po Street, a police constable in a khaki uniform, his silver buttons gleaming and his revolver snug in a leather holster so polished it might have been glazed, would be filling in his beat notes, putting them in the grey galvanised box nailed to the wall of the herbalist's shop. The old man who operated a key-cutting service from a pavement stall like a wooden pulpit would just be setting out his tools: he would be wearing a pair of worn dark trousers and a white vest so bright and clean it would catch the sun.

I opened my eyes and found I was watching the cat. Its paws were twitching in a dream of chasing rats down the alleys or getting to grips with the budgerigar.

'I dream of dragons,' I admitted.

'We all dream of strange things,' Mrs van der Poehl replied, massaging my left knee. 'It's what comes of being old. We've seen it all, the likes of you and me . . . We've been there, done that and sent the postcard.'

The cat got up, idly stretched, left the shadow of the day bed and, leaping nimbly onto the window sill, settled there to await the sunlight.

'How do your legs feel?' Mrs van der Poehl enquired.

'Good. They feel good.'

'It's just a matter of restoring the circulation.'

'What do you dream of?' I asked.

'Me!' she retorted lightly. 'What makes you think I dream? That's a luxury only the innocent can afford.' Then, after thinking for a moment, she went on, 'I dream sometimes. Of handsome young men who dance with me all night long and give me diamonds.'

'Do you know these men?'

'No, not one of them. Figments of the imagination. But,' and her voice took on a hard edge, 'I can tell you there isn't a single man jack of them wears a soldier's kit.' She glanced fleetingly at the photograph on the wall. 'Sailors, airmen, young bucks in well-cut suits. And it's always in the twenties. When I was a girl.'

I looked at Mrs van der Poehl. Her grey hair was wispy where it was escaping from the bun which moved as she worked her hands against my flesh. It was not difficult to imagine her as a flapper girl. Despite her large nose, she must have been pretty, her eyes darkly seductive before the years filled them with caution, her skin soft before the Oriental sun sucked it dry.

'The other night,' she continued, 'I did the Charleston with a blonde, pretty lad decked out in one of those hideous shirts tourists wear. All printed palm trees and beaches. Awful dress sense. But what a beautiful boy he was . . .'

284

'My dragons are real,' I said. 'I've never seen a dragon, of course. But I know they're genuine. Somewhere, they lurk as alive and real as that cat of yours.'

'Just age!' Mrs van der Poehl rejoined. 'Your dragons are no more real than my dandies.'

'They seem it.'

'So they should! What use is a dream if it doesn't seem like reality?'

She finished her massaging and pulled my pyjama trouser legs down.

'Feel better?' she asked, not waiting for a reply. 'You should slow down, you know,' she went on. 'You're past it. Give up your pupil. I'm sure you could get by. I do.'

'It's not just that. I need to be active. You know what the Bible says? The devil finds work for idle hands.'

I looked into Mrs van der Poehl's eyes. There was no hint of condemnation, no suggestion of criticism.

'I have to keep on working,' I explained. 'If I stop, I'll die. I'm like . . .' I searched for an appropriate image '. . . like a shark. If it stops swimming, it drowns.'

'I know,' she said. 'It's the same with all men. Once you start to slow down, you think you're redundant and it scares the hell out of you. But you're wrong.'

She opened the window a fraction, warm air blowing in, ruffling the cat's fur.

'I'll tell you a story,' she said in a mock patronising tone. 'I'm sure it's one you know, being an old China hand. Like me!'

She brushed some cat hairs off the day bed, pushed the dog's malodorous hindquarters aside, smoothed

285

her skirt under her buttocks and sat down. The bed creaked and the budgerigar, assuming the sound to be an intruder flying in through the window, set up a belligerent twittering.

'Once upon a time,' she began, as if recounting the tale to a child, 'there was an emperor of China called Tai Lung. He lived in the Forbidden City surrounded by henchmen and mandarins, eunuchs and concubines and guards. One day, worrying about an uprising by a distant warlord, he was walking in the gardens, deep in thought, when a peacock strutted towards him. It was a magnificent bird. Its feathers were azure and emerald, glistening in the sunlight like a box of gems. To the emperor's surprise, the bird perched before him on a rock statue and began to speak. "You are old and worried about your kingdom just as I am old and was concerned about mine," squawked the bird. "What know you of the affairs of state?" Tai Lung said sharply. "Everything," the peacock replied. "I have subjects I must appease, the whole of the Imperial Gardens to rule over. Just as you have China. But it was getting beyond me. I could no longer chase the younger cocks away, no longer tread the peahens as I did." This struck a nerve with Tai Lung who had resorted to his herbalist of late to remedy a certain lacking in the Imperial bedroom department. His favourite concubine was growing sullen. "So what did you do?" the emperor asked. "I let the young cocks take charge of the garden," answered the peacock. "They chase the sparrows and sort out their own squabbles. I concentrate on my harem of hens and leave them the rest. That way, I still rule but I don't have all the cares." The emperor thought it over, called his

286

council and delegated responsibility for the warlord to his princes. The herbalist was dismissed and the concubine smiled once more.'

'No doubt,' I remarked, 'the herbalist was executed and the emperor ate the peacock.'

'Perhaps,' Mrs van der Poehl agreed. 'Peacock is delicious. But the lesson was learned. You should heed it. Slow down. Let younger men take on the world. It's theirs, you know. Not ours. Not yours. We've had our turn and made a bloody mess of it.'

'That's not a true story,' I said. 'There's never been an Emperor Tai Lung. Big Dragon. You made it up.'

'What does it matter?' Mrs van der Poehl replied. 'The moral holds water even if the narrative leaks like a colander.'

I rose to my feet. My legs felt stronger than they had for days.

'I must go,' I said. 'I've things to do . . .'

I went to the door of the flat and turned the handle.

'We should stick together, us old hands,' Mrs van der Poehl said. 'We're a dying breed.'

'Yes,' I agreed pensively. 'We are.' I opened the door and stepped out into the hallway. The air was cool and smelt of disinfectant and dust. 'Thank you for bringing my legs back to life,' I said.

'Don't go dreaming of dragons on the roof again,' Mrs van der Poehl advised. 'And remember you can't fly. Only Peter Pan and the angels can.'

As soon as the words left her mouth I saw, as clearly as if I was there again, the girls entering the yard in Wuchow, a lifetime away, their white blouses catching the rays of the hot, high sun.

'Stephen! Stephen!'

It was Father Callaghan's voice, urgent and insistent. I put down the censer I was polishing, folded my rag and screwed the top on the Brasso bottle, genuflected quickly to the altar and ran to the chapel door. Just inside the mission gate was a figure sitting on the ground with its back to the stonework. Ah Fong was by its side with Father Callaghan standing over the pair of them.

'What is it?' I called out.

'Come!' Father Callaghan shouted. 'Lend a hand, will you?'

On joining him, I saw Ah Fong was tending a Chinese youth wearing the remnants of a uniform.

'One of the mandarin's cohorts?' I asked.

'No,' Father Callaghan said, 'he's a soldier. There was a detachment in the town yesterday. Moved on now. Something to do with the prefect. Help us carry him in.'

I put my arm round the soldier. He was little more than a boy, perhaps seventeen or eighteen years of age. His clothing stank of sweat and smoke but there was also a faint, acrid stench about him I could not place. With Father Callaghan, I lifted him by the shoulders: I was surprised he was so light. We carried him into our little infirmary, a room once used as a store but equipped to take any of the sick who might come to us. We laid him face down on a *k'ang*. As soon as his skin touched the quilt he began to shiver in rapid spasms, his eyes rolling and his tongue incessantly licking his lips. Beads of perspiration appeared on his nape.

'Malaria?' I suggested.

'No,' Father Callaghan said and, turning to Ah Fong, ordered, '*Dung shui*, Ah Fong.'

This, I knew from the smattering of Cantonese I was picking up, meant cold water. Ah Fong ladled some into a bowl whilst Father Callaghan unlocked our medicine box and rummaged in it. I wiped the youth's neck and he ceased shivering, craned round and, looking up into my face, muttered something I did not comprehend.

'What he saying?' I asked Ah Fong.

'He say you good man. *San foo* good man.'

'Cut the legs off his *fu*,' Father Callaghan instructed. 'Above the knee.'

I took a pair of scissors to the material and cut round his thigh. It was not until I went to his feet to pull the tubes of cotton clear I smelt the unidentifiable stench again, a little stronger.

'Take off his shoes,' Father Callaghan commanded. 'Be gentle.'

I put my hand on the sole of one shoe and pulled carefully. The youth thrashed his arms on the *k'ang* and hissed through his teeth.

'I hold him,' Ah Fong said. 'You pull quick-quick, master.'

I did as I was told and a wave of noxious gas hit my face so strongly that I reeled backwards, the bile rising to my throat.

'Gangrene,' Father Callaghan said ominously. 'Take off his other shoe.'

Holding my breath, I did as requested. Both the

young man's feet were pussed. What was not livid red was a glutinous pale green.

'Can we amputate . . .?' I began but Father Callaghan shook his head.

'If we were the most learned surgeons in Dublin, we'd be at a loss. There's nothing we can do for the poor soul except make his last days a little more peaceful.'

For the next twenty minutes, as Ah Fong held the youth down and talked continuously to him in a monotone, Father Callaghan and I cleaned the wounds on his feet as best we could. Although the flesh was putrid to just above the ankles there seemed no break to the skin except on the soles of the feet.

'He must have walked a long way,' I observed, 'to have so injured himself.'

'Oh, he crawled here,' Father Callaghan said. 'Look at his knees. Raw. He's not walked for some days. The wounds on his feet were not caused by marching. He has committed some trifling wrong and this is his punishment.'

'His punishment?' I replied.

Father Callaghan started to dab iodine on the wounds. I expected the young man to start writhing as the medicine stung but he remained quite still.

'He can't feel it,' Father Callaghan remarked as if reading my thoughts. 'The local nerves are gone. Long gone.'

'What was his punishment?' I asked.

'An age-old one. They lie the miscreant on his front and tie him down. Then a man with a light switch of flat bamboo starts to tap lightly on the skin. Tap, tap, tap. For four or five hours, the administrator of the punishment changing as the arms tire. It does not hurt at first. This is nothing like a caning from a schoolmaster. Thrash, thrash and over with. Oh, no! After a time, all the little veins under the skin rupture. The bamboo carries on its tap, tap, tap. The flesh swells and the bruising spreads so the complete sole will lose its nerves. Then, in no time at all, gangrene sets in. Sometimes it's done to the soles of the feet, sometimes to the thighs and sometimes to the fleshy part at the base of the buttocks. It's called the *light bamboo punishment*. It's a death sentence, though.'

'And his crime?'

'Nothing grand,' Father Callaghan answered, 'you can be sure. Perhaps he disobeyed an order he did not hear. Dropped his gun, perhaps. This is China, Father Stephen, not the Household Cavalry of the Queen of England.'

The wounds cleaned and bandaged, Father Callaghan gave the young man an opium pill and he was soon asleep.

'Surely,' I suggested as we left the infirmary, closing the door behind us and leaving one of our girls to look over the patient, 'we could cut his feet off.'

'No, Father Stephen, we could not.'

'But they do it at sea,' I interrupted. 'They get the sailor drunk, in a stupor, cut off the damaged limb, cover the wound in boiling tar and leave it. The pitch sets and . . .'

I wanted so much to save this man, to bring him back from the door of death, rescue him from the barbarity of his punishment. I could not believe a life could be so discarded because of a petty misdemeanour. Perhaps I also wanted to save him to atone for the captain's victim.

'We're too late. The corruption'll be right through

291

his system by now. Besides, if we cut his feet off and he survived — then what? Another cripple begging in the streets of Wuchow. Another man living in torment and fear of death because he knows he'll go to his ancestors incomplete. No, Father Stephen, we can do nothing but pray for his soul.'

I returned to the chapel and the censer I was polishing, feeling a terrible, bitter rage deeper than any I had ever known. I hated not the Chinese, nor their barbarity. It was not the cruelty I abhorred.

It was my God who had looked down upon His world, at His creation fashioned in His own image and let this abomination happen.

☯

This morning, I took myself along to the forecourt of the temple where I installed myself, sitting quite peacefully on the stone bench, and set about reading today's edition of *Wah Kiu Yat Po*, the oldest of Hong Kong's Chinese newspapers.

I have purchased a copy almost every day since it was first published in the summer of 1925. It is an ironic title where I am concerned for it translates as *Overseas Chinese Daily News*. The implication is that Chinese who live in Hong Kong are exiled from their native lands, which is bunkum. If anything, Hong Kong is more like the true China than its vast neighbour, now the latter has ejected its emperor, its Taoist and Buddhist religions and its village culture and replaced it with a chairman, the doctrine according to Marx and the commune system. In Hong Kong, temples thrive that would, over the wire border, be derelict shells: the hillsides of Hong Kong are scattered with tombs swept clean each year by the living in respect for the dead which, in China, would be just hollows in the bracken.

This aside, it is even more ironic I should read this paper. I am not an overseas Chinese. I am an adopted one.

The newspaper costs me twenty cents. I buy it from a news-vendor who runs a stand in the entrance to a stairway in Ning Po Street. He may be found there only in the morning, until half past nine, his main trade being office and shop staff on their way to work. He does not call out headlines to attract trade, nor does he hang a billboard in the street with the main news hurriedly scribbled upon it with the thickest of writing brushes but relies entirely upon those who know he is there.

His stall is little more than a narrow box of planks screwed into the wall of the hallway which, when not in use, folds flat against the plasterwork so as not to hinder those who use the building. Even when operating, the fold-down shelf projects no more than a foot from the wall.

I know the news-vendor as Lam: his given names are unknown to me. He is in his late twenties and tubercularly thin with a malformed left hand, his fingers being mere stubs of flesh projecting from a club of bone where his palm should be. As if to compensate for this flaw, his right hand is equipped with slender, sensitive fingers like those of a musician. Had he two such hands he could be an accomplished *pipa* player. Not only is his left hand defective but he is also exceedingly short-sighted and wears spectacles with large lenses which look like those of an old-fashioned bicycle lamp. These give him an owlish appearance, magnifying his eyes to at least twice their natural size: when he blinks he might be pulling blinds down over the windows of his mind rather than flaps of skin to clean the street grit from his vision.

Lam is a gentle character, soft-spoken and kind. One morning, I saw him feeding a lame sparrow with crumbs from a bun he had half-eaten. The bird had only one leg upon which it hopped, effectively but clumsily. I was sure this was Lam's only repast that morning and was so moved as to be prompted to speak to him.

'My friend,' I said as I handed over two ten-cent coins, 'I think you spoil the sparrow.'

'How is that?' he replied.

'In this city there is much food to be had by birds. To be served with a fresh sweet bun rather than having to hunt for it is indeed a luxury.'

'That is so,' he said, 'but there is no harm in it. When I am done, the bird will still be able to find his food. Let him share my good fortune for once.'

I left with my newspaper under my arm, humbled and filled with a sense of privilege that I had been fortunate to see such noble justice, a crippled man dividing his precious luck with a crippled bird.

For months after Lam set up his business, I wondered how on earth he made a living from it. He sells about 300 newspapers a day, stocking not just *Wah Kiu Yat Po* but also *Sing Tao* and *Kung Sheung* with a number of lesser, more esoteric broadsides and Chinese comics, but these cannot bring in a living wage when one considers he must pay rent to the landlord of the building for use of the hallway and protection money to the local Red Poles to ensure his wooden lock-up shelves remain attached to the wall. So concerned was I for this gentle young man I once, some time ago, surreptitiously followed him after his close of business.

At nine thirty, he folded away his shelving, sold at a discount what remained of his morning delivery to a store on the corner of Shanghai Street and disappeared in the direction of Mong Kok. I shadowed him to a back alley in Tung Choi Street, where he met a man standing by a large aluminium cabin trunk. Money changed hands and Lam was presented with a wooden box the size of a large attaché case. It was painted green with Chinese characters stencilled on the side but I was too far away and could not make them out.

The case in his right hand, Lam went to Nathan Road and boarded a bus going south: I was fortunate enough to catch another immediately behind his own. At the Star Ferry, he left the bus and travelled across the harbour on the lower deck where coolies and the poor are obliged to ride: it is against the ferry by-laws for cargo to be taken onto the upper deck. Once in Central District, Lam made his way to Peddar Street, where he squatted on the pavement, opened the box and wrapped a black, stained cloth around his club hand, holding it in place with a thick rubber band cut, I should think, from a bicycle inner tube. This done, he undid some catches and, as if performing a magician's trick, transmuted the box from an attaché-type case into a shoe-shine stand complete with a foot-rest. Within minutes, he was in business.

I laughed at myself, at my stupidity, at my allowing

emotions to cloud my certain knowledge of Chinese acumen: that is, wherever there is life there is business to be done.

Today's edition of *Wah Kiu Yat Po* held little to capture my attention. The front page carried news of a bicycle-bomb attack in Saigon, general South-East Asian politics and a report of a kidnapping attempt on Hong Kong Island which had been bungled. The sun was warm but not yet too hot. The old lady in the temple was busy sweeping the stone floors, the scratching swish of her broom loud enough to overcome the traffic. I put the paper down on the bench beside me and leaned forward with my forearms on my legs. As I was wearing my *sam* and *fu*, albeit with an ordinary shirt, and having had my grey hair cut short as Chinese men of my age do, I very much doubt if anyone but the most eagle-eyed observer would have seen I was anything other than Chinese.

When I sit like this in the temple precinct, I let my mind empty. If I were more energetic, or less creaky of joint, I might do a bit of *tai chi*, shadow-boxing in slow motion with the elements of earth, air, fire and water. It has the same effect, clearing the brain of extraneous thoughts in preparation for meditation or peaceful, detached consideration of the metaphysical problems and obstacles of human existence.

My mind thus blank for a while, I became aware of a brief, quick movement on the ground beneath one of the shrubbery pots across the forecourt. I concentrated on the shadow of the pot. It was not until it moved again that I saw the gecko. It was two inches long and coloured in the dull khaki of its kind, its head raised and its front legs holding its forequarters clear of the ground. Aware the reptile is primarily nocturnal, I wondered what it was doing in the mid-morning, risking the presence of sharp beaks and heavy feet.

It bobbed its head a few times: this was the motion which had caught my eye. I looked around the ground near the creature, careful to move my eyes but not my head. There were no tasty insect morsels in view.

Quite suddenly, I saw a second gecko. It was near the base of the banyan tree and facing the first. It, too, was bobbing its head. A cloud shifted across the sun and, as soon as the shadow was over the temple forecourt, the banyan gecko went for the pot gecko, streaking over the open ground between them with such speed my eye could scarcely follow it. The creature skidded to a halt a few inches from the pot and they faced each other. The sun came out and the banyan gecko, realising it was in the sunlight, shifted its stance into the shade which, I presumed, the other thought its own. This was too much for the pot gecko which lunged at the newcomer. They thrashed together, a minuscule haze of dust rising from their conflict.

The confrontation was over quickly. The banyan gecko fled across the open ground towards my bench. I shifted my foot deliberately and it swerved in mid-flight to vanish under another of the pots. The victor, meanwhile, stood his ground then, with less haste, moved under the base of his own pot.

I considered this little contretemps for some minutes, drawing the same conclusion I do whenever I watch sparrows jousting on the tenement roof, dogs circling each other in the side-streets or cats spitting a warning to other feline intruders in the alleyways.

It is this: in the world of nature, where the animals live and rule, you may observe them conducting elaborate rituals but never see them going through the absurd, indecorous fooleries of religion. They have no time for the mystical, the magical, the marvellous. They are not governed by gods or goals. They exist for the sake of living, going about their business of survival without question.

Only men engage in such gratuitous nonsense, abiding by ceremony, governing themselves with liturgies and theologies. Some would say it is the price they pay for being intelligent. I suggest it is the cost of being not sufficiently intelligent to see through it all.

I have today purchased a new dressing gown, a full-length garment in heavy, crimson silk brocade with wide collars and, as it was tailored for a *gweilo*, it is large and generous. I have lost some weight over the past few years and can consequently wrap it substantially around my frame.

The shop in Mody Road from which I purchased it is owned by a man called Lau Kui-shing, whom I first met through Mr Wu. It seems they share the same ancestral village, somewhere in Kwangtung province, and the same vice.

Lau is a jolly man in his early sixties, short and curiously plump, which is uncommon for a Chinese. As they grow older they tend to become sinewy, wiry men, their bones bending as if not designed to carry even such a little flesh for so many years.

In this respect as in many others, I am like a Chinese: for that is what is happening to me. It pleases me. I regard myself as a Chinese for I have lived three-quarters of my natural life in China, spent my years eating the food and drinking the drink, breathing the air and speaking the language. What is more, although I suppose there is sufficient reason for me to wish otherwise, I am proud of it. I do not want to be a European, some high-and-mighty conqueror of the native masses, a patronising colonial with his all-too-perfect laws and his universal language, his wide-eyed pseudo-innocence and his grasping fingers, his hygienic, risk-free life and impeccable gods. I prefer to be one of those men who has discovered enough to know his own mind, to know he wishes to change and be another.

Lau's shop is crammed with merchandise. It is what he calls a general tourist mart, having seen the word in an advertisement in *Life* magazine: it showed a photograph of a Buick car before a glossy showroom over which were emblazoned the words *Stark's Car Mart*. Cars are one of the few items Lau seems not to purvey although I suspect, if you wanted one, he would know a man who could provide it at a discount for cash.

The window of the shop is a rich kaleidoscope of padded cotton coats and brocade smoking jackets, lace blouses, embroidered slippers, sandalwood fans, small boxes of round ivory balls which, it is said, reduce tension if fondled, rattan coolie hats and children's skull-tight red and black silk hats with pom-poms on the top, octagonal card wastepaper baskets with appliqué cotton Chinese dolls on the side and lingerie. A hand-written sign reads *Many good price – pleas appley within*. The counters and shelves carry miniature ancient sword paper-knives in bone and brass scabbards, carved sailing junks ranging in size from a few inches to three feet tall, toys made of cheap plastic and racks of postcards depicting rickshaws, the Star Ferry, a crowded Tsim Sha Tsui street, the Peak Tram, the Hongkong and Shanghai Bank, a temple forecourt (cleared of beggars by the photographer) and two infants squatting on the deck of a sampan shovelling rice into their mouths.

'Good morning,' Lau said brightly as I walked in. His head was bent over an invoice book and a parcel wrapped in green tar-paper tied around with cord. The address on it was in Australia: he conducts a mail order business for former customers.

'Please,' he went on. 'Sit down. Take the weight off.' That is a phrase he picked up as he did *mart*. 'You wan' a beer, soft drink? San Mig? Green Spot orange?' Then he looked up and recognised me. 'Hi, *san foo*! Morning! *Nei ho ma?*'

'*Ho, ho.* I am well. And you? How's business?'

'Business good!' he exclaimed emphatically. 'One week, four cruise ship. Much business done. I run out of cotton hand-ker-cheefs. Never before.'

'That's bad,' I observed.

'No p'oblum. More coming from Tsuen Wan today. I got a friend . . .'

His voice tailed off and he winked. So much business is conducted in Hong Kong through friends and friends of friends. Lau will have paid a little over the odds to buy up someone else's order.

'So! You wan' a beer?'

'I'll have a Green Spot,' I replied.

He shouted out to the rear of the shop and an old woman came hobbling in with a bottle in one hand and a straw in the other. She had bound feet, her legs ending in stubs encased in what looked like painted wooden blocks.

'My mother,' Lau remarked.

I nodded politely to the old lady and made some comment of respect but she merely smirked toothlessly, put the drink on the counter, handed me the straw and hobbled off.

'She no can hear.' Lau touched his ear. 'Deaf. No sound. Good woman.'

I put the straw in the bottle and sucked. The orange juice was sickly sweet.

'So, what can I do for you?' Lau asked.

'A dressing gown,' I said. 'I want a dressing gown.'

'Silk? Cotton? Cotton polyester? Wool cotton mix? Very warm. I got good cotton one. Make in China.'

Before I could reply, he had whisked a packet from a shelf, ripped the cellophane open and spread the garment across the counter. It was light blue with the character *sow*, meaning *long life*, stitched in navy on the back.

'Good quality cotton. From India. Not Madras, not so good. Twelve dollars, for you seven. Old frien', old customer. *Gweilo*, not tourist. Live Hong Kong long time.'

'It's good,' I commented, feeling the cloth, 'but I want silk. Silk brocade.'

'Ah! You got good taste!' Lau exclaimed.

301

I picked my dressing gown from a choice of four. Two were deep blue, one black and the other crimson. They were all heavy, with double thickness sashes and intricate embroidery. The black gown portrayed clouds and hills and was a sober-looking piece, more befitting a man of my age and position, but the crimson one had a highly detailed pattern of trees and lakes, houses hidden in pine copses, people on sampans, temples on islands and bamboo groves beside cottages. Whereas the predominant colour in the pictures on the black item was silver with some blue, the crimson gown was realistic, with greens and browns, yellows and greys. I picked the latter.

'Good choice,' Lau congratulated me, wrapping the gown in brown paper and sealing it with sticky tape. 'Usually fifty-five dollar but for you, thirty-five.'

I handed over the bills. He did not count them. He trusted me just as I trusted him. A tourist would be unwise to do so.

Now, back in my flat, I am sitting in the cane chair, naked except for the gown. It is mid-afternoon and I feel decadent. I might be a latter-day Noël Coward. The silk is cold against my warm flesh despite the fact I have been wearing it for twenty minutes. Silk has a wonderful capacity, like jade, to stay cool, to lose heat quickly when removed from a source of warmth.

The dressing gown becomes me. I would gladly wear it in the street if I were not certain to be justifiably gawked at and, later, arrested. Yet I did not purchase it in preference for the black gown because of its flamboyance or garishness. I bought it because it reminds me of something long lost in the mist of years, something I should not wish to recall for, like so much in life, the joy was tinged with sorrow.

This is a weakness in me. I should not be prone to such madcap purchases. I am not that wealthy a man. The cotton dressing gown with *sow* on the reverse would have done me just as well even if the character displayed on my back would have been not a little ironic. It would just as effectively have covered my scrappy body, given me some modesty should someone enter my flat and it too would be cool to wear. I should reprimand myself. I suppose, by recognising my weakness, I am doing so.

The fact remains it brings back to me, as if it was only yesterday, the sight of Mei-ling in all her finery.

And I bought it because it reminds me of one of God's broken promises.

In the mission yard, between the chapel and the nursery, there hung a barometer in a heavy oak frame beneath which was a thermometer. As I passed it, I tapped the glass with my knuckle: the needle did not shift from a reading of 30¾ inches of mercury. The silver column in the thermometer registered 89°.

In the shade of the eaves by the nursery door, Ah Mee was sitting on a low stool, a sleeping infant in her arms. She, too, was dozing, her eyes shut and her head drooped forwards.

The heat was intolerable. Although I was dressed in my Chinese garb, sweat dripped between my shoulder-blades and soaked through the armpits of

303

my dark blue cotton *sam*. I peered into the water butt which collected rainwater from the chapel roof: it was empty save for a stagnant inch at the bottom, under the surface of which flicked mosquito larvæ.

As I passed the window to the mission office, I heard Father Callaghan talking Cantonese. His voice was quiet as if he was afraid to be eavesdropped upon. The person with him spoke in a gruff, guttural voice from which I could not determine the owner's sex.

My shadow must have darkened the stretched paper pane of the window for, no sooner had I passed than I heard Father Callaghan call me. Without hurrying, for the heat was telling upon me, I made my way to the office.

'Come in,' Father Callaghan said as I knocked upon the door, which was ajar.

On entering, I saw he was in the company of an elderly Chinese woman. She wore the ordinary clothing of a peasant but the material was of a superior quality silk and she wore a fine jade bracelet.

'Please, sit down,' Father Callaghan invited. 'I have some news you must hear.' He said a few words in Cantonese to the woman who nodded in my direction, studying my face as Father Callaghan spoke. 'This woman is a matchmaker. She has come to us with a proposition.'

For a moment, I wondered what a woman was doing making matches and asked, 'What do we want with more matches? We have a dozen boxes in the store. Swan Vestas . . .'

Father Callaghan grinned and said, 'I think you

misunderstand, Father Stephen. She is not a manu-
facturer of lucifers but an arranger of marriages. All
marriages are so conducted in China.'

I laughed slightly at my foolishness and went on,
'All the more reason she should have no business
here.'

'On the contrary,' Father Callaghan replied, 'she
wishes to arrange a marriage between one of our girls
and a young man.'

I was at a loss as to what to say. It was my
impression our girls did not leave us for marriage
but for employment in Hong Kong or Macau.

'The girl in question,' Father Callaghan continued,
'is Mei-ling. You will not know them all as yet
by name, but she is one of our more comely
maidens, in the Chinese concept of beauty, and
certainly one of our most accomplished. She is
also one of those who has offered herself to Christ
Jesus.'

'You mean she wishes to be a nun?' I asked.

'No. Not that. Just she has professed her faith in
Our Lord.'

I considered the situation for a moment: to marry
one of our saved Christian girls to a heathen was a
quandary for which I had not been prepared in the
seminary.

'Who is the intended husband?' I enquired.

'The eldest son of Kung whom you, Father Stephen,
will remember as the purveyor of those particularly
fine eggs and who is the temporary employer of this
good lady before us.'

He grinned and I could, just for an instant, taste
the vile thing once more in my mouth, feel the
consistency of the pellucid green-glass-like albumen

slide down my gullet, followed by the dry cloying of the yolk.

'I do recall him,' I admitted.

'Kung is a Christian and so is his son. A sturdy young man of twenty-three. He keeps the chicken farm from which his father obtains his eggs. The lad has taken the name of Matthew in addition to his Chinese name. He is thus either Kung Chi-ching or Matthew Kung.'

'What shall we do?' I said: I was not sure if Father Callaghan would be in favour of the marriage. 'Need we contact the bishop?'

'No, of course not. It's up to us. To me, as you are so newly come amongst us. And it's my opinion to give the union our blessing. What better way to cement the foundations of our faith than to see it rising from the holy state of matrimony? Do you not agree with this?'

I was in no position to reply in the negative: furthermore, I agreed it was a perfect means by which to bring Christ to the people.

Father Callaghan then entered into a lengthy conversation with the matchmaker. She was not only the broker but also the comptroller of the timetable, the fixer of arrangements and the bringer together of the many strands of the complex affairs of love. The couple, she reported, requested a Christian marriage but along the lines of the Chinese fashion. The right date had been ascertained by studying the two parties' horoscopes and the almanacs, the auspicious day being the following Wednesday week.

In the spirit of compromise I had seen him display over the prayer-flags in the mission, Father Callaghan agreed to all the old woman's suggestions, which greatly pleased her. The wedding, it was decided upon, would be a Chinese service in every respect but the actual religious content.

When the matchmaker had departed, Father Callaghan called Ah Fong and Sister Margaret into the office. There was a discussion lasting several hours, each of us given a series of tasks in preparation for the big day. Sister Margaret was to draw on the mission funds and procure the bridal gown, Ah Fong was to act as the go-between with the Kung family and I was to find a dowry.

This was by no means an easy matter. For several days I spent every spare minute I could afford avidly reading through both volumes of Dr Doolittle's detailed publication, *Social Life of the Chinese*, seeking out what tradition and etiquette demanded be in a dowry purse. I questioned Ah Fong several times an hour and, eventually, decided it was best to put some money aside in the form of *lai see*, coins placed in a vermilion envelope as a gift. And yet I felt, if the marriage was to be at least partly Occidental, I should also provide a bride's drawer. I purchased a fine cotton quilt, some cooking utensils, two hard lacquer pillows and an assortment of lesser domestic items, placing these in a rattan hamper Ah Fong produced from a store-room. By the day before the wedding, I was ready.

The chapel was cleaned from top to bottom by the girls, who were in an increasing frenzy of excitement as the day drew nigh. The stone steps were swept and even the *hutong*, where it passed the mission, was cleared of the garbage usually accumulated in it.

On the evening before the wedding day, Father Callaghan and I sat together on the mission roof, close to the bell, our gins and quinine in our hands. The sun was down, a pale moon low in the sky.

For a long time, we were silent, each of us keeping our own council, watching the twilight deepen and listening to the night sounds. Even though the air was hot, we could hear the call of the boatmen on the river, the cry of peddlers and the humming sound of distant conversation at the food stalls in the street at the end of the *hutong*. At last, Father Callaghan broke our silence.

'You know, Father Stephen,' he said in a quiet voice, 'I feel a strange man tonight. Somehow, I believe this marriage is not just a matter of the old biddy fixing things up, nor is it merely a matter of two young people falling in love – if, indeed, they've seen each other at all, save in a service here or walking in the street. It's not in the nature of the Chinese for intended partners necessarily to know one another. Quite often, they depend solely upon the descriptive powers of the matchmaker. No,' his voice fell even quieter as he gazed into the looming night, 'I think there's more to it.'

'How do you mean, Father?' I asked.

'When that old woman entered my office, I know I should have felt a repulsion. After all, she is little more than a pimp in the service of Venus. And yet, as she came in, I felt a wondrous calm befall the room. When she spoke, she was reason itself which surprised me greatly. We stand in her way with our practices. If Christianity became strong in China, her sisters in the guild of marriage brokers would soon be out of business. And, take my word for it, she's not a poor woman from her employ.'

He sipped his drink, sneezing at the tartness of the

quinine: he had felt a twinge of fever that day and had doubled his evening dose.

'Where I should have felt evil, I felt goodness,' he went on. 'I'm sure she's as wicked as the prong on Satan's tail, but she came to us as a messenger of the Lord. Albeit unwittingly. You know, I'm convinced this marriage upon which we embark tomorrow is one truly made in Heaven.'

I looked at his face. There were tears in his eyes. He sensed me looking at him.

'It's the quinine,' he said, his voice marginally louder. 'It brings not only an itch to the nose but water to the eyes as well. Come, Father Stephen,' he stood up, 'we'd best get down to our beds. It's a long day tomorrow.'

We made our way along the girls' corridor. It was a hive of activity, of happy laughter and giggles. Mei-ling was sitting upon her bunk in the company of a Chinese woman whom I had not seen before: she was certainly not one of our number.

'Who is this?' I enquired.

'She's the wife of the tea-house owner where you did your pants up,' Father Callaghan said. 'I've asked her to do us this service.'

As I watched, the woman entwined two red threads about a hair on Mei-ling's forehead and then, with a deft pull, tugged it free by the roots.

'What is she doing?'

'*Hoi min*,' Father Callaghan explained. 'It is a ritual which means *showing the face*. The hair is pulled out so the bride may be more open to her bridegroom.'

'Why not ask Sister Margaret to perform the deed?'

Father Callaghan laughed briefly and said, 'She somewhat lacks the qualification. For the sake of the bride, it should be done by someone who has borne many sons. The tea-house owner has fathered seven boys. And not a single daughter. I could hardly find a better woman for the job.'

I took to my bed, lying upon my quilt naked save for a towel folded about my waist: this was not a matter of modesty but of wisdom for if the stomach was bare it was considered an invitation to the fever. The night was hot and I fell into an uncomfortable sleep, occasionally bothered by the hatchlings from the water butt.

The following morning, at about eleven o'clock, the ceremony of the wedding commenced. Had we been conducting a Chinese religious marriage, the bride would have gone by sedan chair to her groom's family home but this was dispensed with: instead, the groom came to the mission but not to the girls' building. Instead, he lingered before the chapel door, wearing a black coat on top of a blue *cheong sam* with a red cotton sash draped over his shoulder and tied at the waist: on his head he had a black hat with a red tassel upon it.

'He is wearing five articles of attire,' Father Callaghan said to me as we waited inside the chapel door, 'in accordance with the principles of *yin* and *yang*. Being a male, he must have an odd number whilst she must have even. He has two pieces of underclothing, a pair of *fu* you cannot see, his *cheong sam* and his jacket.'

Mei-ling was to arrive from the girl's quarters as if it was her home. Ah Fong had arranged a sedan chair be hired for this very short but crucial journey.

At the time decreed by the matchmaker in collaboration with a Taoist necromancer, the chair appeared around the corner of the building and halted by the chapel door. Matthew Kung knocked on the side of the chair with a fan, the curtain opening to allow Mei-ling to step out.

I was speechless at her beauty. She wore a scarlet embroidered skirt with a long black silk overcoat and an elaborate wide collar such as the mandarin wore. On her head was balanced an ornate, intricate head-dress of silver and gilt inlaid with small pearls and the azure feathers of a kingfisher. Over the whole of this was draped a red gossamer veil of thin silk.

Father Callaghan smiled much as I would guess a father might at the wedding of his favourite daughter.

The bridegroom lifted the veil and I saw Mei-ling's face was heavily made up with cosmetics, her skin whitened and her eyes and lips accentuated by dark powder and red paste.

Ah Fong, standing to one side, ignited a string of firecrackers which produced an acrid cloud of smoke and a blizzard of charred confetti. The explosions were amplified in the *hutong* so it sounded as if the whole of the thunder stored in the heavens was echoing to celebrate the occasion. Sister Margaret appeared with a tray of smouldering charcoal which she placed upon the steps to the chapel. The groom lifted Mei-ling off her feet and, carrying her, stepped over the fire whilst, above her head, Ah Fong contrived to hold a tray containing a rice bowl, some chopsticks, a tea cup and a small dish such as one spits bones into at a meal.

'All this would normally be done at the home of the groom,' Father Callaghan stated, 'but we decided it should be done here. We cannot entirely avoid their traditions. Besides, they're entering their house here. The house they share with Our Lord.'

'I wonder what Rome would think,' I suggested.

Father Callaghan grinned the same kind of smirk he had when I ate the groom's father's egg.

'They would disapprove, Father Stephen. Be quite certain of it. But, you know my friend, I really don't give a tinker's curse!'

The congregation entered the church. The couple were led to the altar where they knelt. I did not take a part in the service but watched, listening as Father Callaghan stood before Christ on his Cross and uttered the words so familiar to lovers at the time of the consummation of their love before God, albeit in a tongue I could not understand.

'Father,' he began in Cantonese, 'when you created mankind you willed that man and wife should be one. Bind Mei-ling and Matthew Chi-ching in the loving union of marriage and make their love fruitful so that they may be living witnesses to your divine love in the world . . .'

After the service, in accordance with Chinese tradition, tea and sweetmeats were served. Had this been a heathen Chinese wedding, the repast would have been given in the bridal chamber, but our refectory served the purpose instead. Gifts were made, the dowry presented. Each of the mission girls paraded before the bride and presented her with *lai see* provided by Father Callaghan from the sea chest in his room wherein he kept the

312

mission funds. Eventually, at about four o'clock, the wedding party left and the mission became suddenly silent.

'Our first,' Father Callaghan remarked as the sound of the newly-weds and their guests disappeared from the end of the *hutong*.

'First?' I answered.

'Our first marriage. The first, I pray, of many. What a fine start we could have witnessed today, Father Stephen. How good it would be if all our girls could be so accommodated instead of, most of them, heading for a world of servitude.'

'Are you suggesting we start a matchmaking service of our own?'

'Heavens above, no!' he laughed, then, after a moment said, 'But it's an idea. Just think of it! We'd find happiness for all our poor girls, spread the work of Our Lord and earn a good matchmaker's fee for the mission coffers. We could kill a lot of little birds with that one stone.'

We went into the chapel to tidy the altar and make ready for Mass. Father Callaghan went down on his knees before Christ.

'Give them years of happiness in the Light of Your Love, Lord,' I heard him say. 'Let them be an example of Your Goodness to their fellows and bring others unto You.'

It was twelve days later when I next saw Mei-ling. She was lying on the flags in the mission yard, Father Callaghan at her side, her head resting in Sister Margaret's lap and surrounded by all the girls. In her hair was a white woollen flower fashioned like a chrysanthemum. She was fighting for breath.

'What is it?' I asked, falling to the ground by Father Callaghan's side.

'She's killing herself,' he whispered.

'How?' I said. I could not understand it. 'Why?'

'Matthew Kung's been killed. Butchered,' he answered. His voice was dense with anger as he touched the blossom. 'This is the custom of mourning. It is called *dai hau*.'

As I gazed down upon her bloodless cheeks, I remembered his comment to me by the flowerboats: the Chinese are in possession of remarkable methods of self-murder.

'Who killed him?'

'The Harmony Fists. He was found this morning in the paddock where they keep the hens.'

He took the flower out of her hair and handed it to me.

'But why?' I asked.

Father Callaghan made me no answer at first then, through clenched teeth, he said, 'Because he was one of us.'

Putting his hand upon Mei-ling's brow, he stroked it gently and started to recite the Extreme Unction in a quiet, almost inaudible voice.

Mei-ling was sucking hard at the air, her face contorted with effort. Already her skin was as pale as the white woollen flower in my hand, had the translucent quality of a corpse. The inside of her mouth seemed to glisten in the sunlight. About us, all the girls sobbed quietly.

Looking up to Ah Fong who was standing by me, I asked, 'Can we not revive her?'

'No can do, master,' he said.

'We must try.'

'No good. She eat gold.'

'Gold?'

'Gold paper, master. Thin-thin. Go inside her, make air hard to swallow. No can take in air.'

In fifteen minutes, she suffocated and was gone.

☯

Once more, there are American sailors in port. They are not from the main fleet but off three supply ships which are here, according to the *South China Morning Post*, to re-provision and allow the crews some R&R – Rest and Recreation. Sam declares this should be called R&P – Rum and Procreation.

He stocked up the bar of *The Black Pussy* with bottles of good quality bourbon – *Jack Daniel's Old No.7* and *Jim Beam* – bringing in a supply of bread rolls and hot dog sausages. In addition, he employed two friends to act as waiters and a young lad to stand on the pavement by the Fenwick Street pier where the liberty boats dock handing out flyers which I have written and for which Sam paid me $50.

The flyers have been printed on stiff white card edged with gold leaf in order to look like invitations and read as follows:

The Black Pussy Bar and Nite Club
where dames, dancing and dawgs
last the night through.
Free first drink – bear or liquor.
Free jukebox.
Live Band Music after 10 pm.

315

On the reverse is a map on how to reach the bar from the pier, the address and the telephone number. Only the printers' error in the fourth line detracts somewhat from the invitation's authenticity.

'No sweat,' Sam said when I pointed it out to him. 'Nobody expect *bear*. He want beer. Anyway, these guys sometimes no can spell so good anyway.'

He also asked me to be in attendance in the bar. Quite why, I do not know. I can do nothing but I sense he likes me there to add a bit of colour: I suppose an old China hand sitting at the counter lends the establishment a certain *je ne sais quoi*. I am not just an old man but an artefact of the East, as much of an attraction in my own way as the bar-girls and the Hong Kong-brewed lager.

When he requested my presence, and said the drinks were on him, I questioned his uncharacteristic benevolence towards his clientele.

'You aren't usually this generous. With me you're kind, but this seems somewhat extravagant. What are you up to?' I enquired.

Sam tapped his nose: he has learnt this sign from the cinema. He is an avid devotee of the American movie.

'Good business,' he replied, winking.

'How much are you spending? The printing, my fifty, free drinks. Free music. Waiters and the lad at the jetty. And a band! You've never had a band in here before.'

'Must spend money to make money,' he answered obliquely and would not be drawn further.

So, last night, I was in the bar, sitting on my usual stool at the end of the counter waiting to see what

316

was on the cards: Sam was up to something and I was more than curious.

I arrived just before seven o'clock, as he was preparing for the hectic hours ahead.

'Big night,' he announced, pouring my first lager.

'Big night,' I agreed, raising my glass in a toast and saying, '*Yam sing.*'

'Tonight, make good money,' he predicted. 'I do good, girls do good. Everybody do good. Even you, *san foo*, maybe can do good.'

'When do you expect the first customers?' I asked, wondering how he believed I might profit from the evening's activities.

'Eight o'clock. First boat in half past seven. Boy down at the pier now. He ready. Plenty of invitation card.' He rubbed his hands on a length of towelling. 'Tonight, good night.'

I looked at the Johnnie Walker whisky clock over the bar shelves: it was already a quarter past seven.

'Got in good stock of cigarette. All American. *Lucky Strike, Chesterfield, Camel,* king-size *Peter Stuyvesant.* Good quality.'

From under the bar he took out a carton of the latter, split the seal open with his thumb nail and proceeded to place a handful of cigarettes in half a dozen whisky glasses.

'Free cigarettes as well?' I said, not a little amazed.

'Not so free. Jus' until the glass empty. Get people going. Make him feel my bar the best in Wanchai.'

I sensed at that point there was more to this unprecedented evening than met the eye and wondered if Sam was looking to do a competitor out of business, had received a sharp rise in his rent or demands for protection money by the Chiu Chow

317

triads who ran the area. Yet I did not pry: it is best to let a man get on with his own affairs. If he wanted to tell me about it, he would.

As the clock hands shifted to seven-thirty, I thought of the first liberty boat pulling alongside, the sailors checking their wallets, chewing on antibiotic sweets that looked like *LifeSavers* candies, slapping each other on the shoulder and premeditatively boasting about conquests to be made during the next six hours. Those for whom this was a first visit to Hong Kong would be listening to the experienced ones, anticipating the broads, the beers and the bars.

I drained my glass as Sam placed a new bottle by my elbow. I drink my first lager fairly quickly, thereafter pacing myself, sipping slowly, exchanging the odd word with Sam, one of the girls or a client. On rare occasions, one of the latter engages me in conversation: he might be a young sailor afraid of whores, an old one who came ashore just for a drink, a faithful one not wishing to cheat on his sweetheart or a queer disappointed by the shortage of young boys, unaware that colonial culture and Chinese tradition do not openly accept homosexuality.

The curtain of beads rattled and someone entered. I looked up. It could not be a sailor for it was too early: even an Olympic sprinter could not get from the Fenwick Street pier to *The Black Pussy* in under five minutes.

As I surmised, it was not a sailor. It was the boy to whom I tutor Cantonese. For a moment, I did not recognise him, for he was not wearing his school uniform but a pair of tight black trousers, a pink shirt with a wide collar and a scarlet waistcoat with brass buttons. His shoes were black and highly polished, the toecaps pointed and the heels stacked.

His eyes unadjusted to the gloom, he did not see me but waved to Sam standing under the ultra-violet lamp.

'Hi, Sam!' he called out.

'Hi, Gerry!' Sam replied. 'You okay?'

The boy nodded and crossed to the jukebox. One of the bar-girls quit her seat in the end cubicle – all the girls, as usual, were crowded in there, playing cards and chattering to each other like pullets in a coup – and went to his side, putting her arm about his shoulder. This, I considered, was perhaps one reason for his wishing to speak Cantonese, after all.

He thumbed a coin into the jukebox and I expected him to dance with the girl: but he did not. Instead, he entered a cubicle and started to furiously scribble on a piece of paper. When it stopped playing, he returned to the jukebox and, inserting another coin, played the same tune over, returning to his scribbling. He was, I realised, writing down the words of the song. I listened to them. The singer had a falsetto voice.

As I walk along, the jukebox pumped out, the bass thumping, *I wonder what went wrong with our love, a love that was so strong. And as I stroll on down I think of the things we've done, together, while our hearts were young. I'm a-walking in the rain . . .*

'Del Shannon,' Sam said loudly in my ear. He had come along the bar, placing the cigarette glasses. 'New American singer. Many people listen to him.'

The song ended, the boy chose another record. It was a song I have heard played often by the sailors and whores. It is entitled *Are You Lonesome*

319

Tonight? by Elvis Presley: this is the singer Tsoi claims is responsible for encouraging Chinese youths to set light to the hills. As the slow opening bars issued from the loudspeaker, two of the girls left their cubicle, dancing together. Their arms entwined about each other's waist, pulling them together. I could imagine what was going through their minds: for the duration of the lilting tune, they were not bar-girls in a dive awaiting a groping hand and thrusting pelvis but film stars, happy young women in the embrace of a loved one, rich and contented.

Just as Mr Poon was a gambler so are these whores. He chanced his money and his life: they play with the future, throwing their bodies like dice and holding their breath for the six that never rolls.

The boy looked up from his scribbling and saw me. For a long moment, he just stared and, even in the gloom, I could tell he was very surprised. He put away his pen, folded the paper, left the cubicle and, skirting the dancers, came towards me.

'Good evening, sir,' he said.

'Good evening,' I replied.

I did not add anything more. I wanted to see how he would handle our meeting and was, in a mild way, enjoying not so much his embarrassment, but his amazement.

'I was . . . was . . .' he stuttered and, even by the ultra-violet strip light, I could tell he was colouring.

'Not aware I came here?' I suggested.

My words saved him. I could tell, for I have seen it often, he was going to make a confession, a denial or an excuse for being in such a place at such a time.

'Yes, sir.' There was a distinct relief in his voice. 'I usually come early in the evening. Before . . .'

320

Once more, he was lost for words and I waited a moment before replying, savouring his predicament.

'Before business really starts to get under way. As for myself,' I went on, 'I usually come later in the evening.'

He was silent, not quite knowing what to say next.

'Sam,' I called out, 'one more beer.' Looking the boy in the eye, I asked, 'You do drink beer, don't you?'

'Yes, sir. Thank you.'

Sam poured out a San Miguel and I reached for my wallet.

'Okay. Beer free for Gerry, too. I got an agreement with him.'

'You seem to know Sam very well,' I commented, lifting my glass.

The boy raised his own, tilting it towards me to signal his thanks, sipping the froth off before replacing the glass on the counter.

'Yes. I come here at least once a week, usually just after the US Navy's been in. That's the best time. Sam doesn't mind. There's no law against it. So long as I'm over sixteen.' He was suddenly voluble, like every sinner when he sees a chance to justify himself, or repent. 'I don't come here for the girls. I know them, of course, and they know me but I'm not a . . .' He paused, perhaps to catch his breath or to find an appropriate word.

'A customer?' I suggested.

'Yes, a customer,' he concurred.

'So you aren't learning Cantonese in order to communicate with these young ladies of the night?' I answered.

321

'No, sir. Besides,' he said, smiling briefly, 'they all speak English. After a fashion. They have to for . . . for their business.'

'That's true,' I replied, 'so why do you come here?'

'To get the lyrics of the latest songs. You see, sir, Sam has the best jukebox in Wanchai. Probably the best in Hong Kong. He's famous for it. Some of the records are put in it within a week of appearing in the Billboard Hot 100. Like *Runaway*. That was the first I spun just now.'

'And why,' I enquired, 'do you want these lyrics?'

'To sing the songs, sir. To play them. You see,' he sipped at his beer again, 'I'm in a group.'

'A group of what?' I asked.

'Well, a group,' he replied, somewhat nonplussed. 'A group. A band. I'm in with four friends. We call ourselves the Intercontinentals. Because we're from different nationalities – I'm English, the lead's American . . .'

'The lead what?' I interrupted.

This was not a conversation I had expected. The boy, usually so quiet when involved with his studies at my table, was quite talkative, forthcoming even. I found myself taking a distinct liking to him.

'Lead guitar,' he explained. 'We are a rock group – a rock-and-roll group,' he added for my elucidation. 'I play rhythm, the American plays lead, a Swedish friend plays bass guitar, the drummer's a Filipino and the singer's English like me. But, in fact, we all sing at some time or another.'

'And you put on concerts, I suppose,' I said.

'Not exactly. We play at school dances, parties and now,' he looked about himself, 'night clubs.'

322

'This is hardly a night club,' I began, then it dawned on me. 'You mean,' I continued, 'you are Sam's live band?'

'Yes. We start at ten.'

'And is your father aware of your evening's activities?'

The boy avoided my eyes, scanning the dance floor where two more girls were moving sinuously against each other to the tune of the same record.

'Not exactly. He knows we have a band and knows we do parties and things. He thinks this is a party.'

'In a manner of speaking,' I remarked, 'it is. After all, there were invitations printed.'

I had one folded in my pocket, having brought it with me in case Sam insisted it be shown at the door to comply with some obscure by-law. Taking it out, I smoothed the crease and gave it to the boy, who held it at an angle to the ultra-violet strip light and read it.

'May I keep this, sir?' he asked.

I nodded: he wanted it to lend some veracity to his story should his parents discover where he was performing and I saw no harm in assisting him in his petty deception.

The plastic beads of the curtain rattled and five American sailors entered, standing on the edge of the dance floor and surveying the scene.

'Hey,' one said loudly, 'this where the party's at?'

'Come on in, boys!' Sam called from behind the bar. 'Welcome to *The Black Pussy*.'

Over the next three-quarters of an hour, other sailors arrived until the bar was more crowded than I had ever seen it. Sam dispensed a free drink to each sailor on presentation of his invitation which, once

323

the drink was served, Sam tore up. Those who had lost their cards were given their free drink but Sam, not to be cheated, stamped the backs of their hands with a small ivory chop engraved with the two cats from the neon sign.

Most of the time, the boy was lost to my sight in the mêlée but I occasionally noticed, through the mass of sailors and bar-girls – of whom more had arrived, paying a one-night-only permission fee to Sam – a number of figures erecting a drum kit at the far end of the room.

Nobody talked to me. I sat quite alone at the end of the bar, enjoying my drink. Sam and his two part-time waiters were kept busy serving drinks and, after nine o'clock, hot dogs smeared with mustard from a large pot.

As I observed the action around me, I saw one thing that so amazed me I watched for it again. Sam was giving credit to a sailor.

He was a young man, barely out of his teens, with crew-cut blonde hair and a fresh face. This was clearly his first visit to Hong Kong for he was less than au fait with how to handle whores in both the physical and metaphysical interpretations of the word: indeed, he was so forward with one of them that she abandoned him. This was not from prudery but because he had not bought her out: as the girls put it in the vernacular of *The Black Pussy*, no can pay, no can play.

When he arrived at the bar to buy a drink or place an order for his friends, Sam personally served him. This was a deliberate action for, if one of the waiters was approached by this sailor, he directed him to Sam. At one point, he stood next to me.

'What your poison?' Sam asked, cursorily wiping the bar with a cloth.

'Two San Migs., two chasers, Sam,' the sailor called out over the ruckus of the jukebox.

'Comin' up, Pete!' Sam replied and set about opening bottles.

The sailor nodded to me.

'How're ya doin'?' he enquired.

'I'm fine, just fine,' I said.

He looked at my glass. His face was flushed and not just with the heat of the place.

'You wanna beer, pal? Have one on me. Hey, Sam, one more beer down here.'

'Thank you,' I said.

I was surprised at his generosity even though I knew it to be the benevolence of the merry and soon-to-be-smashed rather than an exuding of the milk of human kindness.

'How much?' the sailor asked as Sam delivered three beers and two bourbon chasers.

'On the tab, Pete. No sweat. Pay later.'

As the sailor left the counter, I could not believe what I heard. Sam was running a slate. I interpreted this not as a sign of his growing weak nor an extension of his evening's already astonishing generosity. There was another reason but I was damned if I could figure it out.

By nine thirty, I felt hot and tired and, leaving my stool, made my way towards the door at the rear of the bar which leads onto a rear alley. The door was unlocked, the little battery operated light above it illuminating a plastic fire exit sign, one of the few acts of compliance with the law to which Sam pays more than lip service.

The alley was cool and, as the door shut on a spring the sounds were cut short, quiet. Somewhere overhead, a radio played Cantonese opera, the singers wailing to the clash of gongs and cymbals. At the end of the alley, traffic passed by, the vehicles momentarily loud as they came into view. In the tenement opposite some kind of machine was running, its movements punctuated by a hiss, a sliding of metal, two more hisses and a clunk followed by the first hiss once more.

Leaning against the wall beside a stack of empty beer crates and boxes, I found myself breathless, as if I had been walking quickly for a long distance. I put my hands to my chest, pressing gently in and out to aid my lungs. I was not panicked for I am on occasion breathless, although admittedly only after exertion. The wall behind me vibrating slightly from the music within, I put my condition down to the dense smoke-filled air, the tightly packed crowd, the noise and the heat.

The door opened and Sam appeared.

'*San foo?*' he called, looking round. '*San foo.* You okay?'

'Just tired,' I assured him. 'And hot.'

'If you inside, must drink plenty. If you body get dry, you ill.' He called through the door, '*Wei! Foh gei! Ho lok!*' Then, turning to me again, he said, 'Soon fix you up, *san foo.*'

A hand appeared through the door holding a green fluted Coca Cola bottle. Sam wiped the mouth of the bottle with his hand and gave it to me.

'Drink, *san foo.* Get water in you, sugar. Then you be okay.'

326

I swallowed the chilled sweetness and felt immediately revived.

'Okay now?'

'Yes,' I answered. 'Fine.' I took another swig before continuing, 'Sam, what are you up to?'

'The party? Easy! These sailors work on supply ships, go to all the other ships in the US fleet. You know, sailors like men in a club. All from one ship, talk to his friend there and go ashore with him. But he often don't see other sailors. These guys,' he jerked his thumb in the direction of the door, 'see all the ships and when they go to them, taking supplies, they have a coffee and talk. So! What they talk about? About the last R&R.'

He grinned, putting his hand on my shoulder. It was the touch of friendship: the ex-priest and the whorehouse bar-man joined in amity.

Sam is no fool. This party might cost him a drop in profits but it will spread his reputation. Like every Chinese, he is a shrewd and usually successful businessman at heart, his eye open for opportunity and his energy charged to realise it. I admire this tenacious determination. Other nations lack it in various degrees: the British are idle complainers, the Italians too keen on a walk in the sun after lunch, the Spanish too fond of the *siesta* and the French too set in their ways. The Germans work hard but they are sterile, lack colour and have only gritted teeth: they do not smile.

'That's not what I meant,' I said. 'I understand all that. What's the scam you're running on the sailor?'

I used the word because Sam would appreciate it. He knows this one from the movies, too.

'Scam?' he repeated.

'Scam. Sting. You're running numbers on a sailor called Pete.'

'You clever man, my old frien',' Sam laughed, 'got eyes like an eagle. You see too much!'

'So what's the game?'

'I tell you. I trus' you. But it's a secret,' he exclaimed, moving his hand and stroking my shoulder. 'You tell nobody or I lose money.' He shifted closer to me, resting his elbow on a crate. 'First night the ship in port, I choose one sailor, not too stupid, not too clever. All night, give him credit. Plenty drink, for him and for his frien', something to eat and, later, free girl. I pay for her. She give him quick time only. Ten minute. No more. After, she bring him back and I say, must pay now. But I know he not got enough money.'

'That sounds like poor judgement,' I commented, but knew it was not.

'No, good judgement, *san foo*. I pretend to be cross. Shout, "You got no money, you drink so much. Have girl. Have a good time and now you cheat me. I call the Shore Patrol, Hong Kong Police. Call my frien's. Got tough frien's."' He winked at me. 'He get afraid. Then I say, "Okay. You got no money so must pay me another way." He say he do it so I say, "You bring me record from your ship mess jukebox. All new record only. One just come in from US. You see, *san foo*, every week the US Navy send new records for sailors. All the new hits. And he do it.'

Sam shrugged his shoulders and grinned.

'So that's how you've the best jukebox in Wanchai,' I congratulated him.

'Best in Hong Kong, Gerry tell me.'

It was impossible not to laugh. His scheming was

so preposterous, artful, well planned and skilfully executed.

'But,' I went on, 'what if he doesn't? What if he goes to the Shore Patrol and says he was rolled? What if he goes back on his ship and stays there?'

'He don't,' Sam replied confidently. 'If he call the Shore Patrol, the US Navy want no trouble so they pay. And if he go to the ship he don't want to stay there. His friend' go ashore, he want to go too. But he can only come ashore at Fenwick Street. My guard can see him.'

'Who's your guard?' I asked.

'The boy who give out the invite card.'

The door opened and the waiter called to Sam.

'Now mus' go back in. You comin', *san foo*?'

We returned to the smoke and din but I did not stay to hear the boy's band or see the outcome of the scam yet I am sure it worked. Sam will have selected Pete with all the forethought of a corporate manager deciding who to appoint to a trustworthy position. Men who run whorehouses and bars have all the skills of a top industrialist, a senior manager or a priest. They can smell a sucker, a sap, a sinner and a sound man at fifty paces.

There is no man alive who, given the chance, would refuse to discover his future and there are as many charlatans about selling this information to him as there are priests offering to bless him or save him from himself. The daily newspapers, both English language and Chinese, publish horoscopes whilst the magazines print advice according to the planetary alliances. The temples are invariably busy with fortune-tellers and fortune-hunters, especially before a race day at Happy Valley or at the time of a major festival when people take stock of their lives, assess their sins and make resolutions they know they cannot keep.

Sometimes, when I am out taking the air in the evening, I walk towards the waterfront and, on my way, pass along a street where fortune-tellers congregate to ply their trade.

They are a motley band, yet all cultivate certain qualities which it is beholden of them to maintain, attributes which give them veracity. None of them is under forty years of age for the reading of the future is an old man's game: indeed, some of them have worked upon appearing old so, although their real ages are indeterminate, they look sage-like with long thin beards or Fu Manchu moustaches, straggling hair reaching to their collars and, of course, two-inch-long fingernails to prove they are not manual workers but thinkers, philosophers and poets. They always wear traditional Chinese clothing, the *ma kwa* waist-length jacket over a loose man's *cheung sam* or black *fu*. Several wear skull caps with pompoms on the top and none wear Western shoes but traditional slippers, even if the street is wet. Each man has a small collapsable kiosk on the pavement, little bigger than a telephone box and equipped with a folding seat for the fortune-teller, a small table or shelf and a stool or two for clients.

The inside walls of the kiosks are hung with palmists' charts, phrenologists' diagrams, testimonials from satisfied customers and photographs of

330

the individual fortune-teller's master, the man who taught him the arts of divination. These, too, always show sages or learned-looking men dressed as their disciples are in old-fashioned clothing. A few of the photos have lit joss sticks wedged in their frames.

I am on nodding acquaintance with one of these men. He is called Mr Ng, speaks good English and has a degree in History from the University of Canton. Our friendship is not of a client-based nature. I do not indulge myself in his business. I know my future.

This evening, I was making my way to the water-front with no intention in mind other than to stretch my legs before retiring, when I came upon Mr Ng setting up his stall.

'My friend,' I said, stopping to help him press home a particularly tight metal clasp holding the side wall to the rear, 'how are you?'

'Good. I am good,' he replied, adding, 'Thank you. The metal is bent. Last week – a lorry – ' he slapped his hands together '– boom! Into my stall.'

'You were not hurt?'

'No. No worry for me but much for the driver. I saw his face. He was unhappy. I could tell his fortune. It was not good.'

He unfolded the shelf in his kiosk, arranged the seats and called to a shop nearby for two glasses of tea.

'You sit with me?' he invited, pointing to the stool.

'I don't want to take away your custom,' I replied but he waved his hand in the air dismissively.

'Too early. Nobody will come before eight o'clock. Too many people are eating now.'

A boy arrived with the glasses of tea and I paid for them. Each had a pink plastic lid and red roses stencilled on the side. Mr Ng picked his up, removed the lid and slurped noisily.

'You want your fortune told?' he enquired, his tone joking.

'No. I know where I am going.'

'So do I. You are going to the waterfront at the typhoon shelter, you will walk along it some way, you will go back to your home by another route and you will sleep. I mean, do you want news of your next week or month?'

'At my age,' I declared, 'one does not want to know what is coming. To guess is enough.'

'You will die,' Mr Ng said quite matter-of-factly, as if it was perfectly normal for him to give such information out. 'In the next three months. Already you are tired. Your body is not ill but it is going more slowly. You are like a car with the petrol getting less.'

'Perhaps,' I answered and I sipped at my tea.

'You will go to heaven,' he then declared.

'Possibly,' I said.

'No. You will go,' Mr Ng said with utter conviction. 'I know this because the iron tree flowers.'

At that moment, as if he was standing somewhere over my shoulder, I heard a man's voice say, quite distinctly, 'After nearly a quarter of a century, China still holds surprises.'

Despite myself, I glanced over my shoulder. Had I seen Mr Doble standing there with his glass of gin and quinine in his hand, I should not have been in the least astonished: what I did see was an elderly woman walking past holding her grandchild by the hand. The child was a little girl dressed in a crimson padded silk jacket with a bonnet on her head from which two rabbit's ears stuck upwards.

'You heard someone,' Mr Ng announced as I turned round again. 'A man from your past.'

'Yes,' I said. 'I did. How could you tell?'

'It is my job,' he smiled. 'Would you expect me to give you the secrets of my work?'

'No, I would not.'

He smiled again then, his face becoming expressionless, he said, 'This is a sign you will die soon.'

I was not unnerved either by the spirit voice of Mr Doble or Mr Ng's prediction. What will be, will be. There is nothing I can do, nor want to do, to slow down the clock of my life. A second is a second and that's all there is to it.

'What is an iron tree?' I asked.

'It is a special plant,' Mr Ng responded. 'A little like a cactus but with leaves.'

'Do you have one?'

'I know of one. Not here. In the New Territories, in the valley beyond Tso Shan. They are very rare.'

'And what has this iron tree to do with me?' I said.

'The iron tree only flowers every hundred years. Unless a good man is about to die. Last week, I went to this place and there was a flower upon the tree.'

'Perhaps it is a century since it last bloomed,' I suggested.

'This is not the case.'

'Then what,' I said, 'makes you think it foretells my death?'

'You are a good man.'

'I may dispute that,' I rejoined, 'but even if I were,

333

what is there to say the tree was giving its sign about me? Am I the only good man in Hong Kong who will die in the next few months?'

Mr Ng smiled politely and sipped his tea again before saying, 'No. You are not. But this tree is your tree.'

I did not question the logic and, my tea drunk, got to my feet to leave. Mr Ng also rose, holding his hand out to me. The nail on his middle finger is as long as a talon.

'I will not see you again,' Mr Ng declared as he shook my hand. 'I am going to Macau. My mother is there, come down from China. Do not be afraid.'

'I am not afraid of anything,' I replied and he smiled again.

'That is the way to die.'

I left his stall and passed by the other fortunetellers, some of whom were busy with clients, reading palms, touching heads and studying charts, holding tortoiseshells out or watching as their customers shook bamboo splints out of wooden cups. At the end of the street was a man with a trained finch which, when touched by a customer, hopped from its cage, pulled a card from a deck, accepted a grain of seed from its master and then, with a trust verging upon the inane, hopped back into the cage instead of taking flight for the sky.

At the waterfront, I sauntered slowly along, observing the domestic life of the sampan-dwellers. Children were sleeping on quilts in the arched fabric cabins, men squatted smoking on the decks whilst women busied themselves with chores. The steamy smoke of boiling and frying fish wafted on the gentle breeze, clouding densely as it blew across the glass chimney of an oil lamp.

When I reached the end of the dockside, I halted and sat on a concrete bollard. At my feet were stretched the mooring hawsers of a large junk from the spars of which hung drying fishing nets and racks of gutted fish, their salty stink touching my nostrils.

Mr Ng is right. I am dying although I did not need him to tell me. There have been other signs. I do not refer to the incident on the roof: that was just a coincidence or secondary factor. What does assure me my death is nearing is that, deep inside myself, there is an enceinte quietness. It is the kind one expects at any minute to hear filled with voices, the sort of stillness one experiences when talking to someone with a bad stammer. It is a noiselessness waiting for a noise to fill it.

Everyone, drawing slowly towards death, has this kernel of silence in them. I am certain of it.

What I shall find in mine I cannot tell. Perhaps this is the void I shall hear filled with the song of angels. But there again, it might be filled with the hush of dragons' wings, the hiss of their fiery mouths. Or simply nothing, nothing at all.

On a day-to-day basis, I am all right.

I am not late for appointments and, being a man of some method, I keep an exact mental note of what engagements are forthcoming. The only diary I have ever kept started and ended in the summer of 1900. I reinforce my memory with the aid of a desk calendar, one of those page-to-a-day affairs with the date written large in both English and Cantonese, weekdays in black and Sundays or religious holidays in red, held in place on a plastic stand with metal hoops. Every morning, I tear off the previous day's page and discard it.

Long ago, I learned the future is an unfriendly country filled with disappointment. As for the past, that is best not recorded. In any case, it lingers in the memory, no matter how one tries to eradicate it: it is like an unwanted guest who refuses to leave after all the others have bade farewell. It takes no hints and heeds no pleas, will not put on its coat and stagger off into the darkness.

Today, however, I had another accident, not as drastic as my rooftop interlude and yet, in its own way, more alarming. I was not fighting dragons, nor had I been chasing them. I was merely going about my business, on the way to the market.

It was just before noon. I was making my way up Shanghai Street, keeping to the shadows of the arcades. The sun was high yet it was pleasantly cool in the shade despite the passing traffic: even the din of the motors and the exhaust fumes was unable to filter into the arcades where people walked and shopped, bartered and gossiped.

I was strolling along quite slowly with no need to hurry: life at my age has a certain inevitability.

On the corner with Tung Kun Street, a large crowd was gathered, blocking the pavement and slowing the traffic. Lorry drivers impatiently blared their horns, gesticulating out of their cab windows; cyclists jangled their bells, rickshaw coolies yelled for a clear passage, leaning back in the shafts of their vehicles to brake, but no one paid them attention.

As I approached, I wondered if there had been a minor traffic accident: yet there were no police in evidence. It takes only the slightest diversion to draw a crowd of Chinese onlookers. They are a nation of observers, avidly assembling to watch anything from a public execution to two men with a jack hammer digging up the road.

All my efforts to squeeze past the crowd were in vain. It was packed firmly into the arcade and stationary, everyone chattering and staring in one direction. Having no other alternative, I joined the throng and followed the general gaze.

The centre of attention was a shoe shop across the road. Suspended over the front of the building, three storeys high and twenty feet wide, was a huge decorated *pai lau* of garishly coloured paper flowers and red and gold characters mounted on a bamboo frame. To either side, running from the roof six floors up to the pavement, were two or three dozen strings of firecrackers.

'New shop,' a man standing next to me said in English, in case I was a tourist. 'Opung to-day.'

From his hand dangled two white hens, their feet and wings trussed by twine. They were trying to raise their heads and clucking with indignation. I wondered vaguely if they had been purchased from One-eye.

On the pavement in front of the shop stood the proprietor with a Taoist priest dressed in yellow robes, a black cap tied to his head by a scarlet chin-strap. He was holding an almanac and, when he raised his hand, the shop owner lit a master fuse on the pavement. A rush of sparks ran along the gutter, igniting the base of the firecracker strings which started to explode up the building with an ear-shattering racket. Red flecks of paper fluttered out across the road, blizzarding down on the traffic, thick grey-blue smoke billowing into the air obscuring the front of the building and the *pai lau*. Every other sound was drowned out by the cacophony.

The noise, which I have heard a thousand times without a flinch, began to ring in my head, growing to a painful throbbing. I put my hands over my ears but it continued. I felt giddy and reached out to grasp the arm of the man next to me, missed it, struck the chickens which started to thresh about and fell against one of the arcade pillars. A panic rose in me, my breath came in short gasps and I knew I had to get away from the shattering pandemonium.

Looking round, I saw my best escape was to turn right down Tung Kun Street and into Temple Street. Using my elbows, I fought my way through the crowd and made off at a stumbling jog, working my way through the traffic which was now brought to a standstill. I kept my hands to my ears, drawing curious glances from passers-by: I did not care if I lost face for I was inexplicably frightened.

Turning the corner into Temple Street instantly reduced the sound level of the explosions to an acceptable, distant din. I lowered my arms. My hands were shaking and my head pulsated. I needed a glass of water. Looking round, there was no stall or tea-house but I noticed a snake restaurant on the other side of the street.

The establishment was open but not yet catering for clients. The neon lights were on, the chairs taken

338

off the tables and the frontage open to the pavement but the waiters were dressed in vests and trousers, yet to don their white uniform jackets. The traffic moving slowly once more, I crossed through the vehicles, avoiding being run down by a man on a bicycle with a front platform piled high with bolts of cloth, and stepped towards the rank of glass aquaria along the restaurant wall. They were positioned close to the pavement so they not only provided the snakes with air but were also a means of advertising the menu.

The proprietor and waiters were preoccupied with laying the round tables, spreading white cloths over them and noisily dropping bowls, spoons and chopsticks by each place setting. Overhead, two brass and mahogany ceiling fans desultorily stirred the air. At the rear, a elderly woman vigorously scrubbed a cooking range while a youth in his teens ran a mop smelling tartly of disinfectant over the white and red tiles of the floor.

Most of the tanks contained an immobile knot of snakes, one species to each tank. They did not move except for an occasional flick of the tongue tasting the air. In a smaller tank huddled a group of large lizards, their skins green with minute yellow spots. Their eyes were huge and filled with a great simplicity. If reptiles could be innocent then these knew nothing of the cruelty of the world, were ignorant of what was soon to befall them.

As I looked at them, a sense of terrible foreboding spread over me, centred upon the unfathomable recesses of the soul beyond the reach of the most intricate self-searching. It was followed by a startling feeling of *déjà vu*, the hair on my nape rising as if a tentacle of ice was run across my neck.

From one of the tanks came a sound I had not heard for many years. *Tok-eye*! it went. *Tok-eye*! I turned sharply. The tank from which the sound came was empty.

Feeling faint, I rested my hand against the nearest tank in which there was a single snake, a variety of python three feet long. It was a light emerald creature marked with delicate, random black patterns, the colouring so subtle it might have been painted with water-colours, have been the work of a divine artist dripping indian ink on a green background while the paint was wet.

The distant explosions came to an end. I pressed my hand to my forehead, the skin hot and dry. My cool fingers unaccountably dissolved my fear.

The next tank contained a tangle of many-banded kraits. Their brilliant black-and-yellow or white rings were dulled: in one corner of the tank, a single snake was curled in a patch of white mucus. It was, I guessed, dead and therefore of no use. No Chinese will eat a snake he hasn't seen wriggling before it reaches the cooking pot.

'What you want?' the proprietor asked belligerently in pidgin English, his suspicion aroused by a European in his snake shop. It is rare to see a *gweilo* in such an establishment.

'This snake kill one man,' I replied, pointing to a krait lying close to the glass at the front of the tank. 'Get more money for him.'

The restaurateur was a little taken aback by my response.

'He kill one man,' he confirmed. 'How you know?'

'This snake *ngun keuk tai*. In English call many-banded krait. He tail stop in black band,' I said. 'Chinese say if tail black at end then he kill a man.'

The Chinese laughed and said, 'You know too much!'

'This one,' I pointed to a yellow-and-black snake in another tank, '*kum keuk tai*. Gold leg band snake.'

Moving to a tank to my right, the restaurateur tapped his fingernail on the glass. One of the inmates flashed its head around at the noise.

'What he call?' he asked.

I put my hand to the glass, rapidly bunching and opening my fist. The snake reared up, spread its hood and struck at the glass, a thin stream of venom running down in a colourless trickle like glutinous spittle.

'*Kwoh shan fung*,' I replied adding as a translation, 'More fast mountain wind snake. Very dangerous. In English, we say king cobra.'

'Good snake!' the restaurateur remarked, giving a thumbs-up to lend credence to his statement. 'Can sell for much money.'

'How much?' I enquired.

'Too much. You must have good money for him.'

'*Kei toh*?' I enquired once more, using Cantonese.

'Fi' hundred eightee dollar,' the owner of the snake replied in English, perhaps not believing I could speak more than a few phrases and name a few snakes.

I pretended astonishment and replied, '*Yau mo gau chor ah*!'

At this, the restaurateur and the waiters fell into fits of laughter. Even the woman at the cooking range

341

stopped work to join in and the youth leaned on his mop to share in the joke.

'You speak Cantonese ve'y good. How long you live Hong Kong?'

I looked into the cobra's tank. The perceived threat removed, it had shrunk its hood and lowered its head, but it was still alert, its tongue flicking and its head swaying slightly as if sizing me up for another strike. I wondered how old the snake was. Cobras can live for thirty years: it was not inconceivable to think they might last longer. As I was moving inexorably towards death at the hand of time, so was the reptile doomed, its fate sealed by the first customer to walk in with five hundred and eighty dollars and a desire to fortify his blood, improve his sexual prowess or live longer.

'*Luk saap yat neen*,' I said.

'*Ay-yah*!' the Chinese exclaimed, thought for a minute then added, 'Sixty-one year! So long! You old man now!'

I felt suddenly weak and my head began to throb again. I reached out and held on to the back of a chair by the nearest table.

'Yes,' I agreed, 'a very long time. A very long time, indeed.'

I turned the chair around and sat down heavily in it.

'You Okay?' the Chinese asked.

'Yes. Okay. I buy one glass tea.'

The restaurateur signalled to a waiter who disappeared into the back of the premises. I could hear crockery being moved and reached into my pocket for some coins but the restaurateur waved his hand.

342

'Tea no charge. Free tea for old man live long time in China.'

Smiling my thanks, I leaned forward and stared at my feet. I felt dizzy and rested my arm on the table, knocking over a rice bowl with my elbow. The room shifted as if it was on a pendulum and I was the only fixed point. The snake tanks swayed and, for a moment, I wanted to reach out and steady them in case they should fall, shatter and the irate inhabitants attack me. In a detached way, I wondered what it would be like to be bitten by a deadly snake.

'Take tea slowly,' the Chinese advised. 'You get better soon. You wan' Green Spot orange? Wan' Seven-up? Wan' a Coke?'

'No, no thank you,' I said. 'I be all right.'

The youth with the mop had not yet reached this area of the room and, around my feet, I could see the congealed remains of the snakes which had provided the previous evening's menu. The waiter arrived with the tea in a glass tumbler.

'*Chai*,' he said, placing it in my hands.

Although it was hot, I held the glass and sipped noisily at it. It did not refresh me but it calmed me, stopped the room moving so violently.

Hunched forward with the glass in my hand, my mind gradually filled with disjointed images and vague, half-recollections which passed before me as if seen through an insubstantial dawn mist, the sort that hung in river valleys before the sun could soak them up. I saw a distant fire burning though what was fuelling the flames I could not say: it might have been old car tyres or engine oil for the smoke was thick, black and acrid. From the heart of the fire came a curling dragon. It was not a scaly monster such as one could see on a temple façade but a soft-skinned creature with sad eyes in which I could tell it knew it was going to die. The dragon rose into the sky and as soon as it had disappeared into the mist it was replaced by a butterfly. It was a dark-winged insect but in the centre of each hind wing was an iridescent blue circle which winked on and off as it flew slowly before me, blotting out the fire. As it moved by me, its wings seemed to stroke against my cheek, soft as rich velvet. It reached what I assumed was an iron tree and, as I watched, the tree burst into anonymous, indescribable blossom. I felt a warmth spread through me at the sight of the flowers. The mist disseminated and a hot sun shone out of a blue sky, which I was observing through a screen of tall yellow bamboo stems shot through with green lines, the leaves rustling in the breeze and brushing slightly against me.

The visions ended when I was touched gently on the shoulder: I thought at first it was either the butterfly returning to caress me or the leaves but, when I turned, it was the snake restaurant owner.

'You Okay?' he enquired again.

I straightened my back. My spine ached at the waist but otherwise I felt quite refreshed. The dizziness was gone.

'Yes, I'm okay.'

Yet I could hear the leaves of the bamboo still, rustling in the breeze. The restaurateur stepped aside. Behind him was one of the waiters. His left hand was wearing a thick glove from which dangled a hissing rat snake.

'This for you. Make you strong.'

The waiter put his right hand around the snake's

344

neck and, with a deft downward strike, opened its skin up the length of its body with a razor blade gripped between his fingers. He might have been unzipping the creature. The intestines fell out. Another waiter pushed a small basin under the snake with his foot, the dripping blood collecting in it. The snake's internal organs were cut out and dropped into the basin, which the restaurateur picked up, placed on the table and started to stir rapidly with a pair of chop-sticks, the plastic banging against the metal sides.

Putting my glass of tea down, I was surprised to see I had drunk less than a third of it.

An inch of the snake's blood was poured into a tall wine glass, to which was added red wine from a bottle on the label of which was a dragon similar in appearance to the one in my vision. A waiter stirred the drink with a steel spoon and handed it to me.

I put the glass to my lips and drained it in one. It tasted of sweetness and iron with a bitter tang.

'Good,' the restaurateur said. 'Make you live long time.'

'I already live long time,' I replied after a moment's thought. 'No good for one man live too long. If you live too long, you see too many things. No be happy see too much.'

As I stepped on to the flat roof of the mission, Father Callaghan was standing beside the bell, his left hand resting on the metal, his right in his pocket: we had just celebrated Mass and he was still wearing his

345

cassock. At the sound of my foot-steps he turned sharply and I had the ridiculous impression he was afraid of me.

'Ah Fong said you wanted me, Father,' I enquired.

'Yes,' he said hurriedly, glancing over my shoulder. 'Come by my side, Father Stephen.'

I was puzzled. He was not usually brusque.

'Is there something wrong, Father?'

'There may be,' he replied enigmatically. 'This is why I wanted to speak to you up here. I don't want to alarm the others.'

I felt a twinge of anxiety and wondered what it was he would wish to keep from Ah Fong and Sister Margaret.

'Before Mass,' he began, 'I went into the *hutong* at the rear. The baby posting box was jammed in its runners and I went to free it. Sometimes the wood sticks. There's a worn slide.'

His procrastination increased my anxiety. This, too, was out of character and I wondered if I had done something terribly wrong, upset a local Chinese who had lodged a complaint against me with the mandarin. I could not imagine what my sin might have been but my ignorance of local custom made such an error quite feasible.

'I reached the *hutong* and all looked quite normal,' he continued. 'It is narrow back there and I could not see the box until I was close to it. It was not jammed shut by malfunction. A large splint of wood had been rammed into the side of it, hammered in so firmly I could shift it only with two hands and some mighty tugging. The box, I fear, is now defunct for the splint has cracked the slide. We shall not see so many little souls coming to Christ through our letter-box.'

346

'Can we not have it repaired?' I suggested.

'Not now. There is no carpenter in the town who will undertake the job.'

'I do not understand ...' I started to say, but Father Callaghan interrupted me.

'I fear our days in Wuchow, Father Stephen, are numbered.'

'But who would have done such a thing?' I cut in, not appreciating the import of his words through my anger.

'It's not a matter of who,' Father Callaghan said 'but why.'

He took his right hand out of his pocket. In his fingers was a light brown sheet of Chinese paper, coarse and containing the husks of the rice pulp from which it was manufactured.

'This was attached to the splint,' Father Callaghan said and he handed the document to me.

It was written in characters with a brush pen dipped in red ink, the vertical lines neat and ordered.

'What is it?' I enquired.

'I translated it,' Father Callaghan said, ignoring my question. 'Before Mass.'

He took the paper back from me and held it in both hands as if it was a proclamation and he the crier about to shout its message.

'It says, "May the gods assist the *I Ho Ch'üan*." That is the heading. It goes on, "The foreign devils disturb the Middle Kingdom urging people to join their religion, turn their backs on Heaven and do not venerate the gods and ancestors. Foreign devils are not produced by mankind. If you doubt this, look carefully at their eyes. They are blue." There follows a passage of insults. Then it carries on, "No rain falls in the Middle Kingdom. The moon is made of blood. The earth is dry. The rice fails to grow. This is because the Christian religion has stopped up the heavens."'

Father Callaghan let his hand drop and looked up at the sky. The sun was gaining in height and there was not a cloud to be seen.

'It goes on to make other preposterous claims. One is that we take in babies to steal their eyes to sell. Another is that we cause others to eat them as a part of our rites. A third is that any man who takes the *I Ho Ch'üan* oath shall be impregnable against the bullets of the foreign devils' rifles. And so on. There is more . . .'

There were beads of sweat upon his brow but he made no attempt to wipe them away, blinking as they seeped through his brows to sting his eyes.

'Yesterday,' he said quietly, 'as I was walking towards the river, I met Mrs Tremlett. I think you know her from our party at the Residency?'

I nodded.

'She was accompanied by her two children. Sarah is five, her brother Ambrose three. Their baby amah was with them. We stopped by the market where they sell songbirds. Mrs Tremlett wished to buy some golden finches. I engaged her in conversation as the children looked at the birds. Suddenly, a man appeared from behind the bird stall and, without any warning, slapped their amah so hard across the face she tottered sideways, upsetting a pile of cages. I was astounded for this is quite unlike Chinese behaviour. As the amah picked herself up, Mrs Tremlett assisting her, the man berated the poor servant. "You wicked woman," he screamed, "Look at these children!" He

348

called them *siu kwei-tsi* which means little devils. "Their eyes are as blue as the big devils." He tried to hit her again but Mrs Tremlett was in the way. For a moment, I thought he would strike her but he desisted. Then he shouted in the most insulting of tones, "*T'ien Chu Kiao*," spat on the amah's *sam* and disappeared as quickly as he had arrived, ducking behind the bird stall.'

'What does *T'ien Chu Kiao* mean?' I asked.

'It means Roman Catholics,' Father Callaghan replied.

I sat on the step beneath the bell. Strangely, I was neither afraid nor indignant. My flesh had grown cold yet I was inwardly calm and composed.

'We shall have to take care,' he said after a long moment of silence. 'I spoke to Morrisby last evening. He had already telegraphed Hong Kong. It was just as well I did, for the lines went dead less than an hour later, before he could receive a reply.'

'What shall we do now?' I asked.

'I think our best option,' he almost whispered, 'is to pray that Jesus Christ will look over us and bring us to safety. We are in, I am sure, for a rough time.'

During the night, there has been a squatter fire in the Kowloon foothills. I did not know of it until this morning when I bought my daily paper from Lam, saw the headlines and discovered, according to a sketch map, where the conflagration had occurred. Without bothering to read the article, I walked quickly into Nathan Road and caught the first number 7 bus to come along. It was packed with pupils on their way to school. I squeezed onto one of the wooden slatted seats and was about to unfold the newspaper to read of the disaster when a voice spoke to me from behind.

'Good morning, sir.'

I turned. It was the boy.

'Good morning,' I replied.

'Are you reading about the fire, sir? We saw it from The Peak. It was in the hills behind Kowloon Tong.'

'I am going there,' I told him. 'I have . . .'

I was going to add I had acquaintances there but decided not to admit to this: the boy, however, was thinking ahead of me.

'Friends there, sir. I thought you might.'

He moved aside a little so I could see a very pretty girl standing next to him.

'This is Roxy,' he said, 'Roxy Drawdale.' Then, turning to her, he added, 'This is Mr Galvin, my Cantonese teacher.'

The girl smiled charmingly and asked, 'How d'you do?' in a West Coast American accent, adding, 'Are you going to see they're okay?'

'My friends?' I answered, a little distracted by this sudden conversation. 'Yes. Yes, I'm going to see if they need help.'

'We're going to set up a fund at school,' the boy volunteered. 'Roxy will be in charge of it. For the homeless,' he added.

'That's very noble of you, Gerald,' I replied and realised, I do not quite know why, it was the first time I had ever used his name in addressing him.

The bus lurched into Waterloo Road. By the public mortuary next to the fire station, a funeral cortege was gathered. It was not a grand affair but the ceremony of a poor person. There was only one band equipped with silver trombones, trumpets and tubas, two funereal wreaths mounted on the front of tricycles and one paper orb on a pole through which the devils might escape. A group of about twenty mourners, the deceased's immediate family dressed in white cloaks with the others, the paid mourners, in black, mingled by the door of an ancient Ford hearse. The sight was not a good omen.

'We're hoping to raise money by paying to see our teachers jump into the harbour,' the girl declared. 'A lot of the kids'll pay to see that. We reckon on getting $4,000.'

'A handsome sum,' I said. 'I hope you'll reach your target.'

'We will,' she stated confidently. 'I reckon we'll go over but it's best not to be too optimistic.'

The bus drove under a railway bridge and pulled into a stop. The boy and his girlfriend disembarked, waving to me as the vehicle drove off. I felt touched they should have spoken to me and the encounter, brief though it was, greatly impressed upon me the boy's sincerity.

At the end of the route, the road where the bus usually turned round was blocked by police and fire brigade vehicles. Over a dozen hoses snaked up the path from two hydrants and a water tender on the pavement beside a parked ambulance, its rear doors open and the stretcher missing. Some British soldiers in fatigues were busy nearby sorting out boxes of clothing and military two-man tents.

No one attempted to prevent me from going up the path although there were a number of Chinese being held back by several police constables with whom they were having a heated argument. I suppose, being a *gweilo*, the police thought I was a government official or an aid worker.

I followed the hoses until I came to the edge of what had, until the night before, been a thriving shanty town. Now it was just a smouldering, blackened landscape with hardly any structure remaining standing. Fragments of clothing, charred wood, twisted lengths of corrugated iron, the skeletal frames of chairs, beds and bicycles, and warped or partially melted aluminium cooking utensils were scattered throughout the desolation. The air smelled of singed hair, burnt feathers, wet charcoal and sodden earth, for the ground was soft underfoot from the use of the hoses.

Through this bleak panorama about a hundred people were moving, heads down looking at the ground, sifting through the detritus of their lives, prodding about with sticks, occasionally stooping to pick something up and put it in a straw bag or cardboard box.

Everything was eerily silent. The people did not speak and there was not a single bird in the sky. Even here and there, where there were still a few tiny flames or glowing embers showing, causing no risk and therefore of no concern to the fire brigade, the fire made no sound. Nothing crackled or hissed or spat. It was as if the fire had not only burned down the houses but the very sounds which had emanated from them.

I made my way along what had been a thoroughfare through the shanties. The ground was beaten so hard from the passage of feet that it had not yet broken up under the flow of water. At a junction, I passed the remains of a small shop, the ground littered with broken glass and pottery jars: next to it was what had been a little workshop. The remains of a machine stood in the rubble, surrounded by a scattering of metal discs the size of tap washers but without holes drilled in them: they were discoloured from the heat and I wondered if this had been the site of Mr Yee's counterfeiter.

Ahead of me up the hill was a gathering of men huddled in conversation. They were all Chinese but several wore suits and ties and one carried a briefcase. These, I assumed, were the committee of the local *kai fong* association. As I looked at them, a man detached himself from the group and came towards me, walking gingerly through the ashes. It was Mr Yee.

'*Cho san, nei ho ma?*' he greeted me, holding out his hand which I shook.

'*Ho, nei ho ma?*' I answered.

He nodded, casting a look around us.

'*Kei toh koh yan . . .?*' I began, but he interrupted me.

'*Yee maan . . .*' he said and shrugged, adding in English, 'Not a good place to see today.'

'Twenty thousand people?' I said.

'Maybe more. How can you tell? More than four thousan' house gone.' He rubbed his hands together as if he was cold. 'I expect to see you come.'

'You know I had to come . . .' I started to say.

'They are okay.'

'Are you sure?' I asked.

'Sure. You see up the hill? Some house not burning.

Maybe fi've hund'ed people. They got their house up there.'

His news made me feel immensely pleased, as if I had personally been responsible for stopping the fire from sweeping higher up the mountainside. I would have liked to have sat down for I felt a little weak now: the urgency which had been pumping itself through me was now abated.

'Not all bad news,' Mr Yee said, once more looking about the devastation. 'All the people here now got new houses. New flat some place. Soon, more people come, build new houses and can live here.'

'And when they come?' I replied.

Mr Yee is a businessman. He may not seek to profit from the misfortunes of others but, should those misfortunes place him in such a position as to be able to assist them and himself at the same time, he will be quick to seize the opportunity.

'When they come, business like before. I can get wood, make places here flat for a house, bring in water pipe – even power. I can lend money for him if he want to start his factory. Make something.' He kicked at the discs on the ground. 'Maybe fifty-cent coin,' he added and grinned.

'Did you lose anything here, Mr Yee?'

'Some money. Some small company burn. Five, six, not too many. But no way I can get my investment back. It's a loss. All businessmen mus' make a loss sometimes,' he said stoically and laughed briefly.

'And this fire?' I enquired.

'Maybe start by accident. Somebody knock down a cooking pot, maybe. You know, jus' down the hill there was a factory making soap, hair cream and

354

another making,' he searched for a moment for the English but did not know it, '*yin fa*.'

'Fireworks,' I said.

'Yes. Small one made of gunpowder inside a little ball of earth. For children. They throw them in the street. *Pang*! No too much danger. The name,' he stirred the air with his hand to encourage the words, 'cher-wy bomb.'

'And one of the factories caught fire?'

'Maybe,' he declared.

Yet I could tell he knew this was the official reason which would appear in the fire brigade report: the true reason was that it was caused by deliberate, premeditated and publicly – if secretively – advertised arson. Everybody was aware the best way for a family to be rehoused was to be made homeless. The squatters knew this but were reluctant to risk their homes and livelihoods: Mr Yee and his triad society knew it and were more than conscious of how they might benefit: the authorities knew it but were powerless to do anything about it.

The ploy was simple. As soon as a new block of low cost housing was completed, but just before it was occupied, the local triad societies put their heads together and decided it was time for a squatter blaze. Someone would be tipped off to begin it, setting light to his flimsy shanty after he had removed his most valuable possessions. Invariably, he would tip off his friends and relatives who, in turn, would warn their friends and kin. At the appointed hour, usually late in the evening of a day that had been sunny and bright with, if possible, a brisk onshore breeze, the inferno would commence. The timing was important: a rainy or humid day would mean the fire would not spread as quickly as it might, the breeze was needed to fan the holocaust and the hour of the fire was vital because it would slow the fire brigade arriving through the evening traffic. Furthermore, no one wanted to be made homeless when there was the chance of a rain shower.

Inevitably, ten people might perish in the blaze but that was the cost of having ten thousand relocated into proper abodes. These were odds Mr Yee and his businessmen partners were prepared to back.

'You come an' see me soon?' Mr Yee asked.

'When I need my hair cutting,' I said and we shook hands again.

He walked back towards his group of cronies and I started to wend my way down through the ruins towards the road.

I should hate Mr Yee. He is a manipulator of human lives, a ringmaster in the circuses of joy and tragedy.

Yet I am not one to umpire his little games. When I was young and idealistic, I used to spend my time manipulating people with just as much self-interest as he does, if not for so much profit. All men use and exploit their fellows. It is a part of nature and I know, when the time comes to put the rest of this hillside of shacks to the torch, he will assure my interests are protected just as he will his own.

I have spent this afternoon in Tiger Balm Gardens in the hills behind Causeway Bay. It is a bizarre place described in the tourist guide books as a 'quaint pleasure garden in which a number of tableaux depict scenes from Chinese mythology and religion'. Quaint is not quite the adjective I would choose: macabre might be more apt.

Arranged in the shadow of a tall, white pagoda, the gardens are tucked into a hillside which has been shaped into a series of grottoes, in each of which are hollowed out caverns containing scenes from hell. Half life-size demons, the occupants of the dreams of madmen and murderers, have been fashioned out of clay or plaster of Paris and garishly painted. Some have vermilion dog's faces, puce-and-green snake's heads or the visages of bears and tigers painted royal blue or bright yellow and mounted upon the shoulders of human bodies dressed if not in classical Chinese robes then in the scales of a reptile, with the tail of a shark or the shaggy fur of a wild man and the feet of a beast. These creatures are all armed with tridents, Chinese pikestaffs, swords with serrated blades or spears with wave-edged double-sided points: and every one of them is torturing a living soul, a man or woman who, through some slight folly unworthy of the attentions of the underworld, is being made to pay for their sins. Their faces are contorted with fear, their eyes staring and their mouths wide with silent screaming. Some of these poor unfortunates are shown as past the point of caring about their torture. They have been beheaded, dismembered and are being cast into the flames of eternal damnation, into pits of sulphur from whence there are no exits.

The gardens were erected by a Chinese millionaire from Singapore called Aw Boon Haw who made his money from a medicinal paste he invented which is considered to be a cure-all for a wide range of ailments. It is purveyed in little hectagonal glass jars with a green label upon which, in an orange oblong, is portrayed a leaping tiger. It is a petroleum wax-based ointment and contains menthol, oil of cloves, camphor and tincture of peppermint: it is rumoured to contain opium, too. The lid of the jar is golden like every promise ever made by one man to another. And like all promises, it tarnishes.

I use the balm quite regularly. It has a pungent smell which is not unpleasant and may well be addictive over time but I find it soothes my muscles and, if I have slight catarrh, it clears my nose in minutes even if it also makes my eyes stream.

I am fascinated by these gardens partly because of their utter tastelessness and partly because they profoundly amuse me with their infantile barbarity and simplistic moralising. It also never escapes me that the presentation of all this distress and horror was financed by a medicine which eradicates pain. Perhaps the founder wanted to press home the argument that he could cure the ailments of the flesh but not the ills of the soul.

One of the tableaux is entitled *The Barbarity of Wicked Men*. It depicts the usual scene of torture and disembowelment and is overlooked by an incongruous eight-foot-high white rabbit with bulging eyes and wearing a top hat. He seems to have escaped from an Oriental interpretation of *Alice's Adventures in Wonderland*.

Ignoring the rabbit's thyroid stare, I studied the plaster figures but quite dispassionately. Barbarity is not something which worries me: I have seen too much to be affected by it. I am more concerned with the barbarity upon which God and all his churches depend. If it was not for the barbaric threat of amaranthine damnation the promise of heavenly bliss would be a shabby counterfeit, not worth the striving of being good.

And I do not hate barbarous men. What I really despise is God's barbarity. He promised justice, prophesied peace, held out his hand and offered goodness. He pledged to banish pestilence, expel starvation and ostracise evil. I was bedazzled by his reason, fell for his patter and trusted his word when I should have been on my guard. I assumed that, as he was not a man, I was safe. That was my mistake for God and men are too close for comfort: I have often wondered whether man was made in God's image or men made God like themselves.

Yet another of the plaster scenes has a small notice before it in a wooden frame. Rain and humidity have seeped behind the glass so that the writing has run. It states *A Compassionate Scene in Heaven*. Several vaguely angelic spirits, painted entirely in white with stark blue eyes and red mouths, stand over a sinner who has, presumably, recanted. He bears the marks of the brutality from, perhaps, the tableau by the White Rabbit.

I dislike the compassionate. In compassion there is a grotesque piety I cannot abide, those who show pity seeing themselves as blessed. In their hearts, they relish the misery of others for it affords them an opportunity to earn the attention and praise of their fellows and the generosity of their gods. They are without shame, obloqious vultures without honour or grace.

Only the man who has no god can be truly

compassionate for he can have no ulterior motive of pathos up his sleeve, no deceit hiding in his kind words and actions.

For him, such displays are not compassion. They are merely an in-built animal response to the plight of another of his kind in dire straits.

I would be deemed kind by those who do not share my interpretation, would be considered compassionate and kind-hearted. They would be fooled. I merely do what I believe should be done to protect the order of things, for I am not a sympathetic man but a realist who, on occasion, would soften the impact of reality upon those who deserve better.

The Street of Righteous Enlightenment led from the river to the main square, passing on the way the *kong kwan*, the official inn used by guests and visitors to the mandarin whose yamen was situated next door. Of all the thoroughfares of Wuchow, this was the most pleasant, a wide boulevard with a cobbled way running down the centre and broad sidewalks under an avenue of flame trees. The street was seldom crowded for no market stalls were permitted there and the few shops in the street catered for the richer inhabitants. Whereas in other parts of the town a pedestrian had to side-step barrows of produce, tables of fish, sleeping dogs, rickshaws and laden coolies, here the only obstacles were the trees, loose cobbles, the occasional passer-by and, if he should be on the move, the mandarin in his palanquin.

The gateway to the yamen was an imposing

structure fifteen feet high, a square arch with heavy wooden doors, a glazed tiled roof with curved eaves beneath which was suspended an ornately carved rosewood plaque the size of a narrow bed announcing the name and status of the place. Beside the gate stood two guards. They were not erect, soldierly figures such as one might find in a foreign army but comparative slouches. Admittedly, they did not go so far as to squat on the ground, but they leaned on the wall, chatting or playing toss-the-coin against the curbing stones. Their uniforms consisted of a conical hat tied under the chin by a cord, a cotton jacket died saffron, a pair of short black trousers tucked incongruously into what looked like knee-high puttees and slippers. They were armed with a muzzle-loading rifle and a small sword each. Although they were short men, they were well muscled and held themselves, as soldiers do anywhere in the world, with a certain arrogance.

With Ah Fong accompanying me, I was making my way through the town on one of the circuits Father Callaghan had drawn on a map. Although dressed as a Chinese, I wore my cross about my neck on a silver chain and carried in my hand a woven straw basket in which there were some rice cakes, several packets of dried fish and half a dozen of Mr Kung's aged eggs. It was my business to discover needy souls and present them with the food, bless them in the name of Jesus Christ and tell them briefly of the mission. I had already found two beggars on the river side, had fed them in the name of Our Lord and was walking up the Street of Righteous Enlightenment on my way to the square.

Neither Ah Fong nor I expected to find any needy

folk in the street. The town's sick or lame kept away from it for they knew they were likely to be harangued by the mandarin's guards if they appeared. The comparative reduction in the number of pedestrians also gave the street the reputation of being a poor begging spot.

As we approached the gateway to the *kong kwan*, it opened and a most beautiful woman appeared from within, riding in a palanquin with the door curtains tied back. This was so unusual a sight Ah Fong stopped in his tracks and stared, forgetting for a moment to kow-tow. She was dressed in the finest of brocades, the material coloured ultramarine blue shot through with silver and embroidered with birds and clouds. Her face was impassive behind a heavy layer of alabaster white cosmetics, only her eyes and small red lips accentuated by colour, her hair piled high and draped with a string of pearls: she reminded me of the goddess to which Sister Margaret made her sly devotions. Her feet were bound and contained in wooden clog-like shoes with silk uppers, no bigger than those of a small child.

She was in the company of several officials, one of whom screamed at Ah Fong who rapidly bowed as low as he could, bending at the knees to make himself look even smaller. I followed suit but we still received a verbal tongue lashing as the little procession passed by, another official slapping the curtains closed.

'Who she?' I asked Ah Fong after they had disappeared from the end of the street and we straightened up once more.

'Lady for mandarin,' he replied. His face was red from bending over. 'Famous lady. He got many son with her. Wife no got son.'

'What her name?'

'Her name I no know. Mandarin secret.'

We followed in the direction of the palanquin, passing the yamen guards who leered silently at us. The dusty ground bore the flat, slapped footprints of the palanquin bearers and the shod imprints of the officials.

About thirty yards past the yamen was a *hutong* going off at right angles to the street. It was in deep shadow, for the sun was not yet sufficiently high enough to illuminate it. I gave a studied look into the darkness, increased in blackness by my eyes being accustomed to the bright light. Father Callaghan had, since the attack upon Mrs Tremlett's amah, suggested we keep a cautious eye open for trouble. Neither Ah Fong nor I were armed with so much as a penknife.

The *hutong* appeared empty: I could see, at the far end, the oblong of sunlight where it gave onto the next street, figures criss-crossing it. Yet, as I looked down the alley, I heard a groaning noise of the sort made by animals in pain rather than humans.

'What is that?' I wondered aloud, not so much as a question to Ah Fong as an exclamation of my own curiosity.

Starting towards the *hutong*, I slid the handles of my basket over my shoulder to free my hands. I did not expect to be attacked but it was best to be prepared.

'We be care,' Ah Fong said, as if reading my thoughts. 'No good see bad men,' he went on unnecessarily.

The shadows were cool and the *hutong* seemed to contain no living creature save a cat curled up on an inverted tub halfway to the next street. Some doors opened onto the alley but these were all firmly shut as were the few windows. There was no breeze, a few prayer banners hanging from a lintel not so much as twitching.

My stepping into the alley caused the groaning to cease abruptly. The cat, sensing my presence or awakened by the cessation of the noise, got up. It arched its back, hissed menacingly at me then, appreciating I was no threat, circled about and settled once more to continue its repose.

'There is nothing here,' I remarked to Ah Fong and was about to turn when a movement behind some firewood stacked against the wall of a house caught my attention.

I moved carefully forwards, the space behind the boxes gradually becoming visible. If there was a robber there, or one of the rebellious bandits, I wanted to be ready either to repulse his attack or flee to the street, where I hoped the yamen guards might come to my rescue. Such an expectation was, of course, without foundation: the mandarin was hardly likely to have instructed his soldiers to act upon my behalf and yet he had punished one of his own race over the death of the terrier.

These thoughts rushed through my mind as I edged along the *hutong*, conscious I was disregarding Father Callaghan's advice.

What first came into sight was a bare foot covered in grime and several large scabs. The leg above it was equally dirty, the skin blotched whilst the thigh, when it came into view, was covered by the filthy material of a rolled up *fu*. Just as I was about to take another step a hand appeared trying to smooth down the material. It was an adult-sized hand but devoid of fingers: in their place was a row of gnarled stumps like the roots of an old tree.

Ah Fong, a few steps behind me, whispered, 'What you see, master?'

'I have,' I said in my normal voice, 'discovered a poor soul suffering from leprosy.'

'What *lee-pro-see*?' Ah Fong enquired.

The Cantonese for the sickness was one of the words I had come upon only that morning: I had taken to learning by heart ten nouns every day before Mass, recapitulating them afterwards. If they survived my attention to the Latin of the service, I could be confident they were mine.

'*Ma fung*,' I replied, starting forwards again but Ah Fong grabbed me by the waistband.

'*Ay-ah*! No look see, master.' His voice was filled with alarm. 'No look see. No good look see. We go. Go! Go!'

Leprosy was one disease every Chinese knew: it was more feared by them than any other. They would rather have faced all the dragons of the countryside than expose themselves to it. They were, however, ignorant of its two varieties and regarded every leper as evil, a person who was carrying the punishment of the gods upon himself, a reminder to others of what might befall them if they, too, were to grievously sin. In the eyes of the people, they were so damned even the gods would not let them go to their deaths with their bodies intact. Beggars could expect alms, a bowl of unhusked rice or one or two cash from the sympathetic: a leper had to scavenge like a stray dog, expecting nothing but curses and revulsion.

So firm was Ah Fong's grip, so solid his determination we should leave the *hutong* immediately, I had to struggle to make progress towards the leper. As soon as I took a step, Ah Fong leaned away from me, digging the heels of his soft shoes into the dirt.

'Ah Fong!' I remonstrated with him, trying to twist my head. 'Let me go.'

'*Ma fung* no good. Much bad. You no go, master,' he pleaded at the top of his voice.

Reaching behind, I managed to get hold of Ah Fong's hands and began to prise his fingers off my *fu tau*. The more I sought to loosen his grip the firmer it became. At last, I surrendered, allowing him to pull me into the street.

'We go now, master,' he demanded hopefully once I was back in the sunlight.

'Listen, Ah Fong,' I said, calming him down by putting my hand on his shoulder, 'I am going to see the leper. The man with *ma fung*. This is my work. You do not need to come with me. I understand. But you do not need to be afraid.'

'Mus' be af-aid, master!' he answered loudly. 'If you touch *ma fung beng yan* you too *ma fung*. You finger fall off. You toe fall off. You nose fall off.'

'No,' I said sternly, 'not with this *ma fung beng yan*. He has dry leprosy. Only wet leprosy is contagious.'

Ah Fong did not understand the meaning of the word *contagious* but it did not matter. He was not to be convinced and as I started towards the entrance to the *hutong* he begged me once more to leave well alone.

'No go, master. Please, no go.'

'I must go,' I said. 'This is my work.'

I entered the *hutong* and walked to the pile of firewood. The leper was huddled behind the wood wearing the filthiest rags I had ever seen. His *sam* was in such tatters I wondered if he had deliberately scissored it as beggars were known to do, to enhance the chances of benefaction. Yet, looking at his hands, I knew this was not the case: he had too few appropriate fingers left to use a pair of scissors.

At the sight of me, he cringed against the wall and gibbered something that might have been words but sounded more like the bestial noises of a subterranean creature. Bubbles of saliva formed at his mouth, growing as large as plums before bursting.

'I am come with the Light of Jesus,' I told him in English, with as gentle a tone as I could manage, although I knew he was unable to comprehend a single word I spoke. 'Let His Mercy come upon you.'

I stretched out to lay my hand on the poor wretch but he must have thought I was going to strike him, for he instantly swung his arms over his head and cowered against the firewood, knocking over a bundle of kindling. So as not to alarm him further, I put down my basket and, opening it, removed a rice cake which I held out to him. He eyed it cautiously, uncertain whether to reach for it or not.

A soft voice began to speak over my shoulder but I could only make out a few of its phrases and these meant nothing to me.

'*Sùng lai . . . Lai mât . . .*' it said.

Turning, I found Ah Fong close behind me. He was smiling down at the leper who, encouraged by hearing his own tongue, put out both his stump hands and, grasping the cake between them, thrust it towards his mouth and began to bite into it. He ate in the manner of a rat, his two hands at his face: but he no longer owned the dexterity of either a man or a rodent, crumbs falling down his clothing.

'You touch no get *ma fung*?' Ah Fong asked.

'No get,' I assured him, slipping back into pidgin myself. 'What you say him?'

'I tell him you got present. Can take.'

Once more, I reached out. The leper did not flinch but sat quite still as I put my hand upon the crown of his head. His hair was patchy, such as one might find the coat of a mangy dog, the skin beneath dry and flaking.

'May the Love of Our Saviour, Jesus Christ, come to you, relieve your suffering and bring you to His Eternal Glory,' I whispered.

The leper's head moved under my palm and he gazed up at me. He had not raised his face until now and, as he turned his countenance upwards, I saw his nose was disfigured and his upper lip withdrawn back across his teeth in a permanent, hideous smirk. I felt instantly repelled but fought the emotion and looked into his eyes. The pupils were black but the whites bloodshot and sore.

'*Yee thoo*,' he said, spittle spraying from his mouth onto the front of his *sam*, his tongue grotesquely sticking out below his upper jaw. '*Yee thoo. Gai du. Gai du.*'

'Master,' Ah Fong whispered in my ear, 'he say *Yeh so Gei duk*. Is Cantonese for Jesus Chri's.'

The leper muttered something else and Ah Fong, moving between me and the woodpile, put out his hand and placed it next to mine on the man's scalp.

I made the sign of the cross upon the leper's forehead then, as I began to give him the blessing,

368

there came a clamour from the far end of the *hutong*. A tight throng of people was rushing towards us. At the forefront was a man with a red cloth tied about his brow.

'Master, we go! *Fie di*! *Fie di*!' Ah Fong shouted, grabbing me by the arm.

I turned without so much as a thought and ran after him, down the *hutong* towards the Street of Righteous Enlightenment. As we reached the sunlight, I looked back. The crowd had halted, the leper having crawled into the centre of the *hutong*, where he was kneeling up with his back towards us, his pathetic arms outstretched on either side so that he almost touched each wall. It seemed as though he was protecting us with his hideous illness, knowing the mob would not so much as brush against him. But his delaying tactic was short: the leader grabbed a length of firewood from the pile and, using it as a stave, smashed it down upon the side of the leper's head. He crumpled and the crowd surged forward again, jumping over the prone, misshapen body and kicking my basket aside so the contents spilled over him.

Ah Fong and I had to seek safety and quickly. We spun to our right, fleeing for the gate to the yamen: if we could enter it, we would come under the protection of the mandarin and no canaille would dare enter his premises.

Running at full tilt, we sped up to the two yamen guards who, hearing the approaching shouts and seeing us sprinting towards them, had picked up their muzzle-loaders and stationed themselves on either side of the gate. Ah Fong yelled at them to open the gate but they stood firm and did not respond. Drawing nearer, he hollered again but the only response he got was from the nearest guard who, unsheathing his sword and shaking his head, shouted curtly back at us.

'The *kong kwan*, Ah Fong!' I bellowed, seeing the yamen door was not to open for us. 'Go *kong kwan* side!'

We sped past the guards and on to the second door. It was not open but I hammered upon the wood and the gatekeeper inside, not able to judge what was going on in the street, slid the wooden bar across, pulling the door ajar. I rammed my shoulder against the timbers and we slid in. The gatekeeper was too flabbergasted to stop us. I slammed the door shut, ramming home the retaining beam.

For a moment, all was quiet then there drew near a screaming cacophony and a thumping on the door. The gatekeeper wanted to open up but Ah Fong took him roughly by the arm and demanded he do nothing. I could not tell what was being said but the gatekeeper kept looking in my direction so I guessed Ah Fong was telling him some lie about my importance, my being held in high esteem by the mandarin and so on. At last, the argument was won and the gatekeeper, slipping an iron hasp across the gate as added security, led us across a courtyard and into the inn.

We were shown into a lofty room, large and swept clean but devoid of any furniture with not even so much as a straw mat. After a minute or two, however, several heavy upright chairs were brought in by the gatekeeper, who was accompanied by a young boy with a tray upon which was a pot of tea and two bowls.

'We lucky people,' Ah Fong remarked as he poured the tea. 'If we outside, *I Ho Ch'üan* kill us.'

'Yes,' I answered distantly.

My mind was not on the thought of my danger and escape but upon the sacrifice made by the leper. I could see him still, a vivid and terrible picture in my mind, his arms outspread as if inviting crucifixion, holding back our would-be assassins with nothing more than the abhorrence of his disfigurement and the evil of his awful disease.

☯

'You should buy yourself one like this, *san foo*. Such a thing brings joy to old lives.'

I glance up at the bamboo cage in which Mr Wu keeps his song bird. A light breeze blowing through the tea-house window gently rocks it, sending the bird hopping from perch to perch, trilling and fluttering its wings. It is a pretty little creature, not three inches long with a crimson beak and orange patches of feathers on its cheeks as if a miniature clown had been given instructions in colouring it. Beneath its neck, the plumage is grey with black lines whilst down its sides are rich brown stripes dotted with white spots culminating in a long black-and-white tail.

'So you are pleased with your new acquisition,' I reply. 'Tell me, my friend, what is it?'

'A zebra finch. From Australia,' he informs me. 'Not very expensive. Fifteen dollars.'

'What does it eat?'

'Just seeds. Tiny seeds. Very cheap. And it drinks

water. Very easy to keep. Live three, maybe five years.'

Mr Wu's bird has no name. He is not into calling his companions by anthropomorphic titles. To him it is just a bird and, when he communicates with it, he does so by clicking his tongue and half-whistling.

A waiter stops by our table, replacing our empty tea pot with a full one from his tray. I tap the middle finger of my right hand on the table: this is a sign of thanks, saving on words. At times, the Chinese can be very economical with words whilst, at other times, they are profligate.

The tea-house is, as usual for late afternoon, full of men with their cage birds. There is not a single woman in sight, not even as a menial employee of the tea-house, for this is a man's place. It is not because the conversation is smutty, bawdy or esoterically masculine: it is because, traditionally, men bring their birds here. It is spacious and light with iron-framed windows and seating for a hundred patrons. The waiters are efficient, the range of teas is wide and the sweetmeats are expensive.

Every cage is suspended from a hook, each table having four hooks hanging above it and four seats. The reason for this is so that, as the men sit to chat or gossip, the birds may become acquainted overhead, chirping and singing to each other. As I do not own a bird, Mr Wu's finch has to try and butt in on the avian intercourse two tables away, where an aloof mynah is intermittently squawking in disregard of two canaries.

'The song of birds brings peace to the soul,' Mr Wu announces with quodlibetic authority. 'It is the music of spirits. As the playing of an Indian's flute can calm the snake so can the music of birds soften a man's hardness.'

'The snake is mesmerised by the waving of the flute, not the sound. Snakes have no ears,' I respond pedantically.

Mr Wu is not daunted by the fact. He is old and reality, like truth, is to be avoided when it suits the moment: an old man, like a young boy, prefers fantasies to facts for they are not only more romantic but more convenient. I am old too, so I should know.

'I like to hear the bird sing, *san foo*, because it is free.'

'Your bird,' I say, 'is hardly free. You do not so much as let it out of its cage to fly about your flat.'

'The bird is free,' Mr Wu insists. 'Its spirit is free. Do you know the poetry of Emily Dickinson?'

I admit I do not so Mr Wu sips his bowl of tea, swills the liquid around in his mouth, swallows it noisily and grunts to clear his throat.

'No ladder needs the bird but skies,' he recites, his eyes closed to aid memory, 'to situate its wings, nor any leader's grim baton arraigns it as it sings.' He opens his eyes. 'The song of the bird cannot be reproached. It is like a pure idea, come from the gods, unable to be argued with. What matter if the bird is in a cage so long as its spirit is free?'

I look out of the window by our table. In the street below is a thriving market, a slow-moving wedge of pedestrians flowing by the stalls, eddying where there is a bargain on offer or a parked vehicle causes an immovable obstacle. The view makes me consider how much like life the scene is, a slow progress past temptations and obstructions which are not so much to be resisted as to be smoothed over or avoided.

'Are you afraid of death, *san foo*?'

The suddenness of Mr Wu's question takes me by surprise.

'No, I am not,' I answer with some emphasis.

Mr Wu shrugs and says, 'It was a foolish question. If you have a god you are not afraid.'

'I do not have a god,' I respond somewhat tetchily. 'One does not need such a thing in order to face a reality. Death is merely an unavoidable fact.'

Looking out of the window again, I notice that another at the same level across the street, partially obscured by a large blue-and-yellow neon sign announcing in English and Chinese characters *The Penguin Suit & Garment Mfct. Co. Ltd.*, gives upon a dentist's surgery. In the white-enamel and black-leather chair is seated an elderly woman in a green-and-beige check jacket, her cheeks pushed out with rolls of cotton wool and a chromed tube hanging over her lower jaw. She is gesticulating in the air to the dentist, whom I cannot see for the factory hoarding.

'A dentist I do fear,' I continue, nodding in the direction of the window, 'because he is avoidable. But death? I give it no thought.'

This is a lie.

Death concerns me for it is unknown and the unknown disturbs me. That this ignorance is a condition *sine qua non* of my life is a further reason for worry for I can no more come to eradicate it than ice can embrace a flame. To know it, I must cease to exist: the horror of death is not the act of dying but the irreversibility of it, the finality from which I

374

cannot return any the wiser. When breath stops so does knowledge. That is my ultimate fear.

When I was young, the great mystery was not death but God: I wanted to know him, to be able to recognise him when I saw his signs or words, when I watched an event unfolding and knew his hand was in it. But now that I am old, the mystery is no longer of God but of death and its proximity to me for soon we shall be one.

'Once a *san foo* . . .' Mr Wu begins, impinging upon my thoughts, but I cut him short.

'We are all dying,' I interrupted him. 'Our whole life is but a journey towards death. From the moment we are born, we are on the slide. In the middle of life we are in death. Indeed, we cannot live if we do not accept death. You,' I go on, chiding him, 'as a Chinese should know this. You visit with death twice a year, when you go to the graves of your ancestors. And do not call me *san foo*. I am not a priest and, in retrospect, I was never a priest.'

'You took your vow.'

'I did,' I admit curtly. 'And you promised your wife not to be unfaithful to her. But I'll bet you had a concubine.'

I look into his face, detect the glimmer of memory one sees in the faces of the aged which tells me I have hit the quick.

'I'm not criticising you,' I continue. 'It is not my place either as your friend or, as you will keep on insisting, even as a priest. I'm merely stating a fact. You were not unfaithful to her any more than I was to my supposed faith. At the moment of taking the vow, you and I believed in what we were doing. It is just that men change. Their ideas, hopes, beliefs, moralities alter. It's a fact of life. And death. What does it matter?'

Mr Wu smiles and gazes up at his bird, which is singing noisily and without cessation. Another finch of the same species has arrived, its cage hanging above the next table where two young men in their late twenties are talking animatedly.

'I would be like my bird,' he admits quietly.

'My friend,' I reply, 'you and he are one, both in a cage of which no one opens the door. His cage,' I glance up, 'is made of bamboo and yours – and mine – is made of time. His door will not open until a hand goes in to remove his corpse and our door will not open until, for us, the clock stops.'

He refills our bowls and we both slurp our tea, fresh from the pot and just too hot for our old mouths. The remains of some honey-coated nuts and melon seeds lie in a dish between us, all that is left of the snacks we have eaten.

It is only a matter of time now. I look across at Mr Wu and I know in the instinctive way I suppose any animal knows, that my death is not far off. It can only be a matter of weeks, perhaps days. I have not long to get my house in order, sort out my affairs.

I am sure we do not die at what the doctor or lawyer would term the moment of death. I believe we die by degrees, mouldering away over the weeks before, gradually degrading, faculty by faculty slipping away. We must seek to break our attachments bit by bit for a man should not face eternity encumbered by the trappings of living. We do not die but are torn, part by part, from our existence.

'Forgive me for calling you *san foo*,' Mr Wu says.

'I mean no harm by it. It is habit and a habit is a thing of comfort in old age.'

I smile and he knows he is forgiven.

The zebra finch stops singing. The two young men have finished their intent conversation and are leaving, the one with the bird having unhitched the cage which he now carries at arm's length as if it was an offering.

'I am not an old man,' Mr Wu declares. 'Outside, I am ancient but, within, there are no lines in my skin or a tired heart. Inside, I am a young man.'

At his words, I think of the old flower-seller in the alley and I am suddenly immensely saddened.

☯

The headquarters building of the Hongkong and Shanghai Banking Corporation faces onto Des Voeux Road, across Statue Square and the Cenotaph and, beyond these, to the Star Ferry pier. At least, the rear doors do. Most of those entering the bank through this most popular of portals do not realise they are going in through the tradesman's entrance: the front door of the bank is in Queen's Road which has no view save of the trees surrounding the government offices and the old French Mission building.

Such an enigma could only exist in China: for a business to be successful, the laws of *fung shui* must be obeyed. These dictate that the main door may not face the sea and must be higher than the rear door. Failure to comply with these basic rules ensures instability, insecurity and anxiety, three factors with which no bank may contend.

Beside the rear doors are two bronze statues of lions, each thrice lifesize. They are bold, magisterial creatures, true colonial beasts with solid-sounding British names — Stephen and Stitt, after former senior managers of the firm. Stitt is to the right of the entrance, proudly demure, whilst Stephen is to the left and has his mouth open in a growl. Both statues are pockmarked with shrapnel scars from the Japanese invasion of 1941 and have highly polished paws, for it is customary to stroke them for good luck. I restrain myself from caressing Stitt's paws, preferring to associate with my namesake. He does not sit and watch life pass him by but makes a comment upon it.

Entering the building, I climb some stairs to the banking hall, a lofty, grand temple to Mammon. No matter what the weather, it is always five degrees cooler in here. The marble and the presence of so much money chills the air.

Vast, dark square pillars support a barrel-vaulted ceiling decorated with a huge mosaic portraying the themes of trade and industry between the Occident and the Orient, the God of Wealth surveying steel-workers and aircraft builders, brocade embroiderers and tin beaters, sedan chairs and automobiles.

Often, I momentarily crane my neck to admire the beauty of this roof, remembering it was not made by a famous artist, a Michaelangelo of our age but by a man not unlike myself, a White Russian émigré called Podgoursky who had been eking out a living in Shanghai before his talent and temperament were discovered. I met him once, in the thirties, just as he was about to commence work upon this masterpiece. He was a sad man with a quick wit and a mistress half his age, afraid of something in himself. Perhaps it was his artistic skill scared him so. Art is a god of sorts.

Today, however, I have no time to pause: I am here on business and have not come empty-handed. In one of the narrow lanes — it must have been Li Yuen Street East for there was an inordinate number of stalls selling ladies' lingerie there — I have purchased a cheap suitcase. Where a more expensive item would have leather, this has plastic and the locks are feeble things that could be split open with a flick of the wrist and a twenty-five-cent screwdriver. This weakness is not important. I am not going anywhere. I merely need the case for temporary transportation. After today, I shall give it to Chiu to use as a store for his clothing: he will be pleased to be rid of one of his cardboard boxes.

The enquiries desk is to my left and I head for it, leaning against the counter as a clerk quits his seat to speak to me.

'May I help you, sir?' he asks in a polite voice from which he has striven to remove as much as he can of his Chinese accent.

I want to tell him not to be ashamed, to speak as he would if he were addressing me in the street and selling me dried fish rather than in this austere magnificence and selling me his services.

'I have an appointment to open my deposit box,' I inform him. 'My name is Galvin.'

He runs his finger down the page of a thick ledger and says, 'Mr S. Galvin? Yes.' He places a tick next to my name, swings the book around and asks, 'Will you sign here, please, sir?'

I scribble my initials and a messenger appears at my side to usher me to a private viewing room.

Here, in a cubicle with leather upholstered chairs and a walnut veneered shelf, I am presented with a black steel box, upon the lid and end of which are stencilled white numbers.

The messenger makes no comment but leaves me to my business, quietly closing the door behind me. Putting my fingers under the box, I lift it a little. It is not heavy, weighs not more than ten pounds, not much to show for the end of a life in the Orient. I would wager there are other boxes in the vaults, perhaps right next to mine on the strong-room shelves, which contain fortunes in silver or gold, rubies or emeralds, works of art and treasures carved of ivory, jade and agate.

The lock is easy to open. My key slips in and turns without a snag, the mechanism well oiled.

Opening the lid is a terrible thing for me. I have not done this since Mr Poon offered me the ownership of my flat.

The box is divided horizontally into two halves by a metal tray. The top contains little of importance: my birth certificate, my passport (which must be long out of date for I cannot remember when I last sought to renew it), the deed to my flat which I never need to see and shall soon no longer require, a faded photograph of myself in a cassock, as a smug young man in control of himself and his world and an envelope containing assorted papers, the exact contents of which I have forgotten.

Before I remove this tray, I add to it a new envelope sealed with paper tape over which a Chinese chop has been stamped, the mark of a Chinese lawyer who practises in Saigon Street. Upon the front of the envelope, in a delicate, cursive script, is written *Last*

Will and Testament. I do not place this on top of the items but smuggle it in underneath the old envelope. I do not wish to see it again.

My hands shake as I hook my index fingers into the metal loops at the side of the tray and lift it clear.

The contents in the bottom are wrapped in pieces of felt. One by one, I unwrap them, placing them on the shelf, moving aside an inkwell and dip pen to make room. They are all made of silver: two single candlesticks, a paten ten inches in diameter and a plain chalice with a simple cross engraved upon the side, the gilding on the interior faded and patchy as though struck by metallic serpigo. I handle them gently as if they were made not of precious metal but eggshell porcelain or Venetian glass, liable to shatter at the least touch.

Beneath them is another package, also wrapped in felt. I open this and remove two small wooden jugs. Their sides have split with age and the dry atmosphere of the bank vault whilst the handle of one of them, originally an intrinsic part of the vessel, for they were carved from single blocks of wood, has snapped off at the base and warped badly. Any polish they may once have displayed has long since dulled, soaking into the surface. The inside of the damaged one is lightly coloured whilst the other is stained black.

I place them next to the silver items, removing the box to put it on the floor by my chair, the interior tray resting across the top. This done, I carefully wrap all the objects but one in their felt coverings again and place them in my cheap suitcase. Only the broken jug is to remain in the bank.

My leaving it has nothing to do with its value

although it is true it is worth very little in financial terms. It is simply that I do not want to lose it. The chalice, paten and candlesticks mean nothing to me now, but the secular jugs are somehow special, simple Chinese peasant items. What may happen to the broken one after my death I can neither guess at nor care about yet, whilst I am alive, I want it safe. It is a matter of nostalgia more than anything else, a splinter of sentimentality jammed in the thumb of my thoughts, not to be shifted with the needle of sensibility.

The re-wrapping completed, I lift the box back onto the shelf and remove from it the last item it contains. This is wrapped not in felt but in thin tissue paper which was once white but has turned cream with time. Carefully, I spread open the crisp sheets of tissue to reveal a priest's stole folded neatly along creases that have formed themselves over the years into permanent lines. The material is still white and has not gone the way of the tissue paper. I unfold it until I see the gold and light blue embroidery of a cross: then, I stop.

If I were to continue to open out the stole I should come upon a black patch which resembles a neat ink stain. It is stiff as if made by indian ink, the liquid evaporated and the lampblack left. Yet I do not. I stop, lean forward and very lightly, as if the material was the head of an infant or the brow of a sick friend on their death-bed, I kiss it. My mouth remains closed. It is less of a kiss and more of a touch of the lips.

This done, I quickly replace it and the tray in the box, close the lid and snap the lock shut. The messenger comes at my call and the box is taken away on a little trolley to its secret hiding-place beneath the building.

Suitcase in hand, I leave the bank by the back door and cross the street, taking care to avoid the creaking, squealing trams. At the Star Ferry, I pay my fare, pass through the turnstile, climb the steps and board a ferry, tugging the wooden back of a row of seats across so I can sit facing the direction of travel. Facing backwards makes me feel queasy. At the Kowloon pier, I walk to the rickshaw rank and, leaning back in the seat with my arm firmly on the suitcase wedged in beside me, watch the pectoral muscles of the rickshaw coolie flex and relax, flex and relax as he pulls me homeward through the afternoon traffic.

☯

There are no cruise liners in port, no American warships riding at anchor and only three British naval vessels alongside in the dockyard of HMS Tamar: one is a black, sleek submarine, one a destroyer and the third an unarmed supply vessel. As a consequence, the streets are more thinly populated by tourists than usual.

This state of affairs has both advantages and disadvantages. The benefits are that one is not surrounded by sun-pinked buffoons armed with Baedeker guides and all-but-useless teach-yourself-Cantonese phrase books, sporting clothes they would never wear in their native countries and speaking in louder than normal voices. One does not have to eschew their meandering strolls along the pavements, pausing momentarily to avoid stepping into the frame of their photographs. What is more, with the reduction in potential targets, there are fewer pickpockets and professional beggars abroad and prices are lower. Of the disadvantages, the main one is that the shop touts are out in force competing strongly for customers in order to maintain their cash flow. Shops in Tsim Sha Tsui succeed on high turnover rather than high profit margins.

One tout I particularly dislike. He is an Indian who owns a tailor's shop down the street from Mr Chan's emporium. Most of these store sentinels maintain a station at the entrances to their businesses, calling out to would-be clients as they pass. They may step out of their doorway to press home the point of the magnificence of their wares but nothing more.

This Indian, however, if he believes he has espied an easy sucker, not only berates him from the doorstep but follows him down the street, even going so far as to tug a sleeve. He offers silk ties, silk shirts, tailor-made suits 'to the finest fashionable cut this side of Bombay, sir', Madras cotton vests and sweaters of the purest cashmere.

It is impossible to lightly dismiss this man's pesterings with the usual curt negative response or a wave of the hand. He will not be so easily put off. Trailing a step behind and to one's right, he leans forward to edge himself into the corner of the line of one's sight and blathers.

'Why will you not come in my shop and see for yourself? There is no obligation to buy, sir. No obligation, sir. If you can find nothing you like, please to go. Never mind.' He shakes his head in the falsely deprecating way Indians have. 'What can you lose by visiting the shop, sir? Only a few minutes. Please.' It is at this moment he touches the sleeve or presses his hand against one's arm. 'This way. Just a few steps. I have new Thai silk ties in stock. Just come from Bangkok. Only yesterday.'

He was at it this morning and, to my surprise, attempted to persuade me to enter his shop: after the last time he tried this with me, I would have thought he would remember my face and stay clear but it seems his memory, like my own, is not without voids.

'Sir,' he called from the shop front. 'Good ties, silk shirts, cotton socks, finest quality.'

'No,' I said bluntly and kept on walking, my straw basket in my hand.

He should have been able to judge I was a resident, not a tourist. No visitor carries a locally made bag with the handle repaired with parcel string: but, as well as being forgetful of a face, he is unobservant. Abandoning his doorway, he kept pace with me along the pavement.

'Come, sir. I have very good quality cotton – South Sea Island. Can make you a shirt in two hours. Guaranteed top quality. Your initials embroidered on the pocket for no extra charge.'

'No,' I repeated, a little more assertively.

'If you don't want shirts, I can make waistcoats, smoking jackets. All pure silk from China, made by hand . . .'

I stopped but did not immediately turn around. He thought I was caving in.

'This way, sir, just a few steps . . .'

I rounded on him and said, with as much invective as I could muster, '*M'hai! Ngoh wâ m'hai, m'hai, m'hai. Lun hoi!*'

He reeled back, cursing me under his breath in Hindustani but I knew I had got the better of him. A number of Chinese shop owners in front of their windows laughed and the Indian, having lost face, skulked away. I walked on, pleased at having silenced him.

As I entered the Hing Loon Curio and Jewellery Company, Mr Chan rose from an old armchair at the rear of the shop and came forward to greet me, folding a daily newspaper.

'*Cho san*,' he said, smiling his welcome. 'How are you today?'

'I'm well,' I replied and sat on one of the stools. 'How is business?'

'Not so good,' he confided in me. 'No ship in the docks. Maybe Sunday better.' He rustled the newspaper, dropping it on the counter. 'Big ship coming on Sunday. Two thousan' passengers.'

Along the edge of the underside of his glass counter top are wedged fifty or sixty business cards. I studied them as he moved behind the counter to sit on his own wooden stool, which is marginally higher than those provided for customers. It is considered good psychology for the trader to be taller than the purchaser.

In Mr Chan's line of trade, he comes across every kind and condition of tourist for visitors to Hong Kong always buy curios: it does not matter if they are sailors, businessman, honeymoon couples or elderly folk taking a retirement cruise – whatever they are, they purchase trinkets and, if they have a card, Mr Chan collects it and puts it in his counter. The few I read proved the range of his clientele: *David L. Rodgers, Capt. USN*; *William Corman*,

386

*Corporate Finance Division, The Bank of Australia;
Allan Browning, South-East Asian Affairs, The Daily
Sketch/London; Frederick Fisher, Accountant and
Peter Lowry, Lowry Bells and Diving Equipment,
Djakarta.*

'You brought something for me?' Mr Chan asked,
nodding in the direction of the basket.

'Yes, I have,' I answered.

'Let me see.'

I lifted the basket on to the counter and opened the
handles, removing the contents. Mr Chan unwrapped
the felt to display the two candlesticks, paten and
chalice. He stroked the latter then, removing a yellow
duster from a drawer, began to polish it.

'Where you get this?'

'I have had them a long time,' I said.

I did not look at the four items. It seemed just then
to be an act of betrayal to part with them.

'Yes, but where you get them?' he reiterated.

'I got them when I was a young man. In China.
They are very old. The chalice – the cup you are
holding – was made in 1838. In Italy.'

'They are make of good silver,' Mr Chan commented, turning the chalice over in his hands, 'but
they belong to a church. How you get them?'

'When I was a young man,' I admitted, 'I was a
priest. A *san foo*. These were mine then.'

One of the few tourists walking the street entered
the shop and started to mooch about, gazing at the
cabinets. He had the obligatory camera hanging over
his shoulder, a parcel wrapped in brown paper under
his arm.

'I can help you?' Mr Chan enquired.

'Just looking,' responded the tourist.

Mr Chan, out of deference for my privacy, spoke in Cantonese.

'*Hái pin shùe?*' he asked.

'*Lai pàai t'ong hái Wuchow,*' I said, adding, '*T'ien chu kiao.*'

The tourist's wife appeared in the door and called out, 'I'm through here, honey.'

'Okay,' he called back and left the shop without saying a word to us.

Mr Chan reverted to English.

'Why you take these things?'

'No one would want them,' I said. 'The church itself was finished.'

'What year was this?'

'Nineteen hundred,' I replied.

Mr Chan fell silent and, putting down the chalice, picked up the paten which he studied closely, holding it up to his face and running his finger around the rim.

'This one make in England. See,' he pointed to the base, 'got a hallmark. The silver is very good quality. Not Chinese silver. European silver. Chinese silver got too much tin. But I can't sell it like it is. No one want to buy church silver. But, if you don't mind, I can buy f'om you and sell to a silver merchant. But he will melt it down to make something new.'

I did not care. Not any longer. They were useless to me and meaningless to anyone else. If they were reduced and made into tourist baubles or chopstick rests, cheap brooches, dollar note clips or tie-pins, what difference did it make? None to me.

'No, I don't mind,' I said and any feeling of betrayal lingering in me was dispelled.

Mr Chan brought out a set of scales and weighed

388

the four items together. This done, he opened his newspaper to see what the day's silver rate was and, with a quick flicking of his fingers over the beads of his abacus, made me an offer.

There was no doubt I would take it. He knew I would accept whatever he decreed but he was not to know that had he offered me ten dollars and a glass of beer I should gladly have parted with them.

He removed the money from a thick wad of notes he had in a drawer, slid it into an envelope and snapped a rubber band around to keep it shut. I did not bother to re-open the envelope and count the contents. I merely pushed it well down into the inside pocket of my jacket for safety.

'I see you again soon?' he enquired as I stood up.

'Soon,' I promised.

'Okay. Nex' time you come, we maybe go take tea.'

I smiled and told him I would accept his invitation: and yet I was not sure when I would come his way again for I had nothing left to sell. The well of my life is now empty except for the mud at the bottom.

The chapel was lit by oil lamps, one hanging at each station of the cross and, upon the altar, two candles burned, their light reflecting off the silver of the chalice and paten to the side. The shadows of the roof beams shifted imperceptibly to and fro as the flames moved to the touch of draughts of warm air blowing in through spaces between the pantiles. There was that night, for the first time in over a week, a warm breeze blowing up from the river, carrying on its shoulders the scents and stinks of the banks.

'I wonder if we should not go down on our knees and thank the Lord for this wind,' Father Callaghan remarked, entering the chapel carrying a bottle of wine and some wafers in a porcelain rice bowl. 'After days of having the air as still as it is inside an alms box, it is a blessed relief, to be sure, to have it here tonight. Hot it may be, and distinctly nidorous, but at least it stirs the night.' He placed the wine on the side table. 'So long as it doesn't stir the residents of our fair city.'

'Should it?' I asked, curious to know if the coming of an evening breeze had some supernatural properties for the Chinese.

'Not ordinarily,' he said. 'But these days, who can tell? This drought is doing more than just drying up the land and killing the rice.'

He began to take the wafers out of the bowl, arranging them in the paten and pouring the wine into one of the two wooden jugs that stood behind the chalice.

'When a natural catastrophe strikes the Chinese,' he began, talking as much to himself and the altar as to me, 'such as a drought like this or a flooding of the Yangtse Kiang, they put it down as an act of their gods. Which, I suppose, is fair enough: after all, we speak ourselves of such things in just the same fashion. See the insurance contract on any ship: acts of God are a common commercial risk, it would seem. However, if we suffer a drought, which in Ireland is as likely as a typhoon in Tipperary, we put it down to bad luck. Here, it is considered a visitation from the gods to tell the people that something is wrong. They, in turn, do not blame themselves but the emperor. It is his fault for he has, in their eyes, executive powers in the kingdom of heaven. And so he must atone, fix things so that it doesn't happen again.'

'How does he atone?' I asked.

'Not how you'd think, Father Stephen. Indeed not. You would guess that he'd have a big festival and so on. Mollify the spirits. And that does happen. But it's not that simple. He must be seen by the people to be doing something. The populace, it would seem, are more for appeasement than the gods. Emperors in the past have lost their thrones and their lives because of a month of heavy rainstorms two thousand miles to the west of Peking.'

'So what do they do?'

'Do? They give to the poor to show their humility: of course, they raise taxes to generate the revenue for this generosity. Or they stir up trouble over which they can hold sway, start a fight they know they can win. Or they find a scapegoat.'

He finished laying out the wafers and pouring the wine, ramming the cork back into the bottle and checking that I had done my appointed task of filling the second jug with water.

'That's where we come in,' he continued. 'We are the scapegoats. The *gweilos* in general. The *yang kwei tsi*, the *yang ren*. Which is to say foreign devils and foreigners in general. And especially the *T'ien Chu Kiao* and the *Ye Su Kiao*. The Catholics and the Protestants.'

'How are we to blame?' I said.

'In their eyes, we have come to China with our religion and our One True God and we have upset the lords of heaven. The gods, the spirits, the ancestors are all angry that we are here. The fact that we *T'ien Chu Kiao* first arrived in China in the year 1246 does not seem to dawn upon them. Admittedly we were thrown out a century later, but we've been back ever since the middle of the sixteenth century when the blessed Francis Xavier arrived in Macau. Of course, we've been persecuted but that's all a part of it, isn't it, Father Stephen?'

He placed the wafers upon the altar and put the chalice next to them.

'Now, I fear, we are to be persecuted again. We are seen as the bringers of this drought and, no doubt, the instigators of this hot breeze which you and I know is just air rising off the land but which, to the town's-folk, is the sour tincture of our anger, or the curse of the gods, or the breath of the dragons come to burn their houses if they don't burn ours.' He pulled his watch out of his pocket and, holding it to one of the oil lamps, said, 'Twenty minutes. We had best go and get ourselves up to look like Christians. I'm sure Our Lord would not mind us conducting Mass in *sams* and *fus* but I don't somehow think we should let things go that far. Not yet, in any case.'

We left the chapel, parting on the stairs beside the oil lamp that hung halfway up. I looked briefly at his face as we separated. It may have been the influence of the oil lamp but I believed it was lined more deeply than I had realised before.

As I opened the door of my room, a warm blast blew past me. It was so hot I thought, for a moment, that perhaps Father Callaghan's warning had come true and the building had been set on fire. I rushed to the window but there were no flickering lights outside.

The town seemed unusually still. It was only the early evening but I could not hear the usual clamour that drifted up to the mission from the busy streets. The faint aura of light over the rooftops was there, the smoke of the evening fires wafting through it, but there was no hum of life. I wondered if the hot air was suppressing the sounds but then, to dispel this query, a gong began to sound far away from the direction of the Lung Mo temple. I left the window, lit my own lamp and started to remove my *sam* and *fu*, putting on my cassock and albe.

As I dressed, I considered Father Callaghan's warning that we were to be the next persecuted. He was right. I knew it, had known it in my heart for days although I had not let my awareness or apprehension voice itself to me. I sat in the chair by the table, my cassock unbuttoned, and thought over the events of the past few weeks, closing my eyes the better to concentrate my mind, deliberately conjuring up pictures of those signs I knew foretold our doom – the puppet and the beheaded monkey, the conversations at the Residency and Mr Doble's house, the bloody moon.

When I opened my eyes, they were tuned not to the faint light of the lamp in my room but to the night outside. I gazed across the roofs and wondered then if I was doing the correct thing, if my life was following a pathway that was just and true. I was filled with a surety that my seeking to cure the sick, guide the blind and heal the lame was moral and right but I felt rising in me a terrible question which made me doubt the ultimate purpose of my vocation. I was suddenly filled with an all-encompassing scepticism: it was wrong to bring an alien god to these people.

It occurred to me, looking out over the ancient roofs at the view that must have changed little since the poet Su-shi gazed upon them, that I was not unwelcome here because of my seeking to do good by the people: I was hated because of what I insisted they take in order to accept the goodness I could offer them. In the eyes of the local people, it was not my medicine, my compassion, my sympathy and my desire to assist them against which they reacted. It was my religion.

The gong, which had fallen silent, started up again. It was a monotonous, deep sound, exotically threatening and yet at the same time captivating and exciting. It was like a heartbeat far off in the night, the heartbeat of a people and their history.

Standing up, for the time was drawing nearer to go down to Mass, I commenced buttoning up my cassock. The collar was tight and I had to twist my fingers to get it fastened. When it was closed, it was so firm about my throat that it might have been throttling me.

I contemplated that the Chinese were no more cruel than we. Father Callaghan had intimated as much but the more I thought about it, the more I saw little difference. What was more, any difference I could discern between their cruelty and that of not only my own race but also my own brethren in Christ was insignificant.

Reaching onto my bookshelf, I removed a volume on the history of our faith in China and started to thumb through the pages. It was an old book which had been in my room upon my arrival and must have belonged to Father Callaghan. Bound in brown leather with gold tooling and marbled end-papers, it had suffered much from its time in the East. The covers were mottled with mould, the end-papers separating from the boards and the pages dog-eared from much reading and fingering. Somewhere, there was a reference I needed to read, that would prove my point to me. It was no longer a question of doubting morality but requiring documentary proof to back it up. Sure enough, in the fifth chapter, I found the words I sought.

St Francis Xavier, I read, his name in the text followed by a small × to denote his canonisation, *landed upon St John's Island at Amacao in that year, but his plans of spreading the teachings of Christ were thwarted by the jealousy of his own countrymen and he died thereupon without ever setting foot upon the main land of China.* I flicked several pages over, the paper crisp with age and brittle to the touch: from the edges, the gold dust flaked off upon my fingers. In the next chapter was another passage to confirm my thesis. It went, *After the death of the Jesuit, Matteo Ricci in the Year of Our Lord 1610, there began the prominent controversy concerning the nature of the worship of ancestors by the Chinee. It was undecided whether or not this was idolatrous. The controversy raged for 132 years. An appeal was made to the Holy Father in Rome who sent forth to China his legate, but the Bishop in Macau sequestered him and held him fast with forty priests within the dungeons of the fortress there in which he was detained without favour until his death.*

Closing the book, I placed my albe about my shoulders and left the room, blowing out the lantern. My mind was in turmoil and yet never for an instant did it occur to me that I should go down on my knees and ask God for His advice. Somehow, I knew what it would be: stay and preach, spread the word, change the history of five thousand years. This was not what I wanted to hear. I was beyond divine persuasion.

The girls were already in their places in the pews as I entered. Father Callaghan was standing to one side, the light of a lamp casting its glow down upon him. Behind it, painted on the wall, was a portrait of Christ carrying the burden of his cross to Calvary. The colours were faded and there was a section of the picture missing by his right foot where damp had undermined the plaster.

Sister Margaret was in her usual place near the rear, where she could keep an eye on her charges, and Ah Fong was in the front row, his hands resting demurely in his lap. Another thirty or so Chinese were also present and, amongst them, I caught sight of Mr Kung. He looked haggard, a tired old man without any of the glint in his eye that I had seen when he presented me with his foul egg.

If, I realised as I walked past him, he was not a Christian – that was, if we had not converted him – his son would now be minding his chickens, married to Mei-ling whom we saved from serfdom that she might instead die in agony, suffocating on gold.

Glancing around, the beauty of the scene struck me. The soft light of the oil lamps shone on the girls' hair where they sat in silence, their heads slightly bowed and the gentle movement of the shadows seemed to add an ethereal wonder to the chapel but, whereas a week before I might have said that this was the work of God I now regarded it as a wonder of nature, as a quirk of physics, as a delight accidentally shaped by the hand of man.

Why, I tried to guess, did these people come to the mission, bend their knee to a strange god? What was it that made them dissatisfied with their own ancestors, the ghosts in the hills and the gods in the temples who had served them and their spiritual needs for a thousand years longer than Christ had offered his release to my own kind?

There was something immensely sad about the congregation I had joined. They were, I realised, searching for a dream they felt they could not find in their own world yet which I knew mine could not provide for them. In the course of their search, they had abandoned their history, their people and cast themselves out to be ostracised and martyred.

It was wrong to put these simple people in such jeopardy. They were to die – had already died, in the case of Matthew Kung, who had taken a disciple's name in the place of his own – for a cause they did not understand, which was extrinsic to them and to which they had sold their souls just as much as their neighbours had given theirs to their predecessors or Confucianism, Buddhism or Taoism.

The girls were the ones I felt most for: they had been rescued from death but they had had, with no other choice, to follow Christ. In keeping their lives they had inadvertently traded their souls. They were as much used by myself and my church as Faust was used by the devil. They had been corrupted.

Father Callaghan began the service but I could not keep my mind on it.

This was not what I wanted to do. I had come to China to save people from themselves and I found myself condemning them.

With his back to the congregation, Father Callaghan

stood and faced the altar. The embroidery on his stole shone like dull gold in the lamplight then, as I looked, it seemed to fragment and come loose, drift into the air just as the leaf from the ancient book had come off upon my fingers. For a moment, I was puzzled by this then realised that it was not the gold that was flaking but the light reflecting off it being destroyed by my tears.

Wiping my eyes with the knuckle of my finger, I heard Father Callaghan embark upon the Penitential Rite. He spoke in Cantonese and the response from the people came in the same language but I responded in Latin.

'*Confiteor Deo omnipotenti et vobis, fratres,*' I intoned, the words coming out of my mouth like honeyed lies, '*quia peccavi nimis cogitatione, verbo, opere et omissione: mea culpa, mea culpa, mea maxima culpa . . .*'

I had sinned sure enough. I was guilty of misleading the Chinese towards a foreign god that would not defend them any more than the oaths and rites of the *I Ho Ch'üan* would protect the movement's malcontents from the bullets of the *gweilos*' rifles.

Striking my breast, I continued, '*Ideo preor beatram Mariam semper Virginem, omnes Angelos et Sanctos, et vos, fratres, orare pro me at Dominum Deum nostrum.*'

I did not want my Chinese brothers and sisters to pray for me. I wanted them to rise as one and rush out from the chapel, disappear into the night and find their own gods again, ask their forgiveness if needs be and, later, return to secrete me away with them.

398

Today, my legs have been inexplicably weak. I have not taken any excessive exercise nor have I used the stairs in the tenement in preference to the elevator, but it took me longer to walk from the bus stop to the school than usual. I was obliged to halt twice and would dearly have liked to sit down to relieve the dull hurt in my shins.

Although it was only two o'clock, the popsicle seller was already on station at the corner of the street, seated in the saddle of his machine but dozing with a white pith helmet on his head. When ice cream vendors begin to wear such headgear, one can be sure the really hot months are only just around the corner. I was sorely tempted to purchase one of his popsicles but resisted: it would not have done to go to my interview with a bright red, green or yellow mouth.

The gravel on the street was slippery. I had to cross with extreme care and wished there was something on to which I might hold not so much to retain my balance as to gain some degree of confidence. The individual crystals of quartz on the road flashed in the sunlight: whilst it applies that all that glitters is not gold nor is it so that all which appears beautiful is benign.

I reached the pavement and stood for a moment by the gate. The brass plate had been furbished within the hour for there was a residue of the liquid polish collected in the screw holes which was not yet dry. What is more, the cross and Sacred Heart have been touched up since my last visit to the street, the drops of holy blood crimson and grotesquely shining with gloss paint.

The gate to the school playground is about eight feet high and made of sheets of iron riveted to a frame. This, too, has been recently repainted light grey, the name of the school being written upon it in a wide arc of lettering. Underneath the words *Mission Society* there is a door in the steel beside which is an electric button.

I placed my hand on the gate to steady myself but the metal was so hot from the sun that I quickly removed it and jammed my finger on the button. A buzzer sounded not far away to be followed by soft footsteps. A lock rattled and the door was opened by an elderly Chinese man.

Nodding to him politely, I said in Cantonese, 'I have an appointment with Sister Joseph. At a quarter past two,' adding in case there were two Sister Josephs in the place, 'the headmistress.'

He looked at his watch and beckoned me in.

'Go through that door,' he said, pointing to the entrance of the school, 'and report to the office.'

I set off across the playground, the concrete partitioned with white lines marking out a basketball and badminton court: in the centre was an arrangement of coloured boxes for a game with which I was not familiar. On the inside of the curtain wall by the street was painted a series of circular targets much marked by the impact of rubber balls.

The wide steps up to the main door were shallow and I easily negotiated them. They reminded me of steps in the seminary, so made that priests might mount them without tripping over the hems of their cassooks. Once inside, the building was cool. The walls of the entrance lobby were decorated with infantile paintings and a stone tub in which had been constructed the model of a Chinese garden with miniature trees, little baked-clay houses and pavilions, a larval rock filled with holes and a waterfall down which a trickle was tumbling. It vaguely reminded me of the garden of the Resident's bungalow in Wuchow.

To my left, opposite three low leatherette chairs, was a glass sliding window over which a sign projected from the wall. It was made of lime-green plastic with lettering stuck to it: it stated in both English and Chinese, *School Office & Enquries*. The missing *i* made me think incongruously of the *Black Pussy*. I knocked upon the glass and a Chinese woman slid it open.

'Mr Galwin,' she said somewhat officiously, not looking at me but running her finger down a register.

'Yes,' I confirmed. 'I have an appointment . . .'

'Please,' she interrupted me, 'sit down. Sister will see you in a few minutes.'

I stepped back and sank gratefully onto one of the chairs. My right leg was getting pins and needles just above the knee and I rubbed it vigorously to try and get the circulation going once more. From somewhere deep in the building there started up a chanting. It could not have been a religious intoning for there was a lightness about it, a rhythm that was airy and free. A hum of conversation could be heard too but it was unlike that of adults. Somehow, it was more lively, more joyous.

For a moment, I closed my eyes and no sooner had I done so than I saw, as if in an opium dream, the rows of bent heads of girls long since lost and heard the clack of the foot-treadle sewing machines and, although I could not see her, I could hear Sister Margaret chivvying the girls into Mass.

'Good afternoon, Father,' a voice said but it was not hers.

'Good afternoon,' I replied and, opening my eyes, discovered a nun standing in front of me. She was a European, her wimple as white as her skin and her habit light grey, not more than a shade removed from the colour of the school gate.

'It is good to see you again. Do come into my office,' she invited me. She spoke very clearly with the upper-class accent of a well-to-do colonial madam, yet her tone indicating that she was indeed pleased to welcome me.

I tried to get up but the chair was too low and my legs just would not accept the task of getting the rest of me vertical. My shoes slipped on the polished tiles of the floor and I was stranded.

'Here, let me help you, Father,' the nun said and, with the efficiency of a trained nurse, she shoved one hand under my armpit and the other in the small of my back. With one movement, she had me up.

'Thank you,' I said, a little unsteady but feeling stronger. 'I'm afraid the flesh is somewhat weak.'

'It is the spirit that counts,' she answered, and led the way down the corridor to her study.

It was a bright room, the walls painted in soft yellow and hung with both devotional pictures and more artistic efforts done by the children. Before a wide steel-framed window, through which I could see a small grassy lawn lying in the shade of several trees, were several chairs and an old wooden desk upon which was a black telephone, a stack of exercise books, a section of bamboo standing up like a vase and filled with coloured pencils, a letter tray and a small statue of the Virgin Mary, beside which there stood a slightly larger effigy of Kwan Yin, the goddess of mercy.

Sister Joseph stepped to the window and lowered a light blue venetian blind halfway down the window. The sun was coming in through the mottled shade of the trees outside. As she turned, she must have noticed me looking at the idol.

'A present from one of the girls,' she explained. 'Her father makes them in a little factory at Lai Chi Kok.'

'I knew a priest once who would have approved,' I said.

'Oh!' she exclaimed dismissively. 'It is only a piece of tourist pottery.'

Sister Joseph indicated one of the chairs to me and I sat in it, expecting her to move behind her desk but she did not, coming instead to sit next to me.

'Tell me, Father, how are you keeping? It has been a long time since you were last here. You are, you know, always in our prayers.'

'Well, they seem to be working,' I replied a little facetiously, 'for I am still about and hearty if not hale. But, Sister, you know you must not call me Father. I gave all that up long ago.'

'You have not been . . .'

'Excommunicated, defrocked, call it what you will. No, that is quite true. I am still on the register of holy fathers tucked away in some dusty dossier in the Vatican. But I am no longer a priest so you must not address me as one.'

My speech did not come with any degree of anger nor did I display any petulance.

I am so tired now. It seems hardly worth bothering.

As with Mr Wu, this is a topic she is keen to broach on the rare occasions when we meet, insisting in that stubborn way nuns have of calling me Father. I always refute it, wondering why on earth she does it: probably, she hopes to bring me back to Christ before I shuffle off my mortality and head for the boneyard. How often have I seen priests convince themselves that they see a sign of life in a corpse — on one occasion, in a cadaver — just so that they may absolve the soul and prepare it for heaven with a few quick words. Sister Joseph, I assume, thinks she has more time for I am not yet cooling.

'What may I do for you today then, Father?' she enquired, changing the subject and totally ignoring my request just as she would the unreasonable demands of one of her more fractious pupils.

'I wish to make a provision into the future for the girl,' I told her. 'With the best will in the world, I shall not go on much longer.'

'You are not ill?' Sister Joseph responded with a touching urgency.

'If, by that, you mean am I suffering a specific medical condition then the answer is no, I am not. I am simply getting old and starting to fall apart. It happens to old machines and the human body is nothing more than a machine.'

She opened her mouth to rebut me.

'No argument, Sister. You must leave an old man with his own ideas or, if you will, delusions. But I no longer ascribe to the theory that the human body is a wondrous work of God. Leonardo da Vinci dispelled that one and I agree with him. As for being made in the image of our God – well, if that is the case, I feel sorry for him. My legs don't work properly. What his must be like at his age I dare not think.'

To give her her due, Sister Joseph laughed slightly, though she might have been patronising an old man rather than sharing in his sense of humour.

'I was informed of your natural history lesson,' she said, avoiding a direction of conversation she wished not to follow. 'That was very kind of you. The boy was quite terrified of his catch. Miss Chow, our biology teacher, was most interested and amazed at your knowledge of shore creatures.'

'Your attendant nun was somewhat occupied at the time,' I informed her, hoping my voice contained a hint of criticism. 'She was engrossed in a book.'

Sister Joseph smiled a little bleakly and replied with a somewhat tight lip, 'I could certainly believe it. Sister Margaret is quite a bookworm.'

There was nothing else I could do. I leaned back a little in the chair to give my lungs space and I laughed. For at least a minute, I could not stop myself. Sister Joseph looked worriedly at me: my laugh these days is less of a sound of joyous release and more of a sort of chesty rattle devoid of pain.

'Are you sure you're all right?' she asked earnestly as my laughter subsided.

I nodded to put her mind at rest, gathered my breath and leaned forward again.

'I am sure. It is just that I knew a Sister Margaret once.' I chuckled briefly at the memory.

'Was she a great reader?'

'I don't know. But she was a remarkable woman,'

405

I allowed. 'I met her once in a temple at Wuchow in the summer of 1900. The Dragon Mother temple, it was called.'

'What was she doing there? I know of a fascinating treatise written by a Sister Margaret in, I think, 1911. She came, I recall, from Eastbourne. An Englishwoman who was the daughter of a missionary in Africa. Her essay was about Taoist temple architecture. I wonder if this could be the same woman.'

'I think not,' I said. 'This nun was Chinese and a good age, though not perhaps as venerable as myself. As for what she was doing, she was praying.'

'My Sister Margaret would never, I am sure, do such a thing. She would never bow her knee to another altar.'

I thought that perhaps it was true in that she would never pay her respects to an heathen idol: yet she did, it seemed to me, prostrate herself before the altar of cheap fiction to the detriment of her responsibilities to her pupils if not to her god. For that I criticised her but I was not going to inform on her to the extent of reporting on the quality of her literary taste. Her weakness made her more of a human and less of a nun in my eyes.

'As I was saying,' I began, returning to the reason for my visit, 'I wish to make provision for the girl. To this end, I have here a sum of money to be placed by you in trust for her. If there is any residue remaining after she completes her schooling, please use it for another girl. And, of course, it must be a little girl, as in the past. No boys.'

'You know, Father, I have always wondered about that,' Sister Joseph remarked.

'About what?' I asked.

'About your stipulations. Under any circumstance, no boys. And no mention of who their benefactor might be.'

There was, I thought, no harm in telling her now. It is after all a petty reason really, a mere whim if you like.

'Girls,' I explained, 'because, when I first came to China I taught girls. Not for long. Just a few months. They were strays, orphans or babies abandoned by their mothers. You know how it was.'

'How it still is,' Sister Joseph interrupted. 'Times do not change that quickly in the East, Father.'

'No,' I concurred, 'they do not.'

The telephone on the desk rang once but Sister Joseph ignored it.

'So I have chosen just to help girls,' I went on. 'They are, I suppose, disadvantaged and it is for their weakness that I feel sympathy.'

'You, Father, are a sentimentalist.'

I frowned at her and said, a little sharply, 'You, Sister, are the only person I would allow to get away with such an insult. I am most certainly not a sentimental man. I am a realist. That is why I am no longer a priest. And boys can fend for themselves.'

'And your anonymity?' she asked, impervious to my disapproval.

'That is more complex. But if I remain unknown I am afforded the liberty of being an observer. Such as I was at the beach the other week.'

'Do you often follow her about?' Sister Joseph enquired. 'I catch sight of you sometimes outside the gates as school ends. Under the bauhinia tree, just up the street from the ice cream man.'

'Not very often. Just sometimes. I follow her . . .'

There were so many reasons for my actions. Some I could explain quite easily: some I cannot even interpret to myself.

'I follow her because I like to see her happiness,' I said at last. 'There is a joy in children that we have lost. Both you and I, Sister. Lost forever.'

There were other rationales for my actions of which I did not tell her, dared not even: how my paying for the little girl was in part an absolution, how my anonymity allowed the child to be detached from me, receiving my benediction without the strings of friendship or the obligations of God.

Feeling in my jacket pocket, I removed the envelope Mr Chan had given me and handed it to Sister Joseph. It still had its rubber band around it.

'Open it, Sister.'

She slid the rubber band off it and pulled the wad of notes free.

'It is not very much,' I remarked, 'but I think it is sufficient.'

'It will be more than sufficient,' she replied. Her voice was quiet. 'Will this leave you . . .' she paused to consider her words, '. . . without means?'

'No, no, not at all,' I hastily assured her. 'This was a windfall. You might call it an act of God.'

'You have not been to the races, have you?' she enquired in a tone of mock censure.

'I think you know me better than that, Sister.' I employed her denouncing tone. 'I do not go to the races nor do I indulge in *tien kow*, mah-jong or chess in the park with other aged buffers like myself. You should be ashamed of yourself to think such a thing of an old man. Not to mention, as you will keep on insisting, a Holy Father. As for my regular contribution, that will continue to be paid direct to your bank account from mine as long as I am here.'

'You are a good man, Father,' Sister Joseph said softly and, looking at her, I saw there were tears in her eyes.

'Man yes, Sister, Father no,' I replied.

She stood up, placed my envelope on her desk next to the Virgin Mary and then, to my considerable astonishment, she bent over and kissed me right in the middle of my forehead, as one might a child.

'Man or priest,' she whispered, 'there is much of Our Lord in you.'

I wanted to argue that point strongly but decided against it. Instead, I rose from the chair, discovering that my legs were more firm for the rest.

'One thing before I leave, Sister,' I said.

'You can ask anything of us, Father.'

'What is the girl's name?'

'You know,' Sister Joseph leaned on the edge of her desk, 'I have often wondered how long it would be before you asked me that.'

She was not volunteering the information, but instead looked at me with a half-smile on her lips, her head tilted slightly to one side. I realised that she was not a young woman. It is impossible to judge the age of a nun: she is either very young, very plain or very old. Without looking at a woman's body there is often no way of accurately assessing how long they have lived. In Sister Joseph's case, I studied her eyes and reckoned she was in her early fifties.

'Well?' I demanded as she did not tell me.

'Her name is Julia. Julia Ho.'

'Did you give her this?' I asked.

'Yes. If they do not already possess one, we give all our pupils a European name when they arrive. It makes calling the register so much easier. Besides, most Chinese find themselves a Western name these days. It aids them in business.'

'What was her Chinese name?' I enquired.

'I don't recall. I could look it up in our records.'

She did not wait for me to request this but went behind her desk, opened a drawer and removed a file through the contents of which she thumbed her way, muttering to herself under her breath.

'Here it is,' she announced at last. 'I'm afraid the file is not in alphabetical order. Now,' she put it on the top of her desk, running her finger down a typewritten list, 'Julia Ho.' Here we are. Her Chinese name is Ho Mei-ling.'

From the *hutong* below my window came the characteristic sounds of the honey-cart accompanied by muffled voices. I looked out but only for a moment: if the hunchback was filling one of his barrels I did not want to be overhead as he raised the lid. Gazing down, I could plainly make out the collector of night-soil but I could not ascertain to whom he was speaking for they were standing in a doorway. Their conversation was brief and, at the conclusion of it, the hunchback set off with his cart wheels creaking and the effluent in his barrels slopping around. Just as he reached the end of the alley, I heard a muffled crash. It sounded as if one of his containers of filth had broken open and I made a mental note to assiduously avoid the rear *hutong* for the next few days.

I finished dressing in my cassock for Father Callaghan had declared the night before we should hold Mass very early in the morning as he wanted to take me out of the town and across the river.

'You'll find it quite beautiful,' he had told me. 'We'll go over in a sampan then walk ourselves up the top of Dragon Hill. Where the pagoda is. From there, you'll have a fine panorama of the town.'

'Had we not better take care?' I asked. 'Because of the revolutionaries?'

He had smiled and said, 'I think we should be quite safe up there, out of the town: no radical elements'll bother us in the mountains.' He had rubbed his hands together with glee at the prospect of a day in the country and went on, 'That done, we'll head west for a half hour or so, down through the pine woods. The scent of the bark is unforgettable. There's a flood plain on the far side, opposite *Bak Hok Shan*. All paddy-fields.' He had laughed and continued, 'Has it ever occurred to you, Father Stephen, that China must have been waiting for the likes of us?'

'No,' I had replied. 'Why do you say that?'

'Because it bears our name. Paddy-fields. The fields of Patrick.' He had laughed. 'Maybe of our blessed saint, even.'

'I think,' I remarked, 'the etymology might prove you wrong.'

'To be sure, that's not the root of the name. What it is, mind you, I've never discovered.' He had drunk the last few dregs of his gin and went on, 'You know, Father Stephen, you're sometimes a very serious fellow.'

411

'I am?' I answered.

'Yes, you are. And I like that in a young man but you must also learn to be a little – how shall I put it? – happier. Life is not a sad train of events. It is a joyous span of years upset only by transient sorrows. You must be a less phlegmatic and more accepting of the bounties of Our Lord. He didn't make us in His image to cry and frown but to laugh and smile.'

He had put his hand on my shoulder then and patted it.

'You're a good man, Father Stephen,' he stated. 'A good man. I'm glad they sent you to me.'

The first light of dawn was seeping into a sky devoid of even the merest vestige of cloud. Once more it was going to be a sweltering day. There was no breeze nor even any early bird song.

Leaving my room, I descended the staircase and made my way towards the chapel, tapping my finger on the barometer. The needle jarred but stayed firmly in the area marked *Fair* in Gothic script. Even at this hour, the thermometer registered 78° and the slider in the mercury indicated it had not dropped below 74° during the night.

The mission was very quiet. Not a sound came from the girls' quarters and I was suddenly afraid I was late, that my clock had faltered in the night. It had not been keeping good time ever since I arrived, presumably because the mechanism was not manufactured to stand up to the extremes of the Oriental climate.

The door to the chapel was open. I entered it and, a few steps over the lintel, bent my knee to the altar.

Apart from myself, the chapel was quite empty. The candles on the altar had been lit but there seemed to be no other preparation made for the celebration of Mass although, on the side table, I could see the wine and water jugs in place and the rice bowl in which Father Callaghan carried the wafers was beside them.

I walked down to the altar and, mounting the steps, looked both left and right but there was no one present. Clearly I was not late for Mass but early: my clock, far from being slow must somehow have speeded up although I could not imagine how the spring might have achieved such a trick.

A soft sound drew my attention. It was like a whisper but it formed no words. I looked up at the rafters in case the little devil-lizard had appeared again. As I searched for it a vague, all but indiscernible shadow moved over the beams. I turned and, not ten paces behind me, was a young Chinese man. He was barefoot and wore a black *fu* with a red sash at his waist, another around his brow. His chest was bare and I could see, even in the slight morning light, drops of sweat standing out on his skin like glass beads. In his hands he held a short curved sword.

'What do you want?' I demanded. It did not occur to me he would not understand, any conversation utterly pointless.

He made no reply but remained quite still as if, by my facing round, I had frozen him. It was like a bizarre child's game of statues: if I was to look away, I thought, he would move once more towards me. Yet this was no game. I did not turn my back and he started towards me once more, the sword coming up level to his shoulder. He began to move it sideways in readiness for striking.

'*Ha!*' he suddenly cried and rushed me.

I leapt aside and the sword smashed onto the altar, slicing through the altar cloth into the wood. His first blow made, he stopped and watched me like a predator. I edged my way round the altar to position it between us.

On the floorboards behind the altar lay Father Callaghan. He was on his back, his arms crossed over his breast with his fingers stroking aimlessly at his neck. His throat was cut, his whispering breath bubbling through a pink foam.

'*Ha!*' the Chinese exclaimed again, his sword up and ready.

I waited until he was prepared to run at me, swipe at me with his blade once more. He gathered himself. I could see his muscles grow tight and bunch. Just as he sprang, with the agility and fluid motion of a wild cat, I snatched the cross from the altar and blocked his swing with it. The sword smashed into the crucifix, the force of the impact jerking my arm. The Chinese, not expecting to meet resistance, momentarily lost his balance. His sword, glancing off the cross, was down.

With all the strength I could muster, I swung the cross at his head. One of the bars caught him just behind the ear and he fell to the ground, the sword clattering across the floor and his arms scrabbling. I struck him again on the head, the silver of the figure of Christ flashing in the early light. His skull cracked. It was such a loud sound it might have been the gecko after all, clicking its outlandish noise overhead.

The Chinese tumbled forwards, his legs twitching and hands slapping the floor. Moving quickly to his sword, I picked it up, raised it over my head and

brought it down on the back of his neck. I am not
sure how many times I struck him: I just continued
to hit him, as if I was chopping wood, until his
hands ceased their tattoo on the floorboards and
my rage was spent. My only thought was to kill him,
a cool anger taking over my soul. I was not frenzied
but quite composed, deliberate: there was no other
motive in my mind but to end this life spread-eagled
before me.

Sure the Chinese was dead, I dropped to Father
Callaghan's side. Air was no longer frothing at his
neck. I took hold of his hand and fancied I felt it
tighten on my own.

'*Illumina oculos meos, ne unquam obdormiam
in morte, ne quando dicat inimicus meus. Prævalui
adversus eum,*' I prayed, but then I stopped.

It was a senseless exercise. There was no god
present, no holiness in the chapel. The cross lay
on the floor nearby, the left arm cracked, the
figure of the tortured Christ smeared with the
blood of the dead Chinese. The sword lay next to
the cross, soiled by both Father Callaghan's and his
enemy's flesh.

There was another sound, of soft footfalls coming
down the aisle. I shifted myself as silently as I could
and reached for the sword. The handle was carved
of bone and damp from its owner's sweat. I grasped
it in both hands as I had seen the Chinese do
and, with as much power as I could muster, leapt
from the side of the altar, the sword raised above
my head. What I lacked in sword-fighting skills
I hoped to make up with the element of fierce
surprise.

In the centre of the aisle was Ah Fong. He stood

with his hands hanging at his sides, his face an unearthly white in the grey swelling light of the morning.

'No hit, master! No hit! I Ah Fong,' he said in a wavering voice.

I was not sure whether to trust him so did not relinquish my grip on the sword.

'Where Farfer *Ka Lai Hon*?'

'Father Callaghan is dead.'

I pointed behind the altar. Ah Fong walked hesitantly towards me and peered round the edge of the table. He moaned, just the once.

'He good man,' he said quietly: then he saw the dead Chinese. 'He kill *I Ho Ch'üan*.'

'No. I killed him,' I said, putting the sword down on the floor: it did not seem right to rest it on the altar. Besides, it would mark the altar cloth. 'We must take his body out before the girls come in, and hide the murderer.' I thought for a moment. 'We shall throw the I *Ho Ch'üan* in the river tonight. For the dragons,' I added.

'Oh, Farfer *See Faat Han*,' Ah Fong said: it was the first time he had used my nickname, 'girl gone. All gone.'

'On, no,' I said. A terrible emptiness rushed into my heart. 'Not gone too.'

'Yes, master. All gone. Gone.'

'All dead?' I asked. I could not believe every single one of them had been slaughtered.

'No dead, master. Gone away. Sister gone, too. She one away.'

'Run away?'

For a moment, I found it hard to comprehend what he was saying: then a picture flashed across my mind.

It was of Sister Margaret in the temple, waving her incense sticks.

'What about the babies?' I asked. 'What about the infants?'

I did not wait for an answer but snatched at the altar cloth, tugging it free, the candles falling to the ground and extinguishing themselves, the candlesticks separating from them and bouncing down the steps. I covered Father Callaghan with the cloth then, beckoning to Ah Fong, picked up the sword and ran through the courtyard to the nursery. The heavy door was shut. I pushed on it and it opened. All the cribs were empty, Ah Mee's body slouched against the wall at the end of the room: she, too, had had her throat cut. I went to the baby posting box. It was broken into several pieces and there was a hole in the wall to the *hutong*.

'God damn this!' I swore.

It was evident the sound I had heard from my room was not a honey-cart barrel overturning but must have been the baby posting box being wrenched free to allow the assassin entry.

'More man come,' Ah Fong said, his voice emotionless with terror. 'One come now. Do kill. When he kill, he call his f'ends. If he no hear him, he come too by an' by.'

'Ah Fong,' I ordered. 'Get your possessions. Just enough for you to carry. Put them in a bag and we shall go.'

'Go where, master?'

I thought for a moment, for both of us.

'Hong Kong,' I decided. 'We go Hong Kong side.'

He left the nursery and I rushed to my room, quickly thrusting off my cassock and struggling into

417

my Chinese clothing. Into my leather bag I crammed a few essentials — a pocket knife, some candles, my clock, a hip flask containing brandy for emergencies, articles of clothing, some other odds and sods and my diary. For some reason, I added a photograph of myself taken in Dublin upon my ordination: had I been in my right mind, I should have left it.

My hurried packing done, I returned quickly to the chapel. The blood had soaked through the altar cloth from Father Callaghan's wounds. Quickly, I mixed the wine and water in the chalice, muttered what I hoped would pass as a blessing and a consecration then put a drop upon his lips. The remainder I drank in one gulp to prevent it falling into the hands of the *I Ho Ch'üan*. From Father Callaghan's pocket I took the ring of mission keys and, from around his neck, removed his bloodstained stole and, hastily wrapping the chalice and paten in it, placed them in my bag along with the candlesticks, two jugs and the cross, which I hurriedly wiped clean on a corner of the altar cloth.

In Father Callaghan's room, I unlocked the padlock on his sea chest and flung open the lid, removing all the money it contained. This was quite a considerable sum in letters of credit, bank and promissory notes, some silver sycee and coins, the bulk of the latter in trade and Mexican dollars. I placed it all in a canvas satchel hanging in the cupboard. As I passed his bookshelf, I saw sitting upon it a small opium-smoker's lamp and a few dozen small jade carvings, including a translucent white one in the shape of a tortoise's shell. In an impulse and with panic rising in me, I took these, too.

When I returned to the ground floor, Ah Fong was

standing by the chapel door, a bamboo basket in his hand.

'We go Master Mowisbee house?' he suggested.

I gave this proposal a quick consideration before abandoning it. If the mission had been attacked it was a certainty Morrisby, the Blairs, Tremletts and Mr Doble would have similarly been dealt with: they were either dead or on their way down-river. I did not intend to discover which.

'No,' I repeated, 'We go Hong Kong side.'

'Hong Kong long way, master.'

'Yes,' I acknowledged, 'it is.'

Yet my mind was set: there was no other option, as I saw it, than to make for the safety of the colony, its garrison and its British government.

'How we go, master?'

'By the river.'

'*Lucky Moon* no here,' Ah Fong said. 'Go Nanning side.'

I had not for one moment given the steam pinnace a thought. Even if she had been in Wuchow she would have been useless: the *I Ho Ch'üan* would be watching her.

'We steal a sampan,' I declared. 'Let us go.'

Cautiously, Ah Fong opened the mission gate. The *hutong* was empty. We slipped out, walked quickly down to the street at the end and set off through the town.

There were few people abroad. In the Street of The Cranes, a man was pushing a handcart laden with charcoal and coal dust slabs past a row of closed eating stalls. From behind the shutters of one of them emanated the grunt of stentorian snoring. A dog sauntered in the middle of the thoroughfare, sniffing at wet patches on the cobbles. The further we went from the mission, the busier the streets became. The town's-folk were readying themselves for the day, with shopkeepers starting to open their premises, vegetable sellers setting up their stalls and arranging produce on the pavements.

As we reached the main square, Ah Fong said quietly, out of the corner of his mouth, 'Where we go, master?'

'Go Si Kiang side,' I replied, not turning my head to look at him. 'Take sampan near jetty.'

It occurred to me on the spur of the moment that if there was a trading vessel in mid-stream, we might row out to her and beg asylum.

Halfway across the main square, at roughly the point where my trousers had started to drop, there came a shout.

'*T'ien chu kiao*!'

The voice almost sang out the words. They sounded like a drawn out chant, a mocking melody, a deadly diapason.

'Do not stop,' I muttered. 'Do not look round, Ah Fong. Do not run. Walk all same.'

'*T'ien chu kiao*!' the sing-song voice reiterated. '*T'ien chu kiao*!'

I glanced over my shoulder. There were three young Chinese men fast approaching us. Each had a red scarf around his head: one carried a cudgel and the other two short swords of the sort that had killed Father Callaghan.

'You go, master!' Ah Fong said. 'Go quick. No stop. I talk man.'

'No!' I replied insistently, *sotto voce*. 'Keep going.'

'Go, Master. Go. No af'aid Ah Fong.'

420

He stopped and faced around. I heard him say something in Cantonese which was greeted by a torrent of obvious abuse.

Yet I did not stop. I did not put down my bags and join him. I continued to walk, my mind numb. Perhaps together we could have seen off the three thugs but I did not consider it. I made my way towards the Street of Righteous Enlightenment.

The shouting continued behind me. Other people had now joined in. I could not hear Ah Fong in the clamour: then, over the turmoil there came a shrill voice, high-pitched and querulous.

'*G'oria in ex'lsis Deo et in terra pax homi'bus*,' it shouted. There was a brief pause before it continued, '*Yeh so Gei duk*, I come you bankwet table in fear an' t'embling, for I a sinner, an' no much good . . .'

A huge shout rose from the crowd. A scream echoed round the market place and was then cut off.

The sampan I decided upon was about fifteen feet long, tethered to a stake in the mud not far from the point at which I had embarked from the *Lucky Moon*. There were a few fisherman attending to similar craft along the bank, sorting nets or scrubbing down hulls, but otherwise it was devoid of people. I was thankful most fishing was done in the evening and early night, by the light of lamps.

Without any hesitation, I walked straight towards the vessel, placed my bags in the well with a jumble of fishing equipment and cast off, punting the sampan clear of the bank with one of the long oars. None of the other fishermen paid me the least attention and, within minutes, I was a hundred yards out into the river and a quarter of a mile downstream, riding on a swift current.

My idea that I might seek refuge on a foreign trading vessel was thwarted: there was not a single ship anchored in the river. I assumed they had perhaps already set sail with those Europeans who had received a warning in the night, or avoided assassination by chance.

Once past Dragon Island, I set about tidying my craft, preparing it for the journey ahead. The jumble in the sampan consisted of three nets, a wooden bucket, some lengths of rope, a lantern the reservoir of which was at least half-filled with oil and a grappling hook. Two long oars lay against the gunwale. I retained the smallest of the nets for my own use and threw the others over the side along with some dead and mutilated fish swishing about in an inch or two of bilge-water. This done, I opened a hatch under the small rear deck upon which I should have to stand to row. Behind it I discovered, to my blessing, a smaller bucket of rice bowls and chopsticks, several spoons and a cloth bag containing at least two catties of rice and some dried, salt fish. Wedged under the deck planking was a tinder box, a bundle of joss sticks and, at the rear of the compartment, a pointed rattan hat. As the little hold was dry, I shoved my bags into it and slid the hatch shut.

Tying a length of rope around the larger bucket, I lowered it over the side and was amazed at the strength of the current and the speed at which my vessel was travelling. I watched the shore and guessed that I must be going at least six knots if not faster. Hauling the bucket in, I set it in the well and splashed my face with the cold water.

With my chores done, I decided not to try and row but let the current take me. I lay back against the side of the sampan and found myself convulsed by bone-wracking shivering. My first thoughts were that I had contracted a malarial fever but it was a reaction of shock come upon me now that I was free.

With no preparations for my journey left to do, I found my mind fixing itself upon the events of the day: it was not yet eight o'clock and I had seen murder, and done murder.

This was no proxy killing of an ignorant peasant. I had killed a man with my own hands, giving no thought to the sanctity of life, the creed by which I was supposed to abide. Leaning forward, I saw dark smudges on my shoes. They were not wet, not water spilled from the bucket, but stiff blots.

Tearing them off, I rammed them into the bucket and scrubbed the leather with my hands. A faint pinkness seeped gradually into the water. When, at last, I had removed the revolutionary's blood from my footwear, I tipped the bucket over the side.

Yet what, I thought as the water ran out, if that was not *I Ho Ch'üan* heathen blood, but that of Father Callaghan? It was then I saw him as if he was before me in the sampan, lying on his back with his hands to his throat: the hissing of the water pouring away was his last breath fighting to fill his lungs, whilst the banging of the bucket on the side of the vessel as it rocked over some wavelets was the hammering of swords and cudgels upon Ah Fong's skull.

I leaned back against the fishing net and was shaken by a fresh bout of shivering. The sun was up and hot yet my flesh was as cold as death. My hands could not keep still, my teeth chattered and my legs twitched. I sensed the muscles on my face contorting and tried vainly to control them.

An exhausted sleep must have come upon me for the next I remember was waking up with the sun blazing on to my face and my lips cracked. The sampan was drifting at an increased speed in a current quite close to the south bank. I sat up and surveyed the country through which I was travelling. The hills were close to the river, not a hundred yards from the water, and covered in thick sub-tropical forest. The bank was high and I could not see what lay immediately behind it but, every once in a while, I spied a rooftop.

Every muscle in my body aching, I removed my *sam* and undervest and, refilling the bucket, soaked myself. This done, I put the coolie hat on my head: it was a wise move for not only did it afford me some shade from the merciless sun but it also gave me a disguise.

As there was no need to steer my craft, I had nothing to do and this enforced idleness gave my mind the opportunity once more to dwell upon my predicament, my actions and my future.

'I should have buried him,' I said aloud. 'I should have placed his body where they could not get it, could not mutilate it, could not . . .'

I saw Father Callaghan's corpse hanging from a stake on the dais in the main square, his blood dripping to the ground with small, jet-eyed birds drinking from the puddle. Next to him was Ah Fong, but he was headless and would therefore never get to heaven.

'And the girls,' I went on, talking to myself just as Father Callaghan had recommended. 'Where have the girls gone?'

They were dead. I knew it. If not in the flesh, then in every other respect. Just as Mei-ling had swallowed the thin leaves of gold so had they the false gold of religion. They would soon be syphilitic whores waiting to die in flowerboats, slaves or concubines. Not one would reach the safety of European employ on the coast.

I had sold them out, just as they had sold themselves to Christ.

The sun scorched my legs, even through the material of my *fu*, and the rattan of my hat became so hot as to make it almost painful to touch.

'This is my penance,' I declared to myself. 'The first penance. No Hail Marys, no mumbo-jumbo. Just heat and discomfort.'

Yet what had I to repent, I asked myself. I had committed no sin. I had not killed Father Callaghan nor had I forced Ah Fong to cover my retreat. I had, it was true, done for the Chinese assassin but, I reasoned, he was a heathen and the history of Roman Catholicism was filled with righteous killings. Knights in the Holy Crusades would not have thought twice about what I had done that early morning. All that had happened was that I was the tool of circumstance. If anyone were to blame, I considered, it was God who had made the world what it was. If he really loved

425

his creations, I said to myself, he would have prevented it.

Late in the afternoon, I began to see more craft on the river. I had from time to time passed by cargo junks or low hulled barges laden with timber or bamboo, but, as the sun lowered, more sampans began to appear. To aid in my camouflage, I pretended to fish, casting the net over the side and trawling with it. Much to my amazement, I actually caught a number of small fish, which I brought in and ate raw with some of the rice.

At the bow of the sampan was the customary little shrine such as I had seen on the old lady's boat as she ferried myself and Father Callaghan across to the Residency party. I moved forward and studied it. A simple affair, the shrine consisted of a skilfully printed woodblock of a goddess which had been touched up with gold leaf and red paint. Before her, nailed to the deck, was a metal cup filled with sand and the red stalks of half a dozen burnt-out joss sticks. A child's rice bowl contained a few grains of rice and a fragment of salt fish.

Going to the hatch, I removed two joss sticks from the bundle and, hunching myself forward against the warm evening breezes, lit them with the tinder box. When they were glowing brightly, I stuck them in the cup where they quickly burned. It was not a religious act. I was already past caring about gods. It was more a totemic reflex such as any man might make in order to try and balance fate in his favour: it was no more than crossing one's fingers or avoiding walking under a ladder. Yet, as I sat back with the late sun casting my shadow forwards over the little shrine, I thought how alike I was to Sister Margaret, hedging my bets on the race towards eternity.

On that voyage down the river, I came to serve a new lord: not some ethereal master riding in a chariot of clouds or fire, dispensing love and demanding homage but a dispassionate leader, one for whom love and hate were not demands but facts. The light of Christ was dimmed by the brilliance of reason. I could not justify my actions or the murder of Father Callaghan, the butchery of Ah Fong – and poor little Ah Mee – and the fleeing of the girls within the context of theology, but I could within the tenets of logic.

As night fell, I decided not to moor up but let the sampan drift on its way. Sleep was out of the question, as I had to watch out for other craft engaged in fishing and, twice, I had to take to the oars and steer my way through little fleets of sampans. Just before ten o'clock that night, the stark white quarter-moon disappeared behind dense banks of cloud and, at midnight, it began to rain.

I have always been one to escape and hide.

When I was a child, wracked by some petty guilt I could not understand, when my father had caught me out lying in the trivial ways children have or culpable of some other misdemeanour, I escaped from his wrath and leather belt and hid.

I would to go to the rick behind the byre and tunnel into it, digging with my hands through the close-packed layers of stalks and hay and, back-filling the passage I had made behind me, would disappear and fancy myself invisible, lost to the world. It was dark in there and musty. The further in I went, the warmer and more secure the world became. It was good to be without the searching light of day, the prying eyes of sun and truth. Sometimes I almost suffocated myself in those airless tunnels which I excavated and, when I dreamed my childish dreams of death, I was always in a small dark place where the walls prickled me gently and the air smelled of summer fields, dry dust and mice.

My whole life has been a process of escape and concealment: I believe now I joined the priesthood in order to get away and hide.

Of course, I was not alone. There were others bent on escaping with me. The priests who instructed me in the ways of God, who taught me my duties, schooled me in fidelity or directed me towards righteousness, and my fellow initiates were all, like me, resolute on secreting themselves away.

No one entertains a cause without a deep and secret selfishness. There is no such thing as a true zealot: there is only a man determined to serve himself.

Looking back on my comrades-in-God, I wonder now what it was they were fleeing. For some, it was crushing poverty, rain-swept fields, sore backs after sixteen hours of labour, the cloying mud sticking to their boots. The church was their refuge just as it had been for centuries: peasants have always either sought temporal relief through devotion and prayer or physical relief by surrendering themselves to God, living the rest of their days in comparative luxury by courtesy of the unquestioningly pious and blindly penitent. Others were escaping cruel masters or duplicitous lovers, running from a fear of the flesh which they sublimated by telling themselves that tyrannical men, beautiful women or pretty young boys were instruments of the devil. Some took holy orders because it gave them a purpose in their otherwise purposeless lives and yet still others because the purpose suborned another of which they were ashamed or afraid.

Yet there were a few who trod the path of God because they were good men, a rare commodity. I do not think, in retrospect, I ever knew a truly good man before I came to China and shook hands with Father Callaghan or walked the streets and *hutongs* of Wuchow in the company of Ah Fong.

Maybe it was reality I wished to avoid, from which I was desperate to save myself and from which I am still flinching. My mining in the hayrick was no different from taking a pipe with Mr Wu, sitting on a bench by the banyan tree before the temple, or jumping into a sampan and casting it off to drift at the mercy of the river and its dragons.

My life has been one long journey of drifting uncontrolled but free.

There again, perhaps I always hid because I had no faith and this scared me. Just as I concealed myself from my father that he might not find me out so did I hide from God because I could not truly believe in him.

Nor was it only my God in which I had no faith but also in myself.

I drifted into holy orders, arrogantly believing I was called by God to do his bidding but I was wrong: it was a fallacy, a self-delusion to give justification for my running and ducking, weaving and fleeing. For my hiding. God either did not want me or, finding out the sham I was, abandoned me: or it might have been in the scheme of things to give me no faith, to set me up as a whipping-boy to whom others could point and say that is what happens to a man of little faith. Perhaps it was an object lesson not in the love of God or the cruelty of Man but all an exercise to teach me to keep to my place. I should have remained a simple peasant in Ireland with his cow and two pigs: instead, as I have chosen or it was chosen for me by circumstance, I have lived my life as a peasant in China. What could have been a shack on the edge of a bog in Kerry is in reality a tenement on the corner of Nanking Street with Woosung Street.

Had I possessed a true faith, been more assured of my veracity, more convinced of what I suppose I did believe, events would have shaped me otherwise and my life would have been an altogether different series of trials. Or I should, long ago, have been martyred in the town square alongside Ah Fong, bludgeoned to death with clubs or hacked to pieces with swords, forgotten by everyone save those who took part in the butchery, a mere instant, no bigger than the minuscule flash of a dying star, of a flicker of heat lightning over the mountain, of bestial history lost in the brutalities of time.

This morning, I briefly revisited Mr Chan's emporium. It was a fleeting visit for what I wanted, for the first time, was to purchase rather than to sell.

The cruise ship he was anticipating when I sold him the silver had arrived and the street was so crowded with garishly dressed tourists there was not a tout in sight save for those who sell colour transparency photographs in plastic wallets and offer, to the likely customer, morally dubious examples of other photographic achievement. I was quite unaccosted as I walked the length of Hankow Road except by one of the photograph vendors and a lone tourist wearing a loose shirt decorated with pink flamingos against a backdrop of verdant forests and trousers which, had they not been cream, would have best been described as Oxford bags. He was clutching a swatch of postcards and wished to know directions to the post office. I feigned ignorance, claiming to be a visitor myself which puzzled him for, just a moment earlier, he had heard me address the photoseller in fluent Cantonese.

Mr Chan was busy. Two less exotically attired tourists were mulling over the purchase of some ivory carvings of cavorting horses whilst another couple were considering jade and gold bangles. Mrs Chan, who seldom appears in the shop save to bring her spouse a midday bowl of rice and vegetables, hovered around acting as a sort of store detective.

My greeting today was nothing more than a raised hand and a smile followed by a nod from Mr Chan to imply he would be with me in a moment, but I did not require serving. I knew exactly what I wanted and went straight to one of the heavy cupboards. At a signal from her husband, Mrs Chan unlocked the door. After holding back a number of other items precariously balancing on the front of the bottom shelf, I removed a carved rosewood box with an ornate brass clasp held shut by a long sprung pin.

This was the item I required. When I opened it, I found it lined with deep red brocade padded with down. Turning it upside down, I saw the price was marked at $100 which was, of course, the tourist price. I could buy it for half that and still not dent Mr Chan's acceptable profit margin.

'Good,' I said in Cantonese to Mrs Chan, 'I will buy this one.' The bangle buyers glanced up in surprise to hear one of their supposed number talking the lingo.

She was about to state the price when Mr Chan said in Cantonese over the top of his customers, 'No charge. Just take it. It is not too expensive. Forty dollars.'

'You must let me pay,' I insisted.

'No. It's not an antique. It was made just last year by a factory in Ma Tau Kok. They make over four thousand a week. Unit price is eight dollars. Take it.'

I began to remonstrate but he cut me short, adding, 'Don't upset our friendship. This is just a small gift from one to another.'

'But it is not for myself,' I replied.

'Never mind, take it anyway. I will find a gift for you when you next visit. See you soon?'

'Soon,' I promised, as I had on my last visit, but I lied. I knew this was my final visit to his shop.

Casting a quick look at the laden cabinets and the glass counters with their rows of rings and strings of pearls, gold chains and pendants, I did not feel at all sad. I am done with sorrow now.

At four o'clock, the boy arrived at my flat and,

entering, seated himself at my table, producing his books and arranging them on the table in readiness for work.

'How did your fund-raising go?' I enquired before he opened them.

He grinned in the impish way children have when they are pleased with themselves and replied, 'Eleven thousand two hundred and eight dollars, sir.'

'That's quite a sum. Congratulations,' I said and I truly meant it.

'And they jumped in the harbour,' he went on.

'They?'

'Two of the teachers. Mr Reeves and Mr Cordwell. From the side of the Star Ferry pier. Then they swam across to the Kowloon Pier.'

'The harbour is not exactly a healthy place for a dip,' I commented.

'Mr Reeves is a sport,' he declared and I could tell he was unquestioningly proud of his schoolmaster in the way boys of his age are of someone whom they admire.

He is a good boy: I have decided upon this fact. And he will make an excellent *gweilo*: not one of those who lives in an enclave of European housing on the Peak or the exclusive southern shores of Hong Kong island but in the city, in with the people as I have done.

'Did you like the music, sir?' he asked.

'The music?'

'In the *Black Pussy*. The group's performance.'

'Well,' I began, 'I'm afraid I did not stay. It is not, you understand, exactly my taste in music. The place was very crowded and I had a headache. The smoke got to me. I'm a non-smoker.' I thought to add 'of tobacco' but resisted.

He looked a little crestfallen and I realised he wanted my praise, my approval. I was touched.

'However,' I went on, 'I'm told by Sam you were, in your manner of music, exceedingly good. He was most impressed. How did you father react?'

The boy looked surprised.

'How did you know I told him?'

'I believed you would,' I replied. 'You are a trustworthy and truthful boy for whom deceit is not an acquired art. At least, not yet. You forget I was a priest. A cleric knows much more about the nature of humans than anyone else.'

He grinned a little sheepishly.

'He didn't mind. He said it was good I was doing something on my own initiative and that the racket I made at home practising was translating itself into a worthwhile objective.'

'He did not complain about the venue?'

'No. He just told me . . .' He coloured up slightly.

'To keep your pecker in your pocket?' I suggested.

The boy laughed. It was the magic sound of youth.

'Those were his exact words!' he exclaimed.

'Another of the priest's tricks,' I explained. 'Once learnt they do not die out in a lifetime.'

I sat down at the table opposite him, resting my arms along the edge. I felt tired and suddenly very much older in the presence of this young man but, whereas in the past I had resented or envied him his youthfulness I now felt sorry for him: he has so many years ahead of him to be filled with pain, failure, disappointment and misery.

Some minutes must have passed, one of those lost timespans which have come to me of late, for I was suddenly jerked out of my reverie by the boy's voice.

'May we start, sir?'

'Yes,' I said quickly, 'yes, of course. I'm sorry. My mind was elsewhere.'

'I quite understand, sir,' he said. 'No problem.'

I smiled inwardly at his expression: he was becoming a *gweilo* just as I had done, unconsciously taking in the little nuances of Chinese life that would set him apart from his own kind half a century hence.

'Before we begin,' I said, leaving the table, 'I should like to show you something.'

Going into my bedroom, I took up the rosewood box from my bed and, sitting down once more, handed it to the boy. He was at a loss as to what to say.

'Open it,' I instructed him.

He pulled the brass pin free and lifted the lid. I could smell the vague scent of the wood as it wafted across the table.

'What is it?' he asked, looking inside the box.

'Take it out. Carefully. It is, I should think, fragile.'

He put both his hands in the box and slowly removed the wooden jug I had taken from the bank. Gently, he put it on his Cantonese textbook.

'What is it?' he asked again.

'A wooden jug.' I said. 'Just a wooden jug.'

He turned it round slowly, the veining in the wood moving like hard brown clouds.

'It is of little monetary value, if any,' I continued, 'but it has a history I think you might appreciate.'

I did not elaborate. I fell silent once more and,

although my eyes remained open and fixed on the vessel, my thoughts went blank again.

'Will you tell me its story?' I heard the boy say.

He sounded far away and I did not want to shout back to him. Instead, I watched him as if from a great distance while he twisted the jug in his hands.

'I have wanted to ask you about . . .' he began then paused.

He was looking into my face and I had the sense this was what it must be like for a corpse to stare upwards at a mourner gazing down into the coffin.

'Would you tell me about it, sir?'

I returned from my distant standpoint.

'No,' I replied, 'I think not.'

I opened the drawer in my table and removed the manila envelope containing my black diary. Already, in my mind, it was halfway out of my life.

'This will tell you all you need to know,' I said.

The boy accepted the envelope with both hands as if receiving a libation.

'It has my name on it,' he remarked with some surprise.

'Yes,' I replied obviously. 'It has.'

'May I open it?'

I nodded. He unwound the string and, tipping the envelope up, slid the diary out.

'You asked me – or you wanted to ask me – some questions. This will give you all the answers you sought.'

'May I borrow it, sir?' he enquired.

'It is for you to keep,' I answered. 'With the jug. You will learn about that from the book. It is – it *was* – my diary. Don't open it now. Wait until you get home, to a quiet place.'

'Thank you, sir,' he said, 'thank you very much. I am . . .' He glanced around the room as if looking to see if there were any witnesses. 'May I ask you why you are giving this to me?'

'You will appreciate it. You have done what I did when I was a few years older than you. You are, in many ways, so like me.'

'What?' he exclaimed then, finding his manners, added, 'I don't quite understand.'

Indeed, he did not. He had never had to consider such things, the relationship between the old and the young, the mists of history and the bright, sharp, truthful light of the harsh but wondrous present. He was bemused, unable to comprehend what I was saying. In his own mind he could see no links between himself and an old ex-priest with a failing mind.

'You have committed yourself. To China,' I said quietly.

There was a long silence between us. He looked at the book which he had not yet opened and at the jug whilst I just sat looking at him and seeing, passing before my mind's eye, faces I had not gazed upon for many years.

At last, I broke the silence.

'I'm afraid,' I informed him, 'I am unable to teach you any more. I'm sorry, but I think I have had enough. Of course, this is nothing personal,' I added to allay any insult he might have felt. 'It is just that I find it all a bit beyond me now.'

I got slowly to my feet, left the table and looked out of the window, down into Nanking Street, but it was not a busy Kowloon street any longer but the *hutong* at the rear of the mission: and I could not hear the taxi horns and a blaring radio but

437

the dull beat of a gong and the quiet sobbing of a woman.

When I turned, the boy was still seated at the table, his hands beside the jug and my diary, which I no longer thought of as mine. He was almost crying. His shoulders heaved a little but he made no sound so I could not have mistaken him for the woman. I knew her. She had just decided against posting her baby in case I tore out its eyes and sold them.

It seemed so natural to put my hand upon the boy's shoulder. If I had made the sign of the cross over him, I should not have been surprised. Yet I did not. I let him continue to sit before me in silence. It is better to exorcise pain than let it fester.

'You had best go,' I said after a while which I could not calibrate into seconds or minutes.

I relinquished my hold on his shoulder and he rose to his feet, gingerly placing the jug back in its box and putting his textbooks away in his case. Last of all, he put my diary on top of them. I watched it go as if it was a part of myself disappearing. With the removal of the book I was shedding so much I wanted to be freed from, so much that haunted me.

'If you need me, sir . . .' the boy began to say, tucking the box under his arm and lifting his case off the table, but I held my hand up.

'I need nothing now,' I replied.

Showing him to the door, I once more put my hand upon his shoulder. 'Perhaps we'll meet in *The Black Pussy*,' I assured him. 'Or on the Star Ferry. You know, there used to be a saying that if one travelled daily for the whole of one's life upon the ferry one would eventually meet everyone one had ever known. A mere adage, of

438

course. I am sure the Star Ferry does not carry ghosts.'

The boy stopped just outside my door and turning, remarked, 'I'm sure it does, sir. I'm sure it does.'

Then he was gone. He did not wait for the cumbersome, grinding lift but went round the corner and down the dark stairwell. I heard his footsteps retreating then all that was left was the clicking of typewriter keys in Mr Pao's workshop or in the Pei woman's secretarial college.

It has been a hard climb. The path I took went initially along the edge of the cutting in which the railway line to Canton runs before vanishing into the tunnel under the Kowloon hills. Just by the masonry arch of the tunnel entrance, it veered eastwards, passed through a belt of haphazard boulders and dry scrub noisy with crickets, then began to rise sharply, zig-zagging up the contours of the hillside below the jagged outcrop of Lion Rock. Several times, I had to pause to get my breath or sit down on the hard ground to ease the pain running up my legs.

The grass on the steeper slopes is over a foot high and desiccated by cool winter winds and the lack of rain. It has not been burned for years and carries no signs of any former conflagration although, half a mile or so to the west, the hillside is blackened by the recent fires which I have spied from my tenement roof.

In places, I had to grasp the roots of low bushes to pull myself over a particularly steep part of the path.

This way is not frequently used: indeed, I doubt if more than a dozen people a year avail themselves of it. Twenty years ago, it was probably resorted to by guerrillas fighting the Japanese, and fifty years ago by woodcutters heading over the mountain range to collect kindling in the valleys above Sha Tin, but now it is abandoned by all save small animals and old fools.

Like the Chinese, I have an affinity for mountains: there is even a festival when the main idea is to get up to the summit of the nearest hill and make an offering. I share that attraction and a place such as this I have, over the years, visited when I have felt the need to rise above my place on earth and get a little nearer to the sky. Not to heaven, or to the gods – in the singular or plural – but just to be where cool winds blow and I can be alone to think.

My perch is at the foot of a smooth rock, twenty feet high and as many wide, on a narrow ledge about the depth of an old-fashioned *k'ang*. The rock is warm from the sunlight shining upon me since mid-morning, when I arrived at this spot. At my side is this morning's early edition of the *Wah Kiu Yat Po*, weighted down by a stone, and a picnic of sorts – two bottles of San Mig., a flask of tea, a small cardboard box of Chinese almond biscuits with the outline of a cockerel embossed upon the pastry and three oranges – but I have not touched any of it. I am not hungry or thirsty despite my exertions.

Most of my life, I have had these nine hills as a background to my every move. Wherever I have gone, whatever I have done, they have looked down on me like a row of sentinels. From their shoulders, I can see my entire world. Spread out before me is the peninsula of Kowloon, shimmering in the first really hot day of the year. The streets and alleys, markets and temples which I have frequented are all down there, laid out flat like a relief map. If I had a stick, I feel I could lean forward and tap them as a schoolmaster raps his blackboard with a ruler.

Gazing out to the west, the sun full in my face, I think of how, far beyond the islands and mountains, the estuary of the Pearl River and the mud delta, lie the streets of Wuchow, untrodden by my feet for over sixty years yet visited every day since then in fragmentary moments of reluctant nostalgia, sorrow or guilt.

The harbour glistens, the vessels riding at anchor all broadside on to me for the tide is racing, straightening them into uniform ranks. Beyond, the verdant hills of Hong Kong island rise as a hazy curtain against the distant ocean and a sky bleached by the sun. A few years ago, the airport runway was extended a mile out into Kowloon Bay, the finger of its tarmac strip pointing down Lei Yue Mun passage to the open sea. As I watch, an aircraft passes beneath me, soaring over the rooftops of Kowloon Tong, dropping slowly all the while towards earth. I do not hear its engines until it has completed its turn and is on the ground, a miniature silver bird heading away from me: even then, the sound is only just discernible over the drone of the city.

Leaning against the rock, I feel its heat pulsing into my back. I have removed my shoes, for my heels were blistered during the climb and I have, in the true fashion of the Chinese, rolled up my *fu* to above the knee. My legs are exceptionally pale, the veins running like blue threads just below the surface of the skin. They look so fragile I marvel at how they have succeeded in carrying my blood about my body all these years.

The sun is fierce. I close my eyes but it does not help: all I see then is the pink of my own blood suspended before me, so I open them again and cast my gaze downwards.

I am, I suppose, ready now for whatever the future holds for me, whatever fate thinks of throwing in my way.

There is a wind lifting from the city, running up the face of the mountain, riffling the pages of my newspaper. It is soft and warm but quite blustery. It might be rising from the underworld.

Ever since I clambered into the sampan, cast off the mooring rope and swung the little boat out into the current, I have carried little pieces of hell about with me. At first, they were heavy burdens but, as time passed, they eroded like sandstone, like the karst mountains of China that are forever crumbling, preserved intact only in delicate paintings on silk or intricate ivory carvings.

At my feet, on the very rim of the ledge, I have lined up five quartz pebbles which I collected on my way up the mountain and, as the day has progressed, I have considered them one by one. Each of them is a part of myself, a little bit of China that is in me, a fragment of history that is mine and which I share with the earth. And each one is a regret.

The first and smoothest stone represents Father Callaghan, the man I respected and, in retrospect, loved yet whom I did not wait to bury, over whom I failed to speak the last rites: and I let him down in more than this for I took revenge for his death.

He would not, I often think, have wanted his enemy killed. He was a man of forgiveness and forbearance whilst I was a man for retribution and retaliation. His credo was love thine enemy. Mine was an eye for an eye.

Next to him I have placed a slightly smaller but just as shiny a stone: this is Ah Fong, whom I abandoned to the mob, who died because I was a coward, because I was not prepared to waste myself, to be a martyr for a faith I no longer possessed. How often I have heard his brief scream echo in the halls of emptiness far down inside myself.

I have, many a time, considered my cowardice, if that is what it was. I am doubtful myself. If one believes in destiny then I must regard my behaviour not as the craven act of a poltroon but one of a man of human wisdom. His death and my behaviour have taught me much, not just about myself but about the world in which I have chosen to live and in which I have, in my own way, done some little good.

The survivor experiences death over and over: the slain only knows the end but once. Besides, all men are cowards at heart, if that must be the name for those who weigh up the odds and know when they are beaten.

The third stone is Sister Margaret, who backed both horses and vanished. I do not blame her for, in the final analysis, I followed her example, although I have often questioned why she did not give a warning to Father Callaghan, Ah Fong and me. Perhaps the Dragon Mother's charging stallion was pipping Christ's lame nag as they came to the final jump.

The fourth stone is for the girls for whom I never

searched. Often, as I've walked the streets of Hong Kong, I have wondered if there might have been one of them nearby, watching me. She would not recognise me just as I cannot put a face to the name of teachers under whom I studied, priests under whom I prayed, masters under whom I have served and to whom I've sold myself. Sitting with the city at my feet, I consider what the chances might be of one of them living down there somewhere, an old lady in a tiny tenement room working a sewing machine.

And the fifth stone: that is God, who left me in the lurch.

Another aircraft is approaching from the west, out of the sun that is starting to go down over the far-off hills of Lan Tau. As it glides nearer, it seems to be coming so close I might lean out and swat it. I pick up my copy of the *Wah Kiu Yat Po*, roll it into a cylinder and struggle to my feet. The sound of the engines throbs faintly, reverberating off the hillside. Should it come within reach, I shall knock it down as one might a pestering fly. Yet it does not. Like its predecessor, it passes beneath me and slides off towards the spit of runway.

Looking along the mountainside, I squint against the sun to see if there is another materialising out of the heavens, stealing in on its final approach, but I cannot spy one. All I see are the hot dusty spirals of late-afternoon thermals lifting from the foothills upon which are riding shite-hawks, their heads crooked down on the lookout for snakes, insects, small rodents and, perhaps, dragons.